WHITE CROW

WHITE CROW

BENTLEY LYON

ST. MARTIN'S PRESS
NEW YORK

B-2

Library of Congress Cataloging-in-Publication Data

Lyon, Bentley.
   The white crow / Bentley Lyon.
      p.   cm.
   "A Thomas Dunne book."
   ISBN 0-312-03401-6
   I. Title.
   [PS3562.Y44487W4 1989]
   813'.54–dc20   89-34933
                                                                 CIP

Design by Maura Fadden Rosenthal

First U.S. Edition

10 9 8 7 6 5 4 3 2 1

To Liz, and to Destiny,
for their love
and their encouragement

CHAPTER ONE

The moment Arnold Kent saw the gray-haired man bumping his way through the crowd of passengers awaiting their flights, he knew he had seen him before. The man was of medium build, and walked with a curious rolling motion of the shoulders, He carried a folded newspaper under one arm, and a briefcase. His face was ashen, and with his free hand he tugged at the knot in his tie, trying to loosen it. He disappeared into the men's room.

Kent sat there in JFK's sweltering international departure lounge puzzling over the man's identity. Suddenly, it came to him: from the vantage of the elevated deck of his McLean, Virginia house, he had seen the guy working in his backyard across the street. The man was a recluse, and neighbors speculated about his mysterious and secretive existence. Some thought he was Italian, and one man said it might be a safe house. Kent didn't even know what a safe house was.

Flight 846 to Madrid was announced, and passengers began queuing up at the gate. Kent decided to stay put and get another look at the man, perhaps see which flight he would be boarding. But ten minutes later the Italian had not yet come out of the men's room, and they were making the final boarding call. Was there a problem? Kent entered the men's room. The man was not in view along the row of urinals or washbasins. Kent looked along the row of toilet stalls, peering at the spaces below the bottoms of the doors. Then he saw it: a slumped-over hulk in front of a toilet. He got down on one knee to look under the door, and saw the man's head, face down in a puddle of vomit. The man's hand was next to his head, grasping a briefcase. Kent pulled the briefcase loose and felt the wrist for a pulse. He could detect none. He hurried to the boarding desk and told a startled agent what he'd seen.

Feeling dazed and sickened, he boarded his plane. He found his seat next to a window, and the elderly lady in the aisle seat moved her legs back so he could get by. It was then he realized he was still clutching the Italian's briefcase. He would call a flight attendant and explain. But there was plenty of time, why not take a look inside? Find out the man's name . . . something to enhance the story back in McLean. He snapped it open and rummaged around: a *Time* magazine, two packages of Kools, some newspaper clippings, a small kit with toilet articles, pens and pencils, a stenographer's spiral notebook, an unsealed letter with Spanish postage addressed to somebody in Rome, and a pair of dark glasses. No wallet, money, airline tickets, passport. All those things were probably in the man's pockets.

He lifted the cover on the spiral notebook. On the first few pages were sketched diagrams, meaningless to him. He flipped quickly to the first page with writing on it. Coded information, pure gibberish. Letters and numbers. The neighbors must be right, the guy is a spook. Kent decided to take a look at the letter. More coded stuff, nothing readable. But there was a smaller envelope inside, containing six photographs. He pulled them out, and it was like getting a 220-volt shock. Two of them were pictures of Arnold Kent himself.

It was a joke, he told himself, perpetrated by his prankster friends in the Forest Service. Then the image of the man's face in the pool of vomit snapped him back to reality: it was no joke.

For several seconds his head went reeling, and he thought he was going to faint. Then, his hands quivering, he looked more closely at the photos, grainy black-and-whites with the flattened distortion of tele-photo photography. Despite the blurred backgrounds he could discern the locations. One showed him in front of his house. It had to have been taken from the upper story of the Italian's house. The other photo showed Kent boarding the State Department shuttle number 13 in front of "Main State" for the short trip back across the Potomac to his office in Rosslyn. He recognized the suit he had worn. Both photos were taken only three days ago. It seemed like a dream. What the hell was going on?

He would not turn in the briefcase, not yet anyway. The Italian wouldn't be needing it right now . . . probably not ever. He would take it to the embassy in Madrid. He looked closely at the other photos . . . nobody he knew. He took another look at the diagrams and writing, still

making no sense out of anything. Then he glanced at the newspaper
clippings. One concerned the indictment of Abu Nidal in connection
with the 1985 terrorist attack that killed sixteen people at the airport in
Rome. Another was a Reuters dispatch datelined Madrid and headlined:
THOUSANDS OF SPANIARDS PROTEST U.S. It was about an anti-NATO
demonstration demanding the withdrawal of U.S. F-16 fighter planes
from the air force's 401st Tactical Fighter Wing based at Torrejón de
Ardoz, near the Spanish capital.

The other clipping, from the *Washington Post*, was headlined, ITAL-
IAN FIRM FIGHTS NAVY PLAN FOR 6TH FLEET HEADQUARTERS. It was
an article Kent had noted the week before, and hadn't read closely at the
time. But it dealt with why he had been called to the State Department
last Monday to be briefed by an Agency for International Development
disaster preparedness officer. Kent was about to leave on an assignment
for the Forest Service that would take him to both Madrid and Rome.
AID's Farber Claunch, with whom Kent had worked before, knew of
the assignment and had asked Kent to do an errand for him in Rome.

Claunch had called him into his office; when Kent got there, he had
found another man sitting opposite Farber.

"Arno, this is Otto Frange of State's Italy desk. It is okay with you if he
sits in?"

"Sure, Farber. What's this all about?"

"Tell you in a minute. Coffee? You, Otto? No? Okay. First off, Arno,
what's your clearance?"

"Top secret."

"Isn't that unusual for the Forest Service?"

"Not any more, I guess. We look at a lot of military technology that
hasn't been declassified yet for civilian use . . ."

"Okay, that's great," Claunch said. Claunch was a tall, good-looking
man of thirty-five who liked to get things done. He liked working with
Forest Service people because they were experienced in handling emergency assignments, such as forest fires.

"Arno," Claunch went on, "I was impressed with the report you did
for us last year on how the Italian Ministry for Civil Protection works
with their forest service people during forest-fire emergencies. It was
mostly about use of aircraft, wasn't it?"

"Right. All their large firefighting aircraft, the C-130s, the G-222s
and the Chinook helicopters, are operated by the military under direc-

tion of the MPC, their civil defense ministry, out of Rome. The Corpo Forestale guys work closely with them."

"When you were there did you get acquainted with the military officers involved in that?"

"I met them in meetings, heard them talk. That's about all."

"But your friend, what's his name . . . Tedeschi? . . . of the Corpo Forestale . . . he knows those officers well, doesn't he?"

"They seemed quite well acquainted, yes." Kent glanced at Otto Frange, who hadn't spoken yet. Frange was in his mid-forties, wore rimless glasses, and had reddish-brown hair. He was smoking a pipe, and the tobacco had a curious semisweet odor. He wore an expensive-looking gold chain around his neck, visible under an open-neck sport shirt. The man looked vaguely familiar to Kent, like they had met sometime, or perhaps been at the same meeting. Frange was studying Kent and listening intently.

"Do the forestry guys there talk freely to you . . . about political issues, for example?" Claunch asked.

Kent looked back and forth at the two somber faces peering at him, awaiting the answer. It was obviously not idle chitchat as far as they were concerned. "Yeah, I guess you could say they're fairly open. What are you guys setting me up for?"

Claunch laughed, but Frange didn't. "This is not a big deal, Arno," Claunch said. "I don't know if you read the piece in the *Post* a few days ago, but it was about the headquarters complex of the U.S. Sixth Fleet in Naples. They're presently situated in a goddamn volcano crater west of town in a section called Agnano. Navy's worried about earthquakes, and of course after the bombing of the Marine Corps barracks in Lebanon, security is being scrutinized at all our overseas facilities. Navy wants to move to a better site inland up near Capua. Problem is, the Italian firm, Fiart, that leases out the present facilities doesn't want the navy to move out. They've even hired a big D.C. lobbying firm to raise hell on the hill with Appropriations, Armed Services and Foreign Relations."

"Interesting," said Kent. "But what does all this possibly have to do with me, your friendly forester?"

"The Italians are great little foot-draggers," Claunch continued. "One of the outfits within their rather formidable bureaucracy that has to approve of the move is the MPC, the same guys that work with your forestry friends. Don't ask me why, I doubt if even Otto here understands the inner workings of Italian government, and he's the local expert." Otto smiled, but only just perceptibly. "Anyway, the Pentagon folks figure the deal is being stalled in MPC, for whatever reason."

"And . . . ?"

"The navy wants to get the deal moving before they lose out on their spending authority for this fiscal year. If they can find out who's holding up MPC approval and why, they could apply some appropriate arm-twisting to get things moving."

"I still don't see—"

"Our people don't to make it look like they're interfering in an internal matter. If they started asking questions it might drive the problem farther underground and create other problems for the navy."

"What about State? Aren't they supposed to be the experts in these matters?"

"Ordinarily, yes. But since the lobbyists have come on strong with the politicians, it's become a sensitive matter. The undersecretary's guidance is that it be handled informally."

"Informally?"

"We remembered sending the C-130 to Italy two years ago when they had all those fires, and wondered what's been going on lately. I checked with Phil Perkins of your international forestry staff, and he told me of your upcoming visit to Rome."

"I can't wait for the next part. You're going to ask me to get my Italian forestry buddies to find out who's holding things up."

"And why," Claunch said. "It could be done very unobtrusively . . . on a casual basis."

"What's involved here?" Kent asked. "Why do you think they're trying to tie it up?"

Claunch glanced at Frange, then said, "Could be a payoff. If that's it, and we find out who, there's things that can be done about it. Or it could be a typical bureaucratic problem, pride, power, whatever. But again, State wants to know who and why."

Kent looked at them in amazement. "You mean, like I take one of these fellows aside and say, 'Hey, Mino! So what's the big roadblock down at Sixth Navy?' And he tells me, 'Yeah, it's that pompous land baron Spadolini trying to squeeze some lire out of Fiart and company. One of our national pastimes, you know.' Next thing I know, Spadolini shows up at my hotel room with a couple of hairy-armed friends saying something like, '*Fatti i cazzi tuoi!* Hey, you *americano*, you keepa you hands offa *mia programma*.' Sorry, gentlemen, my position description says nothing about spy work."

Frange's eyebrows shot upward on hearing Kent's use of colloquial (and highly profane) Italian. He couldn't have known that the forester had been reared by an Italian-American foster family, and spoke the language with a regional Italian accent, but no hint of a foreign one.

Claunch took a drink of cold coffee. "Arno, there's no risk here. Just a matter of idle curiosity on your part. You don't have to be nosy, just curious."

"You've cleared this with my boss, Perkins?"

"We thought it best not to . . . complicate things. Arno, we can't pressure you to do this if you don't want to, but we would really appreciate the favor."

Kent accepted the assignment. He left the meeting wondering how the world's largest and most powerful department of state found itself compelled to lean on the assistance of a midlevel forestry career man to do its dirty work. He was also still wondering why, at the last minute, his official passport was denied him based on "visa difficulties," and he had been given special approval to travel with just his personal passport. By now, he was feeling so uneasy about the situation that he wanted to get off the plane. But it was too late; the big jet had already taxied into position for takeoff.

Three nights earlier, Otto Frange left his apartment in Falls Church, Virginia, and drove five miles to a house in McLean, arriving at exactly nine. He walked around to the back of the house, knocked, and was admitted.

"*Buona sera*, Bruno," Frange said. The other man led Frange into the study and turned on the stereo. Bruno Cavalchini was fifty-two, and the 150 pounds on his five-foot-eight frame gave him an average appearance. He was not happy to see Frange, because Otto invariably brought him nasty assignments.

"What is it now?" he asked the taller man, speaking Italian. "Something about the guy across the street you asked me to start watching?"

"Bruno, old friend. You won't even offer me a drink before getting the good news?"

"To you, good news is for somebody else to make a long trip and do a dirty job. Cognac?"

"Cognac is fine. Bruno, what do you think you're being paid for? To live the fine life in the suburbs of one of the nation's most beautiful and awe-inspiring cities, surrounded by political power, the trappings of high office, enjoying the comforts of—"

"*Non me ne sbatto i coglioni!* I don't give a flying fuck about this place. What do I get to see but the walls? What do I get to listen to but the stupid neighbors, having their deck parties until all hours, those two despicable women and their raucous voices talking about the fucking goddamn art shows? *Chi cazzo se ne frega?*"

"All right, Bruno, all right. *Calma, calma.* Let me take you away from all this, then."

"So. What do you have for me, a week on the Italian Riviera, or two weeks in Philadelphia?"

"What would you think about a quick trip to Madrid and back?"

"And what takes place in Madrid?"

"I'll explain it, Bruno. But first, let me ask if he would recognize you?"

"I doubt it. His deck looks into the backyard here, but he's always at work when I go out there."

"Good. I met him myself about a year ago when I was negotiating purchase of this house. Then he shows up at a meeting at State on Monday. Fortunately, he didn't recognize me."

"Why fortunately?"

"Because I told him earlier I was a broker. Anyway, they're sending him to Rome to do something that might gum up a very important operation we have going. We have to interrupt his schedule before he gets there."

"But you said Madrid."

"He's leaving for Madrid on Saturday. After a few days there he flies to Rome. We don't want him to get there. That's where you come in."

"Why me? Angelo tell you to stuff it? He usually gets those jobs."

"He's in Chicago right now. Then I remembered where Kent lived, and realized you already would know what he looked like and be able to follow him easily from his home."

"Well, what about the Lemon Street job you've got me on?"

"Forget about it. This one's much more important right now."

Bruno scratched his head. "How do you want it done? An accident, perhaps?"

"An accident would be fine. However, do whatever necessary to permanently interrupt his trip."

"I don't like it. Why is this so important? What's it all about?"

"Bruno, old friend, just believe me when I tell you it has to happen. You understand I have my orders not to—"

"*Me ne frego dei suoi ordini!* I don't give a shit about your orders. You never tell me anything. Sometime you'll regret that stupidity. It's about the event planned in Naples, a part of Operation Oltraggio, is it not?"

"Stupidity or not, that's how it has to be. And if you are a sane man you will not again mention the event in Naples. And I must say your vocabulary leaves a lot to be desired."

"What's the backup? Who will be there to help me?"

"You will be contacted at the airport on arrival. Don't worry about it until then. You will be on the same flight as Kent."

"I'm to follow him to Madrid, then . . . ?"

"You are responsible for identifying him in person to our contact in Madrid. Then you will be given further instructions. Until then you are not to lose sight of him. If someone is ahead of us on this thing, his itinerary could be other than the one I am handing you now. Naturally, you will memorize the itinerary and these other instructions for our contact in Madrid, then destroy these notes. Do you understand that?"

"Yes, you think I'm some kind of idiot, or what?"

"I also want you to photograph him, then include his pictures along with these. You'll note there's already one photo of him I managed to pick up today. This packet of photos is to be mailed in Madrid to the addressee in Rome."

"And why, may I ask, are photos of him being sent to Rome if indeed he won't be going there?"

"Bruno, you ask so many questions. In this case I can tell you. Should Mr. Kent turn out to have a survival instinct that exceeds even your considerable talents for dealing with him, it will be necessary to have him attended to in Rome. We are not taking any chances on this."

"I appreciate your confidence in me. I have another question, Otto. Why is this man so important, and why is it so imperative that he not reach Rome? After all, I have the need to know what I am dealing with on such a matter."

"That fellow Claunch, at State, tries to pass him off on me as a plain bureaucrat who is merely running an errand for him along the way. He is being sent, so I am to believe, to ask some innocent questions about the delay within the Ministro della Difesa to grant approval for the U.S. Navy's move from Agnano to Capua. But I have reason to believe they know more than we thought they did about Oltraggio. They invited me in, played their little charade, then sent me about my business. *Stronzoli!*"

"And this Kent fellow is going to check it out?"

"Merely my presumption, old friend. And if it's true, you have the answers to the questions you just asked."

"He's not simply a bureaucrat, then."

"It wouldn't make any sense at all. The mission is far too important to employ somebody other than a fully qualified operative."

"Then an accident right here would not be a solution?"

"They'd simply send somebody else."

"Do you know anything about him, what kind of assignments he does?"

"There hasn't been much time since I found out. But I do know he has traveled a lot, always supposedly on Forest Service business. His trips are nominally sponsored by AID, FAO, or sometimes directly by host countries. He was in Mozambique for two months in 1980, and spent considerable time there with people suspected by FRELIMO agents of engaging in espionage for South Africa. He would have been picked off at that time except for the direct intervention of Samora Machel, who didn't wish to discourage the efforts of other western *cooperantes*, as the Portuguese call them."

"He speaks Italian?"

"One must assume that, because he can swear like a Sicilian truck driver."

"Other languages?"

"Undoubtedly Spanish, probably Portuguese."

"Otto, I am not really fond of this assignment. I will do it of course. But wouldn't a serious accident, something debilitating, but not . . . permanent, serve the purpose just as well?"

"Bruno, you really surprise me. But on this occasion I won't be heartless enough to bring your stupidity to the attention of our agency."

* * *

The L-1011 thundered down the runway and into the darkening sky as Kent sat there asking himself why he hadn't just got off the plane and gone home. There had to be a connection between that meeting with Claunch and Frange, and his photos in the Italian's briefcase, and it had to involve that Navy headquarters in Naples. His first thought was that his neighbor had been, for some reason, following him to Madrid, or would be waiting for him in Rome. Three flights had been preparing to board in the TWA departure lounge: Madrid, Rome, and what was the other one? Frankfurt, he thought.

But how would the guy have found out his itinerary? Who was he working for? Or for that matter, was he simply practicing his photographic technique, and just happened to be at the airport by coincidence? Don't start getting paranoid, Arno, he told himself. Let's take another look at the photos.

This time he looked on the back of each one and found them marked in pencil in an upper corner with the letter K, followed by a number. On the back of the photos of Kent the notation was "K-25." The others had different K numbers. This is ominous, he said to himself. I'm K-25, for Christ's sake. He flipped open the spiral notebook again, and found a paragraph beginning with "K-25":

K-25) 29/5-17: T17/3/17 Y-77 (3/11/5/3) Y-79 (3/13/5/0) T23/11/17 Y-79 (3/19/11/0) Y-4, 29/19 (0/29/3/13) HZNERP. 31/5: 13/3/19 Y-4 (3/7/3/15) X-12 (3/17/5/13) FKKQHL.

"That's wonderful," he mumbled. "They give me a spy mission, have me followed to the airport, and now it looks like I need a decoder ring with a secret compartment. Who needs this?"

His first "spy" mission had been a disaster. His boss had sent him to an appropriations hearing in the Senate Office Building to listen in on questions asked of another natural resources agency by certain senators. His own agency would make use of the information to prepare their own testimony, scheduled for the next day. Under no circumstances was Kent to let himself be identified as a Forest Service employee.

He remembered that day quite well. He'd had an upset stomach and a headache, and the hearing room was intolerably hot and stuffy. Witnesses, including the secretary of agriculture, were being questioned by five senators. Kent began feeling faint, and was leaning forward to get blood into his head when he lost consciousness. He awoke a minute later lying on his back, surrounded by a dozen people. A tall man standing there holding his wallet open was saying, "We'd better call the Forest Service and tell them Mr. Kent has a problem." After being whisked away to George Washington University Hospital's emergency room, examined and found to be healthy, he was told by his boss they'd find somebody else for their next undercover mission.

The whole thing had struck him funny, because a lot of his associates had been jokingly accusing him of working for the CIA. His rather frequent trips to different countries, all of them for routine forestry purposes, did nothing to dispel that image. Even Kent's wife, Yvette, was becoming convinced he was an agent. Yvette's studio partner, Sharna Gorv, was the wife of an ex-CIA man who told Sharna there "wasn't any doubt about it." Yvette constantly pleaded with Kent to admit it. One day while he was shaving, she had accosted him through the closed bathroom door.

"Arno, I'm going to ask you one more time, and if you'll tell me the truth I'll stop bothering you about it."

"Bothering me about what?"

"Are you working for the CIA or not?"

He opened the door and stared at her, his face half covered with lather. "Yvette, hasn't it ever occurred to you that you can invariably reach me by telephone wherever I say I'm going to be? Have you ever noticed I can't even keep a straight face when you accuse me of playing a trick on you? What kind of a spy do you think I'd make, for God's sake?"

Her eyes narrowed, and with her lips tight she said, "That is exactly how Bill Gorv said you would answer that question. I really appreciate your honesty with me." She turned away, her long hair swirling in an arc, and walked stiffly down the hall toward the living room. Her mind was made up. Anyway, the marriage was in such tatters it really didn't seem to matter any more what Yvette thought. How their marriage had lasted almost ten years was a mystery to their closest friends, the ones who best understood the fantasy she was living and how little Arno was getting out of the marriage.

Yvette pretended to live in a world in which art was the sole fabric of life, the only thing of intrinsic value. Through years of immersion in her painterly world, daubing out endless canvases, attending untold hundreds of art exhibits, incessantly reading newspaper reviews, art magazines and coffee-table books, her perspective on life had come to be dominated by the thinking and commentary of the pseudosophisticates who made their living impressing the gullibles whose overriding ambitions in life were to be artists in their own right. But Yvette was singularly untalented. Her best canvases could fairly be described as unruly abstractions of congealed pigments. It did not bother Yvette, she said, that the better galleries refused to show her work, because she believed that the true merits of noncommercial art were not readily understood, nor were they accorded the value they deserved until the artist died. She could not recognize that she couldn't paint, and none of her vacuous friends had the guts to put it to her. They would view her work and say things like, "Oh, isn't that interesting," or "Now that's what I call a painting."

Yvette, while seeming to persist in her fantasy, managed to get by socially on her imposing good looks and outgoing personality. She was a tall and stately blonde who looked much younger than her forty-five years, and whose elegant body attracted the stares of most all men, young or old. She was a spirited if shallow conversationalist, but misunderstood the attention paid by her male acquaintances, most of whom were far less interested in her commentary on the art scene than in fantasizing themselves with her long legs wrapped around them in a hot tub at some Mexican seaside resort. Concerning Yvette's own sexual appetites, she had never had an orgasm and doubted whether there was such a thing in women. To her, the sex act was mainly a social function, an expectation of the male that had to be dealt with in a civilized way. The height of social acceptability in her view would have been to be a famous and deliriously successful artist, fawned over by all true art lovers. At least, that's how it all seemed to Kent.

There were no children, so why did they go on living such a hollow relationship? Yvette was too shallow to understand it, and Kent was still blinded by how much he had been in love with her at the start.

Kent's reverie was broken by the pilot's voice on the intercom. He was pointing out the lights of St. John's, Newfoundland, visible to the passengers on the left side of the plane. Naturally, Kent was seated on the right side. Anyway, who wanted to look at the fucking lights in St. John's? The pilot was probably just trying to prove he wasn't lost yet.

The beverage cart had come and gone, meal service was about to begin, and undoubtedly there would be a movie to see at a seventy-five-degree angle from his seat. Fortunately, the elderly lady sitting next to him was skinny and taciturn. This was one evening on an airplane that Kent didn't want to spend elbow-jousting and exchanging life histories.

He flipped on his reading light and stared again at the cryptic numbers and letters in the notebook. It was all done by hand, not like the machine-printed samples of coded text he had seen before. It was probably the Italian's personal system of jotting down information so that it could not easily be understood by the likes of customs agents, police officers, or maybe even the person sitting next to him in an airplane. He thought the numbers curious: almost all odd, rather than even numbers. In fact, the only even numbers were in combination with letters. There were Y-4, (twice) and X-12 in the first paragraph. Maybe the guy just was fond of odd numbers.

Kent looked at the first coded group of letters, *HZNERP,* and began trying letter substitutions. By letting each coded letter represent the following letter in the alphabet, he got *IAOFSQ.* No help there. What about the preceding letter, then? *GYMDQO.* Then he alternated between preceding and following letters, getting: *GAMFQR,* and then *IYODSO.* On his sixth try, adding and subtracting first one letter, then two, then three, in sequence, he got *GALGOS. Galgos* in Spanish meant "greyhounds," and it was also the name of his hotel in Madrid.

Was that a coincidence? He quickly used the same procedure to decode the other word in the paragraph and came up with *ELISEO,* the name of his hotel in Rome. Not a coincidence. What he was looking at, then, was apparently his own itinerary. Okay, that's it, he told himself. I'm definitely going to the embassy Monday morning and stay there until all this is cleared up.

Then it occurred to him the embassy would certainly want to keep the notes and photos. So he tore several blank pages from the spiral notebook and copied down the encoded notes for his own use. Then he flipped off the reading light and tried to relax.

Kent had looked forward to this trip for weeks. He had done an enormous amount of preparation and had developed a plan for international

collaboration in wildland fire management that he felt sure would receive overwhelming support. His meetings on this trip were to be infor-
mal, and among good friends who felt as he did about working together
and making progress. His schedule left time for socializing and sightsee-
ing in two of his favorite cities. But now, instead of a pleasant, agreeable
interlude, away from the inane chatter of Yvette and her art friends, and
from the bureaucratic insanities of the Washington office, he found
himself suddenly enmeshed in something he neither understood nor
had any interest in. In fact, the whole thing was beginning to frighten
him.

By the time the L-1011 landed at Madrid's Barajas Airport, Kent had
pocketed the photos and the several notebook pages containing writing
and stashed the briefcase beneath a pillow in an overhead storage compartment. Two wide-body jets had been unloaded at about the same
time, and there were long lines at passport control. There were few
children among the mid-October passengers; most of them looked like
older vacationers and businesspeople. It was about nine thirty on a Sunday morning, and the travelers were quiet and slow moving, not quite
awake yet after the long flight.

Once past the passport control gates, passengers were funneled
through a single door into the baggage area, a huge room of conveyor
belts and a half dozen or so customs desks. People began scurrying
around trying to find luggage buggies, then gathered around the appropriate conveyors. The relative silence of the big room was shattered by
an announcement on the PA system: "Mr. Arnold Kent, please come to
the information desk. Mr. Kent to the information desk, please," the
voice said in heavily accented English.

Kent looked around, spotting the information desk at one end of the
room. There was an attendant there who had probably made the announcement. Kent's immediate impulse was to comply, but some instinct froze him in place. Who would page him here? Was it a message
from home or from his office? Didn't make sense. They'd call his hotel
or ICONA, the Spanish forest service. Could it be his hosts, trying to
locate him to give him a lift to his hotel? They'd never done that before.
Besides, they knew him on sight. His mind flashed to the contents of
the briefcase and their implications. He scanned the whole end of the

baggage room looking for a clue to the paging, and could find none. He decided to trust his instincts.

In a minute or so one of the passengers went up to the information desk. The attendant listened to him for a moment, then shook his head and the man walked away. Then Kent saw the attendant look toward the greeting area where families and friends awaited the passengers, and shook his head a second time. It seemed clear: the attendant was telling someone, "No, that wasn't Kent." He glanced at the group waiting, not recognizing anyone. But two of them seemed out of place. One was a heavyset man with a square, leathery face, and standing next to him a smaller man with a mustache. Neither looked Spanish. A cold chill ran up Kent's back as all the signs began to confirm that he had become a target.

The taxi driver put Kent's suitcase in the front seat of the compact car and held the rear door open for his passenger. As they headed away from the International Arrivals terminal the driver swiveled his head around and asked, "*¿Señor?*"

Kent was about to say "Galgos," then thought better of it. "Tirol Residencia, *por favor.*" He remembered the small hotel near the university. It was not one of the better-known hotels, and was not near the U.S. Embassy where Americans on government business often put in.

"*En la Ronda de Toledo, ¿no es verdad?*"

"*Urquijo, a la esquina con Princesa,*" Kent corrected him. That was a typical taxi driver ploy directed at foreigners speaking Spanish. Get them to say "*sí*" to incorrect directions, then give them a tour of the town.

Fortunately, the Tirol had a vacancy, and Kent dismissed his driver with a minimal tip.

"How long will you be staying, sir?" the clerk asked.

"Only a few days. And if you would be so kind," he said, sliding a twenty-dollar bill forward, "I do not wish it to be known that I am staying here. A personal matter, you understand?"

The clerk quickly took the money, then said, "Naturally, you are aware we must make our client list available to the police on request."

"Of course. There is no problem about that. And I will pay you again when I check out."

"Yes, sir. You need not expect any problems here."

*   *   *

The phone rang in Otto Frange's Fall Church apartment at seven forty-five P.M. Saturday. He answered as always with, "Yes, go ahead."

"Mr. Overson? This is airport security at John F. Kennedy in New York. A Mr. Bruno Cavalchini was found dead here, apparently of a massive heart attack. Papers on his person requested you be notified in case of any emergency."

"Bruno dead? My god!" Frange hesitated, then said, "Thank you very much. What . . . uh . . . what disposition is being made . . ."

"His body is now at the airport, and he will be examined by a staff physician. We will need instructions from you as to where—"

"Yes, yes. I see. Can you give me your number . . . I want to collect my thoughts for a few minutes, you understand."

Frange hung up, then slammed his fist down on the desk. Shit. Nothing ever goes completely according to plan. He finished his drink, then picked up the phone and dialed twelve digits. In about twenty seconds there was a response from Madrid.

"¿Diga?"

"Forget the diga shit, it's me, Otto."

"Otto! I might have known. Who else would get me up at two A.M. for a piss call?"

"K-25 will be arriving alone. Bruno stretched his paw at JFK. Heart attack. You'll have to get it done without him, understand?"

"What does this guy look like?"

"Tall—about 1.85 meters, athletic build, clean-shaven, good-looking, typically American. Easy to spot. I think your term for it is a white crow."

"Good. What's his hotel? We don't have that."

"The Galgos. Short walk from the embassy where he's supposed to check in Monday."

"And he's to see our man there, right?"

"Correct."

"Okay, no problem then. We'll handle it. What else?"

"That's it. Don't screw this one up."

CHAPTER TWO

Kent took a long, hot shower, feeling fairly secure about not being located by his pursuers, whoever they might be. Then he realized he should call Miguel Escobosa, his main working partner on the forestry project, to let him know about the change in hotels. Miguel always called his hotel to welcome him, and either invite him over or suggest they meet for a drink somewhere.

Miguel could have passed for a university professor. He was tall, slender, studious-looking with his rimless glasses, and soft-spoken. Four years earlier, at thirty-seven, he had risen to the number-two position in the Incendios Forestales or forest-fire section of ICONA, Spain's natural resources agency. He had two ambitions in life: to become chief of the forest-fire section and whip Spain's terrible wildland arson problem, and to have at least two sons. He and Amalia already had nine children, but incredibly, all girls.

"Hello, Miguel, I have arrived," Kent said, speaking Spanish. In the United States they would speak English together, but here their conversation would also, by tacit agreement, be in the home language. Kent's Spanish was not perfect; he had learned it in high school, and later found use for it in the Forest Service training Mexican-American fire-fighters. But already knowing Italian had made it easy to become fluent.

"Arnold! I was beginning to worry about you. The hotel said you had not yet checked in. Where are you now?"

"I'm at the Tirol. You could walk up here and join me for a drink next door."

"All right. I will. Give me ten minutes."

"Miguel, if anyone calls your home asking my whereabouts, do not tell them. It's very important. Do you understand?"

"Someone already did call, asking where you were staying. I told them the Galgos."

"Who was it that called?"

"She said it was a friend, but did not give her name. It was a foreign accent, but not North American. She asked if she could call again later."

"Tell Amalia and your children to say I'm at the Galgos. I'll explain everything when I see you. Oh, something else. Here at the Tirol they will not tell you I'm here. I'll meet you in the lobby."

About thirty minutes later Miguel stepped into the lobby of the Tirol perspiring and looking pale. He embraced Kent and suggested they go immediately to Kent's room on the third floor.

"My friend, you are apparently in grave danger," he told the American.

"Why do you say so?"

"When I was about to leave my flat, Ana, our ten-year-old, had been looking out the window at the street. She said two men in a car were watching the entrance from across the street. I thought it was nothing. You know the children see all those American spy stories and police pictures on TV. Anyway, when I left the building walking east on Ferraz, one of the men got out of the car and walked behind me."

"You think he was following you?"

"There's no question about it. I made several turns and he still was there. I was afraid to come all the way up Urquijo to this hotel, so instead I went around the block and into the metro mouth. I took the first train that came by and he got on also. At the second stop, the Plaza de España, I got off just as the doors were closing, ran across the plaza and jumped into a cab. He wasn't able to follow me, and here I am."

"What did this man look like?"

"He was about your height, but heavier, dressed in a gray suit, and he had a fat face, ugly."

"Clean-shaven?"

"I think so, but I could not see him that well, and was afraid to look back except for a quick glance."

"Miguel, you did very well, and I'm sorry to have brought you this trouble. I owe you an explanation."

Kent gave the perplexed Spaniard a five-minute account of what had been happening to him, and then a stern warning. "Miguel, I think it best that you immediately take your family away from Madrid, or at least away from your home until this affair has run its course. I'm beginning to believe we are dealing with some people who would not hesitate to use force or coercion of any type. Don't you agree?"

"This whole thing seems absurd, but yes, of course you're right. But what about yourself? It seems you're the one in the greatest danger."

"They have no way to find me here, and all I must do is get to the American Embassy tomorrow morning. I can do that by taxi from in front of the hotel."

Miguel picked up the phone, called home, and instructed Amalia to immediately load the girls into the car and take them to the home of her politically prominent brother, who maintained a Madrid estate with a guarded gate. Kent was impressed that Amalia apparently asked no questions, simply agreeing to comply. Had he given such orders to Yvette, there would undoubtedly have been a fifteen-minute discussion concerning the background situation, the various alternatives, and (most important) the impact of the whole thing on her plans for the day. He began laughing.

"You are amused by this?"

"Forgive me, *viejo*, I was just imagining myself telling Yvette to put nine children in our little car, as you just did with Amalia. You must indeed have an understanding woman."

"You must not underestimate her. She could tell by the tone of my voice that I was not to be questioned. But she saves these things up and later unloads them on me in giant heaps at my weakest moments. I tell you, she can crack walnuts in her teeth, or what's worse, between her legs."

"They will be secure at the home of your brother-in-law, no?"

"Oh yes, of course. And by morning you will probably have been killed and we can all go back home."

"¡*Cabrón!* I was about to offer to buy the *tapas* and beer, but now I am thinking about hiding beneath the bed."

"It's not important in any case. I must go to Rubio's and see that my family is safely arrived. Here, let me write the telephone number. Call if you need anything. And if you find yourself in a bad predicament and cannot talk freely, begin your conversation with a remark about your leg being better now. It is something we have agreed on within our family. I should be at my office tomorrow afternoon."

"Miguel, on your way home, be careful."

"*Hasta luego*, Arnold."

Kent hadn't slept on the flight from New York, and welcomed the chance to get a long rest and be ready for Monday. He ordered food and beer from room service, then fell into a deep sleep.

The telephone rang at four thirty that afternoon in a Madrid flat. A woman answered.

"*¿Diga?*"

"I just returned from fishing," the caller said in Russian.

"I hope there were no cod."

"We still have not located him. I followed the Escobosa man, but he eluded me in the subway."

"Has he returned yet to his flat?"

"He did not return, and while I was following him the family drove away to the estate of Rubio Valdez, and now they're behind a guarded entrance."

"*Boltatsya kak gavno v prorubi!* You bob like shit in a hole in the ice! Neither the American nor the Spaniard are as stupid as you took them to be. I assume you have called all the hotels?"

"All of the main ones. There must be five hundred small ones, including the *pensiones*, and the desk clerks are very uncooperative."

"All right, then. The water is already getting too full of turds. Do nothing further until tomorrow. Be at your contact point beginning at eight o'clock sharp. And let me remind you, Aleksey, you have shit your pants twice in one day. There is a limit to my tolerance."

Aleksey Nikolsky hung up, poured himself a tumbler of vodka, then said to his partner, "Yevgeny, that Vera Vlasov is a Manchurian badger in perpetual menstruation. I think it was by a stroke of the demon's vengeance that my father was posted here in the old days and required me to learn this insipid language. I tell you this assignment has been nothing but dry masturbation from the very beginning. The woman has taken me for a second-rate donkey-fucker from the first day.

"She's a *pirdunya*. I can see her now, snapping at her fart bubbles in the tub. But there is no question, my friend, we cannot fuck like crabs tomorrow, or there will be repercussions."

Kent got out of the cab in front of the American embassy at eight fifty-five A.M., Monday morning, and walked immediately to the external booth marked U.S. CITIZENS. He showed his passport and told the attendant of his appointment with Agricultural Attaché Garbert Flenk. He was told to enter the main building through an electronic screening gate, and then he repeated his request. This time the attendant called Flenk's office. In a minute, a tall, good-looking man of about thirty-eight stepped into the foyer. He had brown eyes, prematurely gray hair, and a neatly trimmed mustache. He was impeccably dressed in an obviously expensive suit and shoes.

"Mr. Kent? I was expecting you. Hope you've had a pleasant trip so far?"

A crisply turned-out marine held open the steel door for the two men. They walked down a hall to an elevator, where Flenk punched in four digits on a numeric panel. When they exited the elevator, he used another four-digit code to get through a second steel door that led to another corridor.

"Security is rather beefed up since last time I was here," Kent said.

"More than you would suspect," said the son of a three-time ambassador. "It's a bit boring, but quite important."

Flenk led Kent into a large, tastefully decorated office. There was an enormous American flag in one corner, and an imposing portrait of Ronald Reagan in the center of one wall. A woman, her back turned, was busy at a filing cabinet.

"Excuse me, Cristina," Flenk said casually, "this is Arnold Kent of the U.S. Forest Service. My associate, Cristina del Barrio."

The woman turned and nodded solemnly, with no trace of a smile. Her features were classic Spanish, with a strong Moorish influence. The wide-set eyes were almost black, and her nose was narrow and aquiline. She had straight, black hair tied in a tight braid behind her neck. She was probably thirty-five, Kent guessed, and was astonishingly beautiful, if in an understated way.

"Well, then, Kent," Garbert Flenk was saying, snapping Kent out of his trance. "Sit down and tell me what you're up to. It's about forest fires or something, isn't it?" His tone was somewhat condescending, Kent judged.

"Yes, it is, sir. But first, and maybe much more important, I should tell you about another matter . . . something that happened to me en route, something that might involve national security."

Kent's opening statement produced two distinct reactions. Flenk's reaction was no reaction at all. He just sat there staring blandly at his guest. When he uttered the words "national security," however, del Barrio, who was standing behind Flenk's desk and out of his arc of vision, turned her head toward Kent with a sudden jerk and paralyzed him with a black-eyed glare that struck home like a laser beam. He couldn't believe what he was seeing. The woman was slowly, but very deliberately, shaking her head from side to side, her lips tightly compressed.

Flenk noticed Kent's distraction, and turned to look at Cristina. The moment before he turned, she had turned her own head back to her work.

Flenk smiled at Kent and said, "Do I have the impression I'm boring you already?" He said it lightly, but the message was conveyed.

"Oh, I'm sorry, Mr. Flenk," he stammered. "It's just that . . . I guess . . . uh . . . I wasn't expecting to see . . ."

"It's all right, Kent. Señora del Barrio seems to have that effect on a lot of my visitors. I assure you, she's accustomed to it. Now, tell me more about this . . . national security business that has you all up in the air."

Kent hesitated. Was the woman warning him that Flenk should not be given this kind of information? If not that, what could it be?

"If you're concerned about Señora del Barrio, Kent, she has top security clearance, the same as myself."

"No, sir, it's not that at all, Mr. Flenk. It's just that I . . . uh . . . shouldn't be bothering you with this. Maybe I should bring it to the attention of someone in your security section . . ."

Without shifting his focus, Kent could detect via peripheral vision that the woman was nodding perceptibly.

"Not at all," Flenk said. "We all work together here. If it seems to be significant, I'll see that it's brought to the attention of the appropriate department. What is it that happened?"

"Well, I'm sorry I even mentioned it. My imagination is probably just working too hard. I thought for a while I was being followed, but now it seems absurd to me. It's really nothing."

"Why would anybody possibly be following you? For what purpose?" Flenk asked.

"That's just it. There's no possible reason. I don't even owe anybody money," Kent joked.

Flenk didn't smile. "I really insist you tell me. Inasmuch as you're in my area of influence on this job, I now have the responsibility to track your activities. That would definitely include the matter you just broached to me. Also, it could be very important. Now, when did you first feel you were being followed?"

Kent's head was spinning. It seemed ludicrous that he couldn't talk freely to a U.S. embassy official, and yet the woman's signals, though subtle, had been powerful and clear. He decided against telling this man any more. "Mr. Flenk, I've already told you all there is to tell. Again, I'm sorry to have mentioned it."

"Then what was that about national security?" he demanded.

"Let's just say I was being overly dramatic. Can we get on with the main purpose of my visit here?"

Flenk looked cold and angry. Kent now had the impression the woman had had good reason to steer him off. "All right, Kent. What's your visit here all about?"

Kent began talking about his proposal for international collaboration with the ICONA foresters. During his explanation, Flenk seemed totally preoccupied with other thoughts, tapping his pencil on his calendar pad, his eyes flicking around at the objects on his desk in turn. The woman left the room for about two minutes, then returned with some file folders. Flenk's phone buzzed. He answered it, then said, "Excuse me one moment. There's a call I have to take on another phone."

The moment Flenk stepped out of the office, del Barrio approached Kent and said softly, "Tell this man nothing. Talk to Norbert Whitman in Political Affairs." She then left the room.

"Sorry about that," Flenk said, sitting back down behind his walnut desk. "Now, you're also going to Rome, aren't you?"

"That's right," Kent said, wondering how Flenk knew. "Same sort of get-together there, nothing to add."

"All right then, Kent. I'd appreciate it if you'd drop back to see me before leaving. We like to tie up loose ends, you know."

Kent wondered how many people he'd said that to, and how many actually came back. He was beginning to dislike the man.

"Oh, and by the way," Flenk said. Here it comes, Kent thought. "Where did you say you were staying . . . in case anything comes up?"

"The Galgos."

"The Galgos? Are you sure? Our VIP section . . . they routinely check on expected visitors . . . told me they hadn't checked you in."

"I'm not surprised. My Spanish friends got the same response. They may have me as Kent Arnold or something."

"Okay. That happens. Well, then, I'll escort you to the lobby."

Kent said good-bye to Cristina del Barrio, then turned to Flenk and said, "I wonder, would it be too much trouble to get me in contact with Norbert Whitman?"

"Whitman? Sure. What's that all about?"

"Just a personal message from someone at State."

Flenk dialed a three-digit number on the phone, spoke briefly, then led Kent to another office.

"Norbert, this is Arnold Kent to see you," Flenk said as they both entered.

"Kent? Glad to meet you," said the small, eagle-faced man who was probably about forty. "What's it about?"

Kent turned toward Flenk, who was standing there listening, and said, "Thanks for your help. It was nice meeting you." They shook hands and Flenk left, reluctantly.

Kent turned back to Whitman. "I appreciate your seeing me. I have reason to believe I've been followed since leaving Washington, and that my presence here is somehow tied to a matter involving national security. Are you the person I should be talking to about this?"

"I'm a good starting point. But why didn't you talk to Flenk?"

Kent thought fast. "My intuition was he wouldn't take me seriously."

"Sit down here, Kent. First off, let's take a look at your passport. Good heavens, man. You're traveling on a personal passport?"

Kent told Whitman the whole story, everything except the name of his hotel and the signal from del Barrio. Whitman listened intently, only interrupting for clarification. When he had finished, Kent asked, "What do you make of all this?"

"Damned interesting. And you're sure you have no . . . agenda . . . other than what you've told me?"

n seated, but he could see the desk.
icked up his coffee cup and went into
esk. Kent seized the opportunity. He
lobby looking straight ahead. As he
air, he could see from the corner of
and Leathery Face staring at him in
ut the door, took a left turn on Ur-
of Princesa. He stopped a cab and
ondering if he shouldn't go directly

ly about killing Yevgeny Divnich. To
ss interrogation and delays in leaving
more directly to his assailants. To tell
e embassy might even be worse. And
o involve his dear friend Miguel and
fact. Anyway, how could he be posi-
he Russian?

short of amazing what had just hap-
reign country, where normally one is
of the most minor laws or even social
eign national, Soviet yet, hidden the
wledge of it from the local police and
ngest of all, it had seemed the right
shocked him, yet he felt strangely

g up from his desk. "I was worried
mbassy?"
hey think I am paranoid. I am to go
em later. And your family . . . how is

a problem, and wonders what all the
o back to our flat with the children.

hey have found my hotel. Now is not
What have you told your brother-in-

"I almost wish I did. It might help me to understand what's been going on."

Whitman looked at his watch. "Hmmm. Only about four A.M. in Washington. Look, Kent, before anything else happens I'll need to call State, verify what you've told me, and get some additional information. I will also have to get these notes and photos you brought in looked at. What's your itinerary here in town?"

"My first meeting is for this afternoon at ICONA, at the Ministry of Agriculture on Gran Vía de San Francisco, then all day Tuesday at the same place."

"Okay. I would suggest you attend your meeting this afternoon. Otherwise, we'd be giving the impression we were on to whatever game this is. Here are two numbers. I can be reached at one or the other."

"That's fine, Mr. Whitman. But what do you suggest I do about keeping my health in the meanwhile?"

"You're not worried about somebody trying to do you in?"

"Well, I don't know. It may seem silly to you, but frankly, I'm getting nervous having those goons on my tail."

"Who, other than this . . . Escobosa . . . knows where you're staying?"

"Nobody yet. But I am registered under my real name. Seems like it's only a question of time until . . ."

"Kent, I think you're overreacting. We just don't have that kind of problem in this town. People are followed all the time for one reason or another, and nothing comes of it. I'd suggest, mainly to make you feel better about it, that you stick to taxis instead of the metro, take your meals in the hotel, don't walk around by yourself, and just take it easy. Call me tonight at this number, or here at the embassy at this one. Okay?"

"Mr. Whitman, I may be overreacting, but I don't think that's enough. Why was I given a code number, photographed outside my home and in front of Main State, paged by two hoods at Barajas Airport and all the rest of it, if indeed there's nothing for me to worry about?"

"You don't understand how the intelligence business works, Kent. There is a real spiderweb out there, picking up on anything and everything that meets certain criteria. In your case, somebody decided to monitor the activity. When it turns into nothing they'll simply drop it."

"Whose spiderweb would this be?"

"I should have used the plural. Everybody's got one. Including us. Have you thought about that?"

"Okay, maybe you're right. But this thing seems to be focused on the Naples issue. I don't plan on leaving for Rome until I understand what's going on."

"Up to you, Kent. We'll try to find out, but often these things lead nowhere. Meanwhile, relax and enjoy the city."

Relax and enjoy the city, Kent grumbled to himself as he walked out of the embassy and onto the street. Easy for that sumbitch to say, sitting there in his fortress. Three taxis were poised nearby like vultures waiting for a carcass, and the first one pulled up as he walked toward the curb. He asked to be taken to the Hotel Princesa, a luxury hotel about two blocks from the Tirol. He entered the lobby but went through the gift shop and back out onto the street. When he was certain he wasn't being followed, he headed for the Tirol, but on reaching a point across the street from his hotel, he could see a heavyset man seated in the lobby reading a newspaper. Although the man's face was partly hidden by the paper, Kent decided it could be Leathery Face.

While Kent had been eating breakfast that morning in the hotel's dining room, he had seen people enter directly from the street level via a separate stairway. Therefore, he could bypass the hotel lobby and reach the stairway to his floor by cutting through the restaurant. He decided to do this, rather than chance a confrontation with a possible assailant. If they had indeed found his hotel, there were things he needed from the room: a folder of papers for his meetings, and the copy he had made of the Italian's notes.

He got through the empty restaurant with only a curious glance by a young man mopping the floors, and climbed the two flights of stairs to his floor. The door to his room was ajar. Probably being cleaned, he reasoned. But when he swung the door inward he saw the shape of a man in a suit bending over Kent's open suitcase.

"What are you . . . ?" he started to utter. The man spun around. It was the other goon from the airport, the smaller man, with the mustache. The man reached under his coat in a rapid movement, and as Kent dived at him his hand came out with a pistol. But Kent was on him like a panther. The momentum of Kent's larger, stronger body drove the man against the wall with a thud, the pistol clattering to the floor. As

part where Leathery Face had b
Then, a stroke of luck. The cler
a room immediately behind the
walked rapidly through the sm
passed the heavyset man in the
his eye the newspaper come do
amazement. Kent kept walking
quijo, then a sprint to the con
headed for the ICONA offices,
back to the U.S. embassy.

Kent decided not to tell anyb
tell the police would lead to en
the country, and expose him eve
those less-than-helpful types at
finally, it would be grossly unfai
make him an accessory after th
tively connected to the killing o

It suddenly struck Kent as litt
pened. Having just arrived in a
quite careful to avoid infraction
customs, he had just killed a fo
body, and now was obscuring kr
even his own embassy. And str
thing to do. The whole thing
exhilarated.

"Arnold!" said Miguel, looki
about you. How did it go at the

"Not well, Miguel. I believe
about my business and contact
everything?"

"Amalia doesn't agree there i
secrecy is about. She wants to
What do you think?"

"I'm still being followed, and
the time to let down one's guar
law about all this?"

"That I was followed when I went to see you, and that you have been followed. He thinks I have acted prudently. He also suggests he could be influential in getting police protection for you. Are you interested?"

"Give him my thanks, Miguel. But wait until I discuss it with the embassy this evening. In fact, I'd like to call them from here, before leaving today."

Lieutenant Colonel Vera Vlasov sat at her desk in a basement office of the Russian embassy drinking coffee. She was deputy chief of the Interior Operations group, an auxiliary unit of the KGB, and considered to be one of the toughest operatives assigned to the post. She was fifty-one, and spoke Spanish, English and German as well as Russian. Her father had been shot by the Germans during the war, and her mother taken away by Nazi soldiers, never to be seen again. The Madrid posting hadn't pleased her; it was her ambition to bring down as many high-ranking German officers, civilian or military, as her remaining life allowed, and she was embittered at having her standing request for German duty posts turned down. She felt no particular hatred for Americans, so her current assignment to interrupt Kent's mission was just another job to her. But her comedy team of Aleksey Nikolsky and Yevgeny Divnich was beginning to make her nervous. They had been unable to identify the target at the airport, and then were unable to follow the Spaniard Escobosa to the American's hotel. She herself had then learned where he was staying through a police department cooperator. When the phone rang, she was confident her agents would be reporting the "progress" she had demanded of them.

"Vera," the male voice on the intercom line said solemnly, "you have a problem concerning the American."

"What problem, Anton?"

"We have just been advised by the Spanish police that your man Divnich was found dead in the Tirol hotel. They demand to know for what reason he was there, stuffed in a dirty laundry container on the third floor."

"*Pizdavatiy!* The idiot! How was he killed?"

"They do not yet know, and there are no apparent wounds."

"And what about his eel-fucking partner Nikolsky? Why have I not heard from him?"

"I know nothing of the intricacies of your operations, Vera Vlasov. I merely give you warning. The chief of mission will not be pleased with the inevitable publicity of this mess, nor will he relish the thought of having to advise Korolenko in Rome that the American is still roving about enjoying the Spanish autumn."

"He won't have to advise Korolenko of a fucking thing," she said through clenched teeth. "I may need to make a few reassignments, but I can assure you the job will get done."

At the American embassy, Norbert Whitman was in the office of Counselor for Special Affairs Bradford Baumont. Whitman had just filled in Baumont on Kent's recitation of events.

"So my first call was to Otto Frange, Italy desk at State. He knew nothing but offered to check it out with AID's Office of Foreign Disaster Assistance and get back to me. A half hour later he said they had no knowledge whatsoever of the ancillary mission Kent told me about, that they didn't even recall his being in the office."

"Did you talk to the other guy, the one in the AID office, to verify that?"

"No, I really don't like to do that unless I have to. Creates a lot of antagonism we don't need. But I did call Kent's agency . . . the Forest Service. Guy named Phil Perkins. Has charge of their overseas business. He was aware Kent was coming here, and would then go to Rome. But he knew nothing of the Naples thing."

"Well, what do you think, Norb? Is this guy doing a self-styled James Bond? Delusions of master spy or whatever? What the hell do we really know about him?"

"Damned if I know. He seems sincere and concerned. You know, not the type to hunk up a drama like this, but you never know."

The phone on Baumont's desk buzzed, and he lifted the receiver: "Baumont . . . Yes, sir . . . You're kidding me . . . All right, we'll get on it, sir."

"Parkerhouse?" Whitman asked, referring to the ambassador.

"Yes. You won't believe this. He says an employee of the Russian embassy was found dead in the Tirol Hotel, and that Arnold Kent, a guest of the hotel, is wanted for questioning. Parkerhouse has promised we'd cooperate, and you know how he feels about carrying out promises in country."

"Jesus Christ. The guy is either really involved in something, or he's off the deep end."

"Where is he right now?" asked Baumont.

"Should be at the ICONA offices, forest-fire section I believe he said."

Baumont grabbed the phone, punched two digits, then said, "Nancy, get a call through to the ICONA office on Gran Vía de San Francisco. It's part of the Ministry of Agriculture. Need to talk to an American at a meeting there . . . Arnold Kent . . . forest-fire section. . . . Yes, urgent. Thanks."

"Urgent call for Mr. Kent," said the young Spaniard, sticking his head in the door of the meeting room.

"Sorry," Kent said to the five other men in the room. "This shouldn't take a minute."

"No problem, Arnold," said Miguel. "It's time for coffee anyway. Come join us in the cafeteria when you're finished."

"Hello?"

"Kent? This is Norbert Whitman at the embassy."

"Right. Have you folks got this thing unraveled yet?"

"We're working on it. But right now, we need you to come over here right away. Things are starting to happen."

"My meeting's still in progress. Can it wait an hour or so?"

"Rather not. The ambassador may want to talk to you personally."

"Okay. I'll be there as soon as I can."

Kent gathered up his papers, closed his briefcase, and entered the cafeteria to apologize to his associates. Miguel was escorting him to the elevator when the young man from the dispatch office came running around the corner.

"I am sorry, sir," he said to the two men. "There is another urgent call for Mr. Kent."

"You can't ever escape the telephone," Kent said to Miguel. "It's the price we pay for living in a civilized society." He picked up the phone.

"Hello," he said, this time with a hint of impatience.

"Mr. Kent," said the soft feminine voice he had heard only once before, "this is Cristina del Barrio. Do you remember me?"

"Of course I do—"

"Listen carefully, I have only a moment. You must not, I repeat, must not come to the embassy. There is great trouble here for you. And you must not go to your hotel. Do you understand?"

"Yes, yes, I understand. But then, what do you suggest?"

There was a momentary silence. Then she said, "Take a taxi to the corner of José Ortega and Principe. It's in the Salamanca District . . . a small plaza. I will drive there and pick you up in about one hour . . . a dark green Seat coupe. Then I will explain everything to you. Do you understand?"

"All right. I'll be there," he said, wondering if the whole thing might be a dream.

Miguel waited at a discreet distance. "Is everything all right?"

"No, Miguel, I'm afraid it is not. I must confide in you, and trust you not to divulge this information, do you agree to that?"

"Naturally, Arnold. What is it? How can I help you?"

"Through no fault of my own, I may be in trouble not only with my embassy, but also with the Spanish police. Until this is straightened out, until I know what is happening, I am confiding in a woman at the embassy. Her name is Cristina del Barrio. If necessary, you may contact her, but no one else at the embassy. All right? I mean to say, she will be our link to one another."

"And this del Barrio, she will confide in me?"

"I will ask her to do so."

"But why? How? Your own embassy . . ."

"Miguel, I don't know. I have been marked as an enemy somehow. Somebody tried to kill me this morning. I don't want to tell you more . . . put you in a bad spot."

"Arnold, you have my telephone numbers, and you remember our code?"

"Yes. My leg is getting better."

"I'll see you to a taxi."

CHAPTER THREE

The taxi inched its way along Paseo de Recoletos amidst a late-afternoon sea of trucks, cars and buses. Kent was so busy wrestling with the contents of his two "urgent" calls that he hardly noticed the choking exhaust fumes or the wearying horn-honking of the thousands of vehicles surrounding him. Why did they want him back at the embassy so suddenly, and why had del Barrio warned him away? What bad could happen to him there? It just didn't make sense. And why was the del Barrio woman insistent he not go back to his hotel? Had news of the killing of the Russian been tied to him, then transmitted to the embassy?

Kent thought back about his movements in the hotel and wondered if he had been seen and reported by the man mopping the floor in the restaurant. Unlikely. And nobody had seen him leave, except Leathery Face, who obviously wouldn't report it. Then he thought about his fight with the Russian, how he had almost been shot. Shot! The pistol! My God! I never retrieved the pistol from the floor where the Russian had dropped it. Must have been kicked out of sight during the scuffle. Could the maid have found it? Think, Arno, was the bed made up when you were there? No! Then that was it. She found the gun, and would have led police to the room. The police would have called the embassy to learn Kent's whereabouts.

Holy shit, he told himself as the taxi lumbered along in an unending series of starts and stops. They must have loved that one at the embassy. They already thought I was a goofball, now this. Those sanctimonious bastards would probably just turn me over to the local police. God only knows what might happen from there. Amazing. From garden-variety bureaucrat to international outlaw-spy in two days. Jesus, would Yvette and her friends ever be impressed by this little escapade.

He realized that was only his second thought of Yvette since leaving McLean, Virginia. She was probably going to some art opening in the District, he imagined, where all of the artists' friends would gather to be seen and talk about their own work, while glancing with barely disguised disdain at the work of the featured artist. How many of those openings had Yvette dragged him to, he wondered, where he stood off to the side, clutching his little plastic glass of cheap white wine, wondering when it would all be over and he could get back to his own living room, and maybe the Monday-night football game?

The taxi pulled up at a corner near the small circular plaza, and Kent got out clutching his briefcase. There was a bus stop and a bench, so he simply sat down. He was in a residential area of four- and five-story apartment buildings that were built right up to the sidewalks. Cars already occupied all of the available parking spots, and the late arrivals were beginning to drive their midget cars up onto the sidewalks, completely blocking them to foot traffic.

Why wasn't he panic-stricken? he wondered. He had been followed since leaving home, had been received with suspicion at the embassy, was assaulted by a Russian in his hotel room and had killed the man, and now found himself a fugitive from the Spanish police, the KGB no doubt, and for all he knew the CIA. Furthermore, he was about to be picked up by a beautiful woman about whom he knew practically nothing, and be taken to some unknown destination. Not exactly a routine day in the life of a dirt forester. And yet, inexplicably, he found himself behaving as if everything were fairly normal. Was it, he asked himself, because he had no moral feeling of guilt, and would be able to satisfactorily explain his behavior when given the right chance? Or was he simply going off the deep end and didn't even realize it?

The green Seat coupe pulled up by the curb, and he slid into the front seat. Cristina del Barrio had changed clothes since that morning. Instead of the red skirt and white blouse, she was now in a dark blue jump suit. Her hair was still in the tight braid, and now she had on circular golden earrings. She glanced at him without expression and in faultless English said, "So, what do you think of Madrid?" It was like being asked the question casually by one's tour guide.

"Madrid? This is Madrid? No wonder everybody talks funny. I thought it was London."

"I'm glad you can find some humor in the situation."

"Are you surprised I came?"

"A little. But then, I didn't mean to give you any choice."

"You gave me none at all. Where are we going, to a movie?"

"That would be nice. However, our first priority is to get you out of town and away from the Spanish police. The ambassador promised to turn you over to them for questioning."

"That wouldn't be the end of the world, would it?"

"You did kill that Russian at the Tirol, did you not?"

"He was about to shoot me. And I didn't mean to kill him."

"Do you know what would happen to you, once in the hands of the police?"

"Tell me."

"The Soviets would demand through diplomatic channels that you be held until the matter was resolved, and the Spaniards would comply. You have no diplomatic status whatever, and we could not help you. To have you held longer, the Russians would provide bogus information to the police involving you in some plot to kill their embassy employee. While you were still in jail, you would be discovered hung in your cell, an apparent suicide, and traces of cocaine would be detected in your bloodstream. The newspapers would say, '*Turista Norteamericano Se Suicida Encarcelado.*'"

"Fascinating. But why would they do that? I pose no threat to them, I have no mission against their interests."

"But it is obvious, is it not, that they think you do? Did the Russian not try to take your life?"

"Señora del Barrio, if your presumption of what would happen to me in jail is anywhere near correct, why wouldn't that also be known and understood by the ambassador, by Mr. Whitman and the others at the embassy? Why would they allow me to be subjected to those dangers?"

"Mr. Kent, this may shock you somewhat, because you seem a very naïve and well-meaning person. But we in the embassy have an overriding reality, and that is the prestige and reputation of the ambassador. In conducting our affairs, and I might say both on and off the job, everything that happens, does so to favor the best interests of the ambassador's political fortunes. This ambassador's agenda happens to feature pleasing the regime of the host government, and that is more important to him than risking the life of an American tourist, even one supposedly traveling on official business. After all, how can the ambassador be faulted for collaborating with law and order?"

Kent squirmed in his seat, not seeing the stream of traffic through which del Barrio expertly weaved her way. What she was saying was making a lot of sense. "But why are you helping me? Aren't you risking a great deal by doing this?"

"Of course," she said simply. "I do not wish to stand idle and let you take the consequences of the self-serving actions of some very ambitious, arrogant, and lazy countrymen of yours. I am ready, if necessary, to accept the consequences of what I am now doing. That must sound quite strange to you, but that would be because you do not know my background, the things I have survived, and what that means to me."

"What's the problem with Garbert Flenk? Why did you warn me not to talk to him?"

"I hoped you would not ask that, because I don't wish to make accusations for which there is no proof. He is a very sad man. His father was an ambassador for twenty-two years and one of the most respected career diplomats in the service. Garbert was expected to follow in his footsteps, and made all the right moves as a young foreign service officer. But his talents are only moderate, and he is, well . . . lazy."

"And despite the prestige of his father, his career didn't advance as it might have?"

She nodded, concentrating on the traffic. "Of course he became frustrated, disenchanted and embittered when he realized he was off the fast track. While he was posted in Moscow, as counselor for commercial affairs, he established a liaison with a Russian woman, or more likely, she established one with him. When the matter was brought to light he was chastised for failing to report the affair when it began."

"Was he then reassigned?"

"He was. But it was later found out that the woman had some fairly high-level political connections. His career was, of course, devastated, and he was thenceforth considered ineligible for posting in any of the Warsaw Pact countries."

"But he was never shown to have been compromised, from a security standpoint?"

"You don't understand. Such an association, despite one's apparent innocence, still constitutes being compromised. But for his father's reputation, he would likely have been dismissed."

"But you haven't said why you consider him a present security risk."

"You must consider how the Soviets do their business. Through a liaison such as Mr. Flenk had, there is invariably a minor indiscretion committed, usually unwittingly, by the victim. This is the proverbial camel's nose under the tent flap. Then, bit by bit, using very subtle blackmail, the Soviets gradually coax the camel all the way into the tent. This often happens, and is precisely why he will always be suspect."

"And so you think he still, even here, must cooperate?"

"That is quite possible, in fact, quite likely."

"But you must be aware of other indications . . ."

"I am indeed. I entered his office one morning and heard him giving details of classified information over the telephone. It concerned remote sensing technology used for assessing the Russian wheat crop. I casually asked to whom he had spoken, and he told me it was James Raskin, who was then his boss, the counselor for agricultural affairs. In fact, he had made a point of saying 'Jim' several times over the phone. I became suspicious because they had offices only a few steps apart, and always spoke in person, particularly about sensitive matters. So later that day, I discussed remote sensing things with Raskin and deduced he had not yet received the information given over the phone by Flenk. There have been other incidents."

"But nothing you could use to make a case against him."

"To even try would cause me more problems than him. I'd become little more than a rumor-spreading troublemaker."

"And you think the police may be waiting for me at the hotel?"

While they waited for the traffic signal to change, del Barrio reached into the backseat and handed him an afternoon newspaper. It was folded with page three showing. "There, near the top of the page. Read it."

RUSSIAN EMBASSY MAN ASSASSINATED
Yevgeny Divnich, 42, a chauffeur at the Soviet Embassy, was found dead by asphyxiation this morning in a linen closet at the Tirol Residencia on Marqués de Urquijo in the University District. No motive has been established for the slaying, but a North American, Arnold Kent, a guest at the hotel, is being sought for questioning by the Police.

"I'm impressed," Kent said. "They do nice work. They've probably already thought about watching the airport as well."

"At least they don't have your picture."

"Right . . . Oh shit!"

"They *do* have your picture?"

"Not yet, but the embassy does. I gave that stuff from the dead Italian's briefcase to Whitman. There are two photos of me in there."

She looked at him in surprise. "The dead Italian's briefcase! Really, Mr. Kent, this has been a busy trip for you, hasn't it? And you left home, when was it . . . yesterday?"

"Saturday, actually."

"And this . . . Italian. He was one of your earlier victims?"

"Well . . ."

"No, don't tell me now. I think we should stop here and have supper. We're far enough out of the city . . . at least for right now."

She turned down a road off the main highway and pulled up in front of a small restaurant called La Esperanza. They had just opened, and the couple found themselves to be the first customers of the evening. They selected a table at a window facing the street, and ordered the *cocido* of the house and a bottle of Rioja red wine. Kent explained the matter of the Italian's briefcase and the other events she was not yet aware of.

"What was Whitman's reaction to the encoded information and the photographs?"

"He seemed interested, but I got the impression he didn't believe it was real. It was like he thought I was pretending to be involved in a spy plot. He said he would need to check the stuff out."

"And he didn't think you were in any particular . . . danger?"

"No. He told me just to go about my business, then get back to him. He wasn't at all impressed with my having been followed, with Miguel's experience, or with my pictures in this guy's briefcase."

"And you're sure the Italian is the one who was living in the house across the street from you in McLean?"

"Señora del Barrio . . ."

"Cristina."

"Cristina, I tend to study people I see . . . their body shapes, the way they move around, how they use their eyes, mannerisms, and when I

saw him in JFK walking into the men's room, it was the way he tilted his
head, and a kind of rolling motion as he walked that identified him to
me. I have no doubt it was he."

She broke a piece of bread off the roll and tore it in half carefully. Her
nails were short and she wore no polish. "Mr. Kent . . ."

"Arno, or Kent, as you prefer."

"You visited Manica Province and found out about forest plantations
there. Do you recall what species were being planted, how extensive the
plantations were, and anything about projected growth rates?"

He looked at her in amazement. "I think I've underestimated you
people at the embassy. How would you possibly know I was there?"

"One of my assignments is to check out official visitors who have
been in Soviet-influenced countries . . . such as Mozambique. Your
name was flagged, so I obtained copies of your reports from FAO-
Rome. I also looked into your background generally."

"I see. Now I'm responsible to remember what I said in the reports?"

"Can you respond to my questions?"

"Wow. That was seven years ago, but as I recall it, they had planted
about ten thousand hectares of pine. . . . There were several species
introduced from the southeast United States, Mexico and the Carib-
bean. *Pinus taeda, elliottii,* and . . . *patula,* I think. One other . . .
khaesya, yes *khyaesa.* Anyway, they were talking about annual growth
on the order of about fifteen cubic meters per hectare per year. Also,
they had about six thousand hectares of eucalyptus that dated back to
the fifties and before. But why are you asking me about those things? Do
you question whether it was I who wrote those reports?"

"I'm sorry to have to test you—Arno. I need to find out why you
went there. If it was purely for technical—that is—forestry purposes,
then of course you dealt with Gravato da Silva." She looked at him
expectantly.

"Da Silva, you said?"

"Yes. Gravato da Silva. In the ministry of agriculture. He spoke
highly of your work there, and explained how much you helped him."

"Hm, no, it doesn't ring a bell. Must be some mistake, because I
can't remember anybody by that name."

"Well then, who was John Benchly?"

"John is a biologist. When I was there he was working with agriculture officials on managing the country's wildlife to provide more protein on a sustained basis. But why did you say 'was'?"

"You worked four years in the Sequoia National Forest. Who was Perry Thornton?"

"You people really do dig up ground, don't you? Yeah, okay. Perry Thornton was a retired real-estate guy turned poet in Kernville who led a preservationist movement against logging on the Kern Plateau. Far as I know, he's still there doing his thing."

"What about Stratford Hayes?"

"You know about him too? Hayes was a Porterville civil engineer who owned a piece of land near Springville. During the controversy over Disney's proposed development of Mineral King, Hayes promoted, in lieu of the planned highway, a tunnel that would terminate on his land, thus enhancing its value. But look, Miss del . . . Cristina . . ."

"I'm finished, Arno. I believe you are indeed the person you represent yourself to be. About Benchly, our information is that he was abducted by anti-FRELIMO forces, and not heard from again. That would have been after you left. And there is no such person as da Silva. Will I be forgiven?"

Kent studied her face. The Moorish features, dark complexion, and eyes that looked black in dim light had, until then, projected the forbidding and somewhat saturnine quality seen in the stage faces of flamenco dancers. But now her face was softening and warming, almost showing a small smile for the first time. He liked what he saw in it. "You will be forgiven . . . Cristina, the moment I am convinced you are the person you represent yourself to be."

She blinked several times. "So, now I am being measured as a Soviet agent?"

"Of course," Kent said, finishing his first glass of wine. "What better way to efficiently dispose of me than to whisk me out of reach of the Spanish police? I mean, why bother with all of that troublesome suicide business when you have at your disposal any number of . . . more direct methods?"

"You're right," she said. "This would definitely be the way to handle things. We would then have the choice of either disposing of you straightaway, or of enlisting your services in our cause. But in the meanwhile, how do you propose checking me out, and anyway, what options do you think you have at this point?"

Kent thought she was enjoying the flow of things, and seemed suddenly more relaxed and human. After what had happened so far, he could not imagine this woman as a Soviet agent, with comrades waiting nearby in another car. But on the other hand, who was he to make such a judgment? What did he know of KGB methods, other than the few spy novels he had read, and the documentaries he'd seen on the tube? What he did know was that he had a big problem, namely the Spanish police, along with the KGB threat alluded to by Miss (or was it Mrs.?) del Barrio. "I guess I don't have any options at the moment," he said. "But I would like to know for starters where you picked up your beautiful English. It sounds absolutely American, both in dialect and in idiom."

"Thank you. I've worked very hard on it. My father was a professor of anthropology, and I accompanied him on two sabbaticals to your country. That included my attending two quarters at what was then Chico State College in northern California, and a semester at the University of New Mexico in Albuquerque."

"So you are . . . and always have been . . . a Spaniard."

"Yes. I was born near here and educated mainly in Madrid."

"You must be married . . . have a family . . ."

"My husband was a policeman, a captain in the civil guard. He was murdered by Basques . . . a car bomb . . . about a year ago."

"I'm so sorry."

"Our two children, Filiberto and Teresa, are in a boarding school in the city. It is not the way I would prefer it, however it is not too bad. I think they like the arrangement more that I do."

"When were you in Chico?"

"In the winter of 1971 and spring of 1972. Do you know the place?"

"Yes, it was my winter headquarters for three years. In fact, you and I were there at the same time. What were you doing when the earthquake hit?"

She gave him an amused glance. "That was a nice try, Arno. You are beginning to learn my games. I thought perhaps you were going to ask me about the park with the famous waterfall, the one that does not exist, but in reality has a record-size tree called the Hooker Oak."

He laughed uproariously, slapping the table repeatedly with his large hand. "You know, I think I'm going to like being a spy, even if only for a short time. But eventually you must tell me what you have in mind. I do have the feeling I'm getting in way over my depth."

She waited while the waiter cleared the dishes from their table. "I have relatives in a small village in the Sierra de Guadarrama, not far from here. We will arrive there after dark, and they will hide you temporarily. You must not go out or be seen by anybody other than the family."

"Until . . ."

"I don't know. But tomorrow I shall be at work at the embassy and can learn what is going on. Until it is safe, you must be patient and trust me."

"Okay, but Cristina, I'm very concerned about Miguel and his family—that my assailants will try to get at me through them. He is aware of the situation—he knows I am confiding in you. I trust him completely not to give that away. I told him you are our link, and that he must not communicate with anyone else at the embassy. Would you—"

"I understand. He will be kept informed. Do you think he . . . that is, if it became absolutely essential, could he be called upon to provide transportation and cover to get you out of the Madrid area?"

"Jesus. I'd really dislike having to do that. But yes, yes, I think he'd do it. Just keep in mind he's not experienced in this kind of thing, and . . ."

A quick smile lit her face. "We do what we have to," she said.

They left the restaurant and drove through the darkening night, the road becoming more crooked as they climbed into the mountains. The sparse shrubbery and evergreen oaks of the central plains gave way to the more stately yet scrubby pines of the sierra. Even in the twilight Kent could recognize by silhouette the umbrella-crowned stone pines, the frugal Aleppo pines that could thrive in hotter climes and rockier, drier soil than any other member of their genus, and the sixty-foot-tall cluster pines brought earlier from coastal zones to help afforest the barren slopes of the Guadarrama. It made him wonder whether forestry might ever again be an important part of his life.

Cristina del Barrio broke into his reverie. "Were you able to gain any significance whatever from the coded notes in the Italian's briefcase?"

"Not very much, I'm afraid. He obviously had my itinerary because the names of my hotels in both Madrid and in Rome were there. I suppose they'll decipher the stuff at the embassy. Maybe then I'll be off the hook—at least with our guys."

"Maybe," she said. "But that's the least of your worries. You know, it would be quite helpful to know what we're dealing with. The Soviets have something big at stake here, otherwise they wouldn't be paying any attention to you. What might that have to do with your little assignment from the OFDA people in Washington?"

The copy Kent had made of the notes flashed through his mind. He felt his inside pocket to confirm he still had them. Should he mention it to Cristina, he asked himself? But what if she were, in fact, an agent? She might now be trying to find out if there were such a copy, and if so, where?

"I'd like to know too," he said. "And by the way, I made a copy of those notes, just in case anybody happened to separate me from the briefcase en route to the embassy."

"Fantastic!" she said. "And you have them with you?"

"No, I left them in a safe place in Madrid."

"With Miguel, obviously."

"No. Miguel doesn't even know about my copying the notes. However, should anything . . . happen to me, another person in the ICONA offices will open an envelope explaining the entire situation, and giving the location of those notes."

She drove along through the night for several minutes in silence. Kent studied the line of her forehead, her aquiline nose, her strong chin.

"It is completely understandable that you do not yet have confidence in me, Arno. But you will. Here, beside me. My purse. Open it and find your gift from me."

He complied, withdrawing the tiny automatic pistol. "It's beautiful," he said, admiring the satin stainless steel finish. "But I really wasn't planning any shootings on this trip. And if I were, I'd feel a whole lot more confident with something . . . a bit more, uh, substantial. Anyway, wouldn't this be a big problem if the Spanish police caught me with it?"

"You still don't seem to appreciate that your biggest concern right now is staying alive. Consider it a last resort if you wish. Are you familiar with this kind of automatic?"

"I have one like it at home—an American Arms TP-seventy. It's a little larger and heavier than this one—and it's double-action. This one is not."

"This is essentially the same weapon: twenty-five-caliber, six-round magazine plus one in the chamber. Not much stopping power, but quite lethal if used properly."

"You sound like a gun dealer."

She smiled. "My husband's passion. He made me learn how to handle his entire collection."

She slowed the car, pulling off the paved highway onto a gravel drive that wound around among grape arbors and small cultivated plots corresponding to several private residences. At the end of the gravel lane there was a tile-roofed house almost fully obscured by trees and shrubbery. It seemed to be isolated from the other houses by at least a hundred meters. Cristina drove around behind the building and parked the car next to an old Fiat van with peeling paint and badly worn tires.

"We're here," she said. "I'll be here just long enough to introduce you, then I'll return to the city by another route. Do whatever Pablo tells you—he's my cousin, and he'll try to keep you alive. Other than that, wait until you hear from me, and it might be several days. All right?"

Kent took her hand with both of his. "Cristina, thank you." He thought about grabbing her and kissing her, but she sensed his intention and got out of the car.

As they approached the back door of the house she took him by the arm and said, "In your spare time, try to decode those notes, will you?"

It was three P.M. in Washington, and Phil Perkins, director of the Forest Service's international forestry staff, was still puzzling over his call from the embassy in Madrid. He closed the door to his office, picked up the phone and called Farber Claunch at AID/OFDA.

"Hi, Farber, how goes the war?"

"Quiet today, Phil. No floods, fires or earthquakes, just the usual dozen famines. What's up?"

"Well, I don't know. Thought maybe you could help. What's all this about our man Kent and some assignment you gave him in Naples?"

"Oh, did he call you?"

"No, he didn't, but a Norbert Whitman in our embassy in Madrid did. He said he was trying to verify some statements Kent made to him."

"Did he say there was a problem, or what?"

"No, but he seemed quite concerned. What the hell's going on?"

"I'll find out. All I know right now is, I asked him to get some information from his forestry contacts in Rome relating to something going on in Naples. I'm surprised to hear it was even mentioned at the embassy in Madrid. They're closed up over there by now for the night, but I'll get on them first thing in the morning. Be in your office tomorrow?"

Perkins hung up and picked up his coffee cup to get a refill when his phone buzzed. It was the State Department's agricultural attaché in the Department of Agriculture. His voice was quivering like a violin string.

"Listen, Phil, we've got big problems. You sitting down?"

"I'm listening, I'm listening already."

"The name Arnold Kent ring a bell for you?"

"Sure. What now?"

"You want the bad news, or the bad news?"

"Lay it on me, will you?"

"The Spanish police are looking for him as prime suspect in the killing of a Russian embassy employee. How's that for openers?"

"Oh, I'd place it somewhere ahead of this morning's chief-and-staff meeting on the interest list. You wouldn't shit me, would you, Ferrel? I mean, you sure have a way about making somebody's day."

"Apparently he's mixed up in some trumped-up spy story, they're saying, but won't give out any details. What they're asking you for is Kent's official personnel file, along with anything else that might be relevant. Can do?"

"And naturally they want it by early yesterday, right?"

"I need it in my hands in one hour, max."

"The file is in Rosslyn, but I'll get it sent over on the next shuttle. Kent's boss would be the best source of other info, but he's out of town. You're going to have to settle for just the file until tomorrow. That okay? Oh, by the way, I just talked to Farber Claunch at AID/OFDA. He doesn't know about this yet, but he knows some other things that I don't. Why don't you get him on the line?"

Vera Vlasov buzzed Aleksey Nikolsky into her undecorated office, kept him standing while she sucked the last three drags from her cigarette, then demanded his account of how he had been outwitted by the American. Nikolsky went through the story without mentioning having seen Kent leave the hotel, and leaving the impression the American had already been there when they arrived.

"In all my years of service in this organization," she began, "I have had the dubious honor of dealing with agents singularly unmatched in incompetence and intelligence. But I can assure you that you and that other cunt-lapping jackrabbit Divnich are at the top of the list, and by at least one order of magnitude." Her brow wrinkled, and eyes squinting against the smoke, she lit another cigarette. "I give you an assignment that should have been as easy as pissing on two fingers, and what happens? You commit technical errors with the lightning-like rapidity of one propelled by fart steam. Well, anyway, now I only have one of you turd-feelers left to embarrass me."

Nikolsky avoided her piercing gaze, hoping the lecture would end soon. He had long ago given up any delusions of earning a promotion, and was now merely putting in his time, trying not to get into predicaments like this one. He thought of the vodka bottle back in the tiny flat he had shared with Divnich, and tried to remember how much was left in it.

"Because of your unparalleled incompetence," the wiry little officer continued, "we now find ourselves in a much more difficult situation than it was before you started fucking otters in the snow. If we or the Spanish police fail to apprehend the American in the next twenty-four hours I will have to alert Korolenko in Rome, and that will be extremely embarrassing to me, and disastrous for you, you may be certain. As of this moment I am assigning you two responsibilities. First, I wish to be advised instantaneously when and if Mr. Kent is taken into custody by the police. Second, in the event that he reaches the American Embassy, either on his own or he is delivered there, I must be advised instantaneously. Regarding the embassy surveillance, I recommend you deal exclusively with Anatoly Malik. Do you recognize the importance of what I am telling you I want?"

Nikolsky, still standing in front of her desk, nodded. "Yes, Colonel. You can rely on me."

"I wouldn't be that stupid. Now spare me your presence so I can organize my other people to undo your donkey-fucking."

Vlasov dismissed Nikolsky, then learned by phone from Vladimir Chuvash, another of her agents, that Miguel Escobosa had gone alone from his office on Gran Vía de San Francisco directly to the estate of his brother-in-law where his family had secluded themselves. Chuvash reported that the property was staked out, and that they were working on a phone intercept. Vlasov instructed him to maintain knowledge of Escobosa's exact whereabouts around the clock in case it became necessary to deal with him "on a personal basis."

Vlasov then requested and obtained an immediate meeting with her superior, Colonel Feliks Kratkov, to discuss the Kent matter. Kratkov was an elderly man, slender and stately, and with a full head of white hair. He was regarded as one of the most analytical and prudent KGB officers at any Western European post.

"Vera, you seem unusually upset. Are things going as badly as the furrows in your face seem to indicate?"

She slumped down into a recliner chair and lit a cigarette. "Feliks, we've let the American slip through our hands, somehow. Well, somehow, shit. When this is over I'm dumping Nikolsky, I don't care where or how. Anyway, I'm very unhappy. We just don't have much to go on at this moment. I feel he is hiding somewhere in the city, and he's smart enough, apparently, to blend in with the wallpaper. How critical are we on time?"

Kratkov took off his rimless glasses and began polishing the lenses with a clean white handkerchief. "That depends entirely on how much he might know about Oltraggio. If he's pieced it together, and I really don't know how that could happen, then we're at risk this very minute. We'd have to be concerned he didn't even get to a telephone. Flenk's appraisal is that Kent has seen enough to alert him that something is planned for Naples and that he is somehow involved. But until he put the blocks to Divnich, nobody in their embassy was taking him very seriously. Now they don't know what to think."

"How would he have any clue as to Oltraggio?"

"Flenk says he delivered Cavalchini's briefcase contents to the chief security officer. He obviously had a look at the papers. Otto Frange thinks it highly improbable that Cavalchini would have been stupid enough to be carrying around any reference to Oltraggio."

"But what if Kent held back something, or copied something, or memorized something?"

"Yes, you are right, Vera. We will have to proceed on that assumption and not allow time to slip away. In your opinion, who might be helping the American?"

"There's somebody, obviously, or at least I will be able to make that statement tomorrow after the papers have come out with his picture on the front page. It would most likely be either somebody from ICONA, where Kent has several close contacts, or one of the CIA stooges in the embassy. Among those there are two distinct possibilities, and perhaps a third. Can I be provided with additional help?"

"I have already made arrangements. Can you get by with four more?"

"Excellent, Feliks, provided they may be dedicated to tracking Kent down. I do not, obviously, have resources to watch airports, train stations and all that."

"We'll let the police take care of the obvious avenues. They seem to be reasonably efficient, and I'll see they are sufficiently pressured by the ambassador. Have you contacted Korolenko . . . just in case Mr. Kent gets lucky?"

"I'll do so immediately, but with the full expectation that no actions by his people will become necessary."

"Good. And Vera, what is your plan with respect to Mr. Kent if . . . that is, when you apprehend him?"

"I'll find out everything he knows. Then we'll arrange for him to take the blame posthumously for some atrocity designed to stun the Spaniards. I won't let you down, Feliks."

CHAPTER FOUR

Cristina led Kent through a narrow hallway into a large room in which eight people were seated as if waiting for company to arrive. Two of them were children, a girl and a boy, and the others were adults ranging in age from early forties to very elderly. It was obviously a family gathering, Kent thought, and from the expectant looks on their faces they understood something unusual was happening.

Speaking Castilian, Cristina introduced Kent to José Pablo, the owner of the house and the man who would be responsible for him. Pablo was about forty-three, of medium build, with small eyes, small mouth, and a dark shadow around his jowls from that day's growth of whiskers. His hair was dark brown with no traces of gray at the temples. He was wearing a tan shirt, open at the neck, and sleeves rolled up to the elbow, revealing a gold wristwatch with expansion band and very hairy arms.

Pablo warmly welcomed Kent, and insisted on introducing his family to him, beginning with his grandmother, Doña Cristina, who, he proudly pointed out, had ninety-nine years. The old woman offered her hand, but seemed to focus her eyes off in the distance. She had a full head of white hair, and her eyes, set deep in a sunken face, were outlined in pale red. Her face seemed about half obscured by liver spots, as were her hands and arms, but Kent thought her hands looked strong and capable.

Kent then met the elder Cristina's two children, Antonio, in his early seventies and Francisca, about sixty-seven, Pablo's mother. Francisca, garbed in a traditional black dress of mourning, was a plain, but very pleasant and kind-looking woman with gray hair flattened close to her head and parted in the middle, then tied in the back. She wore small gold earrings and a tiny golden necklace. Francisca's husband Juan José was a stern, fit-looking man of about seventy who had a proud, defiant look; he seemed ready to spring into action at any moment.

Pablo went on. He introduced his wife María, a plump woman of about forty with dark reddish brown hair cut quite short, who wore a flowered print dress, and, like her mother-in-law, tiny golden earrings. José Tomás was eleven, a bright-eyed boy with hair the tone and texture of his mother's. He was wearing a T-shirt with the words AMERICAN BOWLING on the front. José Tomás's eyes danced with the excitement of receiving a foreign visitor in their house. Then, in a red T-shirt and blue jeans, was Paqui, nine, the youngest member of the household.

Still speaking Castilian, Cristina turned directly to Kent and said, "I have explained to them why you are here, and why your presence cannot be made known to anyone outside the household. I leave you in their hands, and will return when I can. Please trust them to do what is in your best interests."

She then had a quick, private conversation with Pablo. He asked a few questions that Kent couldn't pick up, then nodded at her responses. Then she turned toward Kent, looked him in the eye for several seconds, and left.

"Have you eaten yet?" asked María.

"Yes, thank you. We stopped on the way out of town."

"Something to drink, perhaps?" offered Pablo, as most of the others drifted away to other rooms.

"I don't think so. I just realized how tired I have become."

"Nonsense, *joven*," said Juan José. "A shot of cognac will help you sleep better." He produced a half-full bottle of Carlos Primero and poured out a generous portion, having one himself. After downing the smooth liquor, Kent was led away to a bungalow behind the main house. It appeared to be a toolshed, but was outfitted with a tiny bedroom in the ceiling space above the workroom. Access was provided by a retractable ladder that became part of the ceiling when in the raised position.

"I'm sorry there is no toilet in here," said Pablo. "You will have to use the one in the house, or in an emergency, in that little shed back there. There is a little buzzer in the workroom right below you. We use it to call Antonio to dinner. But now we will only use it to signal you that you must stay hidden until we come for you. If it is rung repeatedly, that means you must leave on foot immediately. Sleep well, my friend."

The white bedside phone rang in McLean, Virginia. It was about eleven P.M., but Yvette Kent, having just returned from the District, was not yet in bed.

"Yvette, this is Stan Dawson—"

"Who?"

"Stan Dawson . . . Arno's boss at the Forest Service."

"Oh, oh yes, of course. Uh . . . well, how are you?"

"Fine, fine. Uh, you haven't heard from Arno . . . uh . . . since he left, have you?"

"No, no I haven't. He just left Saturday."

"Yes. Well, something's happened that you ought to know about. I've been trying to reach you all evening."

"Oh, well, I've been out . . . to an art opening, actually. It was really marvelous . . . at Gallery K. Have you been there? It was really—"

"Yvette, something's happened to Arno. I hope it doesn't turn out to be—"

"Did he lose his wallet again, or—"

"Please listen for a minute, Yvette. There is a serious problem. Arno has dropped out of sight in Madrid. The Spanish police are searching for him—"

"Why can't they find him? Don't they know what hotel he's—"

"Let me finish, please. The police think he may have killed a Russian embassy employee in his hotel room, and want him for questioning. But nobody can find him, and—"

"I knew it, I knew this was going to happen. He wouldn't admit it, but I knew all along."

"Knew *what* all along, Yvette?"

"About the CIA, of course."

"The CIA? What about the CIA?"

"That he was working for them. Oh sure. You're going to tell me you didn't know anything about it, but that's not surprising. He wouldn't even admit it to me, his own wife."

"Listen, Yvette. I don't know anything about the CIA, and frankly, I don't think this has anything to do with them. All I know right now is that your husband is missing, and that he's apparently in trouble. We're in contact with the State Department, and—"

"Yes, so am I, Mr. Durstan. And I'm telling you the same thing I told that Mr. Francis or whoever it was who called me, that Arno is in Spain, not Italy. I suppose now there will be a parade of investigators coming here to interrogate me about all this."

"Yvette, I have no idea what's going to happen, but we'll do our very best to keep you informed. Will I be able to reach you by phone at home tomorrow?"

"Well, tomorrow morning I'm having my hair done, but I should be back by around noon. Stay in touch."

Dawson hung up the phone, shaking his head in disgust. "Bitch," he muttered, pouring himself a generous slug of bourbon. "No fucking wonder Arno likes traveling so much."

Garbert Flenk got to his office at the embassy early on Tuesday morning. He got himself a cup of coffee, carried it to his desk, then unfolded the copy of *El País* he had picked up in the lobby. On page three there was a picture of Arnold Kent, the one provided to the police by the embassy, then obviously shared with the press. The article beneath the photo said Kent was being sought for questioning in the death of the Russian Divnich, and that anyone with information should contact the police. An embassy spokesman was quoted as saying that Kent was on forestry business in Madrid, and planned to go on to Rome following the Madrid visit. A Soviet embassy spokesman had said that high-ranking diplomatic officials were concerned and wanted to know why their employee had been viciously slain by the North American spy Kent.

Flenk was looking at the wall clock, wondering when Cristina del Barrio would show up, when she walked through the door.

"Good morning, Mr. Flenk. I see you already have your coffee."

"Have you seen the morning papers?"

"No, I haven't," she said, putting her white jacket into a wardrobe. "What happened? Has Gary Hart made the front pages again?"

Flenk didn't even smile. "Take a look at this," he said, tapping Kent's photo with the eraser end of his pencil.

She quickly scanned the coverage. "So. He's still missing. Must be holed up with one of his forestry buddies."

"Could be, I suppose. What I can't figure is why he didn't come back here when Whitman told him to. At that time he couldn't have known the police were looking for him. He just vanished."

"You don't suppose the KGB got into the act . . . say about the time he would have been leaving the ICONA offices to come here?"

"Why would you think that a possibility? What did they know at that moment?"

"Well, it just seems to me that if that Russian had gone to Kent's room for whatever reason, it makes sense they would have stayed on the trail, for the same reason. Why else wouldn't he have come here immediately?"

Flenk took a long drink of his coffee. "Unless he were warned off . . . by somebody from here."

Del Barrio whirled around to face him. "Did you—?" she asked, eyes opened wide and mouth agape.

"No! Not me, for God's sake! In fact, why would anybody here jump into the middle of that one?"

"You think he's with the Company?" she asked, studying his reactions closely.

"What do you think? You did the background on him. Your suspicions get aroused at all?"

"I thought it through again last night. I don't think so."

"Last night? When did you have time?"

"What do you mean?"

"I called you three times. I was down here working on the commodities report, and I couldn't find the figures we'd worked up last week."

"Sorry. I moved the file to the new section. Late dinner with friends. Didn't mean to inconvenience you. And, as I've said before, I can work late if it's important."

"No problem. I'll be at a meeting with Whitman and others at eight o'clock. It's undoubtedly about our friend Kent. Can you hold down the fort here for me?"

After Flenk left del Barrio slipped down to the lobby area and from the marine sergeant who supervised the night shift of guards found out that nobody had worked after regular hours on their floor the previous night. So where had Flenk called her from, and for what purpose? she asked herself. And why was he lying about it?

Del Barrio returned to her desk and dialed a number. When her call was answered, she said, "Do you have last year's tonnages on perishables for the third quarter?"

"Yes, they're available, but only in round numbers."

"Fine. Send them over when you can, please. Meantime, I have good news on our project, the one we talked about yesterday."

"Wonderful. Things went as you hoped they would?"

"Completely. But I'll need more guidelines as soon as they're available. The present arrangement will probably need a change within a couple of days."

"Okay. Give me a call. If I'm not home, you can probably reach me at Sandra's. Have a good one."

Del Barrio hung up, stretched, then ran her hands over her tightly bound hair. I wonder what it would be like, she asked herself, to someday not have to worry about having your calls listened in on.

It was nine A.M., Tuesday morning, in the Washington, D.C., office of the U.S. Forest Service; it was the regular meeting time of the chief and his immediate staff. Routinely, this included the associate chief, the five deputy chiefs, and the chief's personal secretary. But to be on hand for specific items, staff directors and others were often included. On this day, Phil Perkins and Stan Dawson were told to be there.

When the chief, Cliff Baker, came into the large office, the others were already seated around a large circular table or in upholstered chairs next to the wall. Baker was six foot two and carried about two hundred pounds on what used to be an athletic frame. The succession of buckle marks along his leather belt revealed his gradual weight gain of recent years, but he still looked robust and energetic. He looked around the room, greeting those not normally there for the morning meeting.

"Let's start with you, Sam," Baker said, nodding his head in the direction of his deputy chief for the national forest system. Each deputy chief in turn reported on items of general interest, while the chief's secretary scribbled notes that would, shortly after the meeting, be transmitted electronically to three thousand computer terminals in Forest Service offices around the country. The reports were finished in about fifteen minutes, with no mention yet of the problem in Madrid.

"Okay Phil," said the chief, winking at his director for international forestry. "Here I thought all this time you were developing programs of forestry collaboration over there, and it turns out to be a goddamn spy network. Would you like to tell us what the hell you've got going on?"

Perkins, a rather short, bald-headed man with a red mustache and horn-rimmed glasses, told everything he knew about the situation, which took exactly one minute. Everyone sat there looking intrigued.

"You have anything to add to that?" the chief said, looking at Arno's boss Stan Dawson.

"It blows me away," he said, glancing around the room at the others. "I've never known anyone more normal, conservative, stable, predictable, conscientious, as Arno Kent. It absolutely defies logic."

Baker scratched his head, looking pensive. "Well, how is his wife taking it? I hope the hell you've told her about it."

"She said it confirmed her suspicions that he works for the CIA. Also, she said she can't be reached this morning because she's having her hair done."

"Maybe she works for them too," somebody said, producing a round of chuckles.

The chief wasn't laughing. "We may have a problem on our hands," he said. "Not to mention Kent's health and welfare in this thing, we may come out looking like a CIA front. That's about all I'd need next time I go before the appropriations committee. The secretary already called me this morning. He's not exactly looking for publicity on this. We can't change what may already have happened over there, but let's not let it get blown out of proportion."

"So our line, media-wise, ought to be 'We don't know what happened yet, it's all a big surprise to us'?" asked the director of the Office of Information.

"Well, that's how it is, isn't it?" growled the chief. "Let's just not have any doubts in our minds about why he went over there and what he was trying to get done. Phil, you make sure everybody understands that, okay? And you're the key man here. Let John and me know the minute you have more on it. Anything else? Okay, meeting's over."

The coffee percolated busily on the kitchen sink while Lieutenant Colonel Vera Vlasov squinted through her cigarette smoke at a pile of notes and a map of the Madrid area on her little breakfast table. She never ate anything in the morning, and liked the Spanish custom of having the main meal in early to mid afternoon. Her cat Sasha jumped into her lap, nestled down and began purring. She scratched the animal's head behind the ears, then stroked its fur affectionately. Vlasov was in no great rush to get to her dingy embassy office this morning. She had gotten things fairly well organized, in her view, late last night, in a session with her subordinates, and would now spend her time on contingency planning. She had too many years of experience supervising inept subordinates to suppose that all would go well with a plan that depended even partly for success on human behavior.

Vlasov looked forward to retiring before she became too old to enjoy a more relaxing life than she had known for the last twenty-five years, and had been promised that her last assignment would be in Moscow with the Seventh Directorate of the KGB, the one responsible for surveillance of foreigners in Soviet Russia. That directorate employed many female officers, particularly those with facility in several languages. Inasmuch as the work was classified as hazardous duty, each year served in the Seventh Directorate counted double toward retirement credit. Vera's record of proficiency was excellent in all respects, and she didn't wish what might turn out to be her final assignment in Madrid to produce a black mark on an otherwise spotless record. Should she fail in this mission, and the North American get out of Spain to Rome, he would in all likelihood be picked off by Korolenko's well-oiled machine in Italy. In fact, Korolenko was already aware Kent was still loose in the Madrid area. But she knew that every hour Kent was unaccounted for was an hour during which he might unearth the reason for KGB concern about him and relate this persuasively to the American authorities. Operation Oltraggio, she understood, could not be compromised under any circumstances. And so she was duty-bound to see the American neutralized, and fully intended to redeem that responsibility.

Through Garbert Flenk, she had a list of everyone at the American embassy Kent had been in contact with, and at that very moment two of her officers were pulling together all available information concerning the background, current circumstances, and present movements of those people. Surveillance had been set up covering Garbert Flenk, Cristina del Barrio, Norbert Whitman, and Bradford Baumont. Two more agents had been ordered to assess quickly the Spanish forest service people, particularly those in Incendios Forestales, the forest-fire section, to learn with whom Kent had close liaison and to establish surveillance. Fortunately, the KGB was already receiving collaboration from two ICONA employees. She felt confident that should the Spanish police pick up the American, she would learn of it immediately, and through the Soviet ambassador, gain the cooperation of the police in holding Kent incommunicado. She would know quite well how to deal with him then.

Kent awoke to the crowing of a rooster that, by the sound, must have been perched on the peak of his little shed, not more than a few feet above his head. He glanced at his watch: six thirty. Through the one small window at the east end of his little hideaway he could see that the sun had not yet emerged from beyond the mountain ridge to his east. He had slept profoundly for at least nine hours and felt marvelously refreshed. It took him several minutes to rethink the major events of the previous day and fully appreciate his predicament. He could not hear any human activity other than the occasional passing of a car at a distance, and looking out the window could see nobody. So he dressed, descended the ladder, and used the outhouse behind his shed. Then he went back inside, sat on a stool by the workbench, and dug from his pocket the notes he had copied.

Trying different patterns of number and letter substitutions that he had been successful with earlier got him nowhere now. An hour of effort netted him the date November 15 for something to happen in Naples, but that was as far as he could get. He wondered what the embassy cryptographers had made of it. Surely they must have had it decoded within minutes.

The door to the shed opened and Pablo's wife María entered with a tray of food and coffee. She asked how he had slept, then told him Pablo wished him to stay inside as much as possible during daylight, that their gossiping neighbors and field workers should not be aware of his presence. Later in the morning Pablo brought him a change of clothes and told him his business suit didn't exactly fit in around a rural area like this one. He added that, except for Kent's blue eyes, he could manage to look very Spanish. While Kent put on the clean but well-worn casual clothes, Pablo was hanging a gray blanket on a wall of the shed. He then produced a Polaroid flash camera, lined Kent up in front of the blanket and took several pictures of him from close range.

"And now I will need your passport," Pablo said. "Just think, in a few hours you will be a new man, so to speak."

"That's fine," Kent said. "I wasn't doing too well in my old life anyway. What is to be my new name, and what country will I be from?"

"You will still be a North American. While your Spanish is really excellent, your very slight accent would give you away at any passport control desk. As for your name, that will be selected for you, most likely to correspond with that of a living person whose existence could be verified and whose physical description is similar to your own."

"But I don't understand," Kent said. "Who is doing all this for me?"

"Cristina has helped people before. She has some very good connections. For some reason, she has decided to help you, and that is what we are doing. I cannot tell you any more than that."

"I'm very grateful, Señor Ribera, I—"

"The pistol," he said, holding out his hand. "I need it for a little while."

Kent handed over the small automatic with a bit of reluctance, but knowing he had no choice about much of anything while he was the guest of these nice people. Pablo disappeared, returning a few hours later to hand Kent a leather holster, his small eyes gleaming.

"Juan José made it," he said proudly. "It's for your ankle."

Together, they fitted it to his leg, then slid the gun into it.

"A perfect fit," Kent said. "But now I have one leg heavier than the other."

"In an hour you'll be used to it. And don't forget, this weapon must be cocked before firing it the first time."

"Pablo, is it expected that anyone might come here looking for me?"

"Cristina considers it a possibility. The Russians don't leave any stones unturned. That is why you must be ready at all times to depart quickly and remain hidden. I would suggest going through the grove of oaks behind the shed and to the hillside beyond. From there you can observe the opening behind our house, and the road both above and below our turnoff. If it becomes impossible for you to return to the house, there is an abandoned windmill about two kilometers north of here. That will be a rendezvous point should it become necessary."

"Might the police come and search your house?"

"If they were suspicious, they would likely seal off the road, and then ask the Guardia Civil to approach us. We know those people, and I don't think they would barge in on us without warning."

At that moment Pablo cocked his lead to the left, listening. "There is a car pulling up in front of the house," he said, deep lines forming troughs across his forehead.

He had no sooner spoken, than the buzzer began buzzing ominously and repeatedly. Pablo swept up Kent's discarded suit, jamming it into a wastebasket beneath a worktable, and said, "Out of here, quickly! Into the woods and out of sight!"

Kent slipped out of the shed. Looking around and seeing no one, he made his way quickly into the grove of oaks. He stopped in the shadows and looked back toward the house. Pablo was casually shuffling along toward the house carrying some boards and some hand tools. Kent decided he was well enough concealed where he was, and had a good avenue of escape if needed, so he stayed put to await developments, if any. The escapade was reminding him of some earlier adventures staking out commercial Christmas-tree thieves in a northern California national forest. He thought it a bit amusing that it was now he who was being sought by the authorities.

For about ten minutes, nothing happened. Then Kent saw Pablo walking toward the shed with another man, someone he hadn't seen before. The stranger had on dark trousers and a lightweight leather jacket. Neither man was smiling. Pablo unlocked and removed a padlock from the shed door and they went inside. Kent's skin began getting clammy. He didn't think the stranger was from the police, and he was afraid that his suit was crammed into a place where it might readily be discovered. He felt that Pablo's life was now in great danger, and he eased his way back toward the shed, keeping it in line between the house and himself. It only figured that a second man would be in the house with the family members while this guy was conducting a search of the premises.

Kent reached the oak tree closest to the shed, placing himself within about twelve meters of the building. Then he heard the squeaking of the ladder as it was being raised back into the up position. The stranger had already had a look into Kent's bedroom, and would have seen the blankets and pillow. Kent, fearing the worst, worked his way up to the back of the building and listened. Now he could hear Pablo's voice explaining that his wife had been angered and made him sleep in the shed. He was laughing, and doing a good job of acting.

Then the stranger's voice, speaking Castilian, but with a heavy accent boomed out, "And how does one explain this, my friend?" This was clearly not the police. Kent was sure he'd found the clothes. It was not difficult to predict what would happen next. Pablo and his family would be made to tell what they knew, thereby jeopardizing the entire family, including Cristina and, of course, Kent himself. It didn't escape Kent that some unknown but apparently high-stakes national interests of the United States were also involved. He decided to trust his instincts, impulsive or not, and unholstering the .25-caliber automatic, he jumped into the workroom. The stranger whirled in surprise, his right hand releasing Kent's suit coat and reaching into his jacket for a weapon. Pablo stepped back out of the way as Kent put a bullet squarely into the man's forehead.

Pablo took it in stride. "KGB," he said. "There's another one inside the house."

"You think he heard the shot?"

"Without doubt. You'd better get out of here."

"No way," Kent said, surprising himself with his calmness. "I want you to stagger out of here faking a chest wound and roll around on the ground shouting for help. Do it right now!"

Pablo did as he was told, hollering bloody murder and clutching his midsection. Just the way they do it in the western movies, Kent thought. He watched the back door of the house through the crack between the half-open door and the doorjamb, and in a moment the other Russian came out, with an impressive-looking Luger in one hand and tugging along the nine-year-old Paqui with the other. The girl's face was white as snow. The man spotted Pablo immediately, surveyed the scene for a moment, then, scooping the girl up in his left arm and carrying her along in front of him as a shield, walked through the doorway of the shed. Kent, who had crouched in a dark corner, knew he'd have a couple of seconds advantage before the Russian's eyes adjusted to the relative darkness of the shed's interior. He had the little pistol in both hands aimed at where he calculated the Russian's chest would appear in the doorway. But when he saw Paqui, the Russian's brawny arm clutching her to his front, he froze in terror. The Soviet looked quickly around the little room. His eyes only hesitated a split second on the body of his partner. Then they moved on to pick Kent out of the shadows.

The Russian leveled his Luger at Kent. The hole in the muzzle looked immense from the front. Kent felt suddenly as if his own gun were a water pistol.

"Drop it," the Russian said in Castilian. "Drop it right now!"

Kent dropped the little pistol and slowly raised his hands, still in a crouched position. The Russian moved forward, setting the girl down but keeping hold of her hand. He kicked Kent's pistol aside, then stooped, placing his middle finger on the side of the neck of his fallen companion.

"Son of a whore!" he muttered, staring down at Kent. Kent tried to duck as the man's foot arced upward into the side of his face, sending his head back into the wall with a clunk. Kent's vision went to a black screen, lightning flashes of a hundred colors dancing wildly in front of him. He instinctively covered his face and head with both arms, expecting another kick.

"On your feet, jackal!" he heard. He wasn't aware of whether the command was in Spanish or English. The Russian jerked him roughly along the walkway at the side of the house, the big pistol against his neck. Kent felt blood streaming out of the corner of his mouth, but was yet too dazed to know how badly he was hurt, or exactly where. Then they were at the Russian's car, and the door was open and Kent was being pushed into the backseat. Even in his dazed state, Kent realized his captor would have either to tie him, slug him unconscious, or give him an injection to keep him subdued. He decided to lunge at the man before any of these things could happen. Awkwardly, Kent made his move, diving at the Russian's midsection, trying to throw him off balance. The Russian took a quick step backward, simultaneously bringing his Luger up to a firing position. Kent tried to go under the weapon as he made contact, but it felt like a dream. His motion was too slow, as if he were caught in a sticky web. He saw the flash from his adversary's weapon and suddenly everything tumbled about in a display of warped geometric shapes that quickly fused into absolute blackness.

CHAPTER FIVE

Kent's return to consciousness was like coming out of a dark pit where he had to push monsters from on top of himself and extract himself from a gluelike gel. He was immersed in a sea of pungent odors. His head pounded with pain so great he could not imagine where it was coming from, and he could not yet get his eyes open. Or were they open, but he was seeing nothing? He had a quite vague recollection— or maybe it was a dreamlike fantasy—of having traveled over a bumpy road, and later of being carried by strong hands and maneuvered down a stairway.

As his thinking process began to reshape itself and present him with more logical impressions and questions, he tried to remember what had happened. He brought it back to the muzzle flash from the Russian's Luger. He wondered for a moment if he were dead, and now experiencing the flashback that no dead person had ever before been able to report on. As he pursued the idea, a great wave of pain drove all thoughts away and he almost lost the little consciousness he had regained. When the wave subsided he flexed the fingers of both hands, then moved his arms slightly. They were not bound. I must be in a jail cell, he thought. Why is it so dark? He brought his hands up to his eyes to see if they were open, but there was a bandage there and that was all he could feel. He ran his hand over the rest of his face, but found nothing but bandages.

Kent listened but could hear nothing. There was one dominant odor—the musky, acrid fumes of a fermentation process. Where had he smelled it before? A wine cellar! Unmistakable. Just like the ones he had been in with his parents as a child. But why was he in a wine cellar? Was it a part of the Russian embassy, or some out-of-the-way holding tank the Soviets used for purposes like this? When would they come to deal with him, he wondered. And what would they want from him? Obviously, they didn't want him dead—at least just yet. They would want to know if he had copied the Italian's notes, and if so, where the copies were. They would want to know whom he had told about the Italian, and how it was he, Kent, was involved in it. And after they had learned everything he knew, what would they do with him? Let him go? Hardly. He had killed two of their men, and knew too much about something very important. Then came another terrible wave of throbbing pain that overwhelmed him and, mercifully, deprived him once again of his senses.

It was noon, and Capitán Rodrigo Blanco was becoming irritated. He looked at his watch; the police commissioner would be calling again at any moment, demanding news of the capture of the North American, and suggesting that Blanco had lost whatever effectiveness had resulted in his elevation to the rank of captain. The phone on Blanco's desk buzzed and he grabbed the receiver. It was Lt. Vásquez.

"Captain, we may have something to the north. The Guardia Civil in Alcobendas reports a commotion near Algete . . . some calls about shots fired. Then, fifteen minutes later a fire in a canyon nearby. The *bomberos* are saying a car went off the road and exploded."

"*¡No me importa un carajo!* I don't give a shit about cars and fires. Tell me about the North American. What the fuck are you getting paid for?"

"Captain, I have the Guardia Civil going through the hamlets like shit through a goose. If there's anything there they'll let me know. Meantime, you may be interested to know that the burned car has diplomatic plates corresponding to the Russian embassy."

"*¡Cagatintas!* And you're still flattening your ass in the office? Stop shitting ink and get out there. Take it away from the Guardia Civil immediately in the name of the police commissioner and get to the bottom of it. Get that area cordoned off in the next ten minutes. I want your report in one hour, understand?"

Blanco slammed down the receiver, dialed Lt. Sánchez and learned that only one diplomatic vehicle had left Madrid that morning heading north on route N-1, and that it was probably Soviet. He told Sánchez to notify him immediately if other like vehicles or suspected Soviets passed the roadblock.

Blanco called Lt. Martínez and instructed him to alert the Russian embassy that one of their official cars had been reported off the road in the mountains north of the city, that it was involved in a fire, and that the Spanish police were realizing maximum efforts to rescue the occupants and protect the vehicle from tampering. Blanco then rang up the police commissioner and updated him, adding that the entire area surrounding the incident was controlled with roadblocks and by helicopter patrol, and that the Soviet embassy had been alerted. He then popped two large blue tablets into a glass of water, waited for the effervescence to abate, and downed it in two giant gulps. Wiping his huge mustache with the back of his hand, he moved into the situation room to monitor incoming communications.

Pablo Ribera squinted into the midday sun as the vehicle made its way up the dirt road toward his house. It was an officer of the Guardia Civil, and Ribera was expecting him. He jabbed his short-handled shovel into the pile of dirt he had dug out of a little drainage canal, wiped the perspiration from his forehead and smiled at the officer as he stepped out of the little sedan.

"Good day, Sergeant Olmeda. I suppose you're here concerning the shots that were fired."

"Well, no, as a matter of fact, Señor Ribera. But now that you mention it, we did have some reports from one of your neighbors."

Pablo laughed. "Yes, María warned me I should have told them about it ahead of time. I was just trying out some old ammunition to see if it was still any good. Must be thirty years since I've fired a shot out of the old carbine. You know, not a single round misfired."

The sergeant was neatly attired in his well-fitted bluish gray uniform, and the sun sparkled off the high-gloss black leather of his hat, belt and boots. His eyes scanned the grounds around the front of the house, and Pablo knew he had something else on his mind.

"One of your neighbors also reported a strange car here earlier, a Citroën, they thought, with two men."

Pablo waited for more, but the sergeant clearly wanted a response first. "Yes, there was. Two foreigners, asking questions. They said something about meeting a North American friend of theirs around here, but weren't sure of the exact place. I sent them on their way."

"Did you recognize their accent, have any idea what country they were from?"

"I couldn't tell, exactly. They spoke Castilian, but rather badly."

The sergeant squinted at Ribera for a few moments, then said, "Señor Ribera, did you fire the shots before, or after the strangers were here?"

"Well, both, actually," Pablo said, trying to stay out of a quagmire. "In fact, it occurred to me the shots might have frightened them as they drove up."

Olmeda tugged at his chin thoughtfully. "Hmm. Perhaps your neighbor got it a little confused. She thought she heard the shots all take place while the car was here."

"Well, then, it must have been the Alvárez woman. Crazier than a fruit bat. What's this all about, anyway?"

"They haven't yet told us, only that it's very important a North American visitor be apprehended. I must be moving on, but remember two things, Señor Ribera. There is a nice reward for information, and a very serious penalty for withholding information from the police. Would you kindly relay those things to your family members, just in case they happen to know something of value to us?"

"Of course, Sergeant Olmeda. And by the way, is there a brush fire anywhere near here? We have been smelling smoke."

"Yes, there is . . . in the gorge. Evidently a car went off the edge and caught fire. The *bomberos* are there right now trying to put the fire out."

The Soviet sedan lay on its side at the bottom of the ravine, still recognizable by its shape as a Citroën, but otherwise just a burned-out piece of scrap metal. What was left of the tires still smoldered, the smoke drifting slowly up the canyon in the wake of the fire the car had ignited. Two of the volunteer firefighters from the Algete *cuerpo de bomberos* hosed down the wreckage, as if there might be something there to save. One of them peered inside.

"Hey, Pedro! Look here! Two bodies. My God, what a mess."

"Mother of God," said the other. "They never had a chance to get out. Burned to death right there in their car. I'll get the chief down here."

"Let the poor devils rest in peace for a while. The chief is busy at the head of the fire up there. He wants the hose line pulled back up the hill so the truck can be moved up-canyon."

The Bell G3B-2 helicopter circled the down-canyon end of the fire several times, then headed into the wind for a landing next to the road. Lieutenant Silvio Vásquez jumped out, then made his way down the steep hillside toward the burned car, cursing the ashes, dirt and rocks that were pouring into his low-cut shoes, and the charred stubs of burned shrubs that were leaving black stripes across his uniform trousers. He looked inside the car, shook his head, then knelt down behind the car to try to read the numbers on the diplomatic license plate. Finally, he struggled back up the hill and made his report by radio to police headquarters in Madrid.

News of the wreck made the late afternoon papers. One of them carried this story:

TWO DEAD IN MOUNTAIN ACCIDENT
Two men were killed this morning when their automobile veered off a mountain road east of Alcobendas and burst into flames, causing a brush fire that burned fifteen hectares. The vehicle, a late-model Citroën sedan, was registered to the Russian Embassy, and bore diplomatic plates. Neither victim has been positively identified.

"I don't like it. I don't like it at all," said the tall man with a handsome head of dark hair just barely turning gray at the temples. The others who had been called into his office paid close attention to every word, every facial expression of their boss, the American Ambassador Parkerhouse. He slapped the folded newspaper down on the coffee table and paced around the room, his hands on his hips.

"This fruitcake forestry type pulls into town on Sunday morning, and by Tuesday we've already got one dead Italian, three dead Russians, the local police are furious and there's rumors of a major sabotage incident shaping up for Naples. Tell me, please, ye overpaid bureaucrats, just what in the hell is going on? I mean, does anybody even know for Christ's sake where this character is or what he's trying to do?"

Nobody said anything.

"Now, Brad," the ambassador continued, "yesterday afternoon I asked you to get that . . . Kent fellow in here. What happened?"

"I got him on the phone—he was over at ICONA—and he said he'd be right over. He knew it was important . . . in fact, I told him you wanted to see him," said Baumont. "When he failed to arrive in an hour or so, I called again. The officials had all gone home by that time, but I eventually found out from his main contact there that he left in a cab right after I called. No one there has seen or heard from him since. I'm surmising the newspaper reports concerning the Russian who was strangled in the hotel scared him off, and he went into hiding."

"Or that the KGB latched onto him," said Bruce Charner, the regional security officer.

"What else do you know about this, Bruce?" asked the ambassador.

"When I told the police he left ICONA by cab, they checked that out. A driver reported picking up a foreigner, probably American, late that afternoon, and dropping him off in the Salamanca district. No address, just at a corner."

"Doesn't make sense," said Vernon Prokar, nominally a special assistant to Bruce Charner. "A normal guy would have come right to the embassy on a request like that."

"The police were satisfied the cabby was a regular driver?" asked Charner.

"Evidently. But how would they know if he was paid off?"

"Well, what about Kent's file, the background check, and whatever else we have? Any indication out of the ordinary?" asked Parkerhouse.

"He looked real clean to us until the AID/OFDA folks contradicted his story about the little additional assignment he said he had in Rome," said Baumont. "There's something funny here, all right."

The ambassador whirled around and said directly to Prokar, "Did you check with Langley on him? Those bastards are supposed to keep us informed on stuff like this."

Prokar raised both hands in a sign of surrender. "We have nothing on him. Absolutely zilch. Scout's honor. Maybe NSA, who would know?"

A phone buzzed and Charner took it. Everyone listened to Charner's side of the conversation. "You're positive? Okay, I appreciate it. Keep us posted, buddy."

Charner turned to the ambassador. "You're gonna love this. According to the police, both those Russians were dead before the crash. One was shot in the forehead, the other through the chest and behind the ear."

Parkerhouse grimaced. "Well," he said to Charner, "you get on the horn with your folks, and tell 'em I want this dude off my back before the Russkies decide they need to even the score with us. God only knows what they're thinking over there."

"He's getting some help," said Prokar. "Has to be. The KGB is all over the ICONA guys, so I doubt if it's them. We don't know of any other close contact he has in town, so he's not giving anything away. My guess is this guy isn't just some dumb forester on a James Bond fantasy . . . he'd be dead by now, or wish he were. No, I'd say there's something in the works we don't know anything about, and there's some things about this guy Kent that haven't surfaced yet. We ought to take it seriously."

"All right," said the ambassador. "Brad, I want you in charge of this, at least as far as the embassy is concerned. I'll ask for anything you say is needed. First priority is to get Kent off the firing line, and preferably into the hands of the police. If that's not possible . . . neutralize him one way or another. And just in case he's getting help from inside . . . let's keep this project among ourselves . . . those of us in this room except as absolutely necessary."

The situation was grim in the Soviet embassy. Colonel Feliks Kratkov, the normally relaxed KGB mission chief, overnight had turned into a different person. His jaw now had a hardened set to it, and he spoke in a higher-pitched, more clipped and louder voice. His air of informality was gone, replaced by stiff officialdom and inquiring glances. The deteriorating situation was getting his full concern now, and he had no time for philosophizing or gossiping with subordinates or other embassy personnel. Even the ambassador, who, by ritual, normally received a feigned but de rigueur obsequiousness from the veteran KGB chief, was staying out of his way. Since the news of the death of the two officers had hit the embassy, a crisis atmosphere pervaded the establishment. Colonel Kratkov had found himself obliged to notify Moscow and had received a strong rebuke from Dzerzhinsky Square, and curt orders to immediately rectify the situation.

Kratkov and his immediate subordinate, Lieutenant Colonel Vera

Vlasov, had spent three hours already that afternoon going over all available information and reports about the hunt for Arnold Kent. They had called in and grilled everyone who had been assigned any part of the effort, then cross-checked and evaluated everything available.

"Well, then, it comes down to this, Vera Vlasov. The American is still in the area of Madrid, most likely in the Alcobendas sector, and is being hidden by locals apparently not subject to the interference of the Guardia Civil. That local assistance had to be arranged by someone other than Kent himself, obviously, and therefore either through his ties to the forestry people or the embassy types. And yet your surveillance of the suspect ones in both those groups has not produced results."

Vlasov nodded her agreement as she poured herself another cup of coffee. "Not yet, at least, comrade. But again, the del Barrio woman is likely our best bet. It would simply be too great a coincidence to believe that Ryabov and Amalrik were seen at the home of del Barrio's cousin . . . what was his name? . . . Ribera . . . shortly before their deaths . . . merely by chance."

"And you think, after all that has happened, that she would be stupid enough to lead us to him?"

"Not at all, comrade. But perhaps she would be willing to volunteer some information."

"Out of the question, at least for now," said the white-haired man. "The U.S. embassy is drooling to get Kent into the hands of the police, knowing full well what that would mean to us. Let's not screw that up by getting a flap going with the Americans."

"Then what about somebody from Ribera's family?"

The colonel ground his teeth for a few moments. "I don't know about that. If our estimate of yesterday's scenario is anywhere near accurate, those people have shown themselves to be extremely tough both mentally and physically. They're also very smart. First, we might not even be able to get near any of the children without losing another officer or two. That would be disastrous right now. Second, I don't want to screw up the police effort and get it turned against us. Unless you have some idea that hasn't occurred to either of us yet, I think we're going to have to be patient. That does not mean pulling back on surveillance, reducing pressure on the police, or any of that, you understand."

"The ambassador visited the police commissioner this afternoon, you said?"

"Yes. He made it quite clear, he tells me, that he was bringing the situation to the attention of the secretary of the interior as a strong protest concerning police inefficiency if the American is not immediately brought to restraint. The commissioner was visibly shaken, he told me."

"Feliks," the woman said, forcing a feeble smile, "you know this is the last thing I would have let happen here, with you in command—"

"It is indeed a bad situation, Vera Ivanovna. But I do not want apologies or whimpering in my ear at this juncture. You know what I want, and I leave it in your hands, as you leave your career and your pension in mine. Now, off you go."

Miguel Escobosa, working late at his office, picked up his phone and agreed to take a call from Señora del Barrio of the U.S. embassy.

"Señor Escobosa, you recognize my name?"

"Yes, I do. But, do you mind if I call you back in a moment?"

"Not at all, sir. You can reach me at the embassy."

Escobosa looked up the embassy number, rang it, then asked for del Barrio. She answered immediately.

"This is Miguel. Can you speak freely at this moment?"

"Yes, I am on a secure line. And I appreciate your taking the precaution of verifying my identity. I have only a few moments. Your family is safe?"

"Yes, yes. What about—"

"Your friend is safe at the moment, but suffering from serious wounds to the head and face. He is being actively sought by the Spanish police, the KGB, and the CIA. He can only be protected for another day or two at most. If he is apprehended there is no hope for his life."

"What are you asking?"

"That you provide transport for him out of the Madrid area tomorrow."

"Where is he now?"

"I will arrange for him to be picked up at a location north of Madrid at exactly noon. He will need to be transported at least two hundred kilometers, and he will be unable to sit up during the trip. Can you come up with something suitable that will not arouse suspicions . . . even at a roadblock?"

"I think I can do that. How will I know where to find him?"

"Call me at 57165 from Alcobendas at exactly eleven forty. If it is not I that answers, try the number again at eleven fifty. Do you have any questions?"

"Yes, just one. Through what road block will he be transported?"

"It will be southbound on N-One, then later, to the east on N-Three."

"Through the city, then?"

"Yes. What do you think?"

"Not bad. In fact, that should make it easier. What about the destination?"

"You'll know tomorrow. One other thing. We believe the KGB has an operative in your office, so keep everything seeming routine, all right?"

"Until tomorrow, then."

A strong hand elevated Kent's head gently from the rolled-up blanket on which it had been resting.

"Can you open your mouth?" the voice said in Spanish.

He sucked the water out of the deliciously cold cloth, then asked for more. Within a few minutes he was sitting up and being spoon-fed warm soup. The sharp pain in his head had diminished to a dull ache, and he felt quite drowsy, as if he were recovering from heavy sedation.

"Where am I?" he asked from the darkness of his facial bandages.

"In a wine cellar," said a male voice, "where you are safe from the Russians. You must continue eating the soup. It will make you stronger."

"Who are you?"

"A friend. Keep on eating."

"My eyes. What happened to my eyes?"

"The doctor says you will see again before long. Meantime the bandages must remain."

"But how—"

"Stop talking and finish the soup. I cannot answer all your questions. If you have to urinate, there is a bucket on your left. There is also a bottle of water here by your head. Try to get some more rest, because you cannot stay here much longer. Someone will come for you in a few hours. Good-bye."

Kent listened to the footsteps traverse the wooden cellar floor, then he

heard a heavy door open, then close. He was alone again. He felt the
bandages that covered his face and part of his head. There were two
blankets covering him. He worked his fingers, and began running his
hands over his body to discover any other wounds or sore spots. When
he got to his right ankle he was surprised to feel the leather holster still
in place, and in it, the little automatic given him by Cristina. He pulled
out the weapon and extracted the magazine. He could feel that it was
fully loaded, as it had been when she first gave it to him. He remembered that the last time he had seen it was when the Russian made him
drop it on the floor of the toolshed. The events following that episode
went quickly through his mind again, stopping where he saw the
muzzle flash in his face. How had the Spaniards pulled him out of that
one, he wondered? And what had become of the Russian who had shot
at him?

Still amazed at having the pistol, he felt in his pockets. The wad of
notes he had copied from the Italian's briefcase was still there. And then
his fingers found what felt like his passport. But . . . how? Hadn't he
turned that over to Pablo back in the toolshed? They were going to get
him a new one, weren't they? He ran his hands over his clothing. Everything felt strange and unfamiliar. His head ached again and seemed
to be spinning slowly. Familiar questions again plagued him: Who am
I? Is this really happening? How did I get caught up in all this? Why
aren't there any Americans helping me? Where am I about to be taken,
and why? Then, before drifting off again into a state of only partial
consciousness, he asked himself what it was in Naples that was so important to so many people, and what was his connection with it?

Kent drifted into a state of semiconsciousness, almost as if he were
hypnotizing himself, as he had learned to do many years earlier. Soon,
the Italian's encrypted notes produced themselves on a screen in his
mind, and his letter-number substitution games began rearranging
things involuntarily. But each time he sensed that he was arriving at a
breakthrough, the letters and numbers would fuzz out and turn suc-
cessively through a wide variety of colors. It dimly occurred to him that
he should commit the entire set of notes to memory to facilitate what
was now going on in his subconscious.

And then he was asleep, suddenly dreaming of being trapped by a
flare-up in a brush fire. He ran from the flames, batting at the sparks
that kept landing on his clothes. In a moment he was rolling around on

the street in front of his house shouting for Yvette to throw dirt on him. She ran into the garage for a shovel, but came out with a pitchfork.

"No, no!" he shouted at her. "The shovel, the shovel!" Meantime he kept rolling in the street, trying to keep the flames from engulfing him. Finally, Yvette came out with a snow shovel and tried to dig dirt out of the lawn. It was taking her forever to get a shovelful, and Kent observed all the white grubs just beneath the surface of the lawn. Then she began throwing dirt over him until the fire was out—but she kept shoveling.

"Stop!" he shouted. "That's enough. That's enough!" But she kept at it, the mound getting deeper and deeper over him. He noticed the neighbors standing in their front yards watching with great interest as he was being buried right there in the street. Why didn't they do anything? Why weren't they helping him?

"Help! Help!" he cried, waving his arms, trying to keep breathing. Then somebody with very strong hands and arms was bending over him, stopping him from waving his arms, telling him not to shout. But why was he telling him in Spanish?

CHAPTER SIX

Cristina del Barrio left the embassy at eight thirty, explaining to her boss Garbert Flenk that she was having terrible cramps, and was going to her doctor that afternoon. She had come to work without any trace of makeup and with enough inattention to her hair that several people had already asked if she felt all right. Flenk seemed to take her story at face value. She picked up a taxi in front of the embassy and went straight home. Ten minutes later, she walked from her flat to the metro station at Plaza de España, boarding the number 3 line southbound. At the Sol station she changed trains, taking the number 2 line eastward to Goya. Then, another change westbound on the number 4 line to the A. Martínez station, where she got off and boarded a number 5 line train eastward to Pueblo Nuevo. She emerged from the metro mouth and quickly caught a taxi that carried her to a nearby residential area and dropped her off in a park. When she was satisfied she hadn't been followed, she walked to the borrowed car that she had left parked the night before in back of an apartment house. Then, traveling by farm roads, she managed to reach Alcobendas by ten forty-five, parking near the pay phone whose number she had given Miguel Escobosa the day before. The phone rang a minute after eleven. She answered.

"Yes, who is this?"

"Miguel. Is everything all right?"

"Yes. Are you ready to pick up the cargo?"

"My driver is ready. Where is the load?"

"Two kilometers north of Fuente. There is a road leading west. It is the second *finca*. My man will meet you at the gate to the *finca*. Can you have your vehicle there at exactly noon?"

"No problem. Just tell me the destination."

"Chiva, just east of Valencia. My man will tell your driver exactly where."

"What condition is the cargo in? Can it travel well, or should it be inspected and reconditioned in Madrid?"

"It is in only fair condition, but should continue en route to its destination without delay. You understand?"

"Yes, I understand. Will you be at your regular place of business hereafter?"

"I may be getting ill. I may have to rest with relatives for several days."

"Oh. Sorry to hear it. I hope you get better soon."

"Thank you. And . . . thank you . . . for everything."

Del Barrio hung up, then walked back toward her car. She saw a man sitting on a bench reading a newspaper. He did not look up at her as she walked by, which aroused her suspicion, and moreover, he was not dressed in a fashion typical of the local inhabitants. Not surprising, she thought, in view of what was going on, that the place would be inundated by Soviet agents. She thought about passing her car, but then it occurred to her he might have seen her pull up, and then he would definitely become suspicious. So she simply climbed in the car, pulled out of her parking spot and drove down the street. One block away she made a U-turn, then parked so that she could see the man on the bench. He had already risen, and now she spotted him at the same telephone she had used. It was a frightening indication. After having cleared her path all morning getting up there, she had likely been spotted by some lucky agent who was probably right now describing her car to a whole network of confederates.

Abandoning her car, del Barrio found another telephone and reached María Ribera at the home of a cousin of María's in town. Within ten minutes, María picked up Cristina in back of a grocery store and whisked her out of town down the N-I highway toward Madrid.

Kent, awakening, recognized the voice of Pablo, and gripped his arm. It was still dark; the bandages still were covering his face.

"Pablo, what is happening?"

"Easy, my friend. We must get you out of here right away. The town is swarming with Russians, and we cannot outwit the police much longer, either. How do you feel? Can you travel?"

"Yes, yes. I can travel. Can I remove the bandages?"

"No, not yet. Not until Saturday. Meantime, we are going to put you in a box. You will be in there for many hours, so if you have to take a leak, do it now."

Kent was guided up a narrow wooden stairway, one man in front of him, another behind. He heard the door to the stairway being closed and locked, and then several voices, speaking rapidly in Spanish. There was a short wait, then a truck being backed into position next to the building. A large door opened, and two men carried in a wooden box not unlike a coffin, but deeper. There were blankets spread along the bottom. Pablo explained to him that he was to lie in the bottom of the box, and that a wooden tray would be placed above him. The tray would be full of linen fire hose, making it appear that the entire box was full of hose sections that had been used to put out the fire in the gorge. Kent was to remain silent at all times while in the box. He climbed inside gratefully, saying thanks to anyone who might hear him. The box was then hoisted onto what he imagined must surely be a forest service truck. He listened to muffled voices, the sounds of other cargo being shifted around, doors chunking closed, and finally the engine being started. Some uncertainties went through his head. What about air holes. Surely they'd thought of that. Carbon monoxide? Probably wouldn't be a problem on the back of a truck, he thought. Water to drink? If there was none in his box, he was sure he could survive in this weather for at least a day. Then the truck jolted into motion, and he was going . . . somewhere.

The jolting of the truck over the rough farm road made Kent's head pains almost intolerable, but soon the truck got onto a paved highway, and the agony lessened somewhat. After some twenty minutes Kent felt the truck slow to a crawl, then stop completely with a squeaking of brakes. He heard muffled voices, questions, answers, and guessed it was a roadblock. Then he heard some laughter, and the truck was in motion again. As he lay there in his coffin, as he was calling it to himself, he gave some silent thanks for the friendship of people like Miguel, Cristina, Pablo, and all the others who had succeeded in keeping him alive and out of the hands of his enemies so far. He hoped he would be able to find a way to repay them all someday. Someday . . . if this nightmare ever ended happily.

Before long, he knew from the sounds and smells that they had reached the city. Why was he being taken back into Madrid? he wondered. Were they taking him to a hospital? No, that wouldn't fit what was going on. Was it to the embassy, to be whisked away by diplomatic transport to the United States? Well, not according to the impressions he had got from Cristina. Maybe he was being taken to a U.S. military base, but were there even any near Madrid? He couldn't think of any.

As the city bumping and jostling went on and on he got no better ideas, and was surprised when things smoothed out and they seemed to be getting out into a rural area again. And suddenly there was another roadblock, this time a seemingly more serious one. He heard men climbing onto the back of the truck, looking around. He heard some comments, he thought by the driver of his truck, about moving up reinforcements for a fire that had broken out near Valverde, wherever that was. Then somebody was poking around in the top of his box, and he felt his heart pounding.

"What do you have underneath all this hose up here?" a voice was saying. Kent's spirits began dropping fast. He still had his little pistol, but wouldn't consider using it on a policeman, whatever the circumstances. Hell, he couldn't even see to use the damn thing anyway.

"Just more hose, that's all," came the bored response. "Three more trays, just like that one. If you want to look at it, we'll climb up there and lift the damned things out for you."

Kent was holding his breath.

"No, fuck the hose. All I've been doing all day is looking into boxes. This morning a goose almost bit my finger off, and then just a little while ago I stuck my hand into a pile of shitty diapers. Be off with you, and good luck, my friends."

Kent smiled from beneath his bandages, knowing the KGB would have conducted a more methodical search, had it been theirs to do.

It was Wednesday morning in McLean, Virginia. Yvette Kent, in bathrobe and slippers, ventured out onto the driveway to retrieve the *Washington Post*. Inside at her breakfast table she unfolded the paper and read through the arts section, looking for familiar names, and not-

ing reviews she could comment on later. Her perusal was interrupted by
a call from her friend Sharna Gorv, who was phoning from her downtown studio.

"My God, Yvette, I just saw the paper. What's happening with Arnold? You must be sick. Are you going over there? My God, is there
anything I can do? Just tell me!"

"Sharna! What in the world are you talking about?"

"About Arno. What's all this about his being a fugitive from the police, and about several killings, and all that? Don't you know what's
going on, for heaven's sake?"

"You say there's something in the paper?"

"It's on page five, upper left part of the page . . . it's in the front
section. You do have the paper, don't you?"

Yvette turned to the article, finding it quickly.

> **AMERICAN SOUGHT IN MADRID SLAYINGS**
> Arnold Kent, 47, an employee of the U.S. Forest Ser-
> vice on assignment in Madrid, is sought by Police in
> connection with the mysterious slayings of three
> Russian Embassy personnel, two of them identified
> as diplomats. Police reports include no mention of
> possible motives for the alleged killings. According
> to the Forest Service spokesman Phillip Perkins,
> Kent, a career specialist in forest fire management,
> left the U.S. last Saturday on a routine assignment to
> Madrid and Rome.

"That's just wonderful," Yvette said. "You know, a guy called here
from the Forest Service Monday night. He said there was some problem, and that Arno was gone from his hotel and they wanted him for
questioning, or something like that. You know, big deal. Wanted for
questioning, all right? But God, nothing like this. What do you think is
going on?"

"What do *I* think is going on? What do *I* think is going on? Well,
Yvette, I've been trying to beat into your head for the last two or three
years that man is with the CIA. That's what *I* think is going on."

"Yeah, well I told the guy that, but I don't think he believed me.
They don't know what's happening down there. Do you think there's
really a problem?"

"Well, think about it, Yvette. For God's sake. Regular foresters don't go around . . . finishing off people at the Russian embassy."

"But . . . Arno wouldn't go that far . . . do you think?"

"Bullshit. Face it Yvette, he's into the middle of it now. And so are you."

"Me? Why am I into anything?"

"Listen. Those Russians don't play around. They have plenty of their people over here, especially around Washington. The place is lousy with them. All they have to do is pick up the phone and order you picked up. Then, with you in their hands, they could force Arno to do anything they wanted him to."

"He never told me anything like that could happen. What do you think I ought to do? Can I come and stay with you for a few days . . . until this . . . sort of blows over?"

"Uh . . . well, let me get a reading on that from Bill. And we may be having several people in from out of town . . . to stay over for several days. But I definitely think you should get protection from the CIA. After all, it's their responsibility."

"The CIA? Well, who should I ask for there? Does Bill still have any contacts?"

"Uh, no, I doubt it. You know, when they cut things off with former employees, everything is sort of . . . closed off. Better just call their regular switchboard and explain who you are. I'm sure they'll help you. But if they won't, give me a call, hon. I'm sure you can figure out something. And meantime, don't worry about Arno. Our people will be doing their best. He may be on his way back here this very minute."

"Thank you, Sharna. I just don't know what I'd do without you."

Stan Dawson, Kent's boss, had also seen the news article. He tried three times to reach Yvette, finding the phone busy each time. It bothered him that while the Forest Service hierarchy seemed interested and concerned about Kent's predicament, nobody was doing anything more than just talking about it. The subject had come up again in the chief-and-staff meeting that morning, but only by way of updating and information-sharing. Dawson had sent Kent on the assignment, and felt responsible for his welfare, even though he had little control over the unfolding events. He decided to pin down Farber Claunch of

AID/OFDA concerning the supplemental assignment he had mentioned in their last conversation, and got in to see him at his office in Main State.

"Farber, you saw the newspaper article on Kent. What the hell is going on?"

Claunch looked at Dawson thoughtfully, stroked back his straight black hair for a moment and said, "Okay, Stan, let's get back in my little office."

As they walked through a corridor and then past the receptionist's desk, he leaned over to the attractive black woman and told her he would be out of contact for the next fifteen minutes. The two men sat down on a couch in Claunch's cluttered, windowless cubicle.

"Stan, I had no idea anything like this was going to happen."

Dawson sensed that Claunch was about to unload some new information, and settled back to light up his pipe.

Claunch gave Dawson the whole story, including the part about sending Kent to Madrid on a personal, rather than on an official passport. He told him about Kent's special assignment, and the apparent role of Otto Frange of State's Italy desk. Finally, he threw up his hands and said, "I wish I could tell you some more, but that's it. Apparently, when he got to Madrid, the shit hit the fan. As of when Kent left here, I'm in the dark, and I don't like it any better than you do."

"Does our embassy in Madrid know about the mission you gave Kent?"

"I'm sure they do, but all the communications about that have been between them and Frange. Otto already buzzed me this morning and asked if I knew anything more about Kent than I'd already told him. Said the guy had apparently flipped out and had gone on some kind of a rampage, and that the undersecretary was coming unglued over the whole thing. What's really bugging them upstairs is not the goddamn situation your man is in, but that things may be seen to be out of channels, that something underhanded is going on. You know, sort of a minor diplomatic faux pas or something."

The longer Claunch talked, the more upset Dawson was becoming. During his lengthy career in the Forest Service, Dawson had always respected his agency for not treating its people like pawns to be traded away for tactical gains. And now here was the State Department more concerned about its fucking image than the life of a sincere and forth-right human being.

"Well, Farber, at this point I couldn't care less about channels and faux pas and all that shit. I'm very concerned about what, if anything, our people are doing about seeing to Kent's well-being. What is the embassy doing, for example? Aren't they charged with looking after government employees, hell, even just plain U.S. citizens over there?"

"Yeah, that's exactly how I feel. But let me tell you the realities. Number one, with just a personal passport, Kent is technically not a government employee, not a representative of the United States. Really, he's nothing more than a fucking tourist, to put it bluntly. Number two, tourist or official representative, he's alleged, apparently, to have cut down a Russian embassy driver who's probably a KGB agent, and then been linked to the killing of two Soviet diplomats. Furthermore, Frange tells me he probably had something to do with the death of an Italian emissary in TWA's departure lounge at JFK even before he left the country. Kent is reported to have boarded his Madrid flight with the Italian's briefcase, and said briefcase was loaded with classified material. So if you can evaluate all that shit for a minute or two without barfing, you can appreciate that the ambassador himself would have trouble getting out of that quagmire, and he has diplomatic immunity, which Kent has not. Now then, what kind of help do you think our people, as you call them, should be expected to come up with?"

Dawson sat there expressionless, frozen to the couch. Finally he said, "Farber, what's your assessment? I have known Arno for twenty years, seen him frequently during those years, worked with him on a dozen projects, on and on. He's not a fucking spy, he's nothing but a goddamn forester. Why is he mixed up in all this stuff?"

Claunch stared down into his coffee, shaking his head. "I wish I knew," he said.

"Have you talked to anybody in our embassy over there, or is all your stuff secondhand from this . . . Frange, is it?"

"Yeah, Otto Frange. I guess they called him after Kent told his story about the Naples stuff, and the Italian and his briefcase."

"Well, do you think that Frange might have held back confirming Kent's story for whatever reason?"

"It's possible . . . but almost academic at this point. Kent's in the soup up to his armpits with both the Spanish police and the KGB at this point."

"Well, where do we go from here? Or do I just call Kent's wife and tell her there's nothing that can be done?"

"Good point. Who's your head guy? Baker?"

"Yeah. Cliff Baker."

"I suggest he take it to the State Department via Agriculture. I'd ask him to raise hell about it."

"That's not his style, but I'll give it a shot. Far as Kent's wife is concerned, I doubt if she thinks there's a problem yet. Thanks for your help, I think."

Miguel Escobosa pulled in behind the truck as it passed through Alcobendas, then followed it southward toward Madrid. If there had been a problem at the roadblock, he was ready to jump out and intervene, complaining that the truck was needed immediately at another fire. He was relieved when they waved the vehicle through the roadblock without searching it. When the two vehicles reached the city, Escobosa turned off toward his office, reasoning that to continue the escort might be a tipoff to Russian agents that might be following him. He parked in the underground lot below the ICONA offices, then went to his second-floor office and called his wife Amalia. She and the children were all right, nothing unusual had happened, and she wanted to know when they could go back to their flat on Ferraz Street. He told her not yet, but that he planned to check it out on the way back from the office to be sure everything was all right there.

Miguel called the provincial fire chief who had made arrangements for the truck and crew, and gave him an estimate of their return time. The provincial chief had been Miguel's roommate at the university, and no favor would have been too great for one to ask of the other. The chief did not even ask who was in the box, or why he was in there. To him, it was sufficient that Miguel had made the request. He swore his men to silence, and knew they would obey.

Miguel drove to his flat on Ferraz and parked his personal car a block away. As he approached the building he saw nothing unusual. There was nobody lurking in a doorway, nobody sitting in a parked car, nothing to arouse the least suspicion. So he calmly entered, took the mail out of the box, then took the elevator up to their fifth-floor flat. Ten minutes later he came back down to the lobby and walked out the door. He remembered later it was quite dark on the street as he walked toward his car.

"Wake up, you purple-bellied Spaniard!" The voice was raspy and cold. The words were in Spanish, spoken with a heavy Slavic accent.

Miguel was fighting his way through a mental barrage of shapes and colors, none of the pieces fitting together properly. He felt nauseous, battered, dizzy, and terribly cold. As his vision came back to him slowly, he had to fight to clarify the images, getting the fuzziness off of them, trying to create a single image from the three he was seeing. Everything smelled musty and stale. He found himself sitting on the floor in the corner of a windowless room. He was completely naked, and wet with terribly cold water. A bright spotlight was focused on his face, and it seemed to be burning a hole in him. He discerned the shapes of two men, one on either side of the spotlight. He was not bound, and could have got to his feet. But somehow he had no desire to move. He felt weak and helpless. Was he drugged, he wondered? He felt sore all over but could see no blood, no bruises. Who were these men and where had they come from?

"Miguel," said one of the voices, "we do not have a lot of time to squander. You will now tell us where the American is."

Miguel cleared his throat, wondering if he would be able to talk at all. Squinting into the spotlight, he could not see the face of either man. He knew they were not Spaniards, at least not the one who had spoken to him. "If you mean Mr. Kent, I don't have any idea. I haven't seen him since Monday."

Miguel saw one of the men bend over and pick up something and point it at him. Suddenly, a blast of cold water smashed into his face, knocking his head backward into the wall. Before he could lift his hand, the high-pressure stream was shooting bolts of water up his nostrils. He screamed in agony as he fought to get his head down, but now the other man was grabbing his hair, forcing his face back up into the horrible stream. After a few seconds that seemed like several weeks, it was just as suddenly over. Miguel lay in the pool coughing out water and mucous by the cupful. Finally, he was able to regain his sitting position against the wall.

"We did not come here to play games with you," the voice said calmly. "And again, we don't like to waste time. Now you can make this quite easy on yourself and your family, or you can make it difficult. In either case it will all be over within an hour or two at the most. Have I made myself clear, or must I be more specific?"

The word *family* sent a shock wave through Miguel's body. But they were safely tucked away at his brother-in-law's estate, weren't they? He had just talked to them a few minutes before leaving the office, and that was . . . Jesus God, he said to himself. What time is it now? Hell, what *day* is it now? Could these miserable bastards have them in their dirty hands at this moment?

"If you're sitting there wondering where your dear wife and children are, you had best be concerned about them. Did you think for a moment they were safe behind that elaborate sieve that passes for a security fence?" Both of the men laughed.

Miguel winced. He figured they were lying about his family, but there was no way to be sure. He knew at that moment he would have to at least feign cooperation with these madmen. "All right," he said. "I'll tell you what I know, which isn't very much."

"Before you do," said the other voice, one also carrying a heavy Slavic accent, "be advised that you will be held here until your information is verified. If it turns out to be false, you will never again be able to make love to your wife, or to any other woman. Do you understand?"

Miguel's throat tightened as he considered the threat. His playing field was suddenly much narrower. He would have to come up with accurate information, at least insofar as the things that could be checked out, but information that would fail to compromise Kent's life. It was a difficult order, but one that desperately needed to be filled quickly. He took in a deep breath, then let it out slowly and licked his lips.

"Kent is getting help from somebody at the American embassy," he said slowly, measuring his words and trying to think it out ahead. "They have hidden him out in the mountains north of the city." Miguel reasoned they already had to know all about that.

"Who is it in the embassy?" asked one of the voices. "And how do you know about that?"

"It was Monday. Monday afternoon. Kent was at a meeting there with me. He got two urgent phone calls. The first one, he told me . . . asking him to come to the embassy right away. Then he got the other call a couple of minutes later. He said he was in great danger and could not go to the embassy. I do not know who made either of those calls, believe me, I would tell you."

"Go on," said one of the voices from behind the light.

Miguel pulled his arms closely about himself, trying to control the shuddering of his body and the chattering of his teeth. If only he had a few minutes to calculate how much they already knew. The del Barrio woman flashed through his mind. To give her away would compromise not only her but also Kent.

"The person from the embassy," said the second voice, "was it a man or a woman?"

They must know about her, then, Miguel decided. "A woman. That's all I know about that. My dispatcher said it was a woman who called the second time."

"You are stalling, Miguel," said the first voice, the raspy one, "and our patience is wearing thin. Both of you were in Alcobendas this morning, talking together by phone. What was said in that conversation, between you and Señora del Barrio?"

Again, Escobosa was shocked. Both of them had been followed, so they knew about her already. It was a good thing that he had not personally gone to the pickup point; he had accomplished the instructions by forest service radio using a prearranged frequency that wouldn't be monitored by other stations. He also felt somewhat cheered by the Russian's giving away of today's date. It meant that it was not very likely they had been able to abduct his family yet. But he still had to cough up a credible story, and quickly. It went through his mind that they had probably followed him back to the city from Alcobendas, and would have seen the fire truck ahead of him. He had to work the fire truck into his story.

"Señora del Barrio asked me to arrange transport for Mr. Kent out of his hiding place and into Madrid. So I ordered the crew of a fire truck from Alcobendas to pick him up. Señora del Barrio refused to give me the destination, saying she would have that given directly to the driver."

"And who exactly was to give that information to the driver?"

"I suppose somebody at the place they picked him up."

"And how is it, Miguel, that you escorted the truck all the way to Madrid, and still have no idea of its destination?"

The tone of his interrogator's voice suggested to Miguel that they had more information about that truck and which way it was heading than they were giving out. If they had followed both rigs to the city, they surely would have noted which outbound highway the truck was heading for, or maybe even followed it. He had to give something more away, and hope to hell del Barrio would keep a step ahead of the Soviets.

"The driver said something about Tarancón," Escobosa said, mentally selecting a town on the road toward Valencia, but one the truck must surely have passed by this time. "He was to turn south there, then take the main highway to Albacete."

"Albacete? Why Albacete?"

"I don't know. I swear it. But my understanding is that the truck is to return to its regular station from there. I was only asked to arrange for the transport. I would not have got mixed up in this mess except for my friendship for Mr. Kent. I know absolutely nothing about what is going on. He would not tell me for fear of getting me and my family involved, and now it has happened anyway. Just do what you have to do and leave my family alone. Please."

"How was the American hidden on the truck?"

"I was told he was to be hidden in a box."

"And in what condition was he? Was he wounded or hurt in any way?"

Miguel thought about his family. What if they caught up with Kent and found out they'd been lied to? What would it hurt to tell them the truth? Maybe they already knew what had happened to him at the Ribera place.

"I haven't seen him. But I asked the woman about him, and she said he was only in fair condition. She didn't wish to be specific in case the phone call was being intercepted. That's as much as I know."

The room was silent for a few moments. Miguel took it as a good sign: they were not just dismissing his story out of hand.

"We wish you and your family no ill will, Señor Escobosa. You will be set free in a little while. However, should your story prove to be false, or should we discover you have reported this episode to your government, we will seek you out and cut off your nuts, and your pecker as well. And you might as well kiss your family good-bye also. Do you understand?"

Miguel squinted into the light and nodded slowly.

"All right then, here. Take this pill and swallow it. You'll sleep for a few hours."

He looked at the pill with glazed eyes. The two men pulled his head up by the hair, forced open his mouth, and shoved the pill down his throat.

In the early evening, the forest service truck rumbled smoothly along Highway N-III toward Valencia, the foreman and his driver telling jokes and recounting experiences. A dark-colored Mercedes sedan pulled alongside and stayed abreast of the truck as the man on the right side looked at the official markings on the truck. Then he motioned at the driver to pull the truck off the road. The driver stared back at him, then shook his head. He saw the man in the Mercedes point a huge handgun directly at his face and motion once again to pull over. This time the truck driver complied. The Mercedes pulled in directly behind the truck as it came to a dusty halt off the paved highway. One man came up each side of the truck, weapons drawn and looking grim.

"Stay in the truck and keep your mouths shut," ordered one of them as he perched on the running board. The other man was already on the back of the truck with a flashlight, opening compartments and pulling back tarpaulins. When he came to the hose box he pocketed his flashlight, readied his pistol, then jerked the top open. He saw nothing but a spaghettilike tangle of dirty fire hose. Unconvinced, the man seized a shovel from a pile of tools on the bed of the truck and repeatedly rammed the handle down through the hose until it hit solid bottom each time.

"*Yop tvoyu mat!* I fucked your mother!" he said to nobody in particular as he pocketed the pistol and went on thrashing around. He finally jumped down from the truck, jerked open the right-hand door and dragged the foreman out of the cab by his leather jacket. He forced the terrified man to the ground, then, with a knee in his chest and the pistol pushed against his neck, said, "Where is the American? Where did you drop him off? Speak now, you pathetic bastard, or I'll blow your fucking head off."

"About twenty kilometers back . . . near Motilla de Palancar," he said, his voice quivering in fear.

"When? How long ago?" thundered the Russian, pressing the pistol ever harder into the foreman's neck.

"About fifteen or twenty minutes ago."

"Is he still there, or did he get into another vehicle? Speak the truth, you simple shit, or I'll personally cut out your liver and throw it on your kitchen table in front of your family."

"Please, señor, I am telling you God's truth. He got into a car with a woman."

"What kind of a car? What does it look like? Speak quickly!"

"A small sedan . . . a Seat, I believe. A dark color, dark green or possibly black . . . I couldn't tell in the dark."

"What did the man look like?"

"It would be hard to say. His entire face is covered with bandages—"

"Which way were they heading, in this direction?"

"I don't know. They ordered us to go on east to Utiel, then return to our station at Alcobendas."

"And they have not passed you?"

"No, sir."

The two Russians got back in the front seat of their car. The man on the right turned to face the passenger in the back seat. "He was scared shitless like a trapped hare. He was telling the truth. Our white crow got into a Seat twenty minutes ago with the del Barrio woman. His face is covered with bandages. They're behind us somewhere, but we don't know which way they're heading."

Lieutenant Colonel Vera Vlasov was silent for a minute while she studied her road map in the dim glare of a small flashlight. Then she keyed the mike on her mobile radio and gave instructions to the three other units operating east of Madrid. One of the units was in the outskirts of Albacete; she ordered that officer to immediately advise the Spanish police that their suspect Arnold Kent was just seen in Motilla de Palancar traveling with Cristina del Barrio of the United States embassy. She gave the car description and license number, and added that the American's face was heavily bandaged.

Kent lay curled up like a pretzel on the tiny back seat of Cristina del Barrio's Seat sedan, a blanket draped over him more to hide him than to keep him warm. His head still ached dully, the pain diminished by the sedatives del Barrio had given him when they switched him from the truck to the car. Del Barrio was driving south from the main Madrid-Valencia highway on the road toward Villanueva de la Jara.

"Can you straighten out your legs at all?"

"I think the coffin was more comfortable. How far do we have to go in this . . . matchbox?"

"You don't really want to know. And some of it is going to be bumpy, because we're going to have to get off the main traveled roads. Unfortunately, I couldn't come up with another car, and I'm sure this one is being looked for."

"By the police, or—?"

"Yes."

"Why didn't you keep me in the truck?"

"Too risky. Too much time passed getting you out of Alcobendas. Too much time for people to figure things out. That's why we must keep moving right now, in spite of how you must feel at this moment."

"What happened to me . . . up at Pablo's place? I think I blacked out about the time the Russian was trying to put me into his car."

"María put a rifle bullet into his chest a fraction of a second before he fired at your head. His bullet just grazed your temple, but the powder burns took a lot of skin off your face and very nearly destroyed your eyes."

"Then, who—"

"The doctor? There was no doctor at all. Only a very competent medical technician who happens to be a close friend of Pablo's. We had no choice in the matter, that is, if you value your life at all. Anyway, he was treating you within ten minutes of your injury, and thinks your eyes will be all right. Keeping them bandaged was a precaution, but one cannot be certain, of course. Are you upset with us about that?"

"No, of course into. I owe you my life . . . I think." They both laughed. "That wine cellar I was in . . . how did I get there?"

"Juan José's brother's place. Juan José took you there after he and Pablo got back from the gorge. The diversion caused by the fire tied up the police and the Guardia Civil."

"The gorge? The fire?"

"Oh, sorry. You don't know about that either. I keep forgetting you were out of it. Pablo drove the Russian's car, with them in it, of course, to a cliff not far from his house. He doused the inside of the car with gasoline, tossed in a match, then pushed it off into the gorge."

"You people don't screw around, do you? Supposed to look like an accident?"

"Well, that was the general idea, but it didn't work. It took the Russians less than an hour to find out their men had both been shot."

"That's what I figured. I should stick to strangling those folks. Leaves less obvious marks." They laughed again.

"I'm happy we can laugh, but I'm not sure if we should. After all, we're only one small mistake away from getting you killed. And it's only a matter of time until the embassy knows about what I'm doing. Then I'm all through with that career. Any good jobs open in your organization?"

"Probably not with your record. But aren't you taking that a bit lightly? I mean, you just got your career trashed, for God's sake."

"It's not the *Titanic* going down. Anyway, I managed to find out a few things at the embassy, which isn't really all that easy when you work for a man as distrusted as Garber Flenk."

"The Italian's notes?"

"Right. There was a lot of snickering about that. Nobody around the embassy has ever seen such an absolute hodgepodge of homemade tripe, as they were calling it. I mean, not even sophisticated enough to apply even the most elementary cryptanalytic tools."

"So what did the notes say?"

"They don't have any idea."

"What?"

"Isn't it hilarious? They didn't even take it seriously. They're convinced that you trumped up the whole thing."

"Oh, I see. The James Bond scenario?"

"Along those lines. Photos and the works."

"Is that real? I mean, is that an official posture they're taking to meet political needs, or is that what they really think?"

"Nobody in Washington confirms your story about the Naples assignment. In fact, Whitman thinks your forest service is covering for you."

"How?"

"By passing you off as a competent employee not given to that kind of . . . deception, is the word they used."

"Well, did anybody bother to corroborate what I told them about the Italian guy dying at JFK? And that he was the guy living in the house across the street from me, and that those photos weren't taken by me?"

"I don't know about those things, Arno. Anyway, I got the impression they weren't exactly on the verge of an exhaustive investigation. What they did find out seemed to meet their immediate needs."

"And what do you think?"

"Do you really need to ask at this point?"

"I'm sorry, Cristina. I shouldn't have said that. It was uncalled for."

"Forget it. Have you discovered your new passport yet?"

"I thought that's what it was. Who am I, anyway?"

"Bennet Bryant. How do you like it?"

"Hm. It's all right. Nice sound. Who is he?"

"A consultant from L.A. An expert on motivational dynamics. Think you can handle it?"

"Sure, no sweat. Soon as I find out what motivational dynamics is."

"Stay down now. We're coming to a town. Then I'm turning off onto another road."

"Destination?"

"Valencia, eventually, but with a major stop a bit short of there. We've got to get you healed up enough for some serious traveling."

"And you? That is, after . . . Valencia?"

"I'm not looking that far ahead yet. There are some pretty smart people betting we won't even get that far. Uh-oh."

"Problem?"

"Highway patrol car spotlighting license plates. I've got to pass him. Stay down."

Cristina eased the car ahead into the beam of the spotlight, trying to look calm and questioning. She couldn't see the officers' faces in the patrol car's darkened interior. If they reacted, she would have to stop. She could not hope to outrun them in her little Seat. But there was no reaction, and she gradually increased her speed until she reached her intended turnoff.

"We got by them?"

"I think so. Did you pee in your pants?"

"Afraid to check. So maybe they don't have your tag number."

"Not now they don't. I stole these in Motilla just before picking you up. They probably won't even be reported until tomorrow, but I was worried about them picking up on the make and model."

"I think I underestimated you. You sure you're not with the Mafia?"

"Impossible. I can't eat spaghetti without getting it all over my blouse. Speaking of which, when did you last have anything to eat?"

"Some soup . . . this morning I think it was. What about you?"

"About like that. I'll find a place and pick up some things. Trust my selection?"

"Why change the game now? I'm on a roll."

At the U.S. Department of Agriculture's South Building on Constitution Avenue, Forest Service chief Cliff Baker was still at work after five o'clock. Most of the building's seven miles of corridors had been taken over by the janitors. Baker sat hunched over the old wooden desk that, some seventy years earlier, had served the needs of Gifford Pinchot, the service's first chief. The large office seemed to be half meeting room and half museum, the decorations consisting entirely of framed documents, old photographs, and stand-alone artifacts from early-day ranger stations, lookout towers and logging camps.

Baker fit in well in the museum. He was a large, rugged man who looked the part of an early-day ranger. Except for his polyester suit, he could have appeared in any of the old photos that lined his office walls.

Stan Dawson, Kent's boss, peeked around the corner into Baker's office, hoping to catch him still there. "Cliff? Don't you ever go home?"

"Come in, Stan. Doesn't look like it. You know, those bastards on my staff lied to me. They said this computer system we spent millions on was going to save me work, not create more of it. You know what?" he said, waving his big hand in the direction of his Data General computer terminal on a nearby table. "With this gadget that's supposed to help me so much, I find out about five times more problems each day than I used to. And if I don't look at it often enough, or do what it wants me to, the damned thing scolds hell out of me. I think I'll fire about six guys and get some new ones. You look worried. Why didn't you send me your problem on the computer like everybody else does?"

Dawson noted the tall stack of papers in front of the chief and came right to the point. "Cliff, are you up to date on the Kent thing?"

"Well, as of this morning. What's new?"

"As of this afternoon, Clyde Barlow's calling it a 'serious matter,'" he said, referring to the undersecretary of state. "Latest out of the embassy in Madrid is that Kent's moved out of hiding in an area north of the city, and they've got a nationwide search in progress. They're saying the Spanish forest service is involved in it somehow, the Russians are coming unglued, the U.S. ambassador is livid, and it's getting a lot of attention at State."

"That all? Shit, I thought there was a problem," Baker said, running his hand through his thinning gray hair.

"Oh, yes. And Kent is now believed by the police to be traveling with a good-looking female employee of the embassy, a Spanish national, by the way, and his head is covered with bandages. Other than all that, everything is fairly normal."

Baker shook his head in disbelief. "I suppose we'll read all about this in the *Washington Post* in the morning."

"The news services are beginning to pick up on it. You'll likely be getting a lot of calls."

"That's probably one of them right now," Baker said, pointing at the flashing light on his phone panel. "Hello? Yes, this is Cliff Baker. Kent? Yvette Kent?"

Yvette was sitting on a tall stool at the breakfast bar in the kitchen of her McLean split-level brick house. She was on her second double martini, and becoming more indignant by the minute. She was by now aware her husband's life was in grave danger and that nobody was apparently doing anything about it. Even worse, all of her friends from around town had called and asked what *she* was doing about it. Even the fucking neighbors were getting into the act. She had called several numbers at the CIA and the best response had been, "We'll get back to you, Mrs. Kent." Then she had spent two hours calling the State Department, finally reaching a man at the Spain desk who said they were doing everything they could, or words to that effect. Yvette had almost had it with government types when it occurred to her to call the chief of the Forest Service. Before dialing the number, she placed on the bar in front of her the list of names of senators, members of congress, the governor of Virginia, and other dignitaries that Arno would sometimes write to concerning his views on various issues. It was sometimes useful, she knew, to have a few names ready when talking to bureaucrats.

"Chief Baker," she began, "what, exactly, if anything, have you done for my husband lately?"

"Mrs. Kent, first of all I want you to know how very concerned we all are about what we've heard. In fact, right now, Stan Dawson and I are here in the office discussing—"

"Chief Baker, I don't want to take up a lot of your valuable time, because I know how busy you must be. So why don't we skip all the BS and get down to what, exactly, you're doing about this?"

"I understand how you feel, Mrs. Kent, and—"

"Did you understand my question, Chief Baker, or am I just talking down a well or something?"

"All right. What would you have me do? Your husband is now the object of a nationwide search by the police and probably others. If there were a single constructive thing to do that I thought might possibly be helpful, believe me, I'd drop everything else and go do it. What do you think I can do?"

"Well, Chief Baker, that's sort of your problem, isn't it? You sent him over there, and as I understand it, on a personal passport, for God's sake. That's contrary to your own requirements, is it not, Chief Baker? And why was he apparently given some additional job to do . . . something about the navy in Italy? I mean, what the hell is going on, and what are you personally doing to straighten out the trouble he's in?"

"I wish I could answer your questions, Mrs. Kent. I really do. Frankly, we in the Forest Service are as lost about all this as you are, and that's the truth. Although I wish to God we could do more, I don't know what that might be. I can assure you that the State Department is doing—"

"I spent all afternoon talking to people at the State Department, and as far as I can find out, they're mainly busy getting their butts covered. You need to do something to get that situation turned around. They ought to be helping my husband, don't you agree?"

"Yes, yes, of course I do, Mrs.—"

"Well then, Chief Baker, can I hear from you by, say noon tomorrow concerning what you have accomplished? I'd like to give you more time, but my appointments with Senators Josephson and Donaldson, and with Congressman Paine are beginning in early afternoon."

"Yes, Mrs. Kent, let me—"

"And then I do plan to stop by the *Washington Post* on the way back. They would undoubtedly be fascinated with the Forest Service being a front for the CIA, don't you think?"

"Kent is with the CIA?"

"Mr. Baker, Arno would be the last one to admit something like that. He's . . . that kind of a man. You will help, won't you?"

CHAPTER SEVEN

José Mateo Martínez, director general of ICONA, was having an early morning get-together with Rosendo Luís Echeverría, his subdirector general for protection of natural resources. A morning paper lay on the coffee table. Page one carried the story of the missing American.

SEARCH WIDENS FOR NORTH AMERICAN
The Highway Patrol put roadblocks into effect last night on roads east of the city in an attempt to apprehend Arnold Kent, the North American alleged to have been involved in the slayings of three Soviet Embassy personnel since last Monday. Police are also reported to be looking for a U.S. Embassy employee, Sra. Cristina del Barrio, who was reported seen with Kent last night in Motilla de Palancar.

El Sol was advised late Wednesday night by officials at the Russian Embassy that Kent was assisted in his escape from his hiding place near Alcobendas by personnel of a provincial fire brigade who transported him to Motilla de Palancar where Sra. del Barrio picked him up. Police were unable to confirm the accuracy of that report, however, and ICONA officials said they had no information on the case.

In a late-breaking development that might be related to the above case, Metropolitan Police found Miguel Escobosa Hermosilla, 41, second in command of ICONA's Forest Fire Section, in a dazed condition late last night in the Parque Retiro. Escobosa had been collaborating with Kent recently on forestry matters, but was unable to provide additional information either on Kent's whereabouts, or what he was doing wandering naked in the park.

The article was accompanied by the same photo of Kent that had appeared in the earlier stories.

"Well, what exactly did he say? You did call him, didn't you?" asked Martínez.

"Naturally I called," said Echeverría. "But his wife wouldn't let him come to the phone, even when I insisted. They had a doctor there, working on him. Miguel's wife said he was apparently drugged, his clothing removed, then just dumped there in the park. He's apparently still pretty groggy, raving about the water or something like that."

"When did he come up missing?"

"He never got home from work. She said he called her, that he was going to check out their apartment."

"Well, why—?"

"That's where it gets interesting. Since shortly after this Kent fellow arrived in town, Miguel moved his family in with her brother. He has a big estate with a security fence and all. Anyway, he just never got home."

The ICONA chief read the article again, his mouth set in a downturned arc. "Well, what's all this about the fire brigade in Alcobendas? How the hell did we suddenly get involved in an international intrigue, for God's sake? Please tell me it's just something the Russians made up to save face. Please tell me that."

Echeverría slowly shook his head apologetically. "Afraid not, José Mateo. I called the provisional chief as soon as I saw this. He said Miguel asked him for the loan of the truck and crew yesterday, and he gave it to him. Didn't know what it was for."

"Hasn't he found out yet?" thundered Martínez. "I mean, is the truck and crew still out, or what?"

"Yes, they returned in the middle of the night. The foreman told him he delivered a large box to Motilla de Palancar, but didn't know what it contained. It was a special favor for Miguel. I think Miguel and Kent are old school friends."

Martínez walked to a cabinet, took out a bottle of Gran Duque d'Alba and poured out a small glass, downing it in a gulp. "Well, that's wonderful, just wonderful," he said, wiping his mustache with a handkerchief. "So now we're part of a conspiracy, or so it would seem, along with the North Americans, to decimate the population of Soviet agents operating in Spain. Jesus Christ! Well, we've no time to waste. You get hold of Evaristo and have him find out everything about this from our standpoint, and—"

"Sorry, José Mateo, he's at some conference in Avignon. I'll have to fill in for him."

"All right. Drop everything else for now. I'll give the minister a preliminary briefing, and tell him we're working on a full report. Get back to Escobosa's wife every ten minutes if you have to. And I want Miguel down here the minute he's physically able. Our line for the news media is that we're investigating the reports, and suspect some kind of a mix-up."

"Are we admitting that we were working on a project with Kent?"

"Hm. Well, let's just say for now he was here on a visit requested by the North American forest service, but that the events that have transpired since his arrival have nothing to do with the visit or with us. We're just as mystified as anyone else." Martínez spent a moment looking at the map of Spain on the mahogany-paneled wall. "And one other thing. Take precautions to ensure that Mr. Kent is not 'accommodated' by any of our other personnel along his way to wherever he may be headed."

Lieutenant Colonel Vera Vlasov sat in the backseat of her car parked in a grove of oak trees just east of Requena, about seventy-two kilometers west of Valencia. It was a strategic position, to her thinking, because she now was fairly certain del Barrio and Kent were heading for Valencia, but that they were still to the west of Requena. They could stick to farm roads and secondary highways all the way from Motilla to Requena, she knew, but could not do so beyond Requena because of precipitous mountain terrain with its few, if any, passable roads. She was also aware that the highway patrol had arrived at the same conclusion; they had already set up roadblocks on the major roads west of Valencia and Alicante.

Vlasov had stationed one of the four units under her control just a mile to her west, with instructions to alert her when any green 1982 Seat sedan, regardless of license-plate numbers or number of occupants, was approaching her location. For the first time she felt a growing confidence that Kent would be found. Her only gnawing concern was that the police, with their greater number of units, might get to him first. That would be far better than nothing, of course, but Vlasov wanted it on her record that she had got the job done; she also wanted first crack at him and whatever he might be carrying with him.

It had been a long night, and was becoming a long morning. Vlasov had directed her units to methodically cover all the farm roads, recreation areas and other possible stopping places between Motilla and Requena, and also to check out the cars at all motels and *pensiones* in the dozen or so villages along Kent's possible routes of travel. So far, all the reports coming to her by radio had been negative. This didn't surprise her. These searches were seldom easy, and there were hundreds of places where a crafty person could get a car out of sight for a few hours. But she also knew that time was as precious a commodity for Kent and del Barrio as it was for her. It chilled her to think that should Kent slip through her fingers and get out of the country, her career would be as good as over.

At her embassy, Vera Vlasov had found out a few things about Kent's mission in Rome, and the concerns of her superiors concerning the implications of his interference in the matter. Had it not been for the coincidence of Cavalchini's untimely death at JFK and Kent's intercepting his briefcase, the whole matter wouldn't have deserved much attention. But if Kent turned out to be smart enough to figure out the real thrust of Operation Oltraggio, and if he turned out to be clever enough to reach the American authorities and then to persuade them of Oltraggio's validity, she knew there would clearly be cause for a major rift in American-Soviet relations, or perhaps much worse. There was no question that Kent—and del Barrio as well—had to be stopped, and now.

Vlasov's driver was busy monitoring the highway patrol UHF radio frequency with earphones. He had a road map on his lap. Turning suddenly to Vlasov, he said, "Their helicopter spotted a car of that description heading east near Balsa de Ves, toward Cofrentes. That's on the road that goes south from here."

"Are they intercepting it?" asked Vlasov.

"I couldn't pick up the other end of it," the driver said. "But the pilot said they refused to stop at his loudspeaker command, and that he was getting low on fuel."

Vlasov studied her map. "If they turn north at Cofrentes, we'll nail the bastards," she said. "There's only one place they could turn off coming north, and that leads out into no-man's-land. Their only hope is to try to get lost in the freeway traffic around Requena. What do you think, Vadim?" she said to the short, solidly built man in the right front seat.

"Let's meet them halfway, then, while the police are still waiting around here."

"They might not wait," said Vlasov, glancing at her watch. "Let's get started. With luck, we should intercept them within about fifteen minutes."

"And the police?" said Vadim Leonov, an experienced KGB major. "The helicopter pilot will undoubtedly be watching."

"We'll have to deal with that when the time comes. Meantime, if I have to cram them into the trunk of this car, claim diplomatic immunity and refuse to be searched, that's what I'll do."

The driver spun out from under the oak trees and got going on the main highway back toward Requena, then turned south on the highway toward Cofrentes. There was little traffic on that route, a two-lane paved road in bad repair. They drove fast for about twelve minutes, reaching a point on a little hill overlooking the only possible turnoff that Kent and del Barrio could make from the north-south road.

"Stop here," Vlasov said. "If they pass that turnoff, we'll intercept them, otherwise we will follow them."

"No sign of the helicopter," said the Leonov. "Could they have turned south from Cofrentes?"

"No," the driver said. "I can see the car now, coming quite fast."

"Turn around," said Leonov. "We'll have to take them from behind, just after they pass us."

The green Seat went past them at about fifty-five miles per hour. "Two of them!" shouted Vlasov. "That's the car! Get on the bastards!"

The dark blue Mercedes easily overtook the little Seat, pulling up directly behind it.

"Now watch it," said Vlasov. "We're not dealing with amateurs. Don't get alongside them."

"Ram them," ordered Leonov. "Try to knock them off the road."

The driver stabbed the accelerator pedal, jamming it clear to the floorboard. The Mercedes leaped ahead, dealing a pile-driver blow to the back end of the Seat. The little sedan shot ahead from the impact, then began swerving erratically from one side of the road to the other.

"Again!" shouted Leonov, clearly enjoying the event.

The driver waited a few moments until the Seat straightened out a bit, then rammed it a second time. This time the smaller car went out of control, skidding off the road surface, dropping into a drainage ditch, rolling over several times, finally ending up on its wheels.

"Quickly! Get them out of there," commanded Vera Vlasov. "We've no time to screw around. Hurry! Before the helicopter returns."

The three Soviets jumped from their car and hurried to the overturned Spanish car, their weapons drawn. There was no movement inside the car, both figures slumped, one in the back seat. Leonov got there first and jerked a door open. A man's body fell out into the knee-deep grass. Leonov rolled him over.

"Wha . . . this isn't Kent. Looks like some peasant farmer, for the love of shit."

"Two men," said the driver from the other side of the Seat. "This one looks like a farmer also."

"*Ne pizdi!*" said Vlasov in disbelief. "Don't bullshit me! This has to be them."

"We've been had, comrade," said Vadim Leonov. "Somehow, they managed to switch vehicles with these two clowns."

"Help me. For the love of God, help me," said one of the farmers. Blood was streaming from a corner of his mouth, and he appeared unable to move his arms or legs. The other farmer was either unconscious or dead; he showed no signs of movement.

"That truck! That fucking truck!" said the Soviet driver, pointing back toward the north.

"What truck?" asked Vlasov, trying to hide the tears of frustration.

"About five or six minutes back. A farm truck passed us going like hell. I only saw one person . . . the driver. But . . . shit! I think it was a woman."

"It was a Mercedes, you said?" Kent asked from his cramped position on the floorboards.

"Yes, a dark blue one, with three people in it. The driver looked straight at me. Had to be the KGB, parked out here like that, watching the highway. The bastards."

"They must have monitored the police radio, then. Lucky for us the chopper couldn't stay with us. Must have been short on fuel. How long you figure before those farmers run into the Mercedes?"

"You think I always drive like this? They're probably only about ten minutes back. Wouldn't take them five minutes to put on the spare, and I doubt whether the Russians will spend much time with them. We've got to get ourselves lost on the main highway before this truck is reported stolen."

"And meantime, the police will still be looking for the Seat, I hope."

"Yes, but that won't last long. I just hope this fuel gauge is broken. It reads about four liters less than empty. What are you laughing at?"

"Wouldn't that be the pits? Out here with no gas after all that? Hey, do you know you could be charged with fifteen or twenty crimes by now?"

"Twenty-one, actually, but who's counting?"

"You are taking this rather lightly. Is your father the president, or is your lawyer really that good? Look, until about two days ago you had a good career, you have two young children and God knows how many relatives here. If it turns out I'm on a wild goose chase we're both in the pit."

"Save it for now, Arno. We're into the game now, and there's no begging off. You can tell the authorities I kidnapped you in a fit of wild passion, and I'll say I was saving you from certain death at the hands of the KGB. Should make good reading in the papers, anyway. Then, you could write a hell of a book when you get back."

"I'd sure like to think there'll be a chance to do that someday. How much money do we have?"

"Enough so that we won't be doing a Bonnie and Clyde on this trip. If we can get to Valencia, I can get more. Oh, shit! We're out of gas. We won't even get to the top of this hill."

"Can you get turned around? We could coast back down, maybe find a turnoff or a way into the trees or something."

With the dying gasps of the engine, Cristina maneuvered the truck onto the edge of the road far enough so that, coasting backward and cramping the steering wheel all the way to the left, she was able to get the truck turned around. "I don't know, Arno. I was watching for side roads all the way and didn't see any coming up this grade. We don't have many options. Trust me to do the right thing?"

"Sure. Look where it's got me so far. Anyway, it's your truck. You stole it fair and square."

Del Barrio released the brakes and let the heavy vehicle begin coasting down the grade.

"It's the Mercedes. Must be doing seventy-five, but I think they're slowing down to look us over. Hang on for some crisis management."

The blue car slowed to about twenty-five as the truck rolled slowly down the hill toward them. Del Barrio could see the two men in the front seat looking at her as the vehicles closed. Then, at the last moment, not allowing the Russians a chance to swerve, she jerked her steering wheel strongly to the left and rammed the truck into the Mercedes, the truck's left front fender striking the car squarely in the radiator grille.

Kent, braced for the crash, felt as if he was being shot out of a cannon. Amid the ear-splitting and sickening sounds of tearing metal and breaking glass, he was aware of being bounced around violently between the seat and the fire wall. The terrible din seemed to go on and on, as the greater momentum of the truck continued to push the crushed Mercedes backward down the highway, and off to the side of the road. Approximately six seconds after the impact all sounds had subsided. Kent's first sensation was that his mouth was full of dirt. Then he thought of Cristina.

"Cris? Cris?"

"I'm okay, I think," she said. "What about you?"

"I'm all right . . . at least no new problems. How does the Mercedes look? Think their insurance will cover the repairs?"

"Tell you in a minute, after I check out your friends."

Del Barrio glanced into the Mercedes, then helped Kent out the right door of the truck. "Two guys in the front look dead. Woman in the backseat is pinned in there, but looks like she's not hurt too badly."

It was early afternoon, and several somber-faced men sat at a table in the ambassador's meeting room. Jerome Parkerhouse came in last and took the chair at the head of the table. He looked concerned and slightly angry.

"All right, Brad, you go ahead and summarize where we are locally on this Kent thing, then I'll tell you the latest from stateside."

Bradford Baumont nodded, glanced around at the others. "Yes. It seems impossible, but we just learned that two more Soviet agents have been killed, and another one injured over near Requena."

"What the hell is it now?" said the ambassador. "I hadn't even heard that one myself yet."

"Sorry, sir," said Baumont. "We just intercepted it from highway patrol radio traffic a few hours ago. A farm truck smashed into a Russian embassy car and—"

"Not related to the Kent situation, then?" asked Parkerhouse, leaning forward intently, his expression showing hope and relief.

Baumont was shaking his head and avoiding the ambassador's glare. "Well, that's not entirely clear yet. We don't have all the—"

"God damn it!" thundered Parkerhouse. "What is it that's not entirely clear, then?" The tall man's outburst almost blew Baumont backward out of his chair.

"Easy, Jerome," said Bruce Charner to the ambassador. "Not to shoot the messenger."

Baumont was recovering. "Sir, whoever was in the farm truck apparently fled the scene. When the police got there, two men who stopped to help reported their car was commandeered by a woman with a gun, and she had with her a man whose head was bandaged. The police are looking for that car now."

"Oh, shit! Tell me I'm dreaming," said Parkerhouse. "Jesus Christ! Do you know that's five of them so far? Wait a minute. Where in hell did they get the farm truck?"

"Not established for sure," Beaumont went on. "However, the police radio traffic included the information that del Barrio's sedan was found wrecked, further south toward Cofrentes, and that two seriously injured locals were found at the scene. Sorry, sir."

"We've got a big problem here," said Parkerhouse. "What about del Barrio? Bruce, did you find out how she got hooked up with Kent?"

"I talked to Flenk. He said the two met for the first time in his office when Kent made his appearance here on Monday morning. As far as he knows, they had no private conversations. The only thing that aroused his suspicion at all was when Kent started telling him about being followed. That's when Kent requested seeing Norb," Charner said, nodding in the direction of Norbert Whitman of the security section.

"Any chance Kent and Flenk might . . . that Kent is tied in with the KGB?" asked Parkerhouse.

Vernon Prokar spoke up. "Sir, I've run that through Langley. Their preliminary appraisal is that Kent is straight, but they're doing some more work on it."

"And you're sure he's not CIA?"

"I've been given every assurance, and they say they've checked it out with all the other agencies as well."

"Anyone else?" asked the ambassador, looking around. "All right. This is not going over at all well at State. Barlow has been on me three times in the last day. Says the secretary is becoming concerned about how this might affect our military presence in country. This airbase treaty renewal thing is coming up soon, and the student activities are making hay out of anything adverse that comes up. I can just imagine what the morning newspapers are going to do with this. Christ, they'll be talking about kicking out our F-16s, getting Spain out of NATO, and God knows what else, especially if they play up those nationals getting creamed, and our embassy personnel involved. Brad, what's your plan for control?"

Everyone looked at Baumont, whose face was somewhat less animated than the Rock of Gibraltar. He took his time getting ready to respond, a tactic he used to gain complete attention. "Since we talked yesterday, I put a team on this, myself, Bruce, Vernon, Norb and two others I felt I had to bring in. Our first conclusion was that we can't bring him down throwing rocks at him. This guy seems to be about three jumps ahead of the total resources of Spanish law enforcement and the KGB. We'd just get in their way. The key to this thing, we think, is to understand what Kent, and now apparently del Barrio, are trying to accomplish. The question we immediately came to was, do we take Kent at face value, or look for some other agenda, and if so, what? The feedback from Langley persuades us he's on to something big, isn't sure yet what it is, but is convinced it's important enough to risk his life, career, the whole bag, to bring off."

"To bring what off?" asked Parkerhouse. "You told me those notes from the Italian's briefcase were pure gibberish."

"First impression," said Baumont, frowning. "We decided to take another look this morning."

"And?"

"And . . . we can't find them." Baumont thought it best not to embellish the answer.

The ambassador sat there stunned, a V-shaped vein twitching in his forehead. "You . . . can't . . . find . . . them," he slowly repeated, as if trying to memorize the words.

"They were last seen on my desk," said Bruce Charner, the embassy's security chief. "I ran a complete shakedown in my section. Nothing else was out of order, tampered with or anything like that. Just gone, that's it. Could have been shredded or tossed in the burn bag, but nobody was told to do that. I just can't account for it."

"So you are now telling me that, one, you can't follow up on heading Kent off at the pass, and two, that we have somebody working on us from the inside, is that it?" asked Parkerhouse. "Or is it simply that I'm having a dream, that I'm watching a Three Stooges movie made up entirely of scraps from the cutting-room floor?"

The room was deathly silent for fifteen seconds. Parkerhouse, speaking through clenched teeth, said, "Now all of you listen. I want those notes found, deciphered, and evaluated. I want to know how they got misplaced and who is responsible for it. I want a well-thought-out plan for bringing this situation under control, and I want that all done by four this afternoon. Then, I want a press conference arranged for five thirty here in this room. I expect to tell the press a hell of a lot more about this mess than I know right now, and I expect all of you to prepare me to do this. Now get out of here and get on it."

Thursday morning's Washington, D.C. papers didn't yet have coverage of Kent's latest activities in Spain. But CNN's six o'clock newscast gave the following report:

FOREST SERVICE MAN LINKED TO
FIVE SLAIN SOVIETS ABROAD
Madrid—U.S. Forest Service employee Arnold Kent, 47, of McLean, Virginia, is sought by Spanish Police in connection with the slayings of two more Russian embassy personnel, bringing to five the number of Soviets killed in the Madrid area since last Monday. The latest victims, killed under suspicious circumstances in a highway accident near Requena this morning, were identified as Vadim Leonov and Anatoly Divilkovsky, reported to be Embassy employees working in the Cultural Affairs section. A third Embassy person, who was injured in the accident, was Vera Vlasov, a high-ranking diplomat. Police said two farmers from Cofrentes were found seriously injured several miles from the accident involving the three Russians, and that the personal car of Cristina del Barrio of the U.S. Embassy was involved. Soviet Em-

bassy personnel Yevgeny Divnich, found strangled in a Madrid hotel, and Andrey Ryabov and Igor Amalrik, shot to death and found in a burned automobile north of the city, were the earlier victims in this bizarre case that is rocking diplomatic relations between Spain, Russia and the United States.

Spanish Police officials state that del Barrio, a Spanish citizen in the employ of the U.S. Embassy in Madrid, is also being sought in the case, and that she is presumably traveling with Kent. Embassy officials acknowledged that del Barrio is absent from her post, but declined to speculate further.

Reached at his office late last night, Forest Service Chief Cliff Baker said Kent was in Madrid on a routine assignment, and that Forest Service officials here were at a complete loss to explain what was going on. Baker said he had asked officials at the State Department for help in locating Kent and giving him assistance. Soviet embassies in both Washington and Madrid have declined to make statements.

The news from Spain had brought Kent's office to a standstill as far as getting any regular work done was concerned. Kent's secretary had hung up a huge sign behind her desk saying,

ARNO 5, KGB 0

The sign was decorated with an American flag on the left, and a hammer and sickle on the right.

The main discussions going on were whether Kent was CIA or not, what his real mission in Spain was, and who was this del Barrio woman he was traveling with. Various wagers were being made, the most popular one attracting odds of five to one that Kent would never return to his job in Rosslyn. One co-worker, fond of creating "pools" on sports, elections, promotions or anything else, offered fifty-dollar chances on submitting, in a sealed envelope, the most accurate explanation for what was going on, and the probable outcome. The winner was guaranteed one thousand dollars, with any funds left over in the pool to be donated to Kent or his survivors. By close of business that day, the deadline for the pool, sixty-five entries had been posted. Kent's secretary agreed to make a scrapbook of the submissions after the winner had been decided.

Forest Service Chief Baker, shaken up somewhat by Yvette Kent's call the evening before, had spent an hour conferring by phone with his boss, the assistant secretary of agriculture, with the undersecretary of state, and with an official on the staff of the president's national security advisor. He learned nothing he did not already know, and received little encouragement concerning what could be done to extract Kent from the ongoing situation. When Yvette called at exactly eleven o'clock, Baker told her about his calls, that there was little he could do, and that she might as well go ahead and do whatever she felt might be the most helpful to her husband.

Stan Dawson got the same message from Baker as did Yvette. The day before he had barged in on Otto Frange at State's Italy deck demanding answers about Kent's "supplementary" mission in Rome, and was rebuffed out of hand. Frange complained through channels that Dawson was interfering, provoking a call to Baker requesting that Dawson back off. In his short meeting with Frange, Dawson sensed a hostility that alarmed him. He began wondering if there might be something behind the scenes that might help explain what Kent was involved in. He relayed that concern to Baker, but felt the chief didn't put much stock in it.

Yvette didn't get in to see either of the Virginia senators, but was able to get an audience with a staffer in each office. They had heard the news reports, seemed interested in her views, and promised to relay them to their senators. She made it quite clear in each case that she expected action, and would keep the local news media aware of what, if anything, came of her requests. Then she headed for the *Washington Post*.

Cristina del Barrio avoided the roadblock east of Requena by circling the city on the west, then taking the secondary highway north and west to Liria, then southward into the outskirts of Valencia. This route added about an hour to the travel time but was necessary to avoid obvious police checkpoints. She drove the car into a business district, parked, then found a phone. She got back in the car a few minutes later and they waited until another car arrived. Cristina guided Kent into the backseat, where he lay down, then they were off.

"Arnold, this angel is my cousin Margarita. She is going to find a place for us not far from here."

"Thank you, Margarita. I hope this place is not too far. I've had my legs crossed for hours."

"We'll be there in a few minutes. Then we will try to solve all your problems. I imagine you haven't had much to eat or drink, either of you, no?"

"Eat, drink? I've forgotten what that's like," said Cristina. "What kind of place is this?"

"A small house. One that's vacant right now. Between rentals."

"Yours?" asked Cristina.

"No, but I'm taking care of it for the owners. They live in France this time of year. By the way, who is this gentleman, and why does he have to hide? And what are you doing clear over here?"

"You haven't been reading the papers or watching the news, Margarita. This is the American who—"

"Oh my God! The one who's been killing all the Russians from the embassy?"

"He didn't do it all. I've been helping him. Isn't it exciting?"

"Cristina! For the love of God, how . . . why . . . ?"

She laughed, then said, "It's for a good cause. But it's too much to explain right now. Anyway, I don't want you to know any more about it yet, only that we desperately need your help to hide us out for a few days, then get Mr. Kent out of the country. And, of course, not to say one single word to anybody, not even to Guillermo."

"All right. I'll do whatever has to be done. You can count on me."

The two women got Kent onto a bed in the back room of the little house, pulled off his shoes and covered him with a blanket. He was asleep within seconds. When he awoke it was dark; he had absolutely no idea what time it was, and in his drowsiness, it took a few minutes to figure out roughly where he was and how he had got there.

He felt his face and noticed it was much less tender to the touch. The bandages itched and felt dirty. Why not take them off? he thought. Here in the darkness there shouldn't be a problem concerning his eyes. And what day was this? Thursday? Friday? They had told him the bandages could be removed . . . Saturday, wasn't it?

Gingerly, he worked the ends of the pieces of tape loose from the skin around his neck, and then carefully slid the gauze-wrapped bandage over his head. Suddenly, the whole thing was off. He felt his face. The skin felt rough, as if there were a lot of loose pieces ready to come off. He resisted the temptation to relieve the itching by pulling on any of them. He felt his closed eyes and they felt fairly normal, except for a buildup of crystallized matter around the lids. He slowly and deliberately began to open his eyes, and was surprised at how difficult it was, almost as if they were stuck closed. But after several tries, they came open.

Nothing! He could see nothing! His heart began beating faster. "Cris? Cris?" he called out softly. No response. He lay back down and tried to compose himself. He remembered that during the daytime he could determine direction by turning his head until the brightness through his eyelids told him he was facing the sun. He could get no such impression now, so it had to be dark, he realized. Was it too dark to see with good eyes?

Kent sat up on the bed again and looked all around. Now he could discern vague shapes in the darkened room. Carefully, he rose and felt his way to the wall, then worked along it to a window. The shade was drawn. He felt for the edge of the shade, then carefully pulled it to one side and looked out. The first thing he saw was the silhouette of another house, not far away. Then he could identify the shapes of bushes and trees, and down the road, a streetlight. He covered one eye, then the other. They both were all right, at least as far as he could tell. It was a wonderful feeling, and one he swore he would never forget.

Vera Vlasov was rushed by police ambulance to a hospital in Requena, where she refused treatment until after she had placed a local phone call. She told police she had no idea who had been in the truck that rammed them, and demanded to be released from the hospital immediately. Two Soviets were there waiting for her when she left by the front door. They took her into the business district, briefing her along the way as to what they had learned since the crash, and escorted her to an office with a placard on the door reading, NORTHEASTERN ENTERPRISES, INC.

Vlasov was not badly hurt. She had a black eye, the skin was stripped off the bridge of her nose, and her ribs were very sore. But nothing hurt more than her pride at having been outmaneuvered again by the American and his Spanish companion. She still had little respect for their abilities; it had all been a matter of exceptionally good luck for them. Had they been professionals, they certainly would have finished her off when she was in a helpless state at the wreck. But they would both live to regret that error, she swore to herself. She felt no compassion for her two slain companions. There had been no romantic attachment with either, and in this business you do your job and try to arrange things so that it's the other person who pays the final price. Her deliberate decision to ride in the backseat had paid off for her, as it had on a previous occasion.

Vlasov reached her boss, Colonel Feliks Kratkov, at the embassy in Madrid, and gave him an unvarnished description of what had happened on the highway. He listened without interruption, then asked questions.

"Where do you think they are now?"

"They're hiding in the suburbs of Valencia, most likely on the west side in the Castellón district. The police have turned up the car they stole from the farmers and believe the Kent person and his friend are still in the general neighborhood."

"You apparently have already mobilized the local resources there. What approach are you using?"

"I believe Kent will try to call the United States because he can got no help from his own embassy. Feliks, this is where I need your help."

"Hm. Yes, comrade, that is very good. The Valencia-Washington traffic should be fairly light. I'll have our signal intelligence people focus on that, see what can be done. An intercept would at least tell us what he knows."

"Feliks, I want more than that, you understand?"

"I'm not technically qualified to tell you whether that's possible, but we will at least try. Is there any collaboration locally where you are? That would be more efficient."

"At the telephone office? Yes, I think so. We'll begin on that right now."

"Vera, I still have confidence in you. However, it is time to alert Colonel Korolenko in Rome. I can handle it better from here, but I wanted you to know I'm still just considering it a precautionary move."

"All right, I understand that. But Kent has everything against him if he tries to cross the frontier . . . his photos, passport, money, language.

The police will have every airport, train depot, bus terminal, car-rental agency covered, and all border personnel alerted. I really think he's got to burrow in here for at least a week, maybe two."

"And maybe not. Just look at what he's accomplished so far. It's our appraisal here now that he's a bigger fish than we thought. Don't rule out anything. And don't ask me for any more help. I've had it straight from Moscow that they think we've muffed it, and they're losing confidence fast. We must get this job done with the little we have left, you understand?"

Vlasov quickly set about organizing the KGB resources in the Valencia area. She understood that the organizational priority was finding out how much Kent knew. But her personal top priority was getting to Kent himself. With that in mind, she arranged for police orders to be issued to trace any outgoing calls destined for the Washington, D.C., area, and to receive reports at Northeastern Enterprises on any such calls originating in the Castellón district. This cost a small bundle, but there was no question that it had to be done. It was amazing how quickly one could break through the sticky Spanish bureaucracy with a little money. She knew that such call-tracing might involve as many as six or eight calls per hour, but inasmuch as most of them would correspond to Valencia districts she wasn't interested in, she was confident her people could handle the load.

Vlasov also arranged for proper greasing of police palms at their central headquarters so that she could stay tuned in to anything they found out with regard to their search for Kent. Her other probes concerned information that might turn up at the ICONA offices in Madrid, and at the homes of del Barrios's known relatives around Alcobendas and Valencia. Regarding the latter, she arranged illicit telephone taps, to be monitored on a twenty-four-hour basis. Then she slept on a couch there in the office, ready to spring into action the moment anything promising, or even interesting, came up.

When Cristina del Barrio came into the little kitchen shortly after dawn on Friday, she was surprised to see Kent sitting at the table, hunched over the wrinkled papers he had carried with him all week. She came to him immediately without a word, took his face between her hands and looked at it closely. "Arno, it looks very good, much better than I thought. In fact, it's a miracle!"

"But when do you think I'll be able to see again?" he said, riveting his vision on her right ear.

"Liar!" she said. "I see what you're working on. Didn't I tell you? Didn't I tell you? Well, what do you tuink?"

"That now I can never let you out of my sight."

They embraced for a moment, then she pulled away. "I have salve for your face, and dark glasses, and you must continue the antibiotics, and—"

"And where are we going for breakfast, or are we still going to be on a diet?"

"We're going right here. Margarita brought everything to make it with. Would you like a bath before, or would you prefer to continue smelling like a goat?"

"I thought I'd wait until the other goats began complaining. But now that they have, why not? But before I do, I want you to know you haven't been wasting your time."

"What do you mean?"

Kent gestured at the scraps of notebook paper on the table. "You can burn those papers now."

"You've memorized them already?"

"Yes, but something else. I know what they say."

CHAPTER EIGHT

After four days without a bath or a shave, Kent felt as if he had reached the promised land. He watched the first tubful of water go down the drain—it was more like mud than water—then refilled the tub so he could just lie there and soak in it. He lay back and closed his eyes. Deciphering the notes had tired his eyes surprisingly, and he felt almost like sleeping again. He tried recalling the faces of everyone he had met or seen since this adventure started, and that of Otto Frange kept coming back to him. He had encountered Frange supposedly for the first time at his meeting with Claunch at the AID/OFDA office, but even then it had struck him that it was not their first meeting. During his life, Kent had found that such impressions—of having met someone before—were often valid. But no matter how many times he called up that face, the trace went nowhere.

And then the gold chain appeared around Frange's neck. He had worn an open-neck shirt at their meeting, and Kent had noted the reddish hair on his chest. Suddenly he was looking at that same reddish chest hair and golden chain, but the scene was not Claunch's office, it was Kent's own living room in McLean. "My God, that's it!" he said aloud, almost leaping up out of the water.

Cristina heard him say it. She stuck her head in the bathroom door and said, "What's *it*? Are you all right?"

"It was a wig!" he said. "But the gold chain, the hair on his chest . . . the odor of pipe tobacco . . . it was the same!"

"Arno, will you please explain what in the world you're talking about?"

"Otto Frange. You know, the guy from the Italy desk at State, the one who sat in on my meeting with Farber Claunch?"

"When they gave you the assignment concerning the navy at Naples?"

"Yes. Yes. I knew I had seen him before, you know, like I had talked to him, but somehow he looked different. It was in my house in McLean, for God's sake."

"What? Not really?"

"It was about a year ago. He was bald. He pulled up in front in a big Lincoln or Chrysler. Told me and Yvette he was looking at the house across the street, thinking of buying it, and could we tell him some things about the neighborhood."

"He was looking at the house that the Italian was—"

"Yes. He wanted to know what kind of neighbors would be prying into his man's affairs."

"But you never met the Italian before the house was purchased?"

"Or since. It was only because our deck looked into his backyard that I happened to see him at all. Come to think of it, Frange admired our deck and asked to step out onto it."

"And you're sure it was he?"

"He smelled the same. Now I know why his cologne or after-shave, or whatever it was, struck me in the office. It was an unusual odor, kind of mixed with the odor of pipe tobacco, but I had smelled it once before. Yvette commented on it after he was at our house."

"Arno, the implications of this are fascinating."

"Indeed. In fact, they're frightening. Damn! Things are starting to come together. It's Frange who must have disavowed my story when the embassy checked with State."

"Well, it was just a coincidence, wasn't it, that you were picked out to do the job in Rome? I mean, it didn't have anything to do with meeting Frange at your house."

"Right, just a coincidence. But Frange took advantage of it when he found out I was the one going to Italy. Then, when the Italian had his heart attack at JFK, Frange had to change gears. He had to alert somebody in Madrid I was coming. Fortunately, they didn't pick me out at the airport."

"I've got eighteen more questions, but why don't you finish your bath and get shaved while I put together something to eat. You'll find everything you need, including clean clothes, right out here. But don't take too long. I want to know what it says in those notes."

* * *

The Spanish news media were having a field day covering the exploits of the fugitives and concurrent demise of Soviet embassy personnel in a trail leading halfway across the country. One Madrid daily ran a political cartoon showing an Uncle-Sam-clad Kent with del Barrio in a gauzy negligee zooming along in a Spanish highway patrol cruiser, shooting out the tires on a pursuing Russian embassy car. In the sky above, flying escort, was a squadron of American F-16 fighters from the controversial base at Torrejón de Ardoz. Within hours, the cartoon was showing up in U.S. papers in Washington and New York. Spanish officials from state governors to local police chiefs were on the receiving end of all the criticism, jokes and embarrassment that surround such events, and politicians were beginning to call for results or the expulsion of anyone involved in the breakdown.

The police, therefore, were grimly determined to produce the pair's arrest without delay. Under the aegis of the Ministry of the Interior, the CCAL, or Coordinating Commission for Law Enforcement was hastily activated, enabling federal, regional and local police agencies to pool their efforts without the usual red tape that normally slowed the sharing of information and crossing of jurisdictional boundaries. The main headquarters was set up in Madrid, Captain Rodrigo Blanco in charge, with a satellite headquarters in Valencia at the municipal police station. In Valencia, orders were quickly issued to cover all airports, bus and train stations and car-rental outlets, as well as all points of egress from the general area, particularly at the French frontier. Telephone calls from Valencia to the Washington, D.C., area were being monitored to provide a trace to the calls' sources. In effect, the police were doing the same things as the KGB, but with far more people involved.

By Friday noon, Captain Blanco had arrived from Madrid to oversee operations in Valencia. At the municipal station, a map had been put up on the wall showing the west-side neighborhood where Kent and del Barrio were supposed to be hiding. It was an area of about six square kilometers, containing an estimated fifty-five hundred homes, mostly one- and two-family dwellings. Blanco ordered that a force of one hundred officers be organized to make door-to-door inquiries throughout the suspect area, and to have the job completed in forty-eight hours. He offered a 250-thousand peseta (two-thousand-dollar) bonus to the officer turning up information resulting in the apprehension of the fugitives. The bonus provided the incentive to put in long hours without complaints about the lack of overtime wages. Despite police attempts to hush the media coverage of the local search, the news was on television and radio as well as in all the papers.

News editors at the *Washington Post* thought Yvette Kent's story about her husband being a CIA agent wasn't reliable without confirmation, and none was available through any of their sources, so they heard her out but printed nothing. It would be a juicy story, but they decided to keep it on hold. Instead, they stuck to wire-service reports from Europe and direct quotes from local government officials. But the *Washington Times*, based on Yvette's call to their office, printed the following:

> **WIFE SAYS KENT U.S. SPY**
>
> Yvette Kent, wife of Arnold Kent, U.S. Forest Service employee sought by Spanish Police in connection with the slayings of five Soviet diplomats, claims Kent, 47, is an undercover CIA agent and that the Government is denying this in order to avoid responsibility for protecting him and his family from Russian agents. Contacted at the Langley headquarters, a CIA spokesman said the agency does not comment on its operations abroad, nor on personnel who may or may not be in the agency's employ. To date, Forest Service officials have maintained that Kent is a bona fide Forest Service employee, sent to Madrid on official business of the agency.
>
> According to latest reports from wire services abroad, Kent and U.S. Embassy employee Cristina del Barrio are believed hiding out in a Valencia suburb west of the city. Kent, seen recently with his head bandaged, was reported to have been shot and wounded by one of two Soviet Embassy personnel who were later found killed north of Madrid. The Russian Embassy in Madrid has refused to comment on developments in the bizarre case.

The Kent affair was now making the evening news on the three major TV networks and the cable news channel, and was arousing interest among the country's intelligence agencies, particularly the CIA. CIA officials were of course aware Kent had no connection with their agency, but were at a complete loss to come up with any explanation for what was going on. On Wednesday the deputy chief of EUR, the European Division, had assigned Malcolm Bartledge the job of putting pieces together, and by Friday Bartledge submitted this terse report to his boss:

KENT/SPAIN

10/2—Kent issued travel orders to Madrid, Rome, for routine forestry mission related to prevention and control of wildland fires. Departed U.S. for Madrid on 10/17.

10/19—Kent reported to U.S. Emb./Madrid that he had witnessed the death of a McLean, VA neighbor by apparent cardiac infarction at JFK en route to Madrid, and that he had examined the deceased's briefcase and found photos of himself along with encrypted notes giving details of Kent's itinerary. Kent related to Emb./Madrid the above and also details of "supplemental" assignment for Rome. —Kent says on 10/12 requested by F. Claunch of AID/OFDA to find out from Italian forestry officials who in Italian Ministry for Civil Protection was stalling about approving Navy's move from Agnano to Capua. (He explained that Civil Protection people assist forestry officials in aerial firefighting operations, thus they are well acquainted, that Pentagon declined pursuing this through regular Navy channels so as to avoid appearance of interfering in an internal matter, and that State considered the matter as a delicate one and declined involvement as well.) Late on 10/19 State checked Kent's story and disavowed it.

10/22—Navy denies requesting AID/OFDA assistance, as does State's Italy desk.

10/19–10/22—Spanish police believe Kent involved in slaying five (5) Russian embassy personnel. (See attached news clips.) International attention now focused on the situation. State highly concerned about impact on upcoming lease renewal negotiations for

three strategic air bases in Spain. Am/Emb/Mad.
concerned about safety of American personnel, given
the CIA news slant and KGB loss of five agents there.

Arthur Chafkin, deputy chief of EUR, called Bartledge into his office to chat about it. Chafkin was a tall, lean, unassuming-looking man in his mid-forties. His twenty years in the agency had all been in the DDO, the directorate of operations, and he had been chief of station in three Western European countries. He loved covert work, and it was with great reluctance that he had left the field, at the agency's urging, to take on the administrative assignment in Langley.

"What about this del Barrio woman?" Chafkin asked. "What's her connection with all this?"

"Wish I could tell you," said Bartledge. "She's thirty-five, educated in the United States, widow of a policeman who was gunned down by a Basque separatist. Has two kids in a boarding school, is considered a competent employee at the embassy. It's a mystery to the embassy folks over there."

"Any indication he knew her before this adventure began?"

"None. Met her there in the office his first day."

"What about NSA? Have their SIGINT people been picking up anything between Madrid and Moscow?"

"Those bastards wouldn't volunteer it to us if they did. It's like trying to pry an abalone off a rock with a soda straw. But I'll go over there this afternoon and give it a shot."

"Well, how do you figure this whole thing, Mal? The stuff we've got makes it sound like this Kent has been knocking off those agents mainly to stay alive. Seems like he either has something big, or the KGB thinks he has."

"Could be that first guy he throttled in the hotel was just a chance thing. Because of that they got on his case."

"But wait a minute. By the time that happened, hadn't he already gone to the embassy with that Italian briefcase story?"

"Yeah, that kind of holds his end up a bit," said Bartledge. "But what I don't understand is why he wouldn't seek refuge at the embassy instead of taking off with that gal. Matter of fact, the embassy called him and told him to come right over."

"Well, that was a bit strange. But going back to the hotel killing, if this guy had invented the briefcase bit in order to gin up a spy thriller or whatever, then hadn't been believed right off, maybe he needed to produce a mysterious body to give himself credibility."

"Only thing wrong with that theory, Arthur, is that he handed over the contents of the briefcase, including the photos and encoded notes, to the embassy's security chief."

"Oh? And what did the notes contain?"

"The word being passed along by the ambassador to State is that the notes mysteriously disappeared before they were deciphered. They're probably real happy about that."

"Well, it looks like Kent, if he's legit, would try to put himself into contact with the embassy, or with some other U.S. authorities, or with his wife, or his outfit, or some damn thing, doesn't it? I mean, the guy is sharp enough to still be alive and running loose over there, he must be smart enough to make a telephone call, for Christ's sake."

"One would think so. Must be some kind of weirdo, but apparently a very competent one. How do you want it handled?"

"Not really much to handle at the moment. Why don't you just stay tuned in, try to find out if Kent contacts anyone, and if so what he has to say. Maybe a good idea to talk to his wife, find out what she knows, make a friend of her. Sounds like she needs a little pat on the butt anyway."

"Follow up on the SIGINT possibilities?"

"I don't think so. Best save our chits over at Fort Meade for bigger stuff. I doubt whether this Kent fellow will be loose much longer anyway."

"This is in an Italian dialect I'm not too familiar with," Kent said. They had pushed aside the breakfast dishes and had the notes spread out on the table in front of them. "And it's quite abbreviated as well, and I don't understand all of the coding."

"Stop apologizing," Cristina said. "What does it say?"

"Well, in the first part here it mentions Agnano and Capua, and must have something to do with the subject of that newspaper clipping about the navy's planned move out of Agnano, remember?"

"Yes, their Sixth Fleet support complex."

"Okay. Now this part has my name in it, and the names of my hotels in both Madrid and Rome. That's the part I first decoded. But then in the same paragraph, it mentions a Colonel Golino of the Italian Defense Ministry . . . 'who understands Oltraggio.'"

"*Oltraggio,*" del Barrio said. "*Ultraje* in Spanish, and *outrage* in French . . . and in English. The name of a project or operation, perhaps?"

"That's what I think. Now the first line of this next part is unreadable—it's where the paper was folded and it's worn out there. But right below that, it clearly says, 'fleet from the Mediterranean.' Then it says, 'No delay permissible.'"

"It's so fragmentary, Arno. But you have that gleam in your eye again. What do you make of it?"

"I wish I had hung onto that letter. I think it had some of the missing pieces."

"What letter?"

"From the briefcase. It was an unsealed letter with Spanish postage addressed to somebody in Rome. I meant to take it to the embassy last Monday along with the other stuff, but left it in my hotel room along with my copy of the notes. I got my notes out of the Russian's pocket before I stuffed him in the laundry barrel, but didn't think about the letter."

"Had you read it?"

"I did, on the airplane. Just a quick once-through. It didn't make much sense at the time, but it said something about this Colonel Golino and the desire of . . . some name I don't recall . . . to remove him from the project, so there would be no opportunity for his interference."

"Sounds like orders to liquidate him. To whom was the letter addressed?"

Kent laughed. "You know, I've put myself to sleep three or four times trying to hypnotize myself into remembering."

"I'm sorry this visit has been so dull for you. Could you come up with anything at all?"

"The name Carlo Marasco keeps coming up, but no address. There are likely three dozen of those in Rome."

"Would you recognize the street name if you heard it?"

"Don't know. Perhaps."

"What about the letter. Who would have it now?"

"The police would have looked at it first, but I doubt if they would have connected it with all this. Then, the Soviets would have latched onto it."

"That figures," said Cristina. "The Russians would assume you read the letter, and probably that you had picked up other items from the Italian as well. They would have assumed the worst, and acted accordingly. That explains their great interest in you, I would say. And it also indicates that this Operation Oltraggio is fairly important on their list of things to do."

"Cristina, is there a way I can call Washington from here? If I can get hold of Stan Dawson, my boss, he could get through to someone who would listen."

"It's a good idea, but I think your timing is wrong. First off, any call from right around here to Washington would get us checked out real fast by the police, and probably the KGB. I'm sure they would be watching the lines. Then, what would you tell him anyway? What you know right now would do little more than confirm their opinion that you had flipped out of your orbit."

"You're right, at least about getting traced. But what if I called some friend in California and asked them to relay the message?"

"What message?"

Kent thought about it. "You win. How much time do you think we have here before we have to move again?"

"Are you up to traveling already?"

"I'm up to anything, already," he said.

She stared at him, solemnly at first, then with a reserved smile. "I think we have enough time for whatever you might have in mind."

"Even if it involves committing another crime?"

"I can deal with certain crimes. Which one do you have in mind?"

"One that may involve lack of consent and resistance on the part of the victim."

Del Barrio began unbuttoning her blouse. "My guess is that if you'll give your consent and don't offer too much resistance, nobody will report this one to the police."

Kent was immediately overcome by a wave of passion, of pent-up emotions and fears, and of the need to pull the woman to him and make her a part of him. Suddenly they were both naked and on their feet in the middle of the little kitchen, kissing each other and feeling the other's body for the first time. Then they were on the floor and it was dirty and cold but they felt nothing more than the hot flesh of the other tight against them. Then after rolling around in the dust like two snakes in combat, they were suddenly in a chair, Cristina on top, her breasts teasing his mouth and his eyes as the rhythm went on violently, inexorably. Then at the moment of highest passion, the chair tipped backward spilling the love warriors into an ungainly heap on the vinyl floor. Cristina's scream turned quickly into a raucous fit of laughter as they rolled apart and realized they were unhurt.

Kent lay there on his back, savoring the wave of relaxation that had swept over him. "I never heard you laugh like that before," he said.

"Well, I've never fallen out of a chair during sex before, either, you know. God, that was good. Did you like it, Arno?"

"Oh, about average," he said, dodging quickly to avoid her fist, then grabbing her around the arms and body. Then he kissed her long and hard, and she returned it in kind.

"To answer your earlier question," she said, smoothing her black hair with both hands, "we don't have a whole lot of time. The pressure on the police to find us is so great right now, they'll leave no stone unturned. Margarita says there's a reward for information . . . Some of these nosy neighbors could get suspicious. I think we must leave as soon as—"

There was a knock at the front door. "Get dressed quickly," Cristina said. "Then stay out of sight." She quickly slipped into a terry-cloth robe, looked out the peephole in the door, then eased it open a few inches. Kent had jumped into the little bedroom, had the tiny automatic in his hand, and listened through the space along the hinged side of the door. He heard a woman's voice, then Cristina's responding. Following a short exchange, the door shut and del Barrio came into the bedroom.

She kissed him and said, "A woman from next door. Says she noticed the house was now occupied again, and wanted to welcome her new neighbors."

"What do you think?" asked Kent.

"Not good. She didn't look friendly. She looked nosy and greedy. I told her I was just getting ready to take a bath, and would like to come over to her house to say hello a little later."

"Think she bought it?"

"I won't even guess at it. I think we ought to get out of here right away."

"Fine with me. Any ideas?"

"We can't go to Margarita's. Her place might be under surveillance. I'll get dressed, then go find a phone and get her to come pick me up."

"But her phone might be tapped."

"It's all right. We agreed on how to handle that. I'll have her pick me up from the pay phone. Anyway, it would be better not to have us seen leaving here together. So you wait thirty minutes, then walk north to the second bus stop and wait for us. If necessary, walk to the third bus stop."

"How about another backup, just in case?"

"All right. Tonight at seven, at the Plaza de la Serena. It's known to any taxi driver."

Del Barrio was gone in five minutes. Kent watched her walk briskly down the walk, looking straight ahead as if she had lived there all her life. He put on the clothes that had been provided for him, amazed that they fit as well as they did. Then he placed the notes from the Italian's briefcase into a dish and burned them and dumped the ashes into the toilet and flushed them down. Then he checked his passport. It was still a shock to see someone else's name under his photo; Bennet Bryant was a name he would have to get used to. Cristina had left money: a sheaf of bills inside the cover of the passport, and a small handful of Spanish coins. Another item fell out of the passport, a driver's license in the name of Bennet Bryant, issued in the state of Virginia. It was a clever forgery, obviously his own driver's license reconstituted so that his name, but not his physical description, was altered. How had Cristina accomplished all of this, he wondered? And why? That was an even harder question in his mind.

He checked around inside the house and found absolutely no evidence of del Barrio's having been there. When he had pocketed his few meager items, all that was left was the few toiletry items from the bathroom. He placed these things in the bag they had been brought in and was ready to go. He checked his watch. Twenty minutes to go. Time for a cup of coffee.

While the coffee water was heating, Kent went to the front room and opened the blinds enough to be able to see the street. Movement directly across the street caught his eye: it was a policeman coming down the walk from the front of that house. But when he reached the side-walk, instead of turning one way or the other, he came directly across the street toward the house Kent was in. The officer's movements were casual; he was apparently going to each house, probably asking questions.

Kent's first thought was not to answer the door. But then he thought this might raise suspicions. Maybe one of the neighbors had told him there were people there. On an impulse, he decided to try to remove suspicion by welcoming the officer, then going into his Italian act, one he used humorously at parties and in the office. When the knock came, he put on a casual air and pulled open the door.

"Good morning, sir," the officer said in Spanish. "Sorry to bother you, but—"

"*Scusi, signore, ma io sono italiano. Puo capire lo spagnolo si non parla troppo rapido, capisce?*"

The officer nodded, and began speaking more slowly and deliber-ately. Kent waved him into the house, offering him a cup of coffee.

"No, thank you," said the policeman. "I have many houses to visit. Are you alone here?"

"Excuse me? Am I lonely here, do you say?"

"No, sir. Alone. Is there anybody else living here with you?"

"Oh! Sorry. Yes. I am with my wife here. She went out for the grocer-ies a little while ago."

The officer kept looking Kent over, his clothes, his hands, then star-ing at his face. "What has happened to your face, sir, were you injured recently?"

Kent's hand shot up to his peeling face. He could feel the loose pieces of skin, and was aware his face was reddening. "Oh, yes, officer. It was an accident, where I work, you know. Somebody spilled some gasoline near a burner and it suddenly flared up. I was lucky, I guess. I could have been blinded."

Kent thought he was carrying it off pretty well, but the officer didn't seem convinced. He kept looking around the room, then at Kent's clothing again. After a few more questions about where Kent worked, he asked if Kent would mind showing his identification papers.

✻   ✻   ✻

Captain Rodrigo Blanco's canvassing of the suburban Valencian district was not going as smoothly as he had hoped. The reward offer for information on the fugitives brought forth hundreds of calls from all over the city and the surrounding area, and he found himself short of staff to process the tips rapidly. He gave directions to log in the calls and put red push pins in the wall map corresponding to each call. Within a few hours patterns were forming. For some neighborhoods no calls had come in. These were the more affluent localities where strangers seldom came and went. For other neighborhoods, many calls came in. These were areas in which there were high proportions of rentals, and people were less well acquainted and generally more suspicious. But to Captain Blanco and his staff, the most interesting areas were those in which relatively few calls came in, but in which they were clustered in one or more spots on the map.

One such location of high interest was that in the middle-class Castellón district, where it was already suspected the fugitives were holed up. Only two houses had been reported, but there were three red pins for each of them. The local police had ruled out one of them as a known fencing operation already under surveillance. Captain Blanco asked what was known about the other.

"I took one of the calls on that one, sir," a police sergeant said. Everyone turned to hear what he had to say. "People there are reported staying out of sight in a recently vacated rental house. No car, a woman there, the other person not seen yet."

"How did they know there was somebody else?" somebody asked.

"The woman didn't say," said the sergeant. "Only that she was sure there was more than one person there."

"Have one of your units check that out, Lieutenant," said Blanco. "That's the right neighborhood, and the rest of it seems to fit what we're looking for."

One of the officers working the situation paid close attention, then slipped out of the room and made a local phone call. When the call was answered, he said, "I think they've nailed it. Looks like the third house from the south end of Belén Street on the east side of the street. Can't give you the number. The police will be dispatching a unit within a half hour. You'll have to hurry."

Three minutes later a dark sedan pulled out of underground parking in the downtown area and zoomed toward the suburbs, two men in the front seat and a woman in the back. An unmarked delivery van came behind them, following at a distance of two blocks. Vera Vlasov cursed the maddening noontime traffic that impeded her progress westward out of the city. It would just not do that the police get to Kent first. Not after all she had gone through. At each intersection she checked her watch and uttered obscenities at the drivers who poked along in front of her sedan.

Twenty minutes later, del Barrio, along with Margarita in a borrowed car, cruised Belén Street looking for Kent. Not finding him, they decided to go toward the house. When they got within a block they spotted the police cars and ambulance and a multitude of spectators in the street. Cristina's heart sank. "Wait here, Margarita," she said, climbing out of the car. She walked toward the scene, trying to remain calm, trying to be nothing more than an interested spectator.

"What happened here?" she asked a woman on the opposite side of the street from the little house.

"The police shot a man back there, behind the house. I think they are trying to bring him out to the ambulance now."

"Did they kill him?" del Barrio asked, her face tightening.

"It must be," the woman said, shaking her head. "Because they don't seem in any hurry at all to get him to the ambulance."

"Was it . . . the American that everybody was looking for?"

"Who would know, señora? The world is so crazy these days."

Cristina looked at the scene of people milling around. It seemed like a dream, where people were floating, then fusing with one another, then coming apart and floating again. She felt light-headed, and leaned against a rock wall for support. Then, focusing again on the scene before her, she saw two men in business suits, their backs to the main scene, looking at the spectators. She sized them up immediately as police officers. It would be no good for her to picked up here, she thought, and turning away, walked slowly back up the street, not really caring whether her cousin would be waiting there for her or not. She turned back a minute later to see men carrying a stretcher toward the ambulance. It looked like a blanket was covering the entire figure. Her eyes glazed over as she watched the vehicle slowly drive away down the street, its emergency lights and siren not operating.

CHAPTER NINE

The KGB sedan, racing ahead of the delivery van, headed back from the suburbs toward downtown Valencia. The man in the right front seat turned around, smiling broadly, and said, "It all went smoothly, just as I said it would, comrade. You see, everything is turning out well, no?"

Lieutenant Colonel Vera Vlasov wasn't smiling yet. "We were barely ahead of the police. Our vehicles might have been seen and reported."

"So, what if the van was seen? There are hundreds of trucks just like it in this town. Anyway, we had on the alternate license plates. It will never be traced to our operation. We don't have to worry about that."

"*On ne khuya ne znayet!*" Vlasov thundered at him from the backseat. "You don't know a fucking thing about worrying, major! Until I have that cunt-suffering American in the basement of our embassy begging to be killed, you crab-fuckers keep your optimism bottled up in your asses. One more mistake and we're all swimming in rancid panther piss."

That ended the chitchat in the sedan for the rest of the trip downtown. Soon, the two vehicles were off the street and parked beneath the building that housed the offices of Northeastern Enterprises. Three men got out of the van. One of them reported to the major that Boris had remained behind at the house to search for documents as ordered. The men quickly made sure nobody else was in the underground parking garage.

"All right," said Vera Vlasov, her voice ringing with authority and decisiveness. "Get him out of there and into the trunk of the Mercedes. He's already been put to sleep as I ordered?"

"Yes, Colonel," said the driver of the van. "He'll be out for six or eight hours."

Four of the men dragged their quarry's body out the back door of the van, the sack still covering his head and upper body. They dumped him unceremoniously into the open trunk of the Mercedes. One of the men reached up to close the trunk lid.

"Just a minute," said Vlasov. "I want to see the bastard's face and spit in it." They pulled up the sack. Vlasov stared in shock and disbelief at the unconscious man lying there in his underwear. "But this is not Kent, you Siberian sheep-fuckers!"

"It has to be, Colonel," said the van driver. "He was hiding under the bed, scared as a rabbit."

The KGB major looked blankly at Vlasov. "Then who could it be, Colonel? Normal Spaniards don't lie under their beds in their underwear in the middle of the day, do they?"

"I don't give a weasel-fuck *who* it is, you idiots," Vlasov shouted at them. "Kent is a clean-shaven, green-eyed American twice the size of this person. Look at the mustache! Look at the brown eyes!" she said pushing open one of the eyelids. "All of you donkey-fuckers put together couldn't tell a cunt from a spittoon." The diminutive colonel grabbed the KGB major by the shirt front, pulling his face down to within two inches of her own. "You get this impostor the hell out of here, and you take this bunch of fiddle-fucking clowns with you, and you don't come back until you've brought me what I came here for. And if you can't do that, then don't come back at all, or you'll get a bullet in each ball right out of my own pistol!"

Cristina and Margarita were sitting on a couch in a motel when the local early news came on the television. The first story was about the uproar in the Castellón district, and they recognized the scene as an on-the-spot camera showed the stretcher being carried toward the ambulance. The reporter's voice was saying: "This is yet another bizarre turn in the case of the North American fugitive Arnold Kent, this one taking place just west of the city in the Castellón district. Municipal police, raiding the house shown here, shot and killed a man identified as Boris Suvorov, a Russian citizen in the employ of Northeastern Enterprises, a local firm. Police said they believed the man, who was running from the house, was the fugitive Kent."

"My god," gasped del Barrio, grabbing her friend's arm so hard it almost bruised it. "That wasn't Arno!"

The reporter continued: "Minutes ago, eyewitnesses at the scene told police that a delivery truck arrived here shortly before the police, and that four men entered the house with masks and firearms, and that they dragged out somebody from the house and threw him into the van and drove away. Police are continuing their investigation of this . . ."

"It's even worse, then," del Barrio said, running both hands through her disheveled hair.

"Worse than having been killed?" asked Margarita.

"You don't understand the KGB, what they do to people. And they accuse him of killing so many of their agents. They'll torture him miserably before disposing of him, or he'll rot for years in a Siberian camp. It's the worst thing that could happen."

"Wait a minute, Cristina. How do we know who that was they dragged out of the house, or even if that report was accurate?"

"Who else could it have been, then?"

Margarita was on her feet, changing channels on the TV. Another station was giving the same news. A reporter was interviewing a woman near the scene. The woman was saying: ". . . and they came out a minute later dragging this man toward the van—"

"Did you get a look at the man?" asked the reporter.

"No, because his head and upper body were covered with a sack or something. But it looked like he was just dressed in underwear, and he was barefooted, and . . ."

"Underwear?" said Margarita. "Why underwear? Wouldn't he have been dressed?"

"They must have come right after I left. He . . . hadn't got dressed yet."

"Shhh!" said Margarita, gesturing at the TV. The camera had zoomed in on the reporter's face.

"Police so far have not been able to explain the police uniform and sidearm found in a closet of the house. Stay tuned to this station for late-breaking details on this case as they become available . . ."

The two women looked at each other in wonderment. Then Cristina glanced at her watch. It was six-forty. "Margarita!" she shouted, jumping to her feet. "Kent and I agreed . . . if anything went wrong with picking him up at the bus stop, we were to meet at the Plaza de la Serena at seven!"

"Then you think . . . that he might still be . . . that—"

"I don't know what to think. But I was beginning to think of him as somehow . . . indestructible. Do you think there's a chance?"

"Well," Margarita said, smiling, "you're in love with him, aren't you? Let's go, for God's sake."

Evening traffic was still heavy, but staying off the main thorough-fares, Margarita managed to reach the plaza only a few minutes after seven. They circled the plaza once, saw nothing, then found a place to pull up. Each woman studied the silhouettes of male figures moving across the diagonal paths of the plaza. Del Barrio had her window rolled down.

"Hope you weren't worried," said the resonant male voice not two feet from her ear.

Del Barrio jumped from the little car and almost lifted Kent off his feet hugging him. "Worried? About what?" she said, shoving him into the backseat.

Margarita started the car and swung into traffic.

"We saw the TV news," said del Barrio. "Who was it that was abducted in the delivery truck just before the police arrived?"

"It was a police officer. He came there just before I left to ask routine questions, I guess. I tried to make him think I was an Italian, but he got suspicious and I had to pull my little gun on him."

Margarita looked around from the front seat. "But we saw on television that the man was in his underclothes, and that his uniform was in the closet."

Kent laughed, feeling almost relaxed, even though he sensed he had no right to feel that way. "I was thinking of using his uniform, but it turned out to be way too small for me. Anyway, just about then this van pulled up and four guys with guns and masks were running toward the house. So I ordered the policeman under the bed, and I went out the back way. What else did the news say?"

"That the police shot a Russian in back of the house. Killed him. I saw them load him into the ambulance thinking . . . never mind," Cristina said, choking on the words.

"I didn't know about that," said Kent. "The police must have arrived right after that van left. The Russians must have left one guy behind to search the place. Did they say anything on the news about the first policeman, the one who was abducted by the KGB?"

"Not yet, anyway," said del Barrio. "I suppose as soon as they discovered it wasn't you they got rid of him."

"I hope he's all right," said Kent. "He seemed like a decent man—one who didn't deserve what happened to him. How did the police and those Russian bastards figure out where we were so fast?"

"The Spanish police are very thorough, and very persistent," Margarita said. "You've embarrassed them, too. They'll be right on your trail all the way."

"And the KGB feeds on police intelligence," said del Barrio, "not to mention they don't have to follow any of the same rules."

"So what now?" asked Kent. "Any good movies in town?"

"Back to the motel," said Margarita. "Then I'll borrow your passport and license, and my husband will get you a rental car. You're heading for Italy, no?"

Kent glanced at del Barrio and she nodded.

"So you'll need an airline ticket from Barcelona to Rome, correct?"

"To Milan," said Kent, surprising them both. "And by way of Palma. One learns to avoid international departure facilities."

News of the Spanish police having killed a Soviet citizen brought an immediate and stern protest from the Russian ambassador to the Spanish Ministry of the Interior. By way of response, an official of the ministry sent an emissary to the embassy to state that the killing was unintended; that the police had ordered a fleeing suspect, presumably the American, to halt and he had refused. Furthermore, the emissary allowed, the Spanish government demanded an explanation for the abduction of a police officer whose uniform was found in the house where he had gone to ask questions. Naturally, the Russians denied involvement in the matter and insisted on a formal apology and financial restitution for the family of the deceased. The exchange of statements was made available to the press by both sides.

At the U.S. embassy everyone had heard the latest news from Valencia and they were staying out of sight of the ambassador. At his press conference the day before, Parkerhouse had expressed great outrage on behalf of his country concerning what he was calling the misdeeds of Arnold Kent, and was promising to bring the full resources at his disposal to bear on bringing the man to justice. An editorial in one of the

Madrid dailies the next morning remarked that the "full resources" of Señor Ambassador were apparently quite limited, based on results obtained so far.

Bradford Baumont, the embassy's counselor for special affairs, and the man charged with coming up with a plan to resolve the situation, theorized that Kent would try to reach the U.S. embassy in Rome. There, Baumont speculated, Kent would hope to find refuge from his assailants and a sympathetic ear to what he "fantasized was a Communist plot to create untold havoc of an unspecified nature." Baumont's recommendation was to let Kent's Spain adventure run its course (the report said that "effective containment efforts in country would be counterproductive with respect to current, officially sanctioned activities . . .") and deal with him at the embassy in Rome. The ambassador read the report, popped four large Tums tablets into his mouth, then called Baumont into his office.

"What the hell is this 'effective containment,' 'counterproductive,' 'officially sanctioned activities,' bullshit supposed to mean, for Christ's sake? Who did you write this crap for, some politician running for tax collector?"

"Yeah, sorry. I guess that does sound a bit fuzzy. What it means is that there's nothing we can do anyway, just get in the way of the police."

"And this is what you get paid sixty-eight thousand dollars a year for, to tell me there's nothing more we can do, just get the hell out of the way while this . . . self-styled spy-catcher runs rampant across the fucking country? Get out of my sight, and send me somebody who can prove you're not all idiots in this outfit."

Within five minutes regional security officer Bruce Charner and his nominal assistant, Vernon Prokar of the CIA, were standing in front of the ambassador's desk with serious looks on their faces. After two minutes of quiet instructions, the two men left to do the ambassador's bidding. Bradford Baumont was back in his office downing a double shot of expensive Scotch, wishing to hell he hadn't spent most of the previous night in a hotel trying to impress a good-looking Spanish lady with his sexual prowess and drinking ability. The four months he had spent at this post had definitely not enhanced his career.

A day earlier, Malcolm Bartledge had looked through his file on Kent. It now included copies of the photos Kent had reported taken from the Italian's briefcase, along with the Madrid embassy's report on Kent's account to them. Bartledge was an experienced man, not from having served in bureaucratic desk jobs at the agency, but from his seventeen years on covert assignments in a dozen or more countries around the world. He was a man of average size and build, quiet-spoken, and not one to attract attention to himself through his mannerisms or personality. He prided himself on his ability acquired through much hard work and practice, to observe and remember details of what he saw and heard. Because of its improbable sequence of events so far, the Kent case interested him greatly, and he decided to see what he could unearth locally that might shed light on it. He drove across McLean to Kent's neighborhood of two-story brick houses and streets shaded by the colorful fall leaves of maples, sweet gums, dogwoods, oaks and yellow poplars.

Bartledge parked his green Plymouth across the street from the Kent house, in front of a house with a For Sale sign in front of it. He could immediately see that this was the house from which one of the photos of Kent had been taken, probably from a second-floor window. The closed curtains, uncut lawn and unswept porch made the house look unoccupied. He verified that there was, as reported in Madrid by Kent, a view from Kent's deck into the backyard of this house. As he sat there, he saw an attractive blond woman come out of the Kent house long enough to check her mailbox, then go back inside. He went up to the house, identified himself, and was let in.

"Have you found my husband yet?" was Yvette's first question as he followed her up the stairway into the living room.

Bartledge started to answer, and was cut off.

"You know, I shouldn't even talk to you," she said, gesturing him to a seat. "Your people wouldn't even return my calls until the media started covering the story. Now I guess I'm a hot item, and it becomes necessary to service my account, so to speak. What kind of ghouls are you people, anyway?"

Bartledge smiled patiently. He wasn't sure whether she was ready to hear anything just yet. She was certainly attractive, he thought, much more so than the rather weird art that decorated every wall within view. "You certainly have an interesting home," he said.

"Interesting? Interesting, you call it? You could have said anything else, anything at all. *Interesting* is the kiss of death to an artist. Why don't you just say what you think? You do think, don't you?"

"All right, cluttered, then. Hell, I'm easy."

"And you are uncultured," she said. "What are you doing with my husband over there, and why am I not being given protection? Would you like some herbal tea?"

"Uh, no. I don't think so. Look, Mrs. Kent, we don't know your husband from Elephant Boy. I don't know where you—"

"Sure. Just what I expected. They told me you'd say that."

"Uh, who told—"

"Look. I'm not an idiot. I have friends in your . . . Company, you call it . . . and they said you wouldn't admit anything about . . ." Yvette began crying.

Bartledge's eyes rolled skyward involuntarily. He had been through this drill before. It was no use arguing.

"All right," he said. "I know when I'm beat." She looked at him hopefully. "He's on his way to Moscow to assassinate Premier Gorbachev." Yvette's large mouth fell open. "And on the way back he'll be dropping by Havana to take care of that rascal Castro." Bartledge got up and headed for the door.

He was almost to the door when she called out from the top of the stairway, "Mr. . . . whatever your name is, I'm sorry. Please come back, I need to talk to . . . someone . . . about this."

"Bartledge. Mal Bartledge. I didn't come here to give you any BS, really."

"Why did you come here then?"

"Can I have a minute or two, before you call me a liar or start crying again?"

"I'm listening," she said, leading him back into the living room. "And I'll fix you a drink if you don't want the herbal tea."

"Thanks, too early for me. But go ahead if you want one. Listen, Mrs. Kent—"

"Yvette is fine."

"Okay, Yvette. I got into this case because I was assigned to report on what was going on. You got us involved by telling the media your husband was one of our people. I gather you actually believe that, for whatever reason."

Yvette said nothing.

"I'll tell you right now that's not the case. However, you're not the only one who happens to think so. The U.S. embassy in Madrid started asking us about him last Monday. The KGB undoubtedly believes your husband is an agent, inasmuch as, at last count, six of their people have been killed under circumstances tied directly or indirectly to Kent. Frankly, we haven't as yet figured out just what he's up to, other than trying to stay alive and out of the reach of the Spanish police."

"What about this woman . . . this del Bistro or whatever her name is?"

"It's del Barrio. We don't know that either. We consider it a possibility that your husband has stumbled onto something that has to do with a Soviet plot, and the KGB is on his case. Can you tell me if your husband said anything before he left for Spain that might throw any light at all on this?"

"He never talked about his business things with me. I don't even know why he went over there at all. Something about forest fires. But that doesn't make much sense, in a barren country like Spain, does it?"

"Did he say anything about what he would be doing in Italy?"

"Only that he was going to Rome, and that he might bring back some wine."

"Did he mention anything about Naples?"

"Navels? No, we get our oranges from California."

Bartledge tried to take it in stride. "Uh, right. He didn't say anything about the navy?"

"No. Why should he? How is the navy involved in this?"

"Just trying to put pieces together, Yvette. What about the house across the street, the one that's for sale. Who was living there?"

"Oh, the house of mystery!" she said, lightening up. "There was a man living there by himself. He stayed out of sight, wouldn't even answer his door. They say he's an Italian and the place is a safe house."

"Is he there now, do you suppose?"

"Who would know? He never gets any mail or newspapers, never sets foot in the street."

"Your deck looks into his backyard. Ever see him out there?"

"No. What does he have to do with this? Why are you so interested in him?"

"Well, if it is indeed a safe house, naturally I would be interested in who lives there."

"Mr. Bardridge—"

"It's Bartledge."

"Baldridge, Bartlett, whatever. If we're going to continue this conversation, you're going to have to do a better job of leveling with me. It was you who brought up the house, wasn't it?"

Bartledge's face reddened slightly. "You got me on that one, Mrs. Yvette."

"It's Mrs. Baldridge," she teased. Then they both laughed, the man's face even redder.

"Whatever. Let me explain. Somebody photographed your husband from that house just before he left for Madrid. That's why I was interested."

"Well, the only thing I can tell you is that just a few days before the house was sold the last time, a man came here and said he was looking at it, and asked a lot of questions about the neighborhood."

"Can you describe him?"

"Kind of a solidly built, medium height man about fifty, I would say. Bald, except for a fringe. Hairy arms and neck. Kind of a smooth talker. Didn't seem like your typical housebuyer. More like he was looking us over."

"Any accent, mannerisms?"

"It was about a year ago. I really don't recall. He drove up in a big luxury car, but I couldn't say what it was. What do you think this all means, Mr. uh . . ."

"Mal. I wish I could tell you, Yvette, I really do. I take it you haven't had a call from your husband since he left."

"No, but then he doesn't ordinarily call during just a two-week trip over there."

"Well, when he does call, does he use a credit card, call collect, or what?"

"I don't know. He just calls. Why do you want to know that? You really don't know where he is either, do you? Are you going to tap my phone?"

"No, we're not going to tap your phone, Yvette. It's just that in this business, the more we know, the more we can do to help. Would you be willing to let me know if he does call you?"

Yvette thought for a moment. "Well, Bartlett, that all depends on what he has to say."

Bartledge shook his head, smiling. "I think you just got me again."
He stood up. "Can I visit you again?"

"Sure, as long as you bring good news about what you're doing to
help. Otherwise, I'll be expressing myself publicly. How nice of you to
come by."

Saturday morning Kent and del Barrio had breakfast sent to their
motel room. Margarita would be along with the rental car soon.

"Eight hours," said Kent. "Do you realize we actually slept eight
hours?"

"I know," she said. "I tried to wake you up several times but it was
impossible."

"I wish you'd tried harder. I can get by on four hours."

"Do you have it all figured out yet?" she asked.

Kent poured himself a second cup of very black Spanish coffee. "I'm
still missing a couple of important pieces. But first, it's clear that the
navy wants out of Agnano, and second, that some Italian is stalling it,
and third, that the stalling is extremely important to the Soviets. Tie
that in with the line on the note about getting the Sixth Fleet out of the
Mediterranean forever, and it can only mean one kind of thing."

Del Barrio nodded slowly. "I think you're right. But that's absolutely
diabolical! The Soviets wouldn't do it themselves, of course, so who?"

"I have no idea. But maybe Carlo Marasco does."

"You're planning to track him down first, before you go to the
embassy?"

"Not necessarily. First I'll try Colonel Golino. I've never met him,
but I can at least warn him about Marasco, the guy who's supposed to
liquidate him, and maybe find out some things. You see, I have nothing
persuasive to go to the embassy with right now. They might not be any
friendlier with me than your outfit."

"What do you have in mind for me?" She was staring him directly in
the eye.

"You mean . . . you'd go to Italy with me?" he sputtered.

"You were planning to leave me here in the middle of this gigantic
mess you created? No way."

"But your children . . ."

"They're safe in school. They probably don't even know I'm gone. I'll
be back soon enough . . . I hope."

"And your job," Kent said.

"My job?" She laughed merrily. "My job has recently become helping to get us both out of this little problem we have."

Kent hugged her to him and stroked her black hair. "Cris, it's a lot more than just us. What I think those ghouls have in mind would make the marine barracks in Beirut seems like a peanut shell by comparison. Somehow, we've got to come up with enough to convince an ambassador or an admiral or somebody that this is all real, and God knows how soon it will happen."

Vera Vlasov's boss, Colonel Feliks Kratkov, had already alerted the KGB station chief in Rome that Arnold Kent had been dispatched from the United States to find out who was delaying approval of the navy's move out of Agnano to Capua, and that he had not yet been intercepted as planned. In a follow-up call on Saturday afternoon, he advised Colonel Aleksandr Korolenko that in all probability, Kent would escape from Spain and likely be headed for the U.S. embassy in Rome.

"I suspect General Pelshy is unhappy with your handling of this case, comrade," said Korolenko. "He is not a forgiving person, you know."

"That's putting it mildly, Aleksandr. As I recall, he cashiered the station chief in Lisbon after a similar fiasco. But such is life in the First Chief Directorate. I should have known better than to leave it all up to Vera Vlasov, but then none of us realized what we were up against with this fellow Kent."

"It's too bad for Vera. She was nearing retirement, too."

"Yes, a shame. But listen, old friend. She desperately wants to redeem herself on this case. If Kent and his Spanish girlfriend slip out of Spain, can I send her to you? She is very capable, and would give her life, make any sacrifice to be helpful, to have a part in finishing this."

"Hmm. Does she speak Italian?"

"She can get by. And I don't believe either Kent or the del Barrio woman has ever got a close look at her. Anyway, she is a genius at disguises. I can assure you, she would be helpful to you."

"All right, all right. Send her to me. As a favor to an old and trusted friend. But if she gets in my way or wobbles the shaft on this job, you won't have to worry about paying her fare back to Moscow. I don't accept failure here on my post."

"Good. Good. I knew I could count on you. I'll make the necessary arrangements to transfer her. Have you received those photos of Kent and del Barrio?"

"Yes, we are quite prepared here, as always, Feliks. Much as I dislike taking on this extra workload right now, it will give me the chance to demonstrate to a former mentor how far I have come since my days at the academy. You may let the general know that there will be no problem here. I am personally seeing to it that 'the project' remains uninterrupted and on schedule."

Arrogant bastard, Kratkov said to himself as he hung up. He remembered Korolenko well from the academy. Korolenko always had been on top of his assignments and ahead of anybody else in the scoring books. He was highly rated by the organization for his intelligence, cunning, insight, and energy. As the son of a high party official, he had been expected to perform well, but he had exceeded all expectations. In the army he had, at the age of only eighteen, won a silver medal in freestyle wrestling at the Olympics in Munich. The following year, in international competition, he had suffered a severely dislocated shoulder that ended his wrestling career and got him discharged from the army. From there he went directly to the KGB for special training in penetrating foreign intelligence networks. He learned French, English and Italian and won special commendations for efficiency in his first three major assignments, and now found himself to be one of the youngest full colonels in the organization. His career goal was to head up the First General Directorate of the KGB, a high post that, amazingly, now seemed a distinct and not-too-distant possibility.

Kratkov reached Vlasov in Valencia and gave her the news that she was being given one last chance to salvage something of her retirement possibilities. Vera was tough and smart, and didn't have to have the rest of it spelled out for her. She thanked her boss, and told him he probably wouldn't hear from her again until the case was successfully resolved.

Aleksandr Korolenko had been in Rome for only a year, but was fully on top of his job. When he was a young man, his father had condemned him to probable failure in life, telling him he lacked the qualities of perseverance and thoroughness. It was exactly that condemnation that had led him to his Olympic triumph after only three years of instruction and experience. It was exactly that condemnation that had won him his on-the-job commendations and special assignments that nobody else dared take on. And now, he knew, it would be his perseverance and attention to detail that would bring him success on this assignment, and eventual elevation to the top KGB post in his directorate.

Korolenko had thrown out the lazy and incompetent officers in his Rome residency his first month at the post. Since then, through his leadership, his people had dug into a half dozen major embassies (including the American), and had installed cooperatives in the municipal police, the carabinieri, the Airport Authority, the Ministry for Civil Protection and a dozen other public agencies, with access to records, communications and identification of the citizenry. His reputation for success in his assignments resulted in quick granting of his large budget requests to secure needed collaboration from non-Soviet sources.

Korolenko was known as an officer who was willing to risk his life on behalf of a subordinate officer, man or woman, and as someone who would not give an assignment he would not be willing to perform himself. In return, he demanded loyalty, obedience and, above all, success. He did not smoke or drink, or use foul language. But he did have a weakness: beautiful women. In the KGB, romantic liaisons were frowned on; the danger of being compromised was always present. But he would not deny himself what he felt he deserved. He had his women, treating them as queens, but never confiding in them, never trusting them. Then when an affair would seem near its end, the young woman would just seem to disappear, and another would appear. How Korolenko arranged the magical incarnations and dissolutions of his beautiful and inevitably young companions remained a total mystery to his subordinates, but one they constantly speculated on and discussed among themselves.

Korolenko assigned one of his staff, Major Orlov Myaznikov, to attend to the specifics of the Kent affair, but ordered that Myaznikov get his personal approval on the action plan, and keep him currently aware of what was going on. Myaznikov had his action plan ready in two hours. In essence, it called for intercepting both Kent and del Barrio at the moment of their arrival in Italy—or, failing that, to apprehend them at all cost before one or both managed to reach the U.S. embassy, or the U.S. naval facility in Naples. Before approving the plan, Korolenko asked Myaznikov if he felt he had enough information concerning Kent.

"Colonel, I have studied the background material on him very closely, and I do, in fact, have a major concern."

Korolenko smiled to himself, listening. He did not welcome foolish optimism and overconfidence.

"The analysis we have received from Madrid is to the effect that Mr. Kent is indeed what he appears on the surface to be: a midlevel functionary of their Forest Service. We also have been assured that Mrs. del Barrio is nothing more than a local employee of the American embassy, who somehow has become entangled with Kent. Now, in view of what has happened in Spain during the last seven days, that is to say, six of our agents killed, the rest totally eluded and embarrassed, either we are looking at extreme incompetence among our people, or Kent and his friend are not, after all, what they appear to be."

"Major, you have a remarkable grasp of the obvious, but an amazing inability to articulate it concisely. How do you plan to deal with this paradox?"

The major pushed his glasses up against his face and met the colonel's eyes. "By avoiding both pitfalls. My briefings will advise that we are dealing with journeyman operatives who have already killed six of our people. I am also letting it be known that failure will be dealt with positively, and harshly. Do you agree?"

"Why not?" asked the colonel. "That's exactly how I plan on dealing with you. By the way, have you been in contact with our man in Washington, the one who originally let us know about Kent?"

"Yes, sir. Within the hour. His analysis is that Kent has discovered what Oltraggio is about, but that he's got to get to Rome with it to be taken seriously. Evidently, Kent has not yet contacted anyone in the United States."

"He's too clever to have made that mistake. That's why he's still alive, or at least one of the reasons. Anything else?"

"Frange also thinks the CIA is still lingering on the toilet seat. That's probably accurate inasmuch as our signal intelligence people haven't noted any pickup in traffic between Langley and either Madrid or Rome."

"So much the better, but don't make any assumptions about that. Suggest we monitor their movements here very closely. Any indication yet where Kent and del Barrio will come in?"

"Best guess is they'll try to fly from Barcelona to Rome, probably separately. Kratkov's people might still pick them up at the airport, of course."

"Yes, that reminds me. I just got off the phone with Kratkov, and he has persuaded me to take on Lieutenant Colonel Vera Vlasov, to give her a chance to redeem herself. As far as I am concerned, she will take orders from you, and you can use her in any way you choose. She is as hard as nails, and she knows her way around Rome. Any problem?"

"Not provided you mean what you say about how I can use her."

"What do you have in mind?"

The major smiled, as his mind played with the opportunity. "Let's just say, comrade Colonel, that sometimes it is useful to sacrifice the bait in order to snare the fish."

CHAPTER TEN

Stan Dawson reached out of bed to answer the phone. "The bastards won't even let you sleep on Saturday mornings," he said to his wife. "Yo!"

"Stan? Is that you?"

"Arno? For Christ's sake! Where the fuck are you?"

"I'll tell you later. Can you hear me all right?"

"Fine. What the hell's going on?"

"Listen carefully. I only have a minute. I have not gone crazy, I am trying to stay alive, and the KGB is on my case. There is some kind of a plot to destroy the logistical headquarters of the Sixth Navy in Naples. I haven't found out how or when, but it's soon. Do you know who Otto Frange is?"

"Yes, I do. What about him?"

"He's involved in it. He picked out the house in McLean across the street from my place where the Italian was staying."

"What Italian?"

"The one whose briefcase I found in JFK where he followed me. Do you have all that?"

"Yeah, I think so, but run me through it again. What was it about the Italian and the briefcase?"

"I'll try to call again."

Dawson sat there in bed blinking stupidly at the receiver and listening to the dial tone. "Paper and pencil," he said to his wife.

"It was Kent? Where is he?"

"Get me a paper and pencil. I don't know where he is or what he's doing, but I sure as shit don't want to forget what he said."

"You'd better call Yvette," she said, handing her husband a notebook and pen. "She's supposed to call that CIA guy when she heard from Arno."

"O.K. Got her number?" Dawson reached Yvette, told her the essence of Kent's call, and got the CIA man's number. He dialed and got an answering service. Minutes later the return call came in.

"Malcolm Bartledge here. Understand you have info on Kent, that right?"

"Just talked to him on the phone. You'd better come over." Dawson hung up.

"Stan," his wife said, "you didn't even tell him where we live."

"If he's who he's supposed to be, he'll find me."

Kent walked out of the phone booth, paid his bill at the desk by the exit, and headed for Palma's Gate C-7, where his Alitalia flight for Milan was beginning to board. His auto trip to Barcelona had gone smoothly, and there had been no problem about properly turning in the rental car. There appeared to be no surveillance in the domestic departures area at Barcelona when he was boarding for Palma; he was sure the international departures lounge would have been swarming with police and Russian agents. The selection of Milan rather than Rome, he surmised, would be a further safeguard, even if it cost him extra time en route.

His thoughts moved to Cristina. She would reach Palma the next morning, then fly to Sardinia that afternoon. Her flight from Cagliari into Rome would put her into domestic arrivals, thus avoiding the expected surveillance at international arrivals. Traveling alone, they had decided, would greatly reduce the risk of apprehension. They had agreed on several possible meeting places and times in Rome.

Kent looked over his fellow travelers in the departure lounge. Most of them looked like late-season vacationers, mostly speaking Italian. He saw two couples who he thought were Americans. All were burdened with packages from the duty-free shop and stuffed carry-on bags undoubtedly bearing gifts and souvenirs. There was nobody who looked even remotely suspicious or menacing, and he greatly welcomed the relaxation he was enjoying. He even struck up a conversation with an Italian couple in order to get himself back into the rhythm of speaking the language of his childhood. He was surprised at how quickly he could reimmerse himself into the musical intonation of the language, shutting out the harsher Spanish of the past week.

On leaving the flight in Milan, passengers were herded through passport control and then into the customs room. Kent's new passport went unquestioned, and then he was waved through customs with his one small suitcase. He'd had to return the pistol to Cristina before leaving. Trying to get it through customs would have posed too big a risk. He would have to get his hands on one here, he decided.

He went first to the currency exchange counter and converted all his pesetas to lire. Then he took a taxi straight down the Viale Forlanini into the commercial district and asked to be let out in front of the Galleria, a large glassed-in mall of shops near the Duomo. He quickly went into the crowded mall and purchased a small daypack he could sling over his shoulder, transferred his few belongings and told the clerk he could keep the suitcase. Then he bought a soft hat with a floppy brim and put it on. Once back in the street he entered and left several other large stores, walked through a pedestrian tunnel, reversed directions walking back through, and then caught another taxi to the main railway station, the Stazione Centrale F.F.S.S. According to the information board, the next train with connections to Rome, a *direttissimo*, was departing in an hour. He bought a ticket, then turned to walk toward a café he had seen moments before. But, for some reason he didn't understand himself, he stopped and looked back at the ticket window in the reflection of an information board with a glass cover. He saw a man in a gray coat approach the ticket counter. The man was asking questions and it looked like he gestured in the direction of Kent as he was talking.

Kent's skin crawled. Jumpy nerves, he was telling himself. He turned back toward the ticket window and approached the man. They passed, the man in the gray coat looking straight ahead. Kent got a good look at his face. The eyes were dark and forbidding, the nose straight and narrow, the chin cleft. It was a face without tenderness or humor, but one of seriousness and purpose. The gray coat disappeared around a corner. Kent returned to the ticket window, laid down a ten-thousand-lire note.

"The gentleman who was just here," Kent said to a bemused-looking clerk. "What questions did he ask of you?"

The clerk quickly pulled in the money, glanced in the direction the man had gone, and said, "He asked your destination and what language you spoke."

"And you told him—?"

"He did not offer to pay me," the clerk said with a sly smile. "And I did not like him as well. I told him you were obviously French, and heading for Marseille."

"And did he seem to believe you?"

"*Signore*, he was a man whose face reveals nothing. I wish you well."

"I am in your debt. Many thanks."

Malcolm Bartledge was at Stan Dawson's house in thirty minutes listening to the story of Kent's call. Dawson also filled him in on his less than satisfactory visit to Frange's Main State office, along with a report on what had been told him by Farber Claunch regarding Kent's "supplemental assignment."

"What do you make of it?" Dawson asked.

"Back up a minute. How did Kent sound emotionally? Was it like a routine business call, or was it a national emergency, or like somebody was holding a gun to his head—"

"No, more like intense but controlled, and hurried. He didn't sound spaced out at all, and I would say he was alone at the time. The whole thing sound wild to you?"

"Naturally," the CIA man said. "But then, these things usually do until the pieces start coming together."

"Where to from here, then?"

"The Italian's briefcase, for starters. Here. Take this number. You can reach me at any hour with this. Any message from Kent, or anything else you find out about . . . okay?"

Bartledge zipped back to his office at the Langley headquarters and started making telephone calls. Two hours later he was briefing his boss, Arthur Chafkin.

"Our man in New York found out from the airport authority that a guy did, in fact, die of a CI last Saturday night in the TWA departure lounge. His passport said he was Bruno Cavalchini, an Italian national, but the U.S. address they had on him is nonexistent."

"Who claimed the body?" Chafkin asked.

"That's the interesting part. Papers on his person said to call somebody named Overson, or Overstreet, in Falls Church. We traced the phone number to the home of an Otto Frange, no less."

"State's Italy-desk man?"

"There's more," Bartledge said, nodding. "Mrs. Kent rattled on about the purchase of what she's calling the 'house of mystery' across the street from her place, so I checked it out through a real-estate lady friend of mine. Turns out a guy named Victor Santamaria bought the place for cash about a year ago, through an agent. The buyer himself stayed out of sight, so nobody knows what he looks like. I've got a call in now for the salesman who handled it."

"You think the Italian's agent might have been Frange?"

"Why not? I've also got somebody trying to find out if there's actually anybody around by the name of Victor Santamaria."

"Then, Kent's story isn't as weird as everybody thought. If that's the case, we need to alert the navy. The director has a pipeline to the CNO, so I'll brief him. I'd like you to get things together—a package—for the FBI. They'll be pissed, as usual, that we're as far into this thing as we are, but fuck 'em. What else?"

"I'd like to do something to help this fellow Kent keep his hide intact," Bartledge said to his boss, "but damned if I can think of anything. Shit, I don't even know what country he's in."

The older man laughed, leaning back in his swivel chair. "I think this outfit could use his help. If we find him before the bad guys do, let's make him an offer."

How did they do it? Kent asked himself. Getting away from these people is like trying to extricate oneself from a giant sticky net. He went into the café for a beer and a sandwich, asking himself over and over whether he could have been followed there, or whether it was the result of a chance sighting by one of many observers. One thing was sure; there was no question he had been recognized, and it had to be KGB. An Interpol officer would have confronted him immediately. The KGB wouldn't rely on a clerk's response, they would stay on his tail until the right moment.

He finished his snack, then returned to the giant shed that housed the dozens of incoming sets of tracks. He waited until he saw a train boarding for Genoa, then headed for that platform at the last boarding call. He climbed on, not looking back, then walked through six cars toward the rear. A few seconds after the train got into motion he jumped back off and watched the train disappear from the shed. Nobody else got off, and he enjoyed the thought of some KGB agent having a wonderful time trying to find him on the train. He then stayed out of sight until time to board his train toward Bologna where he would change for Rome. But obviously, he could not now ride by train clear through to the Rome station.

The train whizzed along through the darkening countryside, making brief stops only at Piacenza, Parma, Reggio, and Modena. Kent changed trains without incident at Bologna, settling down for the long run down toward Rome. In Kent's compartment, passengers were drowsy, and by the time the train exited the long tunnel that passes under the Apennines, they were all asleep. The train was due into Rome at eight thirty A.M., but Kent had decided to get off at Orvieto at dawn and find another way into the city. Before Orvieto he managed to get in about four hours sleep, and woke up feeling recharged.

From the train station, he set off on foot, asking directions of early-morning pedestrians and street sweepers, arriving at the bus station in about twenty minutes. Then there was only a half-hour wait for a bus into Rome. His fellow passengers, noting something unusual about his clothing and appearance, eyed him curiously. This bothered Kent; the last thing he wanted to do was stand out in a crowd. He had been seen in Milan, and would need to get different clothes anyway—a first thing to do in Rome. Then it occurred to him that it was Sunday and that stores would be closed all day. Sunday! It was a week ago that he had arrived in Spain. Had all this nightmare been squeezed into just one week? he asked himself.

He was wary getting off the bus, his eyes darting around to see if anyone was watching incoming passengers. He could detect no one, and got out of the station as quickly as possible. He felt he was clear but, to be sure, he walked into a church crowded with worshipers at a Mass, then found a side exit and slipped down a side street. Not knowing the city too well, he had absolutely no idea where he was. But this didn't pose a huge problem at this point. He slipped into a small café where he had coffee and some sweet rolls. He spotted a telephone, asked for the telephone book, and flipped to the Marascos. He was delighted to find there weren't as many with the first name Carlo as he had feared, but he could find none with an address he would have recognized from the envelope he had seen.

Leaving the café, he went in the general direction of the center of the city until he came to a newsstand, where he bought a map of the city. He soon located himself, then walked to a section of town near the Via Veneto, knowing that would place him in the vicinity of the U.S. embassy and the office of his Italian forestry friends. It was also only a short walk away from the Piazza di Spagna, where he hoped to meet Cristina the next evening. He soon found a small, unimpressive hotel on the Via Sardegna and secured a room on the third floor. The room was small and equipped with only minimal facilities, but it was clean, and the price was right. Hardly a place where international spies would be expected, Kent thought. At least that wasn't the way things looked in the movies he had seen.

Kent's few possessions did not include his notebook containing names and addresses, so he went back down to the lobby to get the telephone number for Salvatore Tedeschi, chief of the Italian forest-firefighting service. This time he was in luck. He bought a few tokens from the clerk, went outside and found a public phone, then dialed the number. It was Tedeschi who answered.

"*Pronto?*"

"Salvatore!" Kent was ecstatic to hear the voice of an old friend. "This is Arno Kent. How are you?"

Tedeschi's voice sounded strained and nervous. "Fine, fine. What happened?" he asked in English. "I was expecting you on Friday. Was your flight delayed?"

Kent was astonished. Could it possibly be that Tedeschi hadn't heard the news during the entire past week?

Before Kent could answer, Tedeschi asked, "Where are you now?"

"I'm in town. Uh, can we get together today? I very much need to talk with you. It's very important."

There was a muffled array of background noises and about a six-second pause. "Yes, yes. Where are you? I'll come there."

Kent didn't like it. It just didn't sound right. Tedeschi was not sounding like his sparkling self. He thought fast. "Listen, Salvatore, can we meet in the lobby of the Lombardia Hotel at about eleven this morning?"

There were some more muffled sounds. "The Lombardia . . . yes, that will be fine . . . at eleven. Good-bye."

Kent glanced at his watch. It was only about nine. He looked up the telephone number for the Lombardia and memorized it. Then he walked into the Villa Borghese, a huge wooded park with miles of walkways and roads, and dozens of monuments, museums, fountains and gardens. He spent the next hour and a half reconnoitering the place for a suitable meeting spot, one from which he could observe anyone approaching, and which provided an acceptable escape route if things didn't look right. The park was already familiar to him; he had gone jogging in it several times on a previous visit, not even vaguely imagining what purpose it was going to serve for him later. Finally, he timed the walk from his chosen spot in the park back to the Porta Pinciana, a huge stone archway over the street near a main entrance to the park, and only a block from the Hotel Lombardia.

Then Kent went to a pay phone on the Via Campania and waited until five minutes after eleven. He dialed the Lombardia and asked to speak with Signor Tedeschi, stating it was an emergency call.

"*Pronto. Qui parla Tedeschi.*"

"Kent. Just answer yes or no. Are you with somebody who is threatening your life, trying to find me?"

"Yes," he said in Italian, sounding quite loud to Kent. "Why are you not here yet?"

"Tell them I'm not coming, that I've had an accident. If you can, meet me alone just after dark at the Galoppatoio in Villa Borghese. All right?"

"Yes, yes. I'm sorry you had an accident. Can I wait for you here at the hotel?"

The last part of the question was barely audible, as if the phone were being taken away from Tedeschi's mouth and ear. "Yes," Kent said in English. "I will return as soon as I can, but it may not be for several hours."

Again, the disconcerting silence. Then, "That is all right, I will wait here for you. *Ciao.*"

Kent hung up, wondering how long it would take the goons to figure out he wasn't staying at the Lombardia. Would they then canvass the vicinity, showing his photo to every innkeeper within a mile, figuring he was taking the precaution of using the Lombardia as a convenient meeting place? Very likely, he decided. So he headed back toward his hotel, stopping at a deli where he bought some rolls, cheese, salami and wine. Once in his little room, he added to the plastic grocery bag the most important of his meager belongings, then exited, telling the clerk he was going to visit friends out of town. "In case I don't get back right away, I would like to pay in advance for the next two days so that you will keep the room for me. All right?"

"Certainly, sir," the clerk told him as he accepted the money Kent handed over.

"And if anyone comes here asking for me—my wife has hired some detectives to follow me, you know—please tell them you haven't seen me. I will pay you nicely for doing that."

The bespectacled little clerk cocked his head to one side and smiled. "And how will you be sure I have told you the truth?"

Kent smiled back at the man and said, "I will know by what you tell me."

As Kent trundled off down the street, he rolled it around in his mind. The little clerk had been all too ready to deal. Would he tell Kent's pursuers he had been offered money to keep quiet? They would then ask, "How much?" and offer to double the amount. Why would someone who was willing to lie for a price not be ready to lie for double that price? Kent headed back into the Villa Borghese, where he found a pleasant spot on the grass overlooking a graceful pond. There he sat down, ate some cheese and salami, drank from his wine bottle and fell into a delicious sleep.

The red ball of the sun was slipping down behind the hills west of the city when Kent finally awoke. It was getting chilly, and he slipped on his jacket, thinking about his next move. Tedeschi was a crafty man. If he could elude the goons he would certainly come to meet Kent at the Galoppatoio, a roughly oval-shaped exercise and competition horse track surrounded by shrubbery except for bench seating for spectators on one side. Kent had already sized up the place, so he went to the spot he had selected and concealed himself in the shrubs to wait.

At about eight fifteen Kent picked out the shape of a man walking along the gallop-way. Tedeschi was of average size and build, and it wasn't until he arrived at a point only thirty feet from Kent's vantage point that Kent was sure it was he.

"Pssssst! Salvatore!" Kent hissed.

Tedeschi slowed his pace suddenly, but kept inching along.

"Sit down on the bench there, but don't look this way."

Tedeschi did as he was told.

"Do you think you were followed?" Kent asked him, from his spot in the bushes behind Tedeschi.

"It is quite possible. The men are devils. I cannot remain here but a minute."

"I understand. There are thousands of lives at risk. You must tell me how to reach Vittorio Golino without going to the office of the Defense Ministry."

Tedeschi calmly reached into a coat pocket and extracted a cigarette, lighting it carefully with a wooden match. He exhaled the plume of bluish gray smoke into the night air and said, "I don't know his house. But his father owns a small grocery store on the Via Beccaria about a block east of the river. Vittorio usually helps him open the store at six before going to the ministry."

"Who is Carlo Marasco? Do you know him?"

Tedeschi was silent for a while. Then he said, "The only Carlo Marasco I am aware of was mentioned, if I remember correctly, in connection with the abduction of the American general . . . General Dozier . . . about six years ago. That Marasco, and several of the others from the Brigate Rosse, were never apprehended."

Kent's spine tingled. "The Red Brigades," he murmured. A number of hideous scenes flashed through his mind. General Dozier tied and gagged, crouching in a closet for weeks; the hideous assassination of Aldo Moro in 1978; the killing of Leamon Hunt, a prominent businessman; dozens of other terrorist acts, all aimed against capitalism, the military, NATO, the United States.

"And your family," Kent said softly. "Are they all right?"

"I must return now or they will not be. A word of advice, Arno. Do not get involved with whatever this is. You cannot survive an encounter with these people. They are not like you are. Go to your embassy immediately and get help or you will be dead within twenty-four hours.

Good-bye and good luck to you." Tedeschi arose and sauntered away, continuing his slow loop around the track until he was lost in the darkness.

Major Orlov Myaznikov had learned from subordinates that Kent had been seen in Milan, and had been able to reach Rome. His expectation had been that Kent would head immediately for the U.S. embassy, and he had ordered heavy surveillance in the Via Veneto area. The entering of Salvatore Tedeschi's home in case Kent called there had almost paid off, but Kent had slipped out of the noose once again. Now Myaznikov assumed Kent wasn't ready yet to go to the embassy; that he needed to contact others first to consolidate whatever knowledge he had stumbled onto. But who? Kent would have no knowledge of Carlo Marasco, the Red Brigades operative charged with orchestrating the final step of Oltraggio. Nor would he be aware that Vittorio Golino had been paid off to do the foot-dragging in the defense ministry. At least not, Myaznikov figured, unless Tedeschi had deduced this and was able to communicate it to Kent.

"And what about del Barrio?" Myaznikov asked one of his assistants, Captain Boris Yevchenko. "You say she is here in Rome already?"

"She is, Comrade Major. She tried to slip in through domestic arrivals off a flight from Cagliari this afternoon. I put the Vlasov wench on her. Del Barrio will lead us to the American, probably by tonight, I would guess."

"What orders did you give Vlasov?"

"She's not to lay a hand on either of them, unless it's on the front steps of the embassy. She is to call here as often as necessary to keep me advised. Anyway, I've got her wired with a transmitter. Our direction-finding equipment on the two vans will keep the computer updated downstairs. When we hear Kent and the Spaniard have hooked up, we'll be ready to move in fast."

"What about if Kent decides to call the embassy instead of go there?"

"He doesn't have enough to tell them yet. That's why we're covering Golino and Marasco, just in case. Anyway, anybody calling through the main switchboard saying his name is Kent, and we'll find out what was said on the call."

"We find out yet where he's staying?"

"A dump of a hotel not far off the Via Veneto. Going by the name Bennet Bryant." Yevchenko smirked. "Paid the clerk to keep quiet. But Kent's not that stupid. He didn't leave much in his room. Probably went elsewhere and won't return."

"You figure he'll try to contact Tedeschi again?"

"We gave him a chance. We let Tedeschi off the hook and he drove out to the Villa Borghese and took a walk around the Galoppatoio, but Kent didn't show up, luckily for the Italian." Both men laughed.

"You think Tedeschi will make trouble over this?"

"I told him we're watching his family. They're at her mother's place in Foggia. He's too frightened to fart audibly. We're on his phones. If Kent talks to him, we'll find out what he knows, then fix the Italian."

"Korolenko is worried about this Golino fellow in the defense ministry," Myaznikov said. "Who's looking after that end of things?"

"Marasco doesn't want any interference on that. He indicates that as soon as Golino has done his job he'll see he's taken care of."

"Marasco know what's in store for himself?"

"A lot of money, he thinks, as soon as the operation is completed." The two men laughed again.

At dawn on Monday morning Kent walked past the Drogheria Rivierasco, but it was too early, there being no sign of life. But on his next pass, ten minutes later, he saw an older man in a white apron stacking produce boxes outside the shop. Then a younger man, tall and slender and dressed in slacks and a white shirt and wearing a full-length brown apron, came out of the store trucking more boxes. That had to be Vittorio Golino, Kent decided. He bought a newspaper and leaned against a building, keeping an eye on the scene, until the younger man walked back into the store untying his apron.

When he came back out onto the street he had on his suit coat and was carrying a briefcase. Kent fell in behind him as the man headed in the direction of the Ponte Regina Margherita. As soon as the tall man had walked out onto the bridge Kent overtook him and addressed the man without looking at him.

"Signor Golino, I am the American Kent everyone in Spain is looking for."

The man almost came to a halt, but managed to keep moving as he

stared sideways at the stranger. "I don't understand," he said, his voice
sounding tight and high. "Why are you talking to me?"

"I cannot explain it in only a few words, sir. But I can tell you with
certainty that Carlos Marasco has been given orders to liquidate you
after your job for him is finished."

"I don't have any idea what you are talking about," Golino said.
"Where do you get your information?"

"*Non rompermi le palle!* Don't fuck around with me, I haven't time
for it. I know what your assignment is with regard to delaying the navy's
move from Agnano to Capua, and I'll have your cooperation right now
or take my evidence to your department this very morning."

The man kept walking, his head down. Then he said, "What, exactly, is it you want from me?"

Kent looked around. There were many people walking the bridge,
but nobody seemed to be paying any attention to them. "How long
must the move be delayed?"

"Approval cannot be given until the end of this month."

"For what reason is the delay being made?"

"I have not been told. That is the God's truth."

"Who is Carlos Marasco?"

"He is said to be of the Red Brigades."

"Is it he who is paying you?"

The man did not answer, but neither did he deny it.

"How can I find him?" Kent asked.

"He cannot be found," Golino said. "He finds you."

"Well then, when will he find you again?"

"I have no way to know that. Now please, get away from me. I am
probably being followed this very minute."

"I will," Kent said. "But remember, Marasco plans to kill you when
your usefulness to him is over. Be careful, my friend."

They had reached the other side of the river and Golino disappeared
into a pedestrian tunnel. Kent stopped and looked back. He saw two
men coming across the bridge who immediately came to a halt and
began looking over the bridge rail at the water below. One of them was
pointing at a barge, and they seemed to be laughing. Kent crossed to the
other side of the bridge and began walking back across. The two men
went their way, apparently not concerned about him. When he reached

the end of the bridge, Kent again reversed direction and began to cross a third time. About halfway across he saw the same two men coming back, walking quite fast this time. They were no longer looking idly at the river now, but scanning the people in view ahead of them. Their faces were grim and determined-looking, even from a distance. They were on the opposite side from Kent, and when they reached a point about fifty meters from him, they looked directly at him, then backward and forward at the traffic, as if they were about to come across the bridge to Kent's side.

Kent kept walking, watching them out of the corner of his eye, formulating his escape plan. He could see a slight break in vehicular traffic coming up, and estimated the two men would be directly opposite him when they could get across. When they started their dash across the traffic lanes, Kent did the same thing from his side. As they passed one another in the middle, Kent got a quick look at their astonished faces. There wasn't enough time to stop, turn and pursue without getting hit. When he got to the side, Kent began running in the direction of traffic flow. His assailants were keeping pace on their side, but against the flow of vehicles. Then came Kent's chance. A flatbed truck went by at about twenty miles per hour, and he dived onto it, losing his plastic grocery bag as he did so. On an impulse, he looked back at his pursuers and waved at them as the truck quickly outdistanced them. The truck soon came to a stop for a signal, and Kent jumped off and disappeared in the early-morning stream of pedestrians.

He entered a bar for a cup of coffee and a chance to think things out. Golino hadn't given him much. He still didn't know what was being planned for Naples, who was involved, or when it would happen. The two goons had seen him talking to Golino, and it added up that they would quickly land on the Italian to find out what had transpired. But how and when? Golino was well on his way to his ministry office for the day, and time was of the essence. If it were me, Kent mumbled to himself, I'd go back to the father's store and make him call Golino to come down there immediately.

Much as he disliked the idea of heading back into the arms of the goons, there seemed to be no alternative. In addition, the older (and innocent) Golino was probably about to be victimized. Kent gulped down his coffee and walked back across the bridge once more. Amazingly, he spotted the shorter of the two goons walking ahead of him directly toward the Golino market. He recognized the man by his rolling gait and the sandy hair sticking out from under his hat. The other goon wasn't in sight, which made Kent's spirits soar. The odds had just improved remarkably.

Kent crossed the street, to be on the side opposite the market when Rolling Gait went in. Kent watched him go up to the counter and talk to the older Golino. After what looked like an animated conversation, the old man went over to a wall phone and made a call. It was time to move in. Kent crossed the street, never taking his eyes off the two men in the store. The goon had his back turned, his right hand in a coat pocket. The front door was blocked open, providing a straight avenue to the counter. Kent's last five steps were at a dead run and he plowed into his enemy, driving him with terrible force into and partly over the counter. The man had heard the steps and whirled to face Kent just in time to get Kent's shoulder in the midsection, stunning him so that he sagged to the floor with a thunk.

Kent seized the man's weapon from his pocket; it was a large-caliber automatic. He stuck it in his belt, then grabbed the man under the arms and started dragging him around the counter.

"Help me get him out of sight or we're both dead men!" Kent snapped at the astounded old man. Golino immediately opened the door to a room behind the counter and gestured to bring the goon through. "Did he tell you to call your son to come here?" Kent asked.

The man nodded. "He threatened my life if I didn't call Vittorio."

"Did he speak as a native Italian?"

"He's Italian all right, and he'll have you killed for this."

"Who is he? Have you seen him before?"

"His name is Carlo Marasco," the old man whispered.

"He wants to kill your son. Is Vittorio coming down here?"

"They told me he hadn't yet reached the office. They are to give him the message. Who are you, anyway?"

"CIA," Kent said, sort of enjoying the charade, and hoping the stunned man was taking it in. Marasco was getting his wind back and looking angry, so Kent dropped onto his stomach with one knee and saw the man's eyeballs almost pop out again. As he lay there grimacing in agony, Kent grabbed him at the shirt collars and said, "You've got exactly one minute to give me the answers I want."

"*Fatti i cazzi tuoi!*" the man answered, his eyes blazing with hatred.

Kent took out Marasco's pistol, slammed a round into the chamber, and pressed the weapon firmly into the man's crotch. "I'll mind my own fucking business, all right, as soon as I find out all about yours, asshole." Kent was quite pleased at how impressive his Italian vulgarities sounded. He slid the barrel of the pistol down a fraction of an inch below where he guessed the man's testicles were located and fired a round, blowing a hole in the floor and sending echoes like thunder around the room. The man's face went snow-white and his eyes were blinking like Christmas-tree lights.

"The next one will blow your balls off, *capisce?* After that, you get one in each knee. Isn't that the way your organization marks its victims?"

Marasco nodded rapidly, his face seeming to have aged twenty years in just seconds.

"Tell me quickly, then, what is planned for the navy headquarters in Agnano, when it is to happen, and how. If I think you are lying to me, I'll make you a cripple for life. Now talk! You have one minute or less. What is Operation Oltraggio?"

"November fifteenth . . . at two P.M.," he said, his voice dry and hoarse. "The entire compound."

"How?"

"Explosives, tons of explosives . . . already there."

"Who's doing this?"

"We are," Marasco said defiantly. "And you won't be able to stop it. You or anybody else."

Kent thought quickly. The date was critical. What if Marasco was giving him the wrong date? He moved the pistol up a few inches and poked it into Marasco's crotch. "You had your chance, and gave me a phony date. It's the one thing I already knew. That will cost you your jewels, my friend. Say good-bye to your old friends—"

"No!" the man screamed. "I told you the truth! Don't do this to me, and I will see you are protected. I promise!"

"*Chi se ne frega?* I don't give a shit for your protection. Who are you working for on this project?"

The Italian began mumbling some names Kent had never heard before. It seemed as if he was playing for time. Kent looked around to discover that the elder Golino had left the room. The police, Marasco's accomplice, or any of a dozen others could be on the scene in only moments, Kent knew. A quick decision was needed, and he made it. In a single sweeping motion he dealt what he knew would be a fatal blow with the barrel of the pistol to the Italian's head. He heard the skull crack as he hit him. "Fuck him, the murdering bastard," Kent mumbled as he got to his feet and found his way out a back door into an alley.

CHAPTER ELEVEN

Kent, keeping to back streets, distanced himself from the market and eventually worked his way back to the Villa Borghese, where he napped until midday beneath a tree. He wasn't sure whether it was the sun or the ants that awakened him, but he was sure that he was unshaven, dirty, probably smelly, and definitely hungry and thirsty. Nearby he found a drinking fountain where he slaked his thirst and splashed water on his face. Then, avoiding the fancy shops along the Via Veneto, he walked into a middleclass shopping area where he bought an inexpensive change of clothes. He also purchased toiletries to replace those he'd lost during the bridge episode that morning.

Then he checked into a cheap hotel, long enough to use the facilities, then checked back out, returning once again to the shelter of the Villa Borghese.

The shower, shave and clean clothes made him feel exhilarated, and now he had only to await darkness to keep his appointment at the Piazza di Spagna with Cristina. He walked among the trees and around the fountains thinking about her long dark hair and strong profile, her seductive body lines, her low-pitched voice. He marveled again and again over her willingness to throw everything else aside to help him survive and fight against this terrible plot. Together they would make their way to the U.S. embassy, reveal what they had learned, and seek asylum from the police, the KGB and, now, the Red Brigades.

Kent studied his city map, deciding to approach the Spanish Steps from the east, walking along the Via Sistina. That would place him at the top of the stairs alongside the beautiful Trinità dei Monti. From that vantage he would be able to survey the stairs themselves, as well as the street below. He got there just after dark, and found that the dim lighting around the piazza offered many dark spots in which to sit on the stairs or the marble railing and simply wait. He found such a spot near the top of the stairs that offered a commanding view, and settled in to observe and anticipate.

There was a lot to look at, as the steps provided a wide alley for locals bypassing the busy streets. It was also an ideal place of business for vendors, prostitutes, and others who could do business on the move. And few gawking tourists "did" Rome without coming to the Spanish stairs. No one, Kent reckoned, could feel out of place here.

Kent eyeballed the crowd for an hour without seeing Cristina, or even anyone similar. Then an elderly woman stumbled against him, placing her hand on his shoulder for support. He put his hand on her arm to steady her, and felt the woman quickly poke a small scrap of wrapping paper into the breast pocket of his jacket. Then she moved away down the stairs, steadying herself on the stone railing that separated the two lines of stairs. The woman was dressed as a peasant and was somewhat hunched over. Her head was enshrouded in a dark scarf, and she carried a cane. But there had been something strange about her, to Kent's quick appraisal. Had it been that her arm felt firm and strong as she grasped his shoulder? Was it a kind of phony quality in her old-woman movements?

He remained in place for several minutes acting nonchalant, watching the old woman work her way slowly down the stairs. Then, no longer able to check his curiosity, he pulled out the scrap of paper and read the message.

Woman watching you. Brown jacket, black skirt. Made phone call. Go now. Try later, #2.

"Damn!" Kent mumbled, wadding up the paper. He rose and started down the stairs, then abruptly turned and began ascending, his eyes scanning his arc of vision. He saw nobody fitting the woman's description. Once at the top of the stairs and behind the church, he sprinted through the streets for about six blocks, alternating left and right turns at the intersections. He slowed to a walk, cut through a small park and stopped at a circle of benches surrounding a fountain. The next meeting time was two hours away at the Piazza del Popolo. He decided not to show up there early this time, and spent the two hours on the move, frequently retracing his steps and staying on crowded sidewalks. He was confident he had lost the lady who had been following him.

And then the impossible happened. As he approached the piazza along the narrow street from the west, he found himself walking about two dozen steps directly behind a small woman in a brown jacket over a black skirt. She didn't exactly fit into the scene, Kent thought. She carried nothing, wasn't looking in shopwindows, nor looking as if she was just out for a stroll. There were now few people on the streets, so Kent slowed a bit, falling back to a safer distance. He pulled the front of his hat down and stuck his hands in his pants pockets, trying to look casual, but never taking his eyes off the woman who strode ahead of him.

But what was she doing here near his rendezvous point? Inasmuch as she wasn't following *him*, she must be following Cris, he thought, the idea almost striking him with panic. Then a second wave of fear and disgust swept over him: What if they had captured Cris and tortured this information out of her? He tried to calm himself, to think deliberately, to reason things out. There were, after all, other possibilities. This could be a coincidence, the woman being exceptionally lucky. Or, more likely, this wasn't the same woman at all. Yes, that had to be it, he thought. It's just an Italian woman going home from her job, or to the home of a relative. But he had to find out.

As she turned right onto the now deserted walkway that encircled the piazza, Kent quickly overtook her.

"*Scusi, che ore sono?*" he asked casually, tapping his right index finger against the back of his left wrist.

She turned toward him, revealing a face not unattractive in structure; the streetlights exaggerated her high cheekbones and hollow cheeks, and made her strong and pointed jaw seem smaller than it really was. His impression was of a woman in her mid-fifties, still strong and fit. The expression was neither friendly nor hostile, but a study in cold neutrality. Her grayish eyes narrowed, and her lips compressed into a tight line as she visually bored a hole into his own face. "Don't do anything foolish, Mr. Kent," she said in heavily accented English. "We have Miss del Barrio in our custody, and now you are in mine. Unless, of course, you don't care what happens to her."

The blood drained from Kent's face, and he thought he might faint. Only that they continued walking along the stone pathway kept him intact. He thought quickly, concluding it was a bluff. Why would they even have to mention that to him, unless she were buying time until her confederates got there to help take him?

"Who are you?" he asked.

"It doesn't matter," she said without expression. "Do you wish to see her while she is still alive and not yet mutilated?"

There was something vile in the woman's smirk when she said the word "mutilated," that unhinged the American. All the while her right hand had been in her jacket pocket, and Kent knew why. In a lightning move, he grabbed her right wrist with his own right hand, and reaching around her head with his left hand he clamped his hand over her mouth and dragged the woman into a dark crevice between two concrete walls. He forced her to the ground. She was sinewy and strong, but no match for Kent, who disarmed her, jerked the scarf from her head and stuffed it into her mouth. It was taking all his strength and agility to contain her flailing legs with his own, and to keep her tigerlike claws from making mincemeat of his face. But in a couple of minutes her strength ebbed, and he loosened his grip slightly.

Kent then pulled out his own automatic, the one he had wrested from Carlo Marasco at the Golino market. It was gigantic in comparison with this woman's little gun. He poked it hard into the hollow of her throat, just above the notch between the collarbones. "Who are you?" he repeated easing the scarf out of her mouth.

She said nothing, her eyes flashing hatred and contempt.

"You move one muscle and I'll break your nose," Kent said, pulling back the automatic and jamming it in a rear pocket. With the hand free, he reached out, grabbed her small leather purse and dumped the contents on the ground next to her. There was only one sizable, significant object there, and even in the dark it was identifiable: a Russian diplomatic passport. He stuck it in his pocket, along with a packet of high-denomination Italian banknotes.

"Now then," he said. "You're going to tell me where del Barrio is, or I'll finish you right here, just like I did your precious fucking comrades in Spain." He couldn't believe he was saying these things. It seemed like a dream, or a movie . . . something that never would happen to him in real life. Did he really mean he would kill her, just like that, or was he bluffing? Not even he knew.

"I'll take you there," she said.

"You'll tell me where."

"Then you'll kill me."

"Maybe. How do I know you have her?"

"How did I know to come here for you?"

"What was she wearing?"

"I didn't see her. My . . . associates captured her."

"What did they do to make her talk?"

"She was promised we wouldn't harm either of you."

Now Kent had learned at least one thing: this woman was lying to him. Cristina would never believe such foolishness. Then the woman lurched up and tried to reach the gun Kent had stuck in his pocket, and he had to wrestle her down to the ground again. Doing so, he felt something hard under her blouse. He ripped it open and saw the electronics taped to her abdomen. "A transmitter!" he gasped. The Russian woman was smirking. It was obviously only a matter of minutes before she would be located, On an impulse, he struck her in the jaw hard enough to knock her out, then ripped the transmitter off the woman and stuck it, along with her pistol, in one of his now-bulging pockets. Then, jumping to his feet, he left the darkened alcove and rapidly made his way across the piazza into some gardens that bordered the Villa Borghese.

The gardens turned out to be a very well maintained and very old graveyard. He quickly picked out his spot—a marble tomb. The front of the tomb was open, providing access to a locked wrought-iron gate inside. He tossed the transmitter inside, then withdrew to a spot nearby in deep shadows.

It was late now, and traffic had quieted. But soon he noticed a panel truck making its third pass down the street separating the graveyard from the Villa Borghese. As it passed under a streetlamp he caught a glimpse of the direction-finding antenna on the roof. The vehicle came to a stop about one hundred meters from his hiding place and two men got out and began walking toward the tomb. One of them was carrying what looked like a box, and he had earphones on. The apparatus led them to the tomb. One man stayed outside, looking around, while the other, a weapon in hand, stepped cautiously inside. Kent could hear him rattling the wrought-iron gate. Their voices were muffled, but it sounded like Russian. One of them said something, then they both chuckled.

As they began walking back toward their truck, Kent made his move.

"Stop!" he said, using an internationally understood word. Both men whirled in surprise as Kent moved quickly up to them. One went for his weapon and Kent shot him in the chest, dropping him where he stood. The other stood motionless, one hand still clutching the direction-finding gear.

"On the ground, quickly, face-down!" Kent said in Italian. The man obeyed. Kent disarmed him, admiring the 9 millimeter Luger, which he added to his growing collection. He decided he would have to get rid of some of these weapons before his pants fell down.

"I am about to kill you," he told the man on the ground. "However, if you please me, I will only cripple you, then return to finish the job if you have lied to me. Understand?"

The man nodded, his face pressed into the ground.

"All right, then. Where is the Spanish woman, Miss del Barrio?"

"I don't know, sir. It's the honest truth. She is being followed, is all that I know. My responsibility was only to know the whereabouts of Comrade Vera Vlasov."

"You have lied, and now I must kill you," Kent said.

"No, no, please. My wife, my children. I have told you the truth."

Kent judged the answer to be truthful, and decided to let the man live. He hated what he stood for, but maybe he was not a bad man. Then, Kent thought, would he give me such a break? Fuck no. Kent rabbit-punched him into unconsciousness, then went through the pockets of both men. He added their passports to his collection, though he was not exactly sure how he would use them. He found two pairs of plastic wrist restraints on one man, and used one pair to immobilize the unconscious man, cuffing his arms around the trunk of an oak tree next to where he lay. Then he wiped his prints off the automatic he had shot the first man with and stuck it in the other man's pocket. He tossed Vlasov's little pistol into the tomb and slipped out of the graveyard, heading back toward the piazza. But when he got there, Vlasov was gone, along with her purse and its remaining contents. He circled the piazza twice, but found no sign of Cristina. He and del Barrio had earlier arranged three meeting times and places, and the last one seemed his only chance to find her.

At dawn he was walking the streets and paths near the Porta Pinciana. It was cold, and the early-morning breeze went right through his light jacket and trousers. Then he spotted what looked like an old woman walking with a cane. She kept turning her head back to look at him, but kept walking away. He hurried after her, his heart pounding. The closer he got, the faster she walked; she obviously wasn't a feeble old woman, and this gave him all the more hope. Finally he was just behind her.

"Cris! Cris!" he said.

The woman turned and he could see her face. Both eyes had been blackened and her nose was an enormous bulb. Otherwise, it was the same face he had seen on the woman in the brown jacket and black skirt the night before: Vera Vlasov, according to her diplomatic passport. She was pointing a pistol directly at his chest, and it looked like the same one he had taken from her not eight hours earlier. I should have killed the bitch while I had the chance, he said to himself.

At that moment a car jerked to a stop near them and two men jumped out. They grabbed Kent rudely and dragged him into the backseat, Vlasov jumping into the right front seat. While the two hefty men held Kent's arms, Vlasov reared up over the front seat and belted Kent in the nose with the butt of her pistol.

"*Pizda teby'a rodila, khuy na kolyosakh!* A cunt gave birth to you, you prick on wheels!" she gasped.

One of the men blocked her arm on the second swing. "Easy, comrade, easy. We have some information to obtain from this pigeon-prick. Then you can have your way with him."

They drove around inside the park looking out the windows intently, and chattering in Russian. Kent's nose was gushing blood and mucus, and his eyes were clouded so badly he could only get a dim impression of the blazing hatred in the face of the Russian woman. The three Soviets continued talking rapidly as they drove through the streets, but Kent couldn't understand any of it. He assumed he was being taken either to the Russian embassy or to some other place entirely under their control. What would happen then conjured up some unpleasant images in his mind. He tried to clear his head and come up with something—anything—and it had to be soon.

There was no way he could jump out, both doors being blocked by rather large foreign bodies. The windows were rolled up; no one would hear him scream for help. But there was one thing he could do. He leaned back and relaxed, hoping the men would relax their grips on his upper arms a bit, and soon they did. And then he watched and waited for the right moment. The moment came in the shape of an oncoming truck, both vehicles being on inside lanes. He counted down from three, then jerking his arms free he lunged over the driver, forcing the steering wheel hard to the left. The truck swerved to its right, but too late. There was a grinding crash of crumpling metal and breaking glass, and the car spun 360 degrees counterclockwise, stopping abruptly in the middle of the roadway. One of the Soviets from the backseat ended up on his back in the street; the other was in the front seat pushing the driver and Vera Vlasov into the windshield and dashboard.

Kent tumbled out an open door into a heap on the pavement, dazed but still conscious. As he tried to struggle to his feet, he fell back, not knowing why he couldn't stand. He looked back into the car and saw one of the Russians trying to get out; he was looking directly at Kent and his expression was unforgettably evil. Kent then could see Vlasov. She still had the pistol in her hand and she was trying to pull herself free from the other bodies in the front seat. When she got her eyes fixed on Kent she carefully aimed the pistol at him and he crouched low and instinctively threw his arms up over his head. He heard the shot, knew he wasn't hit, and looked up in time to see the Russian who had been getting out, and who had stepped into the line of fire, clutch at his back, then pitch forward onto his face.

Two men had jumped from a car behind the wrecked one. They quickly grabbed Kent and began dragging him toward their car. When he tried to resist, one of them gave him a judo chop behind the head and he went black. In the confusion of traffic coming to a halt, pedestrians gathering, and those from the wrecked vehicles staggering around, nobody paid any attention to Kent's forced departure from the scene. Within a few minutes the police were there trying to give first aid, organize the flow of traffic and move onlookers back, but chaos prevailed. The driver of the oncoming truck was not hurt severely and police were questioning him. The driver of the sedan had to be peeled off the steering wheel and was loaded into an ambulance, as was one of the two other Russian males. The Soviet who had been accidentally shot in the back by Vera Vlasov was also put into an ambulance without anyone noticing he'd been shot. Vlasov refused to be hauled away for medical treatment, and after identifying herself to police, hailed a passing taxi and headed for the Russian embassy.

Vlasov reported immediately to Major Orlov Myaznikov who was clearly not pleased with the news. Two dark veins twitched in his forehead as he heard out the details of the wreck. Vlasov left out the part about her putting a slug in the back of one of their officers, reporting only that he was severely injured and carried away in an ambulance.

"And the American?"

"I caught a glimpse of him on the ground near the car, but I was pinned inside. By the time I had worked myself free he was gone. He looked like he was injured, like his legs were hurt. I don't think he could get far without medical help. Might I suggest that—"

"Thank you, comrade. I shall attend to trying to sort out this mess that you—"

"It wasn't my fault, Major. I directed his capture, carried it out, and then your men bungled it when they failed to properly restrain him inside the car."

"Yes, I see. It should be most amusing to hear you explain all that to Colonel Korolenko. He accepted your help, you know, as a favor to an old friend. And, by the way, what do you plan on telling him about the Spanish woman, or should I say, the unaccounted-for Spanish woman?"

Vlasov licked her lips and swallowed. "When the American appeared, he became the prime objective. She merely led me to him, that's all."

"That's all?" thundered the major. "You let her just walk away into the park?"

"No, not at all. We searched the immediate area, but she had disappeared. Anyway, I left Antipov on her. I'm sure he saw us pick up the American. He likely has her by now."

"If you read the papers yesterday, you would be aware that Carlo Marasco was killed by an American at the market of Colonel Golino's father. Is there any doubt in your mind who that American might be?"

"Why is this even important to me?"

"Only because, comrade, both of those names figure in Operation Oltraggio, and it will be construed as due to your bungling in Spain that the American is still bounding around on a holiday of wiping out our people and our connections."

"That truck," she murmured, as if she didn't hear anything he was saying. "It was a truck just like that one that swerved across the dividing line and hit us in Spain."

"So?"

"And the Spanish woman was driving it, but Kent was in it. The rotten son of a pig-fucker did the same thing to me again."

"You may not get the chance to even the score, Vera Vlasov. Colonel Korolenko doesn't give out second chances, and you've already had several."

"When will he be informed?" she asked.

"On his return from Naples tonight. I suggest you remain here until that time."

It was clear from the major's tone of voice that Vlasov was now, in effect, a prisoner.

"If it will help any," she said, "I wish it known that I am willing to make any sacrifice—"

"Obviously," the major said.

When Kent began regaining consciousness he found himself covered with a blanket with his hands bound together in front of him. The car in which he was riding came to a halt inside a large garage, evidently beneath some building. He was immediately transferred to another car, which exited the garage and zoomed away. Somebody pulled the blanket off him, and he found himself in the backseat of a large sedan, a man on each side of him. He rolled his head around trying to get rid of cobwebs and began looking at his newest captors. They eyed him with some amusement.

"You play pretty rough, Kent," said one of the men. He had a Brooklyn accent.

"Who are you guys?" Kent asked.

"We're the good guys," the other man in the backseat said. His accent was Southern U.S.

"Not some more of those embassy clowns, I hope?"

The two men laughed, and one said, "You must have met them already."

"CIA then," Kent said. Nobody commented, so he continued. "How did you find me?"

"Look, Kent, or Bryant, whichever you prefer," the one with the Southern accent said, "you'll get a chance to ask questions later. Right now, we're just delivering you."

"To . . . ?"

"The airport, for starters. From there, we don't know yet."

"Or won't say. What about Miss del Barrio?" Kent asked.

"We're sorry about that," the Southerner said. "When those folks carried you away from the park we just lost some of our options, know how it is? But we're workin' on it, all the same."

They sped down the Via Ostiense to the airport, and came up to a gate that led to an area of airport warehouses and shops. One of the men in the front seat was Italian; once he had identified himself, he was given immediate entry. Their car pulled ahead and parked alongside a large metal building until a U.S. Air Force C-130 Hercules cargo plane taxied into view on a nearby ramp and came to a halt. The car pulled ahead and came alongside, where Kent was escorted aboard and strapped to a cot by American airmen. A sergeant with an automatic weapon was posted to guard him.

"Tell me we're not going to Spain," Kent pleaded to the airman. The young man smiled at him, but said nothing.

The flight lasted four hours, during which Kent was given food and coffee, but told absolutely nothing. When the big cargo plane touched down, Kent stretched his neck up far enough to get a glimpse out of a small window and saw, to his great chagrin, the arid, treeless plains of central Spain. He was escorted from the C-130 to an air force van and taken to a nearby building, where he was untied, completely searched, given a shower, and then made to put on military fatigues. Then he was escorted to a mess hall, fed again and, after a four-hour wait, put aboard an air force jetliner along with several dozen military personnel bound for Andrews field near Washington, D.C. At no time before or during the trip was he approached by anyone of any apparent authority, nor given any information by anyone else. He sat between two air force sergeants the entire trip, and was not allowed to talk to anyone on the aircraft.

An unmarked van waited for Kent on the ramp at Andrews. Two men in civilian clothes escorted him to the vehicle, loaded him into the back where there were no windows, and drove away to join the endless stream of cars on the Capital Beltway. Kent was numb from his sleepless trip across the Atlantic and had given up trying to gain any information from his captors. He would just wait and see what developed. He was now only a few miles from his home, but it didn't seem that way to him.

He felt as though he were still in Europe, or at least ought to be. The only real relief he felt was at not having to guard against being attacked by enemy agents or foreign police, but this was more than offset by his concerns about Cristina, and about the fate of the hundreds, or maybe thousands of lives at risk at the navy headquarters at Agnano. He wanted desperately to lie down with his head on a soft pillow and be allowed to sleep, but somehow he knew this was not to be, at least for now.

After about twenty-five minutes the van made a sharp turn, slowed and came to a halt. Kent could hear a gate rolling open, the vehicle moved ahead. A minute later it stopped and he was escorted from the van through the doorway into one of the several large buildings of the compound, down a corridor, then up in an elevator, and finally into a small room with no windows nor decorations on the walls. There were two men in the room.

"Hello, Kent," the tall man said. "I'm Malcolm Bartledge." He held out his hand. "And this is my associate Bill Percival." He pointed to his companion, a man of average stature wearing a turtleneck sweater and brown corduroys. "I hope you had an enjoyable trip?" Bartledge said, winking at Turtleneck.

Kent sized the two men up. Here they were, warm and cozy in their plush surroundings, getting ready to play games with him while the KGB, Red Brigades and who knows who else were getting ready to demolish a lot of American lives. They looked relaxed, pleased that they had been able to orchestrate his abduction, and most likely expecting him to be grateful for being rescued from what looked like certain death. Bullshit, he thought.

Several choice epithets occurred to Kent, but he decided to clam up and let them get things started.

"Sorry about your treatment en route, actually," Bartledge said. "We insisted nobody talk to you. Also, you seem to have acquired a reputation for making trouble with your hosts, so we had little choice—"

"Fuck you," Kent stated. "Do you assholes know what the hell is going on at the navy headquarters in Naples?"

"That's exactly why you're here," said Bartledge. "I know you're tired, frustrated and bent out of shape, but frankly, we don't have a hell of a lot of time to dedicate to making things nice for you. We're going to start right now with your telling us everything you know about this whole damn thing, and right after that, we're going to make sure it's all true. So save all of us some time and don't give us a screwed-up version, because we'll soon enough find out."

"I'd be amazed."

"Can we get on with it?"

"I have a condition, just one goddamn condition, and I'll personally hold you to it one way or another."

Both men looked at him, waiting.

"Get del Barrio out of there and make everything right for her."

Bartledge thought for a moment. "We'll do all we can," he said.

"Not *we*," Kent said. "*You*."

"You got it," Bartledge said, turning on the switch to a tape recorder. "Now, let's get started."

Kent reached out and flipped the switch back off. "Del Barrio?" he asked.

"I'm beginning to see why they had problems with you," he said, shrugging his shoulders. "Be back in ten." When he returned, he had to shake Kent awake to show him the text of his message to Rome. "Okay?" he asked?

Kent shook his head. "Acknowledgment?"

"No can do," Bartledge said. "They're closed for the night."

"So am I, then," Kent said, slumping down in his chair.

"Well, fuck a duck!" thundered the CIA man, stomping out of the room. He was back in twenty minutes with an official-looking acknowledgment. "Is this good enough for you, Your Highness?"

Kent scrutinized the machine-printed text. "If this is a fake, you'll wish to God you never laid eyes on me."

CHAPTER TWELVE

Cristina del Barrio had watched with growing horror as Kent went scurrying after the old woman with the cane. Del Barrio was aware of the sedan waiting nearby and dared not cry out. From behind a tree she picked up a stone and threw it at Kent, hoping to get him to look around. But the pebble bounced unnoticed behind him. She was about sixty meters from Kent when the woman whirled around and drew out her gun. It was then that del Barrio, even from that distance, recognized the woman: the same one she had seen in the wrecked Mercedes back in Spain. She cursed the Soviet's cunning in mimicking her own disguise from the night before.

Terror-stricken, she considered her options. When she glimpsed the two men running up to the pair from the car, it was obvious she could do nothing but try to stay hidden, protect herself so that she could make a move later. Moving as nonchalantly as possible, she hurried toward the parked sedan, then memorized the license number and car description as she passed it. Then she slipped off the pathway and into some shrubbery. As soon as the car pulled away, she hurried out of the park, got to a pay phone, and made two calls. The first was to the Italian police, the second to the American embassy. In each case she made the same succinct statement: "This is Cristina del Barrio. I just saw KGB agents abduct Arnold Kent of the United States at Porta Pinciana in a dark blue Renault sedan bearing license number CP7 N443."

Refusing to give further information, del Barrio headed for the U.S. embassy via the back streets, staying clear of the Via Veneto until the final cross street before the embassy. She checked her watch: six forty-five. The main entrance would not be open for over an hour. So she ducked into a café and made a pretense at reading the classified section of a day-old newspaper over four cups of coffee and some rolls. Then, with her scarf pulled low to shield her face, she walked into the main entrance of the embassy and proffered her valid Spanish passport beneath the heavy glass that shielded the young man at the visitor's entrance desk. The man looked at the passport without a change in facial expression, then addressed the woman.

"Do you have an appointment?" he asked, his eyebrows forming thick, inverted Vs over his dark eyes.

Answering slowly and deliberately in Italian, she said, "This is a matter of life and death. Tell your regional security officer I must speak with him immediately."

The young man surveyed her face momentarily, then, pointing a finger at her, said, "You wait." Then he picked up a phone, punched a button, and held a quick conversation with someone on the other end. He had no sooner set down the phone than a steel door separating the lobby from the corridor beyond swung open. A marine in dress blues came quickly out and escorted del Barrio through the door. He passed her through a metal detector and into a room that seemed to be a working area for security people. When she was escorted in, the other marines and civilians glanced up, scrutinizing her. She was told to sit down, and in a few minutes two women in civilian clothes entered and led her to a small room where they told her it would be necessary to be searched. She readily submitted, telling the women their apologies were not necessary.

She was kept in the small room for fifteen minutes, then escorted upstairs to a large office in which four men and a woman were already seated, apparently awaiting her arrival. She was quickly introduced, offered a cup of coffee, which she refused, and then everybody was quiet, waiting for her to begin.

"Do you know who I am, and why I am here?" she asked in her excellent English.

After several seconds' silence, the middle-aged man behind the desk smiled vaguely and said, "Perhaps you might tell us."

Del Barrio looked quickly at each one of them; it felt like their eyes were all penetrating her body, poking holes, seeing if anything might leak out. Not surprising, she reminded herself mentally. She looked a fright and knew it. Maybe they were even noticing the smell, she thought.

"Did you get my telephone call this morning—the one about Arnold Kent being abducted by the KGB?" she asked, again looking from face to face. She noted there were no surprised expressions, no raised eyebrows, no glances between her listeners. Her impression was that all these people were quite ready for her.

"Would you mind starting at the beginning?" asked the man behind the desk. "When did you first become involved in this situation?"

"I will be most happy to do so, sir," del Barrio said, "but at this very moment Kent's life is in great danger, and it is he who has the key to what is shaping up to become the biggest catastrophe to American interests here since World War II. I simply mean to suggest that—"

"We appreciate your concerns, young lady, we truly do. Please rest assured we are acting in a timely and appropriate manner in the matter of Mr. Kent. Now then, if you would simply start at the beginning, we can get on with this."

Del Barrio looked at each face again. Nobody seemed on the point of contesting the security officer's game plan. None of them even seemed overly concerned about her great catastrophe projection. Were they that far ahead of her, or that far behind? So she launched into her story, beginning back at the American embassy in Madrid, leaving little out. They all listened intently and without interruption for the twenty minutes it took her to get the story out. Then they asked questions of her for what seemed like more than an hour. At first, it seemed to her the questions were aimed mainly at checking her out, ensuring that she was real and to be taken at face value. Then it became apparent that they were accepting her story and were now trying to fill in the blank spaces.

Finally the security officer, who had identified himself as Clayton Oliver, looked around at the others, satisfying himself there were no more questions to be asked. Looking at del Barrio, he said, "You have been quite helpful to us, and we very much appreciate your coming here. Thanks kindly for your cooperation." Then he simply stood up and offered his hand, as if to say good-bye. Most of the others said good-bye and began filing out the door as if they had just concluded a routine morning staff meeting and were heading for the coffee room.

Del Barrio's head began spinning; everything felt like a dream. She whirled around, finding only Clayton Oliver and the woman present, shuffling through papers on his mahogany desk. "You mean," she sputtered in disbelief, "you mean I'm just to walk out of here onto the street and go about my business?"

Oliver straightened up to face her, a look of questioning on his face. "Of course," he said. "You're not a prisoner here, after all."

"What? Do you realize, after what I've told you, that I'd be nothing but dead meat, to use your expression, out there on the street? Do you know you haven't given me one shred of information about Kent, and frankly, I think I deserve one hell of a lot? Do you understand I've thrown away my job, and perhaps my citizenship and freedom, on behalf of the safety of American citizens in general, and of Arnold Kent in particular? And you're standing there giving me a 'Thanks a lot, we appreciate it'?"

Oliver had turned half away, and didn't seem the least bit ruffled over her tirade. "Yes, of course, I can see your point," he said, "but you realize, of course, the restrictions we are operating under when it comes to foreign nationals. We have very limited means of handling things without bringing sanctions down on us. If it would be helpful, I can make an embassy car available to transport you over to the Spanish embassy, and let them know you'll be coming."

"What about Kent? Where is he, and what are you doing about it?" she demanded.

Oliver walked back and sat down at his desk. "I'm afraid that we can't give out information that might compromise our operations," he said, making it sound final.

"Meaning that I can't be trusted, after what I've done for you?"

"Not at all," he said, shaking his head. "Simply that if you don't have information, it can't be obtained from you."

"But you don't mind if somebody tries, is that it?"

Oliver didn't respond to that question. "Can I get you the car?"

"In a minute I'm going to tell you where you can put your car," she said. "But right now, I must reveal to you that I held back a few details from the story that you desperately need."

Oliver's eyebrows shot up, and he looked at her out of the corner of his eye without turning his head. "For example?"

"For example, a couple of Italian names from the notes in the briefcase. Also, a date that you might find interesting."

"I'm listening," he said eagerly, glancing at the other woman as if seeking signs of her approval for his astuteness.

"Fuck you, you bureaucratic stuffed shirt," del Barrio said. She noticed the other woman smile and turn her face down to hide what it revealed. "I'll tell the ambassador, nobody else."

Oliver's face turned pink, and his jaw became set. "Out of the question. He's not available," he said with finality.

"Fine," del Barrio said. "I'll wait until he is."

"I'll have you escorted to the street at once," he threatened.

"Fine," she said. "If I'm fortunate enough to reach my embassy, I'll see that my information is given directly to Mr. McAllestair by our ambassador, along with my report on your hospitality, courtesy and concern for my welfare. I will then place a call to the *Corriere della Sera* and provide them with the entire story."

Oliver's face turned noticeably redder, and he got to his feet stiffly. The fortyish woman glanced back and forth between the two, obviously enjoying the exchange. "I . . . I'll see what can be arranged," Oliver sputtered.

Cristina was led into the office of Ambassador Donald McAllestair, followed closely by Clayton Oliver, the security officer. McAllestair received del Barrio most cordially and offered her a chair.

"Mr. Ambassador, I have been received with a great deal of hostility by your staff, in particular by this gentleman. May I discuss my information with you without his presence?"

"Of course," he said, glancing at Oliver.

"But, Mr. Ambassador—"

"If you please," McAllestair said coldly, nodding his head toward the door. Oliver stalked out without so much as a glance at del Barrio.

Del Barrio didn't waste time or words. She succinctly summarized what had happened, orally documenting the key parts of her story. McAllestair listened with interest, without interruption, until she had finished.

"What do you think is the purpose behind this . . . Oltraggio event?" he asked.

"It's clearly what all anti–U.S. terrorism is about in this part of the world. Diminishing the American presence, the American influence. In this case the immediate objective is to get the U.S. Sixth Fleet out of the Mediterranean. Secondarily, I would assume that any erosion of U.S. participation in NATO would be sought. The ambassador is of course aware of efforts in Spain to oust the F-16s from Torrejón de Ardoz."

McAllestair regarded her with growing respect. "What, specifically, do you think is planned with regard to the headquarters at Agnano, and when is it supposed to come down?"

"Sir, that's why Mr. Kent and I came here. Somebody has to find those things out, and so far, nobody in your government seems interested."

"And why should you be?"

"Mr. Ambassador, I value American lives as I value the lives of Spaniards or anybody else. It became evident to Mr. Kent that hundreds, perhaps thousands of lives were at risk here, and he had the decency, he had the guts to try to do something about saving those lives. In return, Jerome Parkerhouse tried to throw him to the wolves to avoid causing diplomatic ripples that might have been injurious to his career. I saw that happening and interceded."

"You're in love with Kent?"

She looked at him steadily before replying. "If that's the case, it's something that didn't start until we were both already in great trouble over this thing. My personal feelings toward him had absolutely no influence on my behavior."

"And I take it you approve of everything he's done . . . killing those people . . . stealing cars . . . causing wrecks—"

"He's tried to stay alive long enough to find somebody to convince that American citizens by the thousands may be killed by terrorism. Yes. Yes, I approve of that."

The ambassador still didn't seem convinced. "And where is Mr. Kent right now? Why isn't he here?"

"Excuse me, sir. I assumed your people had told you. Kent was captured in the Villa Borghese this morning at dawn by agents of the KGB. I reported that fact to your embassy by phone within a few minutes after it happened. I really don't expect to ever see him again." She choked on the last words, and tears were showing in the corners of her eyes.

"It was, in fact, reported to me. It was also reported to me that the vehicle was involved in a head-on collision, and that a passenger was killed."

Del Barrio straightened up in her chair, her eyes wide.

"He wasn't killed in the accident, but just afterward, shot in the back by a woman who was in the car."

Del Barrio clapped her hands over her eyes. "Oh, God, no." She started to slump forward, out of the chair. McAllestair leapt forward and caught her.

"I'm sorry. I had to see your reaction. The man who was killed was a Soviet agent."

"But . . . what about—"

"Witnesses told police two men from a following car dragged somebody out of the wreckage and drove away with him. We don't know who that was."

Del Barrio thought about it for a moment. "Do you—are there American intelligence operatives in town who were looking for Kent?"

He declined to answer that one. He offered her a cigarette, and she refused. "How can I best help you?"

"Promise to verify my story, then take action on it quickly. It's what Kent would have wanted."

"I meant, for you personally . . . for your welfare."

"I don't know. I haven't had time to think about it. I have two children. They're being cared for, but I must get back eventually. I've undoubtedly lost my job, but it seems unimportant to me now. Is there anything I can do . . . any way I can help on this Agnano situation? Let me help. Then I can go back and face the music, whatever it is."

"How can you help? What do you have to offer?"

"I know generally what this whole thing is about, and believe it. I speak Italian. I've seen and can identify the Soviet woman who shot the man in the back. They've seen me and have my picture. They surely want me dead by now. I'd at least make respectable bait, wouldn't I?"

"How long do you think you'd last on the street?"

"I'm here, aren't I? By the way, I didn't dress like this to win any beauty contests, obviously."

The ambassador laughed. "I wasn't going to mention it. You could do with a bit of tidying up." He poured them each a cup of coffee, taking his time adding sugar and cream to his own. "I'll need a bit of time to get you checked out. Then we'll see what needs to be done. Think you can put up with our hospitality for a day or two?"

"Of course. In the meantime, if it is at all possible, Mr. Ambassador, Kent may have been able to obtain critical information. If there is any possibility of—"

"I can assure you that idea has occurred to me, and it will be delivered immediately to the appropriate people. I'll also personally see to it that you are given any information we are able to get about Mr. Kent himself."

Del Barrio got to her feet, but only for a moment. Her face white, she put both hands on the desk to steady herself, then collapsed on the floor before the ambassador could get to her.

Aleksandr Korolenko strode purposefully into the foyer of his well-appointed office in the Russian embassy, where Major Orlov Myaznikov and his assistant Boris Yevchenko awaited him, along with three other staff personnel. Korolenko had cut short his visit to Naples after getting the news that Kent had reached Rome on Sunday, but was still loose as of Monday evening. Now it was Tuesday and he asked Myaznikov for his report before even saying good morning to him. Myazkikov braced himself, then told his young boss how Kent and del Barrio had slipped through their hands that morning. In describing the episode, he made it clear that Vera Vlasov had orchestrated the fiasco, in defiance of his instructions to her to stay in the background and in contact with Miss del Barrio.

"Thank you very much, *Captain* Myaznikov," Korolenko said coldly, clearly indicating his intention to have the major's rank reduced via the next diplomatic pouch to Dzerzhinsky Square. "And what, exactly, is your statement regarding the present whereabouts of these two individuals?"

Myaznikov glanced at Yevchenko, as if for moral support, then said, "Comrade Colonel Korolenko, I have learned from our people inside the American embassy, that the woman appeared there this morning, and has not yet left. Kent himself has not been seen since this morning's . . . unfortunate episode."

"Yes, unfortunate indeed," the colonel said, quickly glancing at each person in the room, "and for all of you as well as myself. Do you realize that our entire project has been compromised by your effeminate blundering? I simply cannot fathom the depth of incompetence demonstrated here in the last few days during my absence. You have shown yourselves unable to deal with two untrained foreigners who are little more, really, than tourists. And in the process I am told one of our officers has been killed, three of them seriously injured, and the rest of you humiliated."

"Somewhat more than tourists, sir," ventured Yevchenko. "They are reported to have decimated our mission in Spain, after all."

Korolenko whirled toward the young captain. "Should you make the mistake of contradicting me one more time, *Lieutenant*," he thundered, "I will personally arrange to have your testicles poked so far up your nostrils, you'll be seeing out of your bunghole. Now, what about this Vlasov disaster?" he asked, looking back at Myaznikov. "Where is she right now, and what are your plans for her remains?"

"At your command, Colonel, I am prepared to bring about her disappearance."

"Not yet," Korolenko said. "I am still hopeful that we can dispose of her in such fashion as to derive some benefit from it. Right now, because of your collective and appalling buffoonery, I will immediately be involved in high-level planning aimed at redirecting our project to ward off the damage you have allowed. In the meantime, Myaznikov, you can attempt to salvage what little value is left in your career here by coordinating our local resources toward the end of neutralizing whatever damage Kent and the Spaniard have managed to accomplish. By the way, I want both of them dead at the earliest opportunity, and I don't care how you do it."

Kent was alone in the leather chair when he awoke. It surprised him, because in seemed like just a moment ago that three men had sat opposite him with their folders spread out in front of them, and the technician had begun injecting him from an IV bottle on a stand next to his chair. Earlier, they had questioned him for over three hours before putting him down with the chemicals. He looked at his watch. He had been out for five hours.

"Don't try to get up yet," a woman's voice said to him from behind. "You'll fall down. Just sit there for a while. I'll get you something to drink." She was back in moments with orange juice. Then Malcolm Bartledge came in.

"You stumbled on a big one, pal," he said jauntily.

Kent looked in the direction of the voice; he was still seeing things as if in a cracked mirror, one that produced many overlapping images.

"How does the navy like it?" Kent asked.

"Well, you know how those guys are. Remember Pearl Harbor? Same attitude forty or fifty years later. Problem is, we aren't able to give them anything tangible, anything they can get their teeth into. I think they lie around on their bunks reading so many spy stories, everything kind of mixes together and nothing is real any more. You'd think after the marine barracks incident they would jump on anything. But it seems like they're pissed off we'd suggest there might be a slight chink in their fucking armor or something."

"Well, what do you think they'd like to have?"

"Oh, I don't know. Maybe a set of plans and a copy of the instructions. Their intelligence types will undoubtedly crawl around and try to dig up some verification, some indication that there's something to it. But they might wind up fucking up what we've got nailed down so far."

"What about you guys?"

"Convinced? Yeah, maybe seventy-five percent—"

"I meant, what are you planning to do about it?"

"It's in the cooker. Know more about it soon. Meantime, about this fellow Otto Frange. He might be the key to this. That is, he probably has stuff we badly need."

"That would be my guess, too," Kent said. "But how would you go after it?"

Bartledge smiled. "That's where you come in," he said, adding, "that is, unless you're tired of playing the game."

"Shit no!" Kent said, straightening up in the chair. "I owe that sucker a big one, the way he set me up. Speak to me."

Bartledge got serious. "Right now he apparently doesn't know we're looking at him. The son of a bitch has been sitting there on that desk at State for two years pulling the rug out on us whenever he could. He's no big fish in their outfit, but evidently they rely on him to poke thorns into us from time to time. We could probably let him sit there and keep an eye on him, but there might be nothing for months. Our view is we ought to reel him in, bleed him, then ship the fucker to Leavenworth."

"What if he won't cooperate?"

Bartledge laughed heartily. "Oh, he'll be happy to oblige us," he said, winking at Kent. "Only thing is, we've got to cover his disappearance for a week or so, keep things from clanging closed prematurely on the other end."

"And that's where I come in?"

"He lives in your neighborhood, right?"

"If you say so."

"Well, I thought it might be kind of fun to have him run into you in the neighborhood—like maybe at a social gathering or something—where we could check out his reaction. He would recognize you, wouldn't he?"

Kent smiled, beginning to like the way things were progressing. "He sure as hell would. What would I do, play it straight?"

"Right. Cozy up to him and the lady we're having invite him. You and Yvette invite him to your house for a drink after the party. He wouldn't be able to resist, just out of curiosity."

"Who is this lady, and how persuasive is she?"

"Works at Main State. Says Frange's eyes come out of their sockets whenever she's within view. He's been after her for a date for months."

"Now that you mention it," Kent said, becoming more and more fascinated with the idea, "there's usually a wine and cheese party about this time of the year—"

"It's tomorrow night," said Bartledge with a smirk. "We didn't even have to get it rescheduled."

"You bastards are oily, you know that? I'm not really all that curious, but is Yvette planning to go?"

"Absolutely," Bartledge said. "She's a local celebrity, and very much in demand at all social occasions these days. In fact, we have it on good authority she'll be the guest of honor. It'll be a good chance for you to surprise her too."

Kent laughed. "She'll probably be disappointed to lose her top billing. But do tell me more about your little plan. Are we coming as a couple, or do I wait until the last minute, then waltz in there in these fucking military fatigues and try to act casual?"

"We did, as a matter of act, already talk about that. If you're willing to go along with it, we'd rather not say anything to anyone, not even Yvette, about your being back here. The news media still have you out of sight in Rome, still trying to do your thing, whatever that is, and nobody seems to know. I took the liberty of getting Yvette to come up with one of your suits, etc., telling her we might need them for you in Europe to come home in. Hope the pin-striped job is okay."

Kent sat there shaking his head in disbelief. "What happens after we all get to my place?"

"We thought a surprise party would be nice. You know, lights out when you come in, all that?"

"Charming," Kent said. "But if he's so hot for this animal you got him lined up with, he'll probably say screw the neighborhood, where's the motel?"

"I told you, this gal Donna is persuasive. Trust me."

"With all due respect for the legendary capacities of your agency," Kent said, "I have to say this sounds a whole lot like a high school play. You know, this guy Frange has made a career out of outsmarting the competition. This well-endowed lady might be able to con him into going to the party, but once the guy gets a close look at me, it won't take him more than about three and a half seconds to figure he's been set up."

"Why should he?" Bartledge asked. "Is there any way he'd possibly know you fingered him to us?"

"Well, it might occur to him that I heard that he'd refused to confirm my account of the little meeting in Claunch's office. But of course that would take more like four or five seconds, than the three and a half I mentioned."

"Kent, you're a worrier. He'll be so fucking surprised he won't know what to think. You should have a lot of fun answering the innocent-type questions he'll have for you."

"Where the hell is the FBI in this deal? I thought this kind of thing was their responsibility."

"We don't have much time. Anyway, they think the Naples thing is a wild goose chase. Fuck 'em."

They stood up and shook hands. "Let's eat," Bartledge said. "Then we can get together with my boss and talk about your next assignment."

"You mean about tomorrow night?"

"Shit no, man. That's all set up. I'm talking about finishing this job you began at JFK eleven days ago."

Kent glanced at Bartledge's face as they walked down the corridor. He was absolutely serious. "But, what about—"

"Relax, Kent. You've been with a conservative agency too long. Hang loose. Don't sweat the bureaucracy. Just nod your head up and down when I ask you, and I'm asking you now, if you'd like to give us a hand for a couple of weeks. Should be a lot of fun, just like what you've been doing lately. Includes three fun-filled days of special training, shitty hours and questionable companions. What say?"

Kent's wide grin was all Bartledge needed. It didn't occur to him that Kent's main motivation had little to do with the excitement of working, even if just temporarily, for the CIA.

The wine and cheese party was one of the three annual events dished up by the Westridge Women's Club of McLean, Virginia, an organization apparently dedicated to the proposition that residents of a subdivision should cling together, even if they didn't happen to have any good reason to do so. On the third Sunday in July, invariably a day of temperatures and humidities in the high nineties, there was the infernal swimming and barbecue party in somebody's backyard, terminating with the auction of ghastly castoffs from members' attics. Then in midwinter there would be a pot-luck supper, generally consumed on wobbly card tables scattered around the house and garage. In recent years, these suppers were highlighted, to say it charitably, with such show-stoppers as a magic act by a real-life federal judge and a flamenco dancing performance by an army wife who'd just had her third lesson.

The fall wine and cheese party was the most formal and least structured of the three events. The only regimentation was the labeling of guests with little stickers saying: HELLO! MY NAME IS _____! Not all guests chose to so adorn themselves, however, believing they were already well enough known, that only a blithering idiot would wear one, or that they didn't, in fact, give a shit if anyone could figure out who they were anyway.

The men of the Westridge neighborhood would come in suits or sport outfits wearing ties or turtlenecks. In this affluent neighborhood, their clothing ran to conservative styles and colors, save for one gentleman taken with the idea that trousers should look roughly like plaid horse blankets. Women came in fashionable winter or fall outfits ranging from dress casual to formal gowns. There would be no entertainment, auctions or special events of any kind at these fall affairs; it was strictly a stand-up-with-the-wineglass-and-see-who-else-is-there-and-what-they're-wearing kind of a do. Conversations around the house

ranged from the asking prices of neighborhood homes to the latest political jokes being told around Washington. A major theme among the
men was the Super Bowl prospects of the Redskins; among the women,
how much time their husbands spent watching football.

A great variety of wines would appear on the table. Most of them
were modestly priced vintages, to put it kindly, no connoisseur being
dull enough to waste his better stuff on barbarians who probably
wouldn't know a Mouton-Rothschild from a Mogen David, nor have
the foggiest about who might have provided it. Consequently, the swal-
lowing of wine was accompanied by only slightly masked grimacing,
particularly on the first sip.

But inevitably the wine did its job, loosening tongues and lowering
barriers so that faceless commuter robots and occluded house plants
would come to life to reveal previously unseen facets of their personae.
It was into this ambience that Arno Kent made his appearance on a
Thursday night in late October.

"That's the place right there," said Kent, pointing out a white-painted
brick house on Westridge Drive.

Malcolm Bartledge passed the house, made a U-turn, then parked
the Plymouth on the opposite side of the street about a half block away.
He looked at his watch. "Only seven fifteen," he said. "You won't go in
until Otto's there."

"What about your people?"

"They'll go in a little after seven thirty."

"What's their cover? These folks tend to know one another."

"No problem. Negotiating to buy one of the homes for sale in the
neighborhood. Sellers suggested they drop in and get acquainted.
They'll keep their eyes on Frange, just in case anything looks like it
might get out of hand."

"I appreciate it," said Kent. "You sure Yvette doesn't have a clue
about this? What do you think I ought to say to her, like, 'Sorry I didn't
have time to call. How have you been?' Or how about, 'I stopped for a
drink on the way home from Italy and forgot what time it was'?"

"Yeah, I know this will be a bit awkward," Bartledge said, in a world-
class understatement, "But if this thing is going to have real punch, we
want everybody to be really shocked and amazed. By the way, you'll
need to clue in Yvette about our little private surprise party at your
house, so she'll be ready to go along with it."

"I figured that out. I suppose you guys already have the key to my house and have familiarized yourselves with the floor plan."

Bartledge laughed. "You won't run us in on breaking and entering, I hope."

"It's really nice working with you guys, you know that?"

"You'll learn to love it, Kent. Who's that going in?"

"Retired army colonel. Real asshole."

"Which one?"

Kent snorted. "The one with the lousy haircut. His wife is taking lessons."

"Wonderful. How about that couple coming down the walk?"

"Uh, the Postens. British embassy, navy attaché, I believe."

"There he is," Bartledge said with delight, pointing to a square-built man accompanying a slim lady in a dark wrap. "This'll be the last night on the town for that son of a bitch."

"I'm nervous," Kent said. "After what he's put me through in the last two weeks I may not be able to restrain myself. Think your people would accept him with a flattened face?"

"Relax, Kent. Just think of it as the high school play, where you're one of many supporting actors. We want to get him out of there under controlled circumstances, and without any kind of fuss that would make it noteworthy, or even start rumors. We need several days before his people start digging into it."

"Okay. But tell your folks if this guy makes any fast moves, the play is over."

"If he does, Donna will be all over him like a flash. She's not only a knockout, but also a third-degree black belt in judo. Ready for Act One?"

"Yvette's not there yet," Kent said.

"It's okay. In fact, better. We'll get two reactions out of Otto this way."

"Sounds good. By the way, who are you supposed to be?"

"Anybody know you don't have a brother-in-law?"

"Let's go."

When the two men entered the house they were greeted by the hostess, Fran Whiting, a woman with whom Kent was not yet acquainted. He mumbled his name and that of Bartledge, and her face showed no sign she thought anything was unusual. She seemed so intent on making a cheerful welcome that it went right by her. Kent winked at Bartledge, then they stuck on their little labels and entered the main room. There were at least twenty people standing around in groups of two, three and four. Otto Frange and Donna had their backs turned; they were talking with another couple. Kent felt the blood rushing to his face when he saw Frange. Even from the back he knew he had been right about this being the guy who had come to his house that day a year ago.

Then somebody recognized Kent. It was Parker Lindsay, a physicist for one of the "beltway bandits." First his mouth sort of dropped open and his eyes widened, then he quivered for a moment or two trying to make sure he was seeing something in real life. "My God!" he uttered, not loud, but in a way that arrested everyone's attention. Everybody looked at Lindsay, then followed his line of sight to Kent, who simply stood there smiling.

There was a collective gasp, a moment of stunned silence, then one voice, then another, soon a whole chorus of "Arno Kent! Arno Kent!" Nobody rushed up to him; they were too shocked to believe their eyes. Here was the man whose name had been on the front page of the *Washington Post*, and repeated daily on almost every radio and television newscast for the last ten days. Kent glanced furtively at Frange, not making a point of it. The man's face was white as chalk, and wine was spilling out of his glass as he tried to steady his hand. Kent noted that Donna was watching Otto's face.

Kent held up both hands, palms facing his audience. "Greetings, everyone," he said, smiling broadly. "I wasn't sure I'd be able to make it tonight after such a busy trip, but here I am. Don't let me interrupt your enjoyment. Please, just go on with the party. I'm real happy to be here."

Everyone swarmed all over him, a hundred questions coming at once. Backed into a corner, he told them, "I'm sorry, everybody. I've been asked not to give out any information until the folks at the State Department are finished with me, which should be in about a year."

"Bullshit, Arno," screeched a forty-five-ish woman clutching a high-ball glass. "How many commies did you put away? We've got bets on this, you know. Was it eight, nine, how many, Arno?"

Before he could even think about answering, somebody else chimed in with, "Come on, Arno. We don't get many celebrities around here. Give us at least what the *Washington Post* will have tomorrow morning."

The fusillade went on and on, the questions falling on top of one another with no gaps for responses. Finally, Kent managed to wave them into relative silence and said, "I just want to tell you all how great it is to be back here where people aren't trying to shorten your life and—"

"Yeah, well you must not be spending much time downtown . . . ," began a black diplomat, grinning widely.

"Shut up, Clarence," said his wife. "You've been spending way too much down there, as far as I'm concerned." Everybody laughed.

"Anyway," Kent continued, "I can't tell you about it now, but there's a big deal going on over there, and they tell me if I play my cards right, they may let me go back."

"So what is it that's going on?" persisted another man.

"For God's sake, give the man a rest," said Lindsay. "Back off and let him enjoy himself. You'll find out soon enough all about this thing."

After a few other attempts to gain information failed, people began drifting back to more normal wine-and-cheese-party behavior, but they kept staring at Kent as if hoping some gems of knowledge would magically emanate from him.

Then Yvette Kent came in with a couple from the neighborhood. She didn't see him immediately, so he slipped up behind her and said, "You're late. I thought you'd never get here."

"Oh, hi!" she said, whirling around to face him. "What are you doing here? I thought you were . . ." He caught her as her knees went limp, scooped her up and carried her into one of the bedrooms. Mina Lindsay went quickly ahead, opening doors, then getting the guests' coats off the bed and out of the way.

"It's all right," Kent said to Mina. "Just leave us for a while. She'll be fine, she's tough as iron."

Back in the living room–dining room area, three sets of eyes kept vigilance on Otto Frange, who was trying to get his nerves back on track after the shock of seeing Kent in the flesh. One set of eyes belonged to Donna Schenk, who had arranged Otto's appearance.

"Otto, what is the problem?" she said. "Did I say something that upset you?"

He didn't even hear the question.

"Otto? Otto?" she said, waving her palm back and forth in front of his eyes.

"What? Oh, sorry. I got distracted there for a while. You know, that's really amazing."

"You mean about Arnold Kent?"

"Yeah. You know, I sat in on a talk with him just before he left to go over there. Then, after what's happened, I guess I really never expected to see him again."

Donna took a sip of her wine. "Well, you must be glad to see him. Aren't you going to welcome him back, say hello, go to hell, or whatever?"

"Yeah, sure," he said. "Thought I'd let the crowd thin out a little. Listen, sugar, I just remembered a phone call I have to make . . . the guy will only be there for a little while. Be right back, okay?"

Otto slipped through the crowd, which by now was becoming substantial, found the phone, then dialed a local number. Getting nothing, not even a dial tone, he took the receiver from his ear and stared at it dumbly. "Phone out of order?" he asked the hostess, who happened to be standing nearby.

"Well, if it is, I didn't know about it," she said. "Let's try the one in the kitchen."

They did, and it didn't work either. Frange, growing somewhat concerned, returned to the living room and found Donna. "Listen, sugar," he said, "the phones here aren't working. You mind if we get out of here, find a phone, then go somewhere and have a good time?"

"Can't it wait just a little while, Otto? There are a ton of people here we haven't even said hello to yet."

"You don't understand how important this is, sugar." He was beginning to perspire. "Listen. How about if I make a quick run to a pay phone and come right back?"

"Well, I . . . ," Donna began, trying to stall, looking for a good way of doing it.

"Otto Frange, isn't it?" said Kent, stepping up in front of them.

"Yes, yes, it is," Frange said, forcing a wan smile and extending his hand. "I really—"

"You really didn't think you'd ever see me again, right?" Kent said with a hearty laugh. "Aren't you going to introduce us?" he said, smiling at Donna, whom in fact he had not yet met.

"Oh, yes, of course," he said.

"Otto needs desperately to make a phone call," Donna said, her eyes sparkling. "But the ones here are out of order. Do you happen to live nearby?"

"How does a half block away sound?" Kent asked. "I want to get out of here anyway. You know, jet lag and all that. Why don't the two of you come on down, and we'll have an honest drink before you get back on your way?"

"But . . . your wife, Kent," Donna began innocently. "She apparently just saw you for the first time since—"

"Oh, she's fine now. Anyway, Mr. Frange, I'll be able to tell you a few things I couldn't discuss with all these people from the outside. Shall we get our coats?"

Frange finally put things together, or at least his early-warning system began functioning. It was the combination of things: being dragged to this party in Kent's neighborhood, seeing Kent dramatically appear, the phones suddenly not working, and now this invitation to Kent's house. It was all too much to be coincidental. He had been set up, and was about to be taken. There were undoubtedly agents here ready to nail him. Shit, he thought, now he couldn't get back to his office, even to his home. The bastards would have his car watched too, maybe even wired with a locator beacon. Then the final bit of irony occurred to him: the bitch Donna was a part of the trap. He wasn't about to make out with her this night. He needed to find a way out, and quickly.

CHAPTER THIRTEEN

Otto Frange glanced furtively at the kitchen door that led into the carport. He could see it was being casually guarded by a well-built man in his mid-thirties, a guy trying to act like he was merely enjoying the party. He decided he'd have to get out the front door.

He glanced back at Kent, now with a steely gaze. "Yeah, thanks, Kent," he said. "That would be real helpful. I'll get our coats and meet you at the front door."

As Frange moved through the crowd in the living room he edged toward the front window and glimpsed out at the street. He clearly made out the silhouettes of two men in suits standing in shadows near his car. Must be another way out, he thought, looking around. All he could see was a set of windows facing the backyard. They were small panes of glass, sixteen of them, each about fourteen inches square, separated by narrow wooden dividers. He waited for people to move out of his line of approach. Kent, watching him, sensed his intent and stepped in front of him, saying, "Mr. Frange, I—"

"I have something here for you, Kent," he said, stepping toward him. Before Kent could react, Frange grabbed him by the arm, swinging him around toward the middle of the room, then without a second's delay belted him in the jaw with his huge fist. Kent reeled backward, smashing into the wine table with a terrible crash, and collapsing with the table and three dozen wine bottles at the feet of six or eight people trying to jump out of the way. While the onlookers stared down at the chaos in amazement and surprise, another great crash was heard as Otto Frange hurled his own impressive bulk through the windows and into the garden, leaving a gaping hole through which a strong stream of cold night air began pouring into the living room.

Women were screaming and men were shouting. Some were pulling Kent to his feet, others gathered at the hole to look out into the night. Bartledge dashed out the front door shouting at his men in the street to circle around behind. Yvette, hearing the commotion, came out of the bedroom and looked around at the disaster area. She found herself standing next to the hostess, who was in a state of shock, and said, "Fran, did Arno do this to your house?"

Mrs. Whiting shook her head philosophically. "Nobody did it, hon," she said. "We've just been too lucky all our lives. I guess it was just our turn, that's all. Shit, it was just a damn house." Then she began crying.

Frange's plunge out the window was fairly successful, as window plunges go. When he hit the ground he knew immediately he wasn't hurt except for minor abrasions. He got to his feet like a cat and zipped away, sticking to adjacent backyards. When he was a block from the scene, he saw the door of a house open, and a young man came out, keys in his hand. A Buick waited in the driveway. Frange timed his move. Just as the man unlocked the driver's door of the car Frange pounced on him, knocking him out with a rabbit punch. Within a few minutes he was speeding along the Capital Beltway heading for Hyattsville, Maryland.

Most of the guests hastily departed, a few of the Whitings' closer friends staying behind to deal with the debris on the floor and the gaping hole where the windows had been. Kent offered to help, but Bill Whiting asked him to "just kindly get the hell out of our lives."

Kent walked Yvette home. Surprisingly, she seemed completely back to normal, but deeply fatigued. She wanted to know nothing from her husband, only to get to bed and go to sleep. Kent gave her a tranquilizer, put her to bed, and watched over her until she had drifted away. Then he downed a double bourbon and collapsed on the couch in the living room. His eyes had no sooner closed than there came a loud knocking on the front door. He pulled himself up, stumbled to the door and looked out through the little glass window at the top. It was Bartledge.

"The son of a bitch got away!" Bartledge said twice, gnashing his teeth. "Just like Hollywood, for God's sake. Can you beat that? The guy diving out a fucking window?"

"Wonderful," Kent said sleepily. "So much for the grand plan. So what happens now?"

"Whatever that is you're drinking, I'll have a double," Bartledge stated. They continued their conversation in the living room, drinks in hand.

"He won't be stupid enough to come back for his car, go to his house, or anything like that," Bartledge said. "All we can do now is stake out his known contacts in the area."

"So now he's got some kind of a fix on what we know," Kent said, staring down at his whiskey.

"Yeah, but all it means is that we've got less time than we wanted. The son of a bitch is undoubtedly on the phone by now."

"You figure he'll hole up somewhere in the area?"

"I doubt it," Bartledge said. "He knows we'll be on his case. He'll probably try to get out of the country at the first chance. How's Yvette holding up?"

"She's just kind of overwhelmed right now. I think she needs some rest and no stress for a few days."

"Listen, Kent. We don't have time for you to screw around here. Can you get some help in for her?"

"You guys are nothing but compassion, you know that?" Kent said sourly. "Yeah, I guess so. I can get one of her friends to come over tomorrow."

"I was thinking about right now," Bartledge said.

"Fuck you," Kent said. "You'll see me tomorrow sometime if everything works out okay."

Bartledge finished his drink in a gulp. "All right, all right." He looked at his watch. "Got to get moving. Listen, I'll send a car out for you at . . . eight."

"Noon, and that's the best I can do," Kent said, standing up. "You know, like sleep . . . shower . . . clean clothes . . . wife?"

Bartledge looked up when Kent was shown into the agent's Langley office. "Guess where Frange is right now," he said.

"Probably on an airplane for Italy," Kent said.

"Try the Montgomery County General Hospital. Ran into the back of a truck on the beltway."

"When?"

"Couldn't have been more than fifteen minutes after he left the party."

"So there was no time for him to call anybody?"

"That's my guess. But better than that, he wasn't identified at the scene. The car had just been reported stolen in McLean, and the Fairfax County Police made the connection. We identified him and asked the police to sit on it for national security reasons. They said okay. Anyway, he's unconscious, and the medics think he'll go into a coma."

"Well, so what? News of my being back here will be out by now anyway. Whoever's running things over there will figure their plan has been compromised."

"Maybe. But we're planting the line around Rome and Madrid that the 'Kent Returns' story is a CIA hoax. In case you didn't know it, you're hiding out in Rome right now. Aside from that, some good news for you. The del Barrio woman turned up at our embassy there not long after we got you out. Our station chief checked out her story with us and we verified it based on what you gave us."

On hearing her name, Kent felt an enormous surge of relief and an overpowering feeling of joy. "Thank God," he said. "Will she be going back to Madrid?"

"Word is, she wants to stay there until things get cleared up. I don't think there's a plan yet."

"Does she know what happened to me? I mean, last time she saw me, if I figured things out right, I was being dragged into a car by that KGB bitch and two heavy-handed accomplices."

"Doubt it, Kent. Our people in Rome understand the story that you're cooling it there, so they won't tell her."

"I don't like the sound of that. If she thinks I'm holed up in some filthy KGB cage over there, no telling what she might try to do about it."

"Kent, like I say, they don't have anything figured out for her yet, and you can be sure they'll take good care of her."

"I can't be sure of a fucking thing when it comes to our embassies. The sooner we get over there the better I'll like it."

"That will happen before you know it. Right now, let me give you an idea of how you're going to spend the next few days. There obviously won't be time to send you down to the 'farm' near Williamsburg for a regular training course. So we've put together a little thirty-two-hour course to get you through the essentials of survival and some other good things.

"This is Sam Devon," Bartledge said, introducing him to a studious-looking black man dressed in khaki pants and a pullover sweater. "Sam is our foremost expert in high-tech weaponry. We stole him from Toys-R-Us in their off-season." Devon glanced sideways at Bartledge as if he had heard the line several times before. "You might start him off with something to help him avoid the right cross," Bartledge said, winking at Kent.

"Come with me, Kent," Devon said. "I've got some stuff here that'll light up your life."

"You've got him for four hours," Bartledge hollered after them. "Then turn him over to Benson, okay?"

Devon led Kent into a room that looked like an electronics shop. The workbenches accommodated impressive-looking test equipment and a wondrous assortment of tools, storage compartments and unidentifiable contraptions. "Look, Kent," Devon began. "My understanding is that what you need to know about are the little people-to-people gems that affect longevity, limited to the items you can pack around with you through customs, etc., without raising suspicion. That sound about right to you?"

Kent laughed. "You know, Sam, I spent the last couple of weeks keeping alive without even the benefit of Rolaids. Hell, a rusty jackknife would look good to me."

"Okay," Devon said with a slight smile. "But I kind of hate to hold back on the good stuff. We'll start with this little gadget," he said, pulling open a drawer. "I call this one the Tiny Tim." He held up what looked like a ballpoint pen. "World's most innocent-looking blowpipe," he said proudly. "Carries a dart so small and so sharp, the victim doesn't know he's been hit."

"It kills him?" Kent asked.

"Not unless a medical team fails to arrive within twenty seconds," Devon said dryly. Then he showed Kent how to arm the device and use it accurately. "We've got some genius in the lab . . . been working on gene-splicing and all that. Says he's working on a chemical agent capable of dart injection with this blowpipe—" At that point Devon interrupted himself laughing. "It's a delayed-action deal. Victim doesn't realize what's happening to him, but within about three days he finds his sexual preference changing. Suddenly he finds himself cozying up to one of our dudes. Then of course, our options widen."

"But isn't this kind of research, this kind of monkeying with genetic materials—"

"Illegal?" Devon asked, almost laughing about it. "You are new here, aren't you?"

"And if the victim is a woman?"

"Curiously enough, it doesn't seem to have the same effect, and we don't know why."

"How in hell did you find out what effects it would have?"

"Sorry, Kent. My security clearance is only top secret. They wouldn't even tell me that. Okay, let's move along. This little item here is called the Buster Brown. Looks just like an ordinary wallet, right? Okay, what it's got inside, other than the routine kinds of things you'd have in your wallet, is six ounces of a plastic explosive and a hundred fifty tiny buckshot pellets. Lethal as hell within about five feet. Working this zipper here starts the fuse, and you've got either two seconds or twelve seconds depending on which direction you pull the zipper."

"And you can carry it through the metal detectors in the airport?"

"Right. The buckshot is spread all around inside the explosive so that it doesn't form a solid mass like a gun would. We tried using plastic pellets, but they just didn't produce the kill success we were looking for. Nothing like old-fashioned lead for pellets."

"What do you use it for?"

"Operations folks asked for a short-range hand grenade. That's the two-second fuse. The twelve-second fuse provides the option of planting it on somebody, then getting the hell out of the way."

"Very nice," Kent said. "What else do you have?"

"Just getting started. Okay. This is a tin of aspirins you can carry in your pocket. Most of them are the real thing. All look alike to you?"

"Yeah, I guess so," Kent said, peering into the little box.

"Look closer. Two of them have a tiny dimple right in the center. Those have been treated."

"Let me guess," Kent said. "If I screw up, I take one and it's all over, right?"

"Not quite," Devon said. "What you get is instant epileptic seizure, grand mal type, one each. Pretty nifty, what?"

"Truly a marvelous achievement, but why in hell would anybody in his right—"

"An escape mechanism. Produces dramatic convulsions . . . guaranteed to draw a crowd when you really need one. One of our guys used it recently to get an airliner turned around on the taxiway."

"He didn't want the plane to take off?"

"Ice on the wings. Flight attendant wouldn't listen to the passengers. So he popped a pill. Next thing he knew they had him in the airport dispensary."

"The airplane finally took off okay?"

"Yeah, but they de-iced it first, he found out later. We've got simulated-heart-attack pills too, but they're pretty risky. Too much like the real thing. We mainly use those on other people."

"How do you guys go about developing stuff like this?"

"We don't," Devon said. "We got people in the FDA picking up on the big drug companies' fuck-ups. Okay. Now this here comes as a kit. Pills and powder, or just PP for short. You take the pill first, wait at least an hour, then put the powder on your palm. Shake hands with the victim, then pretty soon you get to watch the blood start to pour out of his ears."

"Pass," Kent said. "What's next?"

"Electronics," Devon said, leading Kent into an adjacent room. "You remember the old Dick Tracy wrist radio? Well, in its day, that was visionary stuff. Now we're far beyond it. For example, this cute little device is a transmitter-receiver designed for surgical implant behind the ear. Two-year battery. The on-off switch actuates when you whistle a four-forty A tone, even for a hundredth of a second. So if you happen to be tone-deaf, you just make like a slide whistle. You can even change frequencies by pinching your nose and applying pressure to the eustachian tubes. You don't have time for the scar to heal, so forget this one."

"I can live without it," Kent said.

"We can fix you up with one of two models that are fairly popular right now. This one is the eyeglasses–hearing aid model. It's reliable, powerful and easy to use, but of course can be detected if you're searched. By the way, it has a self-destruct switch with a forty-second delay. This other one is a real dandy, a triumph of miniaturization."

"That's not an Oreo cookie?" Kent asked in amazement.

"That *is* an Oreo cookie," Devon said, popping it into his mouth. "*This* is the radio," he said, opening a small box. "A Chapstick for the men, a lipstick for the ladies. You talk into it while you're using it. The electronics are about the size of a pea, built right into the middle of it. It's sound-activated and fixed-frequency. Improper disassembly destroys the electronics. There's no receiver. It's designed for line-of-sight transmission, and if needed you can get an acknowledgment by hand signal."

After two hours of gadgetry, Kent was given two hours of familiarization with conventional weaponry. Then came four hours on use of disguises and covers. At ten P.M., he was told to get six hours of sleep and be ready for more beginning at four. The next day's instruction, which lasted until ten P.M., included training in clearing his path to avoid being successfully followed, encoding simple messages, dropping messages or materials, undergoing hostile interrogation, rigging and disarming explosive charges, and other subjects. On the third and last day, he was instructed in how to kill or disable people using commonly available items such as a pencil, a peeled banana, a roll of toilet paper, a woman's high-heeled shoe, a necktie, and even a candy bar.

Then Malcolm Bartledge had him whisked away to a house in the Virginia countryside for last-minute preparations with what they were referring to as the O-Team.

Friday morning's *Washington Post* didn't yet have the news of Kent's reappearance in McLean. But on Saturday morning, his picture was back on page one with a story that began:

KENT BACK, BREAKS UP MCLEAN PARTY
Arnold Kent, alleged slayer of at least six Soviet foreign agents and fugitive from justice in both Spain and Italy, made a surprise appearance at a fashionable McLean wine and cheese party Thursday night. According to guests at the home of William and

Frances Whiting at 6525 Westridge Drive, Kent made
a dramatic appearance and quickly became involved
in an altercation with an unidentified guest who fled
the scene after diving out a window. The unidentified man, believed wanted for questioning, apparently escaped authorities reported to be on the
scene. Whiting, 58, said that Kent was slightly injured in the fracas, and left immediately after the
incident. The Post has been unable to contact Kent,
a U.S. Forest Service employee in the agency's Washington, D.C., office, and Forest Service authorities
said they have no knowledge of his whereabouts or
recent activities.

When contacted by the Post last night, a CIA
spokesman issued a standard statement that the
agency does not comment on current situations that
may or may not involve agency personnel. Officials at
the State Department say they have no information
on the case.

News media coverage during the next three days consisted of rehashes
of the entire incident, invariably adding that Kent had again slipped out
of sight. Some writers, frustrated with the utter lack of hard information, were advancing the theme that unauthorized covert operations
were being conducted, and that the entire matter should be brought out
into the open for public scrutiny. At Kent's office, co-workers kept their
transistor radios handy to catch the hourly news broadcasts. They had
enshrined Kent's office, covering his ugly steel desk with a huge American flag, and draping red, white and blue crepe paper from corner to
corner of the room. On the walls were gaily painted WELCOME HOME
signs, a WE'RE LOOKING FOR A FEW GOOD MEN poster, and even one
from World War II featuring Uncle Sam saying LOOSE LIPS SINK SHIPS.
So many of the agency's eight hundred or so Washington office employees were trooping in on official time to visit "the shrine," that the deputy chief for administration issued a written edict forbidding entering
the offices of that staff group except on official business. Several other
Department of Agriculture agencies also warned their people to stay
away. Wags from the BLM, BIA, Fish and Wildlife Service and other
"sister" agencies took delight in calling their cohorts and asking if this
was the "Central Forest Agency," or sometimes, the "Forest Intelligence

Service." To the thousands of civil service bureaucrats shuffling through endless boring paperwork, the Arnold Kent case was the greatest thing to happen since Watergate.

Aleksandr Korolenko sat behind his ornate oak desk in a third-floor office of the Russian embassy in Rome. As usual, the desktop was clear except for the telephone, a neat pile of papers, and a tray with a pitcher of water and a glass. He was rereading for the third time a message that had been delivered from Colonel Feliks Kratkov in Madrid relaying the reported appearance of Kent back in the United States. This possibility seemed absurd to Korolenko, and his first thought was that the CIA was shoveling out a line of disinformation aimed at scuttling their plans for the navy headquarters. There was no way, in his thinking, that Kent could have slipped out of Rome without his knowing it. But still . . . where was he, then?

The young colonel knew his sparkling career was inching onto shaky ground, but he didn't dawdle long contemplating defeat. He had faced adversity like this before, and knew that the boundary between failure and success was often a narrow one, one that could be leapt over with sufficient intelligence and energy. It was only a matter of a few hours before he would be confronted by his superiors in Moscow, asking him to clarify reports they undoubtedly were receiving about Kent's appearance in Washington. Inasmuch as he could not, in fact, state precisely where Kent was, this would probably lead to a KGB conclusion that their plans had been compromised. Therefore, in those few hours it would be his job to prepare a bold revision in the plans for Operation Oltraggio that would capitalize on *Glavniy Vrag*, the "Main Enemy"'s probable calculation of Soviet intent with regard to the navy headquarters near Naples. The revision would mean that many things would have to be done in the space of a few days, not only in Italy, but also on the part of collaborators in Yugoslavia. He was confident that he could gain the support of his superiors, and set to work immediately.

Korolenko's staff didn't yet know that Kent had got out of the country, only that they had muffed their assignment. They were staying out of Korolenko's way, pretending to be chasing down important leads in the city. Korolenko let it stay that way for the time being, not wanting the clods in his way anyway. Soon enough he would give them their new assignments, ones that he knew they would perform with expectation of being shot if they failed.

There was a subdued knock on his door, and Major Orlov Myaznikov entered. Korolenko looked up at him without elevating his head, his expression one of impatience and disdain. He waited for the major to speak.

"Comrade Colonel, our surveillance team reports that the Spanish bitch is still at the American Embassy, and since her arrival there has had a private meeting with the ambassador. Our information is to the effect that she is being treated with respect and that her report has been taken seriously."

The young colonel only nodded. This report was indeed bad news, but it provided solid information that he badly needed. He got up and paced around the room, then sat back down, composed himself, and said to Myaznikov, "All right, Major. Now we have an assignment for Lieutenant Colonel Vera Vlasov."

"I am certain—"

"Silence! I don't give a runny shit what you're certain of. Now, as I was saying, Vera can have this one last chance to redeem herself. As a matter of fact, it will also be your last chance to redeem yourself. So if I were you, Major, I would be very decisive in issuing the appropriate instructions to her."

Myaznikov opened his mouth to ask a question, then closed it, deciding to wait.

"Simply stated, Vera is to personally, I repeat, personally penetrate the embassy grounds and remove the Spanish woman alive and deliver her here. This is to be accomplished within the next twenty-four hours, Major, and remember, I am holding you directly responsible for results."

Myaznikov was nodding his understanding, but it was obvious by his furrowed brow that some things troubled him about getting this job done. He tugged at his shirt collar, swallowed hard and said, "Yes, sir. However—"

"Get out!" thundered Korolenko. "Twenty-four hours!"

When the major had retreated into the hallway, Korolenko kicked the door shut with a bang and sat back down behind his desk. If the Vlasov bitch succeeds, he told himself, several new opportunities would thereby materialize. First off, he would have in his hands one of the two fish that needed punishment for their atrocities against his comrades and his state. Second, he would be able to quickly ascertain how much both she and Kent had found out about Operation Oltraggio, and what had become of that information. Finally, wouldn't she make a fine piece of bait for a trap into which the vile American Kent might yet be lured? He began smiling at the prospect.

CHAPTER FOURTEEN

The Lockheed C-141 Starlifter touched down at the Italian airbase in Pisa shortly after dawn and then taxied back to the ramp where an unmarked tan van awaited. Four men in civilian clothes climbed down a ladder from the huge plane and walked to the van. Then the aircraft taxied for departure.

The van headed immediately for the main gate of the airbase where it halted long enough for the Italian captain, who had been riding in the right front seat, to get out and wave the vehicle on its way.

"Who's the driver?" Kent asked Malcolm Bartledge.

"Alessandro Bovio. Alex, meet our man Bruce Bennett," he said, winking at Kent. "Alex is a native of Rome, and the guy we mainly rely on to do our talking for us, find our way around, keep us alive, all that good stuff."

Bovio was in his early thirties, dark-haired, with a mustache, prominent nose, and a good smile. He looked back over his shoulder at Kent. "Welcome, Bennett. I know about you from your last trip over here," he said, laughing. "The vodka-drinkers are still looking for you. I think you have a pretty good price on your head. And how the hell are you, Mal? Haven't seen you for more than a year. Thought maybe they clipped your wings."

"Naw, they let me out on good behavior every year or so. Anybody brief you yet on our scam?"

"Sort of. They sent me here to pick up a team of auditors to look at the embassy's financial management. I guess that's you guy's, right?" he asked with a chuckle.

"That is correct," said Bartledge. "And we'll probably have to do the same thing for the navy in Naples."

In addition to Kent and Bartledge, the O-Team included Joe McCord and Vince D'Amico, both agency regulars, both fluent in Italian. Their mission had been defined two days earlier in Virginia. D'Amico and McCord would proceed immediately to the navy headquarters near Naples, where they would tie in with navy brass and organize a countersabotage effort. They would also lay groundwork for a surprise evacuation of personnel, in case that became necessary. Meanwhile Kent and Bartledge were to meet the CIA station chief at the U.S. embassy in Rome and attempt to unearth sources in the city who could shed light on the plot. While not having been said directly, it had become evident to Kent that the KGB's interest in him would be the magnet essential to this strategy.

The navy was not yet acknowledging that there might be a threat to the headquarters compound, or the Naval Support Activity, as it was officially known. Preliminary reports, based on CIA information, had been sent by navy headquarters at the Pentagon to headquarters, Sixth Navy at Agnano. The reports alluded to a possible security breach that threatened, at a minimum, the central administrative facility, and potentially, the entire compound. Admiral Carl C. Hixon, commander in chief of the Sixth Navy, was initially very disturbed at the report. But after conferring with his staff and the chief security officer for the base, he had concluded that there was minimal possibility of such a breach, and that the report was likely based on disinformation aimed at lowering morale at the facility, masking other subversive operations or both. However, Pentagon brass got his okay to have D'Amico and McCord pay a call and discuss their evidence with him.

The men napped during the four-hour run to Rome. Vince D'Amico sat next to Bovio in the front seat, and got caught up on KGB activities around Rome. Kent watched the Italian landscape zip by, reflecting on his train ride along a parallel course only a week and a half earlier. Since then he had not been together with Cristina; they had only touched briefly when she passed him the note on the Spanish Stairs. He couldn't wait to see her at the embassy, and now it would only be a matter of another hour or two. Did she know what had happened to him since she saw him abducted in the Villa Borghese? Did she know he was now on his way back from the United States and about to take her in his arms? Should he take off the phony mustache, or let it mystify her, along with his slick-looking new suit? He dozed off again, grateful for the opportunity to make the minutes disappear quickly.

Cristina del Barrio awakened feeling better than she had in a week. It was Tuesday, six days after her "crash" from what the doctor said was simple exhaustion and stress. Embassy staff had made a room available for her in a building behind the embassy structure where the contingent of marines and other live-in staff were also housed. Mary Tompkins, an embassy translator, had been shopping for her and now for the first time in more than a week Cristina had presentable, clean clothes to wear, and some comfortable shoes to go with them. It was ten in the morning, and Mary came to accompany Cristina to the embassy PX, situated on the compound toward the rear of the property. Del Barrio looked forward to selecting some basic cosmetics and other personal items. She was unaware, as were even the security personnel at the embassy, that the entire northwest side of the compound was being watched from an apartment window of a building on the Via Boncompagni, the avenue skirting that side of the embassy compound. Normally, the embassy would not be concerned about that possibility, inasmuch as that portion of the grounds accommodated only the PX, the post office, the gardening shack, and some walkways. Anyone could walk into that area off the street and not be challenged by guards.

The two women had been in the PX for about ten minutes, and had become separated as they browsed among the book racks, displays of foodstuffs, bottled goods, clothing and gift items. Del Barrio was reading the label on a bottle of perfume when she became aware of a smaller woman standing very close to her. She felt she was being scrutinized, and slowly turned her head toward the woman. The jolt of shock and surprise froze her in horror; it was the face again, the one she had seen first in the wrecked car in Spain, then again in the Villa Borghese. There was no mistake. The Soviet's mouth was a tight little line of grim determination and resolve, her dark eyes little more than narrow slits below thinning eyebrows devoid of makeup. Her cheeks were sunken, her little jaw thrust forward. It was a face that would intimidate most men.

Del Barrio lowered her gaze to the woman's hands and saw the small but lethal-looking pistol the woman clutched in her right hand just inside the open jaws of a handbag. There was nobody else nearby. The Spaniard waited for her to speak.

"I have absolutely nothing to lose," the Soviet said. "If I fail, I will be executed. You will do exactly as I say, nothing more, nothing less. Any attempt to attract attention to yourself will result in your death on the spot. Do you understand?"

Del Barrio glared at the cold, dark eyes, appraising the woman. Was she bluffing? What would be the consequences of being abducted by her? Should she take her chances here and now, or look for a way out later?

"Do you understand?" Vlasov repeated impatiently, but still with her voice muted against being overheard.

Del Barrio slowly nodded, noting that the Soviet stood just far enough away that she could not be grabbed suddenly before getting off a first shot.

"All right. You will walk out of here the way you came in, speaking to no one. You will walk directly toward the Via Veneto, and then turn right on the sidewalk. I will be either at your side or right behind you. Now move."

Del Barrio turned toward the store entrance, her eyes scanning the place for Mary or anybody else. But it was like a bad dream. Everyone was busy looking at items, writing things down, or had their backs turned. It was a clear, straight shot right out the front door. She thought about bumping into a display of wine bottles, knocking them over, attracting attention. But now the Russian woman was right behind her, ready to put three or four bullets into her back, and there was no doubt she was willing to do it without a second thought. She had no choice but to walk out of the PX and down the curving walk through a garden toward the street. There was only one small consolation in letting herself be taken so cleanly: nobody else would be getting hurt because of her.

She quickly formulated a plan of action, and she knew it might be her last chance. When they reached the sidewalk along the Via Veneto, she would jump into the busy thoroughfare and take a chance on being hit by a fast-moving car. That would be better by far than a hideous death by torture in some dirty basement at the Russian embassy. Or perhaps it would be a lengthy and showy trial in Moscow at which she would be found guilty and committed to a Siberian work camp for twenty or thirty years.

Now they were only ten meters from the sidewalk. Vlasov was to her right and a step behind. In three seconds, she told herself. Three or four quick steps, then into the street. *Now!* she said almost aloud and made her move, hoping the first car to hit her would have a moment to hit the brakes first. But what happened was even worse. Before she took her first step off the curb, she felt a strong arm catch her firmly around the waist. She was held tight against a man's body. In a matter of a few seconds, as she writhed against his superior strength, a car pulled to the curb beside them and she was hurled into the backseat, the man alongside, and Vera Vlasov in the front seat talking to the driver in rapid Russian. Del Barrio was crushed down out of sight at the man's feet, her world having just caved in again, and this time maybe for good.

At exactly nine o'clock, Admiral Carl C. Hixon, irritated at having to come ashore over what seemed to him an unimportant matter, entered the small conference room in the building accommodating Naval Support Activity headquarters. He slammed the door behind him, his signal for those present to come to their feet until he bade them be seated. He glanced around the room quickly, noting an empty chair.

"Where's Johnson?" he asked of nobody in particular, glancing at his Rolex to confirm that nine A.M. had indeed arrived.

Nobody answered. A few of the officers were aware that Captain Johnson had called in sick that morning. But they were also aware that to offer any excuse to the admiral would bring a stinging rebuke for not having made sure that Johnson's next-in-command would be present. Nothing argumentative could be offered the admiral by a subordinate without fear of a verbal lashing. And so, like a team of obedient sled dogs, the staff did the "old man"'s bidding, no more, no less, and tried to stay the hell out of his way. Nobody could decipher the source of Hixon's sour nature. He had a distinguished service record dating back to the waning days of World War II. He credited his underlings fairly for good work, and had the reputation of advancing the careers of those officers who served him well. But he was considered a hip-shooter. On having an issue broached to him, he would without hesitation announce his view, thereby casting it in bronze for all time, even if the presentation of additional facts should reveal his first decision to have been a wrong one. His staff soon learned not to alert him to an emerging situation until they could give him the complete picture in writing, even if that meant a significant delay. They also learned not to be the harbinger of bad news, keeping in mind the adage about shooting the messenger.

Hixon's isolation from reality was compounded by his on-shore secretary, a female warrant officer who had the impression that her prime function in life was to shield the old man from all intruders, including representatives of the media, the Congress and even his immediate subordinates. On one occasion she had physically restrained a rear admiral bent on seeing the fleet commander concerning movement of hostile warships in the Mediterranean.

Morale at the base among the officers was understandably low, and descending. Most affected were the more senior officers; their intake of spirits was noteworthy, as were their requests, generated through indirect channels, for transfer to some other post. To *any* other post.

One exception to this rule of hiding from the admiral and not making waves was in the person of Lieutenant Commander Harold Scheer, second in command for base security. Scheer did not have frequent contact with the admiral, inasmuch as he stayed ashore and reported directly to a Captain Bryan Rosewell, chief of base security. But he didn't miss any opportunities to greet the old man, pass along useful information or volunteer to run errands. Such brass-polishing would have been scorned by Scheer's peers, had it not been for the young officer's pure guts: he was the only one in sight willing to take the old man on regarding the merits of whatever issue was up for discussion. War veterans in blouses with four, five and six stripes on their sleeves would blanch in awe as the young lieutenant commander would tell the admiral he was wrong about something, then stand his ground under the old man's withering stare and explain just why. It was said the admiral would never tolerate that from anyone of higher rank or more years. Maybe the old man had a special tenderness toward youth and inexperience, the discussion went. It was clear that Hixon was stung repeatedly by the young man's interventions, but for unknown reasons he never banned Scheer from standing in for his boss at the staff meetings.

The main agenda item at this meeting was base security, and so Captain Bryan Rosewell had chosen to bring along Scheer. Rosewell idled away most of his office hours calculating the amount of his retirement pay and the number of work hours remaining until he could begin collecting it. Details of the base security situation were getting beyond his attention span, and he increasingly relied on his subordinates for needed data for response to questions from higher authority. Things had come to the point at which Rosewell feared attending one of these meetings by himself, simply because he realized he no longer understood what the fuck was going on around him. This greatly amused Scheer, and it gave him much greater room to be innovative and influential. He was ready at any moment to detail existing base security measures or to recommend changes.

Admiral Hixon despised small talk, regarding it a waste of time and a revelation of a fear of confrontation on main issues.

"Well, God damn it, I expect full attendance at these meetings," he began, looking directly at his base commander, Rear Admiral Ian Mac-Pherson. "Where the hell is that overpaid officer who's supposed to take Johnson's place?"

MacPherson caught the eye of a yeoman seated at a desk to take notes, and nodded at him. The sailor went out the door.

"All right," Hixon said. "Base security."

Everyone looked at Captain Rosewell to see if he was paying attention, and if so, how frightened he might look.

"Pentagon advises we may have a problem here," Hixon began. "They say the intelligence types have stumbled on some sort of a scheme to run us out of here like the marines were run out of Beirut. They can't specify details such as exactly when this might happen, who all might be involved, or just how the hell they expect to carry it out." Hixon let that sink in for a minute while he went through all the elaborate preparations necessary for firing up an expensive cigar. Nobody ventured to ask any questions at this point.

"Rosewell, you're still awake, aren't you?" There were some subdued chuckles from the others, and Rosewell's upper lip was quivering as he tried to decide whether to smile or not.

"Captain, bring us up to date on what you've accomplished for base security since Beirut. You know, like what have you done for us lately?"

Rosewell was already beginning to panic, his hands trembling and mumbling sounds beginning to burble out of his mouth. Lieutenant Commander Scheer gave him an elbow in the arm and shoved an open binder in front of him. Rosewell managed to read the itemized list of actions taken, and, as he stumbled through them, it was obvious this was his first look at the document. He even registered surprise a few times, as if the item were news to him.

Hixon glared at the captain sidewise, his mouth curled and eyebrow raised in an expression of contempt and disdain. Most of the other officers seated around the table avoided eye contact with one another for fear of bursting out laughing. All of them had seen the list weeks earlier when it was first endorsed by the admiral and routed around headquarters. Scheer put on an air of agreement and support, nodding his head thoughtfully as his boss read along haltingly. It was obviously Scheer's work, and everybody knew it. Rosewell finally got through it, and looked up at the admiral for some sign of approval or acknowledgment. But there was neither.

"You never could read worth a damn, Rosewell," the admiral said. "Anyhow, so much for ancient history. The question was, What's been going on lately, like in the last two weeks? You were here during that time, were you not?"

"Yes, sir. What's been happening is that, since these actions were taken, I've been evaluating their effectiveness." Rosewell glanced at Scheer, hoping for a sign of confirmation. But the younger man was staring at the pad of paper on the table in front of him, trying hard not to start laughing.

"And what have you found out, then?" asked the admiral.

"Well, sir, there hasn't been time yet for a complete analysis, of course. However—"

"However, nobody has succeeded in blowing up the compound yet, is that it?" said the admiral. If Hixon had said it smiling, everybody would have howled in merriment. But his face was a giant scowl, and all the officers gritted their teeth and looked sideways at Rosewell, wondering how in hell he could have victimized himself so effectively.

Hixon was remorseless. "I'm concerned about air defenses. Explain to me that item about distinguishing between friendly and hostile aircraft approaching our location."

Rosewell hastily located the item in the binder and began to read it aloud again.

Hixon raised his huge fist, then slammed it down on the table with a force that rattled the walls and started the framed pictures of famous warships oscillating. "God damn it! How many times do I have to listen to you try to read that thing? Will you for Christ's sake close the fucking goddamn binder and tell me from your knowledge, limited though it obviously is, what the hell it means?"

At that point, Rosewell was in such a state of shock he couldn't even remember what day it was, let alone what the item he had just read said. His lips were quivering again, but no sounds were coming out. Scheer was ready to fill in, glancing rapidly back and forth between his boss and the admiral, waiting for a cue. He didn't want to see this go on any longer, but the admiral was enjoying it too much.

Hixon leaned back, took a long drag on his cigar and sent a blue plume of smoke wafting into the silent air. "Okay, Rosewell, I know you haven't had much time to work on all this, what with all your other responsibilities, which are . . . ?"

It was another gut shot from the admiral. "Base morale, sir," Rosewell said.

"Well, I won't ask you what you've done about *that* lately. You probably don't have that list with you, and then you wouldn't be able to read it to us anyway. But tell me this, Captain. If you were to retire from this outfit on the very first day of your eligibility, what would your monthly annuity amount to?"

Everybody saw this one coming except Rosewell. "Thirty-one eight-five, approximately, sir." All the officers shook their heads in dismay.

"Thank God," said Hixon. "And here I thought you'd been sitting there at your desk doing nothing all this time. This meeting's about over. I may be getting sick. As I stated earlier, after I meet with these . . . gentlemen . . . tonight, we may have some things to do. Meanwhile, if they approach you, you are to treat them civilly, and discuss with them anything within your particular sphere of responsibility. You will not, repeat not, get outside your own area or volunteer general information or opinions you happen to hold. Is that clear? All right, meeting's over. Scheer, I want to talk to you in my office."

A delivery truck pulled up to the main gate of the Naval Support Activity compound and the driver held out a sheet of paper to the armed marine. The sign on the side of the truck said INSTALLAZIONI MORONI, and the marine smiled at the driver as if he recognized him on sight. He glanced cursorily at the paperwork, then waved the vehicle to a parking area just inside the gate. Another marine approached the truck, looked at the same paper, then went around to the rear end and climbed into the truck bed. The driver accompanied him and, on request, pried open the lid of one of the twenty-four wooden boxes that filled the truck. The guard looked inside the box, nodded his head, then jumped down off the truck and waved it on.

"Toilet bowls and tanks," he told the other marine, logging the delivery on the clipboard. "Same outfit that was here a week ago with all those fuckin' washbasins and urinals."

"They know where to take 'em?"

"It's right there on the delivery order. Looks like a coupla boxes for every goddamn building on the compound."

"You look inside the boxes?" said the first marine, a sergeant.

"Just one of them. They're all the same, just wooden boxes all nailed shut. Look like they just came out of the factory."

"Well, I don't know. You remember what the lieutenant said about inspecting deliveries."

"Oh, fuck the shit-ass lieutenant," said the corporal in disgust. "Who the fuck is going to off-load every goddamn truck that comes in here and open every fuckin' box. Let the shit-ass lieutenant come down here and supervise the shakedown if he's so goddamn concerned about it. Anyway, I seen that same outfit come in here a dozen times in the last coupla months. Fuck the shit-assed lieutenant."

The sergeant didn't carry it further; he too had seen the Installazioni Moroni truck come and go a number of times. What the lieutenant had ordered was simply unreasonable, even if the order had been signed, as it had, by Captain Bryan Rosewell, chief of base security. The sergeant didn't even know who Captain Rosewell was, never having seen him before.

The van pulled up to the side gate of the embassy compound shortly after noon, and before the heavy steel gate was rolled open, two marine guards looked into the van and checked the passports. Once inside the main embassy building, Kent and his companions declined a lunch invitation, explaining they had stopped for a bite in Viterbo. While they were waiting for Fred Dawkins, the CIA station chief, Kent asked the protocol officer about Cristina. He was shocked by the look of concern on the woman's face. She studied him a few moments, then said, "How is it you know —"

"We all know about her," said Alessandro Bovio.

"Well," she said, "it's something that has everybody here very concerned. We don't know exactly what's happened yet."

"She's not here?" asked Kent.

"She was here this morning. She went to the PX with Mary Tompkins, one of our translators, then simply disappeared into thin air. Nobody even saw her leave."

Everybody stood silent for a moment, evaluating the story, not being able to think of any rational scenario.

"Did she have a passport, any papers on her person?" asked Bartledge.

"No, a passport was being prepared for her. As far as we know, she didn't even have a purse or wallet with her. Mary was going to buy cosmetics and things for her."

"Well, is anybody looking for her, or doing anything to . . . ?" asked Kent. His stomach was beginning to tighten up and he felt a little bit dizzy.

"Where's to look? What's to do?" asked the woman, turning up the palms of her hands and shrugging her shoulders in a gesture of helplessness. "Our security people have searched the compound, questioned everybody around the PX, post office and grounds."

"Is the PX accessible to, let's say, somebody coming in off the street?" asked Bartledge.

Bovio answered. "Yes and no. There's a guard shack between the Via Veneto and the PX, but they don't necessarily challenge everybody. Their job is mainly to politely tell strangers wandering around that they're technically on embassy grounds, and that the PX and the post office are for employees and their families only. If any outsider got through, and that wouldn't really be too difficult, they wouldn't be permitted to buy anything without a red or a black passport, or a PX card."

"So what's the supposition about her disappearance?" asked D'Amico.

The protocol woman again shrugged. "No idea. Clayton Oliver is handling it. He's telling us she just walked off. Said he figured she'd do something like that."

"Why did he say that?" asked Kent.

"Maybe you'd best ask him," she said, heading for the door.

When Dawkins showed up, they were all introduced by Bovio, then led into a small conference room.

"Before getting into things," said Bartledge, "we're all concerned and curious about this del Barrio disappearance. What's your slant on it?" Dawkins was in his early forties, and he seemed to be squinting out at his visitors from behind thick, rimless glasses. He was neatly dressed in a gray suit without vest, his hairy wrists protruding from his coatsleeves. "Wish I had one," he said. "Didn't meet the woman, so it's hard even to make a guess."

"We picked up that your Mr. Oliver, whoever he is, wasn't surprised," Bartledge said. "Any idea what that means?"

"He's the regional security officer. Apparently, the two of them didn't get on too well when she first came in here the other day. I understand through the grapevine that he more or less tried to brush her off after hearing her story. So she insisted on seeing the ambassador, and somehow got her way on it. I take it Oliver got his tail chewed by the old man later."

"Let's hypothesize she got abducted," said D'Amico. "Not likely, but possible, right? They have plenty of motive, like revenge, bait for a trap, going after what she knows, right? So their next move, what would it be?"

"Yeah, okay," said Dawkins. "Far as I know, they're still in the dark about Kent, that is Bennett, here."

"You mean, that I never got out of Rome?" asked Kent.

"Yeah. They'd play that through just in case."

"Meaning they'd need to contact Kent somehow. But how?" said Bartledge.

"Tedeschi," said Kent. They all looked at him. "Salvatore Tedeschi, my friend in the Corpo Forestale. "When I first got here, I called him and the KGB guys were already sitting on him, waiting for my call. He's scared shitless, and would probably do anything they asked in order to protect his family."

"Not bad," said Dawkins. "Any other ideas?"

"Golino," said Kent. "Colonel Golino's father, the old guy that runs that store where I ran into Carlo Marasco. Then two locations they would think about; places where Cristina and I tried to rendezvous.

Spanish Steps and the Piazza del Popolo. We also have another rendezvous point they don't know about."

"Where is it?" Dawkins asked.

"You don't need to know that, it's a family secret," Kent said in a mocking Sicilian brand of Italian.

Kent glanced at Bartledge, who sat there with a smirk on his face leering at Dawkins.

"I'm beginning to see why you brought him along," Dawkins said. "He related to the Gambinos by chance?"

"If you're looking for a way to get this thing started," Kent said, "give me some backup, and I'll check out the possibilities."

Dawkins sat tapping the eraser end of his pencil on his desk for a few moments. Then he said, "Well frankly, we haven't been able to stumble on anything even hopeful looking around town. Those clowns have really put a lid on it. Tell you what. As I understand it," he said, looking at D'Amico, "you and McCord are heading out for Agnano this afternoon, right? Okay. Bartledge and Kent here can have Alessandro and whatever else I have that they might need. I'll set up a separate phone number here, and we'll call this the main contact point. Think that will meet your immediate needs?"

"We'll need radio communications," said Bartledge. "Small stuff."

"Yeah, we can do that too," said Dawkins. "What else?"

Kent spoke up. "How did they find out Cristina was here at the embassy?"

Dawkins got an annoyed look on his face. "Speculation on my part: they've likely got somebody in here. Obviously we haven't been able to root it out. By the way, Kent, or Bennett, you're in here on a faked-up assignment specifically designed to thwart that kind of penetration. That little conversation you all had with our protocol lady is not especially helpful, you know. She's all right, take my word for it. But I did have to tell her to keep a clamp on it."

"All right, gentlemen," said Dawkins. "Bovio here will be my representative on this program, but it's your show. Standard rule applies: you guys are on government business, but not diplomats. If anything goes sour, we'll treat you just like any other government employee who got crosswise with the locals. You know, transport the body back to wherever your wife wants it, that sort of thing."

"Air freight, I hope," said Bartledge, winking at Kent.

"Right. Nothing but first class," said Dawkins as he stood up and stuck out his hand. "You guys deserve it."

Kent's first call that afternoon was to Salvatore Tedeschi, and he was told by an associate at the ministry of agriculture that Tedeschi was sick and had been hospitalized for an indefinite period. When Kent asked about the nature of the illness, the respondent said he was unable to give out the information.

Kent called Tedeschi's home, and was told by a woman that the family was out of town, and they weren't accepting any calls, period.

Kent then called the elder Golino at his store. He identified himself, and asked if there were any messages for him. The response was that he never gave messages or other information over the phone. "But is there a message?" Kent persisted. The old man simply hung up. It sounded at least like a possibility.

Kent and Bartledge selected clothing from a wardrobe maintained at the embassy for visitors who needed to look Italian. They both picked out casual street outfits that were neither too pretentious nor too downscale, but definitely Italian in cut and fabric, right down to the shoes. Then Alessandro Bovio checked out an embassy car, one licensed as a normal Rome passenger car, and pulled up in back of the embassy compound. Then they drove the two miles to the Tiber and cruised past the Golino market. Everything looked normal. On the second pass, they found a place to park a half block away. Kent smoothed his fake mustache and slipped on the noncorrective horn-rim glasses. Then he and Bartledge got out of the car and walked past the store while Bovio waited and watched.

A dozen steps past the store, Kent said, "Looked like a couple of customers in there. What say we step inside, look around at stuff until they leave?"

"You go in, Kent. I'll hang around outside with this newspaper. If you hear me whistle, head out the back way."

Kent stepped inside and began looking at merchandise on the shelves. In a few minutes he was alone in the store with the old man.

"It's me, the American," Kent said, removing the heavy-rimmed glasses.

The old man squinted at him for a minute, then nodded. He leaned forward across the counter and said in a low voice, "The woman . . . the Spanish woman wants you to meet her."

Kent waited for him to continue. He looked afraid and his voice was tight and dry-sounding. "Where?" Kent asked.

"At the Porta Pinciana, at ten tonight."

"Who told you this?"

"She sent a messenger. I did not know him. Now please go. I am in great danger with you here."

"When was the messenger here?"

"Only an hour ago. Now get out of here quickly."

Kent went out the front way and headed for their car, Bartledge not far behind.

"They've got her, the bastards," Kent told the other two men as they drove away. "Supposedly, she wants me to meet her tonight at the Porta Pinciana."

"She wouldn't have suggested that on her own?" asked Bovio.

"She would have simply asked me to meet her at the agreed place. She was warning me away."

"Meaning that if you go there, you get introduced to the Russian army," said Bovio.

"And even if you don't, they now know you're in Rome," added Bartledge.

"Well, it's what we wanted, isn't it?" asked Kent. "How else will we get a chance to pick off somebody who knows what's going on down at Naples? Not to mention getting Cristina back."

Bartledge and Bovio said nothing as they drove along thinking about it.

"What kind of help you think we can get from Dawkins?" Bartledge finally asked Bovio.

"I've found him to be very resourceful, once he's convinced you've got a valid plan with a good chance of payoff. He'll take the risks, give you the horses. But first he's gotta be convinced."

"So, what've you got in mind, Kent?" asked Bartledge.

"The Soviet bitch," Kent said.

"What?"

"The one that chased me around Spain, then ambushed me in the Villa Borghese."

"Figures," said Bartledge. "She'd be the one they'd have to recognize you, then two or three hairy-armed ones to give you the heave-ho. You suggesting we try picking her off, bleed her for information?"

"Not at the moment, anyway," said Kent. "She's too tough, too smart to give us anything worth taking seriously."

"What a put-down," said Bovio. "And after all the money we spent on our new chemistry set."

"Anyway," said Kent, "they're probably figuring by now I won't be coming alone. Bovio, they know what our people look like?"

"Not a problem. We do disguises real good. Better than Halloween, yet. And if you want some special skill we don't have, we can hire it. So what's your plan?"

"Okay," said Kent. "It's fairly devious, and a bit on the risky side."

"We do devious," said Bovio, leering into the rearview mirror. "But what's this risky shit?"

"Like I'll do it myself if you guys aren't interested," Kent said.

"Be cool, man," Bovio said. "Hell, what are friends for?"

CHAPTER FIFTEEN

It was a windy and chilly evening in Rome, and the sidewalk cafés and bars along the Via Veneto, normally well-populated at nine, were mostly vacant and being closed for the night. Merchants were lowering canvases around their streetcorner newsstands, and shopkeepers had already lowered steel gates over their store fronts and were turning out lights. It was a night when the tourists went straight back to their hotels from supper, and even the pimps and streetwalkers had given up for the evening. It was a night on which anybody standing around in a public place would draw attention by their presence, and it gave Kent an eerie feeling just thinking about it.

The three men timed their first pass by the ancient gate of Porta Pinciana at five minutes before ten. Bartledge was driving, Kent in the right front seat, and Bovio manning the radio in back. As they turned the corner from Via Campania onto the Via di Porta Pinciana, Bartledge took it slowly so Kent could recon the area. He saw no one just standing around. They turned up a side street, parked and waited a few minutes. A last-minute radio check provided no new information from the two other CIA vehicles cruising the area. They drove back toward the historic gate that separated the developed area from the Villa Borghese. A block from the gate they stopped, and Kent got out. Bovio handed him a bag of groceries with a loaf of bread sticking out the top. "Remember, think Italian," he told him with a wink.

Kent pulled up the collar of his cheap dark-colored coat and pulled the cap down low over his fake glasses. He felt nervous and charged up, an uncomfortable feeling, but one he somehow relished. He went over the plan in his mind as he made his way down the street. When he spotted the Soviet woman, he knew what he would have to do. But would he be able to recognize her, not make a mistake? And could he prevent her from recognizing him, at least for the first few precious moments? He put the thoughts out of his mind, leaving these things to his instincts.

Walking northward along the Via di Porta Pinciana, he scanned his environment, looking for human shapes in doorways, parked cars, or standing at bus stops. Everything seemed normal. Then, as he passed the entrance to the Lombardia Hotel he glanced into the lobby. Nothing unusual, just two desk men shooting the breeze at the main counter. Then he saw the woman sitting on a divan next to the wall in the lobby. As he strode past she turned her head in his direction. He only got a quick glance, but there was no mistake. To his shock and surprise it was not the Soviet woman, but Cristina del Barrio.

It terrified him. She was not supposed to be there. Instinctively, he didn't react, but kept walking, his head pointing straight ahead, his eyes searching the shadows to each side. This wasn't foreseen. The plan was off. It was time to improvise. When he reached a point about forty meters past the hotel lobby he activated his eyeglasses radio and reported to Bovio and Bartledge what he had seen. There was a silence, then the response: "Suggest you find a secure observation point and wait for developments. Don't make an approach. We'll be standing by."

Stand by for what? he asked himself. He pressed the transmit button. "I'm going into the lobby and check it out," he said, knowing that, as usual, he was jumping into another alligator pond.

As he approached the hotel again, he could see that the lobby opened into a dimly lit adjoining room to the right. If somebody had Cris under guard, they were likely in that room. So he switched his bag of groceries to his right arm to shield his face from that side, the loaf of bread brushing against his cheek. He walked boldly into the lobby and up to the desk. Now there was only one clerk, and he asked how he could be of service. Kent stood only about five or six feet from del Barrio, and he was sure she would be able to recognize his voice, even as he spoke Italian. He would know in seconds if she were free or captive at that moment.

Kent asked whether a Mr. Aprilanti was registered there. He slowly turned his head toward del Barrio as the clerk checked the list of hotel guests. She showed absolutely no sign of recognition, merely continuing to stare out at the street. Then, turning half toward the dimly lit room on the right, he could discern an ominous-looking man in a dark suit staring directly at him.

The clerk was saying something about nobody by that name, but Kent's attention was riveted on the dark suit now moving toward him, his hand in his overcoat pocket. Then he could see yet another man beginning to appear out of the shadows. He heard del Barrio say clearly, but in a very calm, quiet voice, "Look out!"

Still clutching the grocery bag, Kent extracted a pen from a shirt pocket, pushed a tiny switch on the clip, then put one end in his mouth. He turned directly toward the first man and gave a quick little puff. He saw the little dark spot appear on the man's forehead: a perfect hit. The man stopped in his tracks, a look of bewilderment coming over his face, and then simply fell forward into the lobby.

The second man, a younger guy in a leather jacket and a short hair-cut, was momentarily stunned by the older man's fall. After a moment, he looked straight into Kent's face as if trying to decide if this was the quarry. Kent looked back at him, shrugging his shoulders in an Italian way, and showing that he had nothing in his hand but a pen.

"How many of them?" he said in English, not taking his eyes off Leather Jacket.

"Two inside, two outside," she said.

He glanced toward the street, but could see no one. The clerk, think-ing the Soviet had stumbled, came rushing from behind the counter to give help. Meanwhile, Leather Jacket had figured things out and was pulling a pistol from his waistband. Kent saw it in time and lunged into the clerk, driving him into the Soviet, and the three of them went to the floor in a heap. Kent, on top, scrambled to his feet first, stamped hard on the Soviet's gun hand, dislodging the weapon and producing a loud grunt from the agent. Kent grabbed the pistol, whirled around, grabbed del Barrio by the arm and made for the stairway, just left of the main desk. They bounded up the narrow passageway, taking the stairs three at a time.

Colonel Aleksandr Korolenko was standing by his car across the street with Orlov Myaznikov, and they saw the whole thing.

"Get in there fast," Korolenko told the major, "before one of those idiots calls the police. Move!"

Korolenko then picked up his radio and ordered two units standing by in the area to move up to his location. They did so immediately, and he gave them new orders.

When Bovio and Bartledge learned Kent was heading into the hotel, they alerted their other two units, then hurried there on foot. As they rounded the corner onto the hotel street, they saw the two men by the car across the street, then saw one of them run into the hotel.

"That broad-shouldered guy by the car," gasped Bovio. "Korolenko. He's their big gun here."

"Then they did bring their army," said Bartledge.

"Maybe just a battalion. They've probably nailed Kent by now. You think if we confronted them—"

"Forget that idea," said Bartledge. "There'd be a war out here. Anyway, you underestimate Kent, and the Spanish lady apparently isn't all that shabby either when it comes to good old-fashioned grab-ass. Let's just sit tight and be ready to jump in, if and when."

The two Americans watched in fascination as two carloads of obvious KGB agents arrived, got orders from Korolenko, then marched into the hotel, almost as a group. Two of them stayed in the lobby, the other six, with Major Orlov Myaznikov leading, heading up the stairs. Korolenko and two other men remained by his car across the street, a position that offered a view of the hotel's fire-escape ladders.

Kent and del Barrio got to the third level above the lobby and raced down the corridor. The only door open was that of the chamber maid, and they dashed inside. The maid was sitting at a little table drinking coffee and smoking a cigarette. She jumped up when they entered.

"Don't be afraid, miss," Kent told her, "but there is a fire on the second floor. Can you sound the alarm?"

"Yes, yes, the alarm!" she screamed, rushing out the door into the hall.

"It won't stop them," del Barrio said, grabbing his arm tightly. "They're unbelievable bastards."

"What? And I thought you liked them. Quick. Find me a big wastebasket full of trash. Let's make this realistic."

They found what they needed right there in the maid's cleanup cart. At about that moment the fire alarm began wailing from a dozen horns around the hotel. Guests began pouring out of their rooms in pajamas, underwear, and a few in tuxedos and evening gowns. Kent dragged the maid's cart into the open door of a room on the street side of the hotel. He ripped the trash container off the cart, hauled it into the bathroom and dumped the contents into the tub.

"Matches! Matches!" he shouted. Del Barrio found some on a bed-side table and socked them into his outstretched hand. In moments, smoke was pouring out of the bathroom. Then Kent seized a chair and broke out the window. As he hoped, air pressure from the hotel's heat-ing system forced a stream of air through the window, carrying with it the choking smoke from the bathroom bonfire.

Kent looked around for del Barrio and, not seeing her, rushed into the hallway. She came hurrying out of an adjacent room in a silk dress-ing gown, her hair pulled down loose, and barefooted.

"Take off your clothes," she said.

"Really? Right now? I was thinking maybe later—"

"Get the hell in there and put on the guy's robe, dummy, before we're the only ones left in here."

When they reached the stairway, there were so many people coming down from the upper floors, they had a difficult time crowding into the stairway. Now the guests could smell the smoke and many of them were becoming hysterical. Some were shouting "*Calma, calma!*" trying to slow things down, to avoid anybody getting crushed or trampled, but those few were nearly drowned out by the general commotion.

Hanging onto each other, the pair became part of the crushing flow of human bodies down the stairwell. The Soviet agents had just begun working the first level above the lobby when the alarm sounded, then realized they would have to try to screen the guests coming down the stairs. But they lost that battle in moments and simply got pushed back-ward down the stairs into the lobby along with everybody else.

By the time del Barrio and Kent got to the lobby, two policemen were on the scene trying futilely to break up the traffic jam that had already blocked access to the approaching fire engines. Even in that maelstrom of humanity, the Soviet agents were obvious to Kent simply because they were facing the crowd instead of the street. He almost laughed as he looked at them: wide-eyed, pissed off, obviously distressed and con-fused. The Russians appeared not to even give a second look as del Barrio and Kent surged ahead, their heads shielded in their hands, feigning coughing from the smoke.

As if by a miracle they stumbled into Bartledge and Bovio just away from the hotel, and the two agents had trouble recognizing them.

"It's us!" Kent said to them with a grin. "How do you like the new getups?"

"Smiles and shit later," Bartledge said. "This place is alive with the slime, including Colonel Korolenko. Get into the back seat of that Citroën by the corner and I'll see if we can squeeze our way out of here."

Traffic was still tied up, and cars were having to exit the hotel street one at a time. A police officer was directing the flow, but a bit farther down the line, somebody seemed to be checking into each car with a flashlight.

"Uh-oh," said Bovio from the driver's seat. "That ain't the carabinieri down there checking cars out."

"There's two of them," said Bartledge. "One on each side, looks like."

"You sure they're not plainclothes police?" said Kent.

"Can't tell from here," said Bovio. "No way to know until they're right on top of us. But I doubt it. Look at the bastards, flashing their lights right in everybody's face."

"I would suggest orthochlorobenzalmalononitrile," said Bartledge. "What do you think, Alessandro?"

"Perfect. Glove compartment."

The two men approached the Citroën simultaneously, one on each side. "Identification papers!" ordered one of them. The moment he opened his mouth it was obvious he was not a native Italian. Before the next full second had elapsed, each of the KGB agents had been sprayed in the face with a model M-120 police magnum Mace cylinder, and the French sedan sped away leaving the agents rolling around in the street clutching at their faces with both hands.

"Shit!" Kent said, looking back through the rear window. "We just missed a chance to grab one of those goons. How the hell are we going to find out—"

Kent stopped short when he felt del Barrio give him an elbow to the ribs. He shot her a glance and saw her sly smile. "We don't need them," she said. "Major Myaznikov was careless enough to leave his jacket where I was being interrogated. While he was out of the room I got a look at something in one of the pockets. We need to get to Naples fast."

*   *   *

"I'm Vince D'Amico, and this is Joe McCord, sir. We appreciate
your cooperation."

"Come in, gentlemen. You too, Scheer," said Admiral Carl Hixon,
waving his visitors to a leather couch in base commander MacPherson's
handsomely appointed office. "Lieutenant Commander Scheer here is
standing in for Captain Rosewell, our chief of base security. Rosewell is
an asshole."

D'Amico and McCord glanced at each other, then at the young officer, who seemed to be nervously brushing lint off his trousers.

"Now, those people in the Pentagon seemed to be convinced I've got
some kind of a security problem here, but wouldn't discuss it with me
further," Hixon said. "Instead, they persuaded me to hear it from somebody who apparently is a hell of a lot better informed than anybody in
the U.S. Navy. If that's you people, I would sincerely appreciate knowing, within the next thirty seconds or thereabouts, just where the hell
I've fallen down on my job." Hixon reached up with his left hand and
unbuttoned the top button on his white shirt, never taking his eyes off
those of D'Amico, who sat directly opposite him.

"How long have you been in the Mediterranean?" asked D'Amico
without blinking an eye.

"What, if anything, does that have to do with it?" Hixon thundered.

"Well, Admiral, if you've been here in charge for, say, five years, you
can't expect me to fully answer your question in just thirty seconds."

It took the admiral a moment to recall just how he had worded the
question. He stared hard at the civilian for several seconds. "Spare me
the goddamn fencing match and get on with it."

D'Amico gave him a five-minute summary of events, along with the
CIA analysis of their implications. He concluded by stating that the
most likely scenario involved a direct attack using high explosives to
destroy all or part of the NSA complex.

The admiral almost laughed in his face, but restrained himself. He
turned toward Lieutenant Commander Scheer with a sarcastic smile
and said, "What do you think, Commander, is that possible?"

"Yes, sir," he said, surprising the fleet commander. "Are you ruling
out use of chemical and biological agents, Mr. D'Amico?" Scheer
asked.

"Not at all. We're just talking probabilities. At this time, even the most radical Arabs are frowning on those weapons for terrorism, mainly because they understand the magnitude of the backlash that would be unleashed against them. Use of high explosives, on the other hand, seems to them like a game of tennis."

"What about aerial attack?" Scheer wanted to know.

"Too high-profile," said McCord, speaking for the first time. "They can't manage logistics on that scale without the world finding out who's behind it."

"Look," said Admiral Hixon, "I can understand how you types at Langley can pick up some weird rumblings, then concoct a scenario that would make Beirut seem like a cocktail party. Then somebody in the Pentagon makes the usual assumption that we're all sitting on our duffs over here enjoying the benefits for which this country is renowned, and fails to give us any fucking credit for being able to do our jobs or pay any attention to what the hell is going on around us. I'm sorry, gentlemen, but you just haven't said a goddamn thing that impresses me for sour owl shit, and frankly—"

"I'm not so sure, Admiral," said the younger officer, cutting off the fleet commander in midsentence. The admiral, astounded, sat there with his jaw hanging open at a forty-five-degree angle. D'Amico and McCord, both former military officers, concluded instantaneously and independently that the young man's naval career would likely be a short one. But at least for this fleeting moment, they were holding him in extremely high regard.

"Since Beirut," Scheer went on calmly, "we've overhauled our entire security system. What happened at the embassy or the marine barracks isn't going to happen here. We know it and they know it. That's why we've got to anticipate some new means of penetration."

Hixon had managed to get his mouth closed, but opened it again. "Such as?"

"That's exactly the point, sir," Scheer said. "We're never smart enough to figure that out before it happens. That's why we've got to take this seriously."

"And you regard yourself as more serious than I am, young man?"

"No, sir. Nor am I as experienced or as knowledgeable. But neither am I arrogant nor obstinate." He made the statement in an unemotional but firm manner, his eye contact with Hixon unrelenting.

The admiral's face reddened noticeably as the two men stared at each

other, the old bull of the pasture challenged by the yearling. "You saying to my face that I'm arrogant, mister?"

The younger officer let three seconds tick by, perhaps wondering
what life as a civilian would be like. "With all due respect, yes, sir."

It was deathly quiet in the room for what seemed to Lieutenant Commander Scheer like several months. Finally, the admiral shook his massive head slowly and said, "You know, young man, that's exactly what
my wife tells me." Then he threw back his head and laughed uproariously. Everybody laughed with him except Scheer. Then the admiral simply turned toward the two civilians and said, "Gentlemen,
exactly what do you recommend?"

It was midnight, and there was considerably more activity than usual
in the U.S. embassy on the Via Veneto. Bartledge, Bovio, Kent and del
Barrio were sitting around a long coffee table with Fred Dawkins in his
office. Del Barrio had again been outfitted with clothing from the embassy's supply.

"Now then, Miss del Barrio," Dawkins said. "This delivery schedule
you got a look at . . . how much can you recall from it?"

"You know, I didn't have a whole lot of time, as it was clear the major
was only stepping out of the room to find his cigarettes. Anyway, I had
seen a subordinate hand him a paper a few minutes before, and he was
probably going to destroy it after reading it. It was a copy of a delivery
schedule on the letterhead of an Installazioni Moroni. There were five
or six delivery dates specified over a period of several weeks, and the last
date on the list was November third, that is, today. Or I should say,
yesterday," she said, glancing up at a wall clock.

"What, exactly, were the items being delivered, and where on the
base were they to be delivered?" asked Dawkins.

"'Installazioni fissi dal gabinetto,' it said. Bathroom fixtures. I
couldn't tell anything else about the delivery, except it was stamped
'delivery completed' at the bottom."

They all sat there for a few moments thinking about it. "Jesus
Christ," said Bovio. "Why would a major in the *Komitet Gosudarstven-
noy Bezopasnosti* give a flying fuck about a toilet delivery to the Navy
base . . . unless?"

"Five or six deliveries, you said?" asked Bartledge.

"Yes."

"Any idea what size truck, number of items, weight, anything like that?"

"No, sorry. There wasn't time."

Bartledge glanced at each person. "Folks, I don't think there's a hell of a lot of time to waste."

"I would agree," said Dawkins. "I can alert their base security right now."

"Let's think about that for a minute," said Bartledge. "If the folks on base panic, get into a flurry of activity, somebody might decide to trigger the stuff."

"Well, just what the hell alternative is there?" said Dawkins. "For all we know, they might be timing it for seven in the morning."

"All I'm saying is that we don't want them to panic. Yeah, I agree, they need to know. Can you suggest they sample the containers right away? Shit, maybe they've already opened them and installed the stuff, and there's nothing wrong with it."

"The KGB wasn't looking at delivery orders for entertainment purposes," Kent said. "Could be the first few deliveries were legit to establish an innocent pattern. I'd recommend a discreet but immediate evacuation of all personnel except the security types."

"Such a decision would be up to the fleet commander, or the base commander of course," Dawkins said. "But I agree with the idea. Meantime, is there anything that can be done through this . . . Installazioni Moroni outfit?"

"We want a shot at it," said Kent, gesturing at Bovio, Bartledge and del Barrio. They all looked at each other and began nodding.

"All right," said Dawkins. "I'll get base security alerted. Then, first thing tomorrow morning we can get together here and—"

"Negative," said Kent. "We're leaving now."

"Okay, then," said Dawkins. "I'll see if they're finished with Miss del Barrio's new passport. Anything else?"

"Yeah," said Kent. "Get somebody on duty and next to a phone at our consulate in Naples. When we get there I'm going to be asking how to locate and recognize whoever runs this Moroni plumbing outfit. One other thing. I could sure use some spare nine millimeter rounds for this Russian pistol."

*   *   *

The phone rang at about one A.M. in the off-base residence of Captain Bryan Rosewell, chief of base security. He had sucked up three or four double Scotches after supper and didn't hear it for the first twelve rings. Finally, he hauled himself out of bed, found the lamp, then stumbled over to the phone. "What the hell is it?" he said.

"Sorry, sir," said a voice. "U.S. embassy, Rome. Says it's urgent."

"It damn well better be. Put the bastards on," he said, squinting at his digital watch.

"Fred Dawkins, station chief. Sorry to awaken you, Captain."

"Yeah, I'll bet. What's this all about?"

"Did our men D'Amico and McCord bring you up to date this evening?"

"D'Amico . . . McGraw? I don't even know who the hell you're talking about."

"You know, the guys we sent down this afternoon to talk with you folks about the base security problem?"

"Oh, yeah. Well, I haven't seen them. The skipper said he was going to talk to them himself. I wasn't invited. Maybe you better talk with him about it."

"Yeah, well I wasn't able to get through to him. Listen, Captain, this is pretty important. We think you've got about four or five truckloads of high explosives stashed on the base."

"Are you serious? Shit, we've got a hell of a lot more than that. We got a whole goddamn ammo dump here. Everybody knows that, for God's sake."

"No, no. Listen. I'm talking about stuff you're not aware of. Stuff hauled in and labeled toilet fixtures and who knows what else."

"Oh, Jesus Christ. One a-fucking A.M., and some wino prankster wants me to shake down the goddamn heads for bombs. Who the hell are you, anyway?"

"All right, Captain Rosewell. Tomorrow morning I will personally contact Admiral Hixon and tell him you refused to cooperate in an emergency threatening the lives of everybody on the entire base. I have recorded this conversation, so that if you should survive this emergency, the recording can be played at your court-martial."

"Listen, you son of a bitch. I don't even know who the hell you are, and I'm not about to evacuate this base on this kind of a report. You can shove your recording up your goddamn ass."

"Captain Rosewell, why don't you look up the number of the American embassy in Rome, give us a call, and ask for Fred Dawkins. Tell the operator it's code forty-three, and they'll put you through. If I don't hear from you in fifteen minutes, I'm calling the base commander. Do you have his number?"

"Yeah, let's see . . . it's . . . Shit. I can't read this stuff without my glasses. Why don't you just ask at the base switchboard? Anyway, I can't do anything like that without authority from higher up. Why don't you just call him now and get it over with?"

Colonel Feliks Korolenko transmitted a coded order to all his officers on the scene to secure operations and regroup at the Soviet embassy, leaving Major Orlov Myaznikov to deal with the police regarding the body of the slain Soviet agent in the lobby of the hotel. While last evening's mission had broken down severely, Korolenko accepted it as only a temporary setback. He had not yet decided whether Kent and del Barrio had outsmarted him by staging the fire to cover their escape, or whether it was just a lucky break. What bothered him the most, however, was simply not knowing whether the thrust of the Naples plot had been calculated by the Americans. This meant, in effect, that the project had been compromised and that a quick decision needed to be made.

Once inside his embassy office, Korolenko phoned his station chief in Naples and was told everything with regard to the project appeared to be normal. Inasmuch as open discussion on the subject was inadvisable, he concluded from the remarks that the explosives were in place, and that detonation would be possible as previously scheduled, that is, as early as the day after tomorrow. He advised his man that the schedule might have to be moved up twenty-four hours, and to make whatever arrangements were necessary to accommodate that change. Then he called Vera Vlasov into his office. She came in looking somewhat haggard and gray.

"I'm sorry you missed all the excitement last night, at least inside the hotel, but you must have seen it from a distance."

"Yes, Colonel," she said. "When I heard the fire alarms I guessed what was happening. So you see, I'm not the only one to fall victim to the American weasel and his Iberian consort."

The colonel smiled, expecting such commentary. "Indeed, Vera Vlasov. But yet, according to my notes, you have fallen victim five or six times in succession, and after all, you were a part of this evening's fiasco. But I did not call you in here to scold you again, even though that would be well deserved. I called you in here because maybe we can learn from your repeated failures. You must be getting to know this Kent fellow pretty well by now, and the Spanish whore as well. What do you think they will do now?"

Vlasov pulled cigarettes out of her purse and lit one. "Comrade Colonel, it is you who has at his disposal all the local intelligence reports. They undoubtedly went immediately to the embassy after disabling two of your clowns. Haven't you had that confirmed? Perhaps you should be asking, what will the officials at the embassy do?"

"I'm having that appraised at this very moment. What I want is your intuition."

"First of all, from what I've been able to learn in the last couple of days, the bureaucratic Americans are not reacting to the imminence of events going on under their noses. That will be entirely obvious to Mr. Kent, who, I have learned, knows how to make things happen fast. I have drastically changed my opinion of him, and now understand he is perhaps one of the Americans' foremost and most capable operatives. Disguising himself as a plodding forester has enabled him to make absolute fools of us. Unless I am badly mistaken, Kent, Miss del Barrio and undoubtedly other CIA agents will be heading for Naples early this morning in an attempt to head off our planned event."

"And what do you think they'll do when they get there?"

"There are two avenues. One, of course, has to do with the headquarters complex itself, with security precautions there. Not having been told of the details of the plan, I cannot evaluate that avenue further."

"And the other avenue?"

Vlasov frowned as she sucked on her cigarette. "Uncovering local knowledge of your collaborators."

"Our operations have been highly restricted. He wouldn't have time, unless he had something fairly tangible to go on."

"Maybe. But you asked for my intuition, and it is that Kent either already has something tangible, or will get it, and probably by this morning."

"Let's say the possibility exists," Korolenko said. "If so, that would have to be in connection with our delivery people. They have been highly paid to be discreet, and made aware of the consequences of being otherwise."

"When will their services no longer be required?"

Korolenko laughed. "Orlov tells me the deliveries have been completed. But it is too soon, because the Americans would become suspicious if they tried unsuccessfully to contact them with regard to the merchandise."

"How many of them are aware of the real nature of the merchandise?"

"None, to my knowledge. That's the beauty of it. The switch was made in a Yugoslav warehouse in Split, and not even those people knew where the stuff was going."

"So you have no need to deal further with the people of the Naples delivery firm?"

"Yes, but only as a precaution, and at the appropriate time."

"Then I don't follow what you have been telling me, Colonel. Why was it necessary to even contact the delivery people, not to mention paying them handsomely and requiring their being discreet?"

"Vera, you are a very tiring person, and you don't at all understand the Italian businessman. It is practically standard practice here to steal expensive imports before delivery, replacing them with similar, but much cheaper merchandise. Therefore, it was necessary to explain to them that the Yugoslav fixtures had been exchanged in Split for vastly inferior Russian stuff, and that the Yugoslavian merchandise was headed for the Kremlin. Under no circumstances were they to open the crates, or to make reference to the swap. Now, in view of all that, what can the CIA make out of that in one or two days?"

"I don't really know, Colonel. But the longer these Moroni brothers are around, the less secure you ought to feel."

"You think Kent and company might track them down?"

"I'd like to be there when they do, and you understand why."

"Are you ready to leave right now?"

"Yes."

"Good, because with your record of failures, I wouldn't think of leaving you unsupervised in my jurisdiction. If I find an assignment within your limited capacity, perhaps you'll be given your opportunity. Our vehicle will be leaving the garage at precisely one fifteen. That's twenty minutes from now."

"Colonel, it's about a two-hour drive. What are we going to do at three fifteen in the morning in Naples?"

"For one thing, that is the only time of day suitable for reviewing the major streets of the city. For another, it is a good time not to be observed or followed leaving our embassy. Finally, it is an excellent time to learn what our competitors may be up to. If you're concerned about getting your beauty sleep, you began worrying about thirty years too late. Now if you'll excuse me, I have some preparations to make."

At two twenty A.M., a black Mercedes-Benz sedan with diplomatic plates of the Soviet embassy passed a tan-colored van with Italian plates on the autostrada near Cassino. The driver of the van turned his head toward the sleepy passenger in the right front seat and said, "You see that?"

"Yeah. Dumb bastards never have learned to travel incognito."

Kent, coming awake in the backseat, said, "Was there a woman in there?"

"Looked like there was," said Bovio. "Friend of yours?"

"Yeah. She's been trying to date me for weeks. I think she lusts for my body."

"Kind of confirms things," Bartledge said. "I mean, why we're busting our ass getting down here early. I hope the hell Dawkins got the job done with Admiral Hixon. He's got at least one thousand sailors there every day. God knows how many civilians."

CHAPTER SIXTEEN

Fred Dawkins poured himself a fourth cup of coffee as he sat alone in his embassy office on the Via Veneto. After failing to reach the commanding officer of NSA, he tried several other numbers in the chain of command. In each case, he was told, the officer could not be reached at that hour despite whatever emergency might exist. In two cases, the phone rang unanswered. In another, it was answered by a domestic who claimed not to understand either English or Italian. Finally, Dawkins asked the base switchboard operator to give him the officer of the guard.

Lieutenant J. G. Farwell came on the line.

"Farwell, this is Fred Dawkins, security section, American embassy in Rome. This is an emergency concerning your base. I want you to confirm who I am by calling the embassy and asking to speak with me. Tell them it's Code forty-three. Do you understand?"

"What's the nature of the emergency, sir?"

"It's life-and-death. Please call me immediately."

Two minutes later Dawkins' phone buzzed, and Lt. Farwell was on the line. Dawkins quickly summarized the situation, emphasizing that large quantities of high explosives were believed to be in place on the base and could likely be detonated at any time.

"Sir, I was alerted by Lieutenant Commander Scheer last evening that such a possibility existed, and understood that action was underway."

"What action?"

"Well, he said, there were two CIA men on base suggesting a search be made throughout the compound, and that we were cooperating with them."

"Is a search in fact being made now?"

"I haven't heard any more about it, sir."

"Well, was there any discussion about an evacuation of personnel?"

"Evacuation? No, sir. There's nothing like that going on, no orders issued. Have you been in contact with Captain Rosewell? He's in charge of base security."

"He was my first call. He wasn't at all responsive. Listen, Lieutenant Farwell, I wasn't able to reach the base commander, his exec, or any other high brass down there, and this Rosewell fellow went back to bed. In my view, all of your night duty personnel are at this moment at high risk of being blown sky high or by some other means wiped off the face of the map. You need to get into immediate, I say immediate, contact with the base commander and give him our concerns. He may wish to evacuate personnel, and frankly, that would be my recommendation."

"Well, sir, my assumption would be that the skipper would already have been informed about all this by your men last evening. Is your present concern based on new information that he wouldn't have yet?"

"Lieutenant, I have absolutely no way to know what he's been told. And by the way, where exactly are our two men right now? They haven't talked to you about this?"

"No, sir. I haven't even seen them."

"Let me get this straight. You're the officer of the guard tonight, and you have no indication there's a search going on right now? And would you necessarily be aware of it if there were?"

"Sir, I've already made two motorized patrols around the base to inspect the guard. There's nothing going on, just like every other night around here. There's not been a single report from a posted guard concerning any unusual activity. If a search is in progress, it's a damn well concealed one, sir."

"Where would our men D'Amico and McCord be staying tonight?"

"At the VOQ, that is, if they stayed on base. If they went off base, they could be anywhere in the city."

"Is there some hotel where visitors are usually booked?"

"I wouldn't know about that, sir."

"All right, Lieutenant. Priority one, get in touch with the admiral right now and relay my message. Priority two, shake down the VOQ for D'Amico and McCord, and tell them to call me. I'll be at the same number all night. Your actions during the next hour could result in either saving or losing the lives of everybody at that goddamn base. Do I make myself clear?"

Lieutenant Farwell rang the number of the Admiral MacPherson's residence and got no answer. He grabbed his driver and they jumped into a jeep parked outside the guard shack. Their route of travel took them by the Visiting Officers' Quarters, so Farwell dashed inside and awakened the petty officer sitting behind the counter.

"Officer of the guard, sailor," he told him as the man jumped to his feet. "You got a coupla civilians here tonight, a D'Amico and a McCord?"

The sailor consulted his log. "Yes, sir. They're registered in, but neither of them showed up for the night yet, sir."

"You mean they were here, but went out and haven't returned?"

"They stowed their gear in their rooms, sir, then headed out with an officer who brought them here. If I remember right, they were talking about going to some restaurant in town."

"Who was the officer?"

"I didn't get his name, sir, a lieutenant commander."

Farwell glanced at his watch: three thirty A.M. "Okay, sailor. As soon as they get back, have them call a Mr. Dawkins at the U.S. embassy in Rome, urgent." He gave him the number.

Farwell's visit to the base commander's residence was, at least from his point of view, a disaster. It was the admiral's wife who finally answered the door, and she made it clear that her husband could not be disturbed until morning, and that she was quite certain whomever was in charge during the night could make the appropriate decisions regarding any emergency. But a split second before she could get the door closed in Farwell's face, the young officer managed to blurt out, "Yes, ma'am. We're preparing to evacuate all night duty personnel from the base immediately. By your leave, ma'am." He turned purposefully and began striding down the walk toward his jeep.

"Just one minute, Lieutenant," she said through the screen door. "Don't go away."

In about two minutes the admiral, his sandy hair standing out at all angles, came to the door in bathrobe and slippers. Instead of inviting the young officer inside, he came right out on the porch and peered inquisitively at his visitor in the semidarkness of the early morning.

"Now just what in the hell is all this about an evacuation of personnel from my base?"

"Sir, I have received an urgent call from the embassy in Rome stating their conclusion of the likelihood of a major explosion on this base at any moment, and—"

"Lieutenant . . ."

"Farwell, sir."

"Do you realize I've been up to my ears in talk of some goddamned explosion here since day before yesterday, and that, in fact, our security people are shaking the place down at this very moment, and now you come here at 0340 hours to give me this great news?"

"Sir, I am OG tonight, and I can tell you there is no search now taking place on the base."

The admiral peered at the lieutenant for a few moments, wondering whether he was hearing this from a competent officer. "Where is Captain Rosewell right now?"

"Sleeping, sir."

"What about Lieutenant Commander Scheer?"

"Is he the officer who was accompanying the two civilians?"

The admiral nodded.

"Unaccounted for, sir."

"What the fuck does that mean?"

Farwell explained the situation at the VOQ. The admiral just stood there, his hands in the pockets of his robe, his head slowly shaking from side to side.

"Jesus Christ," he said. "Isn't this a hell of an organization I got here? The cream of the navy running the place and they can't figure out how to get through the fucking night without me. Now then, just what was it that got the people in the embassy so stirred up in the middle of the night, some new guy just coming on shift who saw the paperwork for the first time, or do they have something new and dramatic to get worked up over?"

"I can't respond to that, sir. The gentleman I talked to, a Mr. Dawkins, said he tried to contact you personally but couldn't get through. Then he went down the chain of command until he got me. He said it was life-and-death stuff, sir."

"And it was this Dawkins who suggested the evacuation?"

"His recommendation. But he understands it's your decision, sir."

"He got that one right. All right, Lieutenant, you got your job done. Carry on."

"Aye aye, sir. Any further instructions?"

"Yeah, come to think of it. Go down to Rosewell's place and tell him I said to get his lazy ass out of the sack and find out what's going on around here. I want his report on my desk at 0800 concerning everything that's happened on base security during the last twelve hours. Then I want you to find out where Scheer and those two spooks are, and what they've been doing all night. Get back to me on that by 0700. That's all."

It was still dark, but traffic had already picked up along Via Arco Mirelli, where Arnold Kent and Cristina del Barrio sat in a small sedan watching the upper floor of a small apartment house. A man finally came out, got in his car, and drove north to a side street. "That's Moroni," Kent said, following. The man parked behind a shop building and went inside. Three minutes later, Kent and del Barrio were there knocking at the same door. Arturo Moroni, looking a bit perplexed, stood facing the two strangers and asked what they wanted.

"I'm sorry to bother you so early, Mr. Moroni," said Kent, speaking the more northerly Italian of his parents. "We are Americans, and we've been sent down here by our embassy in Rome on an urgent matter related to the navy base at Agnano." Both Kent and del Barrio were smiling, trying to keep it light and friendly in order not to put the man too much on his guard, at least to begin with. He waved them inside.

"So what is it about the navy base?" Moroni asked.

"It's about the delivery of some bathroom fixtures your firm has made recently. You are aware of the deliveries, no?"

Moroni looked at each visitor's face, his own face still registering a question mark. "Yes, of course. We made a number of deliveries. I don't understand. What is this all about? And why at this time of the morning?"

Moroni was a thin, friendly-looking man with a pale complexion and a receding hairline. He wore thick, rimless glasses, and a hairline mustache. He had on a white shirt and necktie beneath his blue coveralls, and gave the first impression of being a professor or scientist rather than a plumbing contractor. His thick, spatulate-tipped fingers were the only outward feature that seemed to match his profession.

"Mr. Moroni," Kent said, "there may not be any problem at all. But we received some information that there is a great security risk at the base, and we are checking out all possibilities."

"So, what has that to do with me, with our deliveries?"

"Probably nothing at all," Kent said, trying to put the man at ease. "We have been told you are an honorable man who runs an honest business. But we need to ask you a few questions about the merchandise you delivered. May we?"

"Of course. Of course."

"You delivered a large number of crates, as we understand it, to several buildings on the navy compound, and these crates contained things like sinks, toilets, and so forth. Is that not correct, Mr. Moroni?"

"We did, in fact, deliver a large number of crates to the buildings, in accordance with the delivery instructions issued to us by your government, Mr. er . . ."

"Bennett," said Kent. "Excuse me. And this is Miss Ochoa."

"And the crates were all marked to indicate they contained the items you have mentioned," Moroni continued. "However, I cannot say definitively what were the actual contents of those boxes."

Kent and del Barrio glanced at each other. "Why not?" asked del Barrio.

"Simply because we were, in effect, asked to act as a forwarding agent. The crates were shipped to us from Yugoslavia, and we were instructed to deliver them directly to the navy base."

"Oh, I see," Kent said, nodding. "And you did not verify that the contents were in satisfactory condition, as most delivery firms would do?"

"Ordinarily, yes," stated Moroni. "But in this case I was instructed not to do so. I suppose the shipper feared we might substitute inferior merchandise for the original contents. It happens all the time, sadly enough."

"Yes, I see what you mean," Kent said. "And in this case, who, exactly, gave you such instructions?"

Moroni tensed up on hearing the question. His face tightened, and he folded his arms defensively in front of him. "I'm sorry," he got out finally. "I'm really not at liberty to give information about my clients. Anyway, is this some sort of official interrogation? I have tried to be friendly with you people, but there is a limit—"

"Mr. Moroni," Kent said softly, "you do not have to tell us anything you don't wish to. And we do not wish to bring this to the attention of the authorities, please believe us. But here is the deplorable situation. We are working against the clock. We have reason to believe those boxes contain explosives, placed there by an enemy of the Americans, who wishes to destroy the naval compound and kill thousands of innocent people. Such an explosion could occur within the next few hours if we are not successful in learning who might be involved and what their intention might be. Can you, as an honorable man, sympathize with our need to find out about this? Can you help us save thousands of lives?"

"Please, Mr. Moroni," said del Barrio. "Their lives may be in your very hands."

Moroni's pulse was racing now, and he was beginning to perspire. He didn't yet understand the depth of his involvement in this thing, but having received a payoff not to talk about it gave him a clue. Thoughts of his wife and children flashed through his mind. Then he thought of a massive explosion on the naval base. He was beginning to panic; he needed time to think.

"Their lives are in your hands," del Barrio repeated.

Moroni wiped the palms of his hands on his trouserlegs. "The shipping agent was a foreigner," he said.

"A Yugoslav?" Kent asked.

"No. I know the Yugoslavs. He was not a Yugoslav."

"A Soviet, perhaps?" del Barrio said.

Moroni looked down, but did not shake his head. "I . . . I am just not certain," he said. But the two visitors didn't even have to glance at one another to know that he was, in fact, certain.

"Mr. Moroni," Kent said. "You have been most helpful, and we will go away and leave you alone. But just one other question or two, if you don't mind."

The Italian gave Kent a blank stare.

"You are in the plumbing business. Do you happen to know who will eventually install all the fixtures you delivered to the base? Will it be some local firm, or will the Americans do it themselves?"

Moroni relaxed a bit at this question. "The Americans? They don't do anything themselves. They always hire things done. They don't know anything about plumbing, that's for sure. Why don't you ask your own people? The American contracting officer could tell you what's going on."

"We just don't have time. Don't you understand, this may be a matter of minutes we're talking about."

"I will tell you this much. When we made the deliveries, we naturally inquired whether we could do the installation. And, as usual, we were told it would all be handled by Fiadini, the guy who gets all those jobs."

"This Fiadini," Kent said. "Where can we find him?"

"Vincente Fiadini. His place is on the Via Francesco Crispi, not two kilometers from here."

"Mr. Moroni," Kent said, "is there anything else you could tell us . . . anything unusual or otherwise that could possibly help us?"

The Italian wrinkled his brow, and his eyes seemed to wander back and forth. "It might not be important," he said, "but I have heard that Fiadini recently has taken on a new man to supervise installations at the base. It seemed strange to us."

"Strange? In what way?" asked del Barrio.

"An outsider. Not from the family, or even from Napoli."

Kent and del Barrio thanked the man and returned to their car. "How do you figure it, Arno?" del Barrio asked as Kent eased the car away in the stream of traffic.

"Well, Fiadini's got to know what's going on, or he's an idiot. Let's get to a phone, find out what Bovio and Bartledge have found out."

They stopped at a pay phone and Kent dialed a number at the American consulate. A woman answered, exchanging passwords with Kent.

"Anything from Alessandro or Malcolm yet?"

"They're at police headquarters. You didn't yet hear about Joe and Vince?"

"No. What is it?"

"It's awful. Their bodies were found about an hour ago in an alley. There was an officer from the base as well. I think he's still alive."

"Oh, shit. What happened?"

"We don't know yet. They were all apparently shot sometime last night. I'm really sorry."

"Damn. Listen, del Barrio and I are en route to the place of business of a Vincente Fiadini on the Via Francesco Crispi. Tell them the bathroom fixture crates were delivered unopened from Yugoslavia, and that Fiadini has a new man engaged to do the installations. Got that?"

"Okay. Everybody know who Fiadini is?"

"Good for you. He's a regular plumbing contractor at the base. He may be involved in this thing. What's going on at the base? Is there an evacuation underway?"

"Not that we know of. Malcolm wants you to call him when you can at 6037412. It's the number of base security. They're heading over there from police headquarters."

Kent got back into the car and gave the bad news to del Barrio.

"The bastards play rough," she said, shaking her head in disgust. "And guess who's next on their list . . . if they can find us. It's beginning to look like their timetable's been tightened up. Where next? To Fiadini's?"

"Unless you have some other idea, Cris. What do you think about a scam to get in touch with this new guy who's working for him? How creative can you be on short notice?"

"I think I could get away with being a messenger from the Russian embassy, maybe with some special instructions for their installations man. What do you think?"

"Let's do it. But you'd better go in alone. I don't think they'd believe I'm really the slovenly Italian I'm trying to portray. What are the special instructions, by the way?"

"Repeatable only to the installer . . . find out where he is. If he's right there, get him outside to talk to him alone."

"Good. Get him on the street, and try to talk him into getting into the car with us. We'll force the issue if necessary. Shit! It's still only six forty-five. Let's hope there's somebody there."

"There's the place, there on the right. And there are lights on," del Barrio said.

"All right, I'll pull up here. And listen. If it doesn't feel right to you, don't hang around. Just start heading down the street to the west and I'll come by. Be careful . . . I love you."

She winked at him, putting a little kiss on his lips, then jumped out and walked toward the shop bearing the name FIADINI in large black letters above the door. Below Fiadini's name, Kent was a bit surprised to see the line that said, LAVORI IDRAULICI ED ELETTRONICI. As he watched her striding down the sidewalk, Kent felt queasy without knowing why. Everything seemed okay at the moment; perhaps it was the D'Amico-McCord tragedy chewing at his insides. In the hurry to get to the bottom of the impending disaster at the base, he hadn't yet even had time to let that one sink in and tear him apart.

Del Barrio knocked at the door of the shop. The door swung inward, and he saw her step inside. Then Ken saw something that unnerved him. About a minute after del Bario had stepped inside, the door opened again, and from his vantage point a half-block away, he saw a man stick his head out and look up and down the street. The head looked familiar, but he couldn't place it for agonizing moments. Then it crashed home: it belonged to one of the men in the lobby of the Hotel Lombardia in Rome, the man whose hand he had tromped during the scuffle with the Soviet agents.

Kent's face went pale, then blood started rushing back upward and his scalp tingled. His first impulse was to charge into the shop, gun in hand, ready to do mayhem or whatever necessary. Then he got a grip on himself, and repeated silently an often-quoted piece of survival logic: Don't do the expected. He started the car immediately, drove past the shop to the end of the block and swung right, looking for an alley. He found it, but drove slightly beyond, then double-parked, leaving the engine running. He jumped out and hurried down the alley, counting the shops as he had done from the car on the main street. On his left there was a row of apartments, their back sides facing the alley, and housewives were gaping at him as they hung out their wash or swept their porches.

Kent was within twenty meters of the Fiadini shop when he spotted a Mercedes sedan turning into the alley from the cross street directly ahead of him. He ducked into the shadow of a masonry wall between two of the apartment buildings. He heard the Mercedes stop behind the Fiadini place. He waited several seconds, then peeped around the corner of the wall in time to see two men in suits go in the back door. He noted that the driver of the sedan remained at the wheel.

He knew what would happen next: they would come out with Cris, get into the car, then speed away to God knows where to interrogate her, perhaps torture her, then get rid of her for good. He thought about ambushing them as they came out. He would have the element of surprise, but would be badly outnumbered and outgunned. And Cris might be used as a shield and it would all be over. What else could he do? Then his mind leaped to the car-wreck tactic that had got them out of tight spots twice before.

He looked around and found some discarded boards about five feet long, picked them up. As casually as he could, he walked out from behind the wall and retraced his steps back out the alley, trying his best to look like a workman. As he walked through the alley toward the cross street, he worked out his plan. First he would back up far enough to see down the alley, then wait until the Mercedes came toward him. Then he would enter the alley and smash into the sedan with sufficient impact to stun everybody inside. Cris would anticipate the crash and lean forward bracing for it. From there, he would take things as they happened.

When Kent reached the end of the alley he glanced back over his shoulder and noted that the Mercedes was still motionless in the alley. Then, as he hurried toward his own car, he saw a boy of about fifteen getting into the driver's seat. Kent broke into a sprint, but it was too late. The car zoomed away into traffic and was gone. Almost panic-stricken, he looked around for a vehicle to commandeer but there was none. So he took the only option left to him: he ran back to the alley and headed toward the Mercedes, gun in hand.

But the faster he ran, the faster the sedan seemed to distance itself from him. The goddamn thing was backing down the alley toward the other cross street, and worse, he could see there were either five or six people inside, two of them women.

By the time he reached the back of the Fiadini shop, the Mercedes had disappeared into the stream of traffic. Panting heavily now, and in a black rage, he went to the back door of the shop determined to kick it in. But he found it unlocked. He plunged inside in a low crouch, holding his pistol in both hands. He found himself alone in a supply room. At first, silence. Then footsteps, coming to see who had entered. He jumped behind the door that led inward from the supply room, his pistol ready. The door swung open, trapping him in a corner behind it. The footsteps marched to the outside door and he heard it being slammed shut from the inside. He pointed the pistol toward the footsteps that were coming back through the supply room. His heart was pounding, and he was sure his breathing could be heard as well.

The door swung away from him, but there was nobody. The door slammed closed from the other side and he was again by himself. He waited a few seconds, then gently opened the door and slid through. Voices were coming out of a nearby room; sounded to him like two men, but they were speaking low and he couldn't understand what they were saying. He eased up to within inches of the doorjamb and listened. Now the voices were audible, but he couldn't get it all. They were talking fast, and it was in the local dialect. But it was about transmitters, detonators, radio frequencies and electronic interference: strange jargon for plumbing contractors. One of the voices seemed to be explaining things to the other person, then they both laughed and exchanged comments Kent could not understand, but that he judged to be crude jokes about what was going to happen as a result of their project.

He could wait no longer, and jumped into the little room. The two men turned their heads toward him, their faces blank. They were both leaning over a table strewn with papers and electronic paraphernalia. The man on the left was a wiry, dark-complexioned person of average height, dressed in coveralls bearing the decal of the Fiadini firm on the right breast. He had a hawkish nose and a thin black mustache that seemed to be twitching on one side. The man on the right was of lighter complexion, with a wide face and sandy hair. He looked square-built and muscular, and was dressed in brown slacks and a beige sport shirt. He did not look like a plumber, or at least was not dressed like one. They remained motionless, their eyes darting back and forth between the American's face and his lethal-looking automatic.

"On the floor, face down!" Kent ordered. The man in the coveralls immediately complied, but the other man didn't move, staring malevolently at Kent, his wide mouth slowly forming a hateful and defiant grin.

"*Non capiso un cazzo,*" he muttered dryly, his Italian crudely spoken. "I don't understand a fucking thing."

"*Non rompermi i coglioni!*" Kent threatened, aiming his weapon directly at the man's chest."

"*Vai in mona di tua sorella,*" he said. "Go to your sister's cunt."

Kent put a 9-millimeter slug into the man's chest. The shot knocked him back against the wall, and he slid to the floor, his face showing amazement and shock. It was an act of impulse that fully startled Kent as much as it did his adversary. Kent pushed the man down onto his face and did a quick pat-down that produced the typical contents of a man's pockets, but no weapons. Then he searched the other man and found nothing of interest.

"You!" Kent said to the darker-complexioned one, pulling him up to a sitting position by the collar of his coveralls. "You will answer my questions this moment, and answer them truly. If you do not answer quickly, I will shoot your hands into splinters. If you do not answer truthfully, your family will be found dead before you can get home to them. Do you understand me?"

The man's face was a portrait of fear. He glanced at the pool of blood flowing from beneath the other man, then quickly nodded.

Talking fast through quivering lips, he told Kent that he was Fiadini and that he and his partner Giulio Petrini had contracted with "these agents" to do what they believed to be a legitimate job. But by the time they discovered what it was really about, there was no backing out, at least if they valued their lives and those of their families.

Kent, continuing to press his weapon against Fiadini's neck, asked, "Who is this man I just shot?"

"Fochner. Eric Fochner. They brought him in to keep an eye on me. He's also an electronics technician."

"And what was the job they had you doing?"

"We installed a high-powered radio transmitter on the volcano. It is concealed inside an abandoned shack."

"A radio transmitter? But you are a plumber, are you not?"

"Yes, *signore*. But we also do electronic work. Anyway, we had nothing to do with the electronics, just the installation of the equipment."

"The transmitter—with whom are they communicating, and why do they need it?"

"We figured out it is not for communications . . ."

"Then . . . ?"

"It is set up to direct a very strong signal at the naval base."

"*At* the naval base? For what purpose?"

Fiadini licked his dry lips and breathed heavily. Kent judged him too frightened to lie convincingly. "I don't know, *signore*. But it is designed to self-destruct after sending out its signal toward the naval base. One can only guess . . ."

"Yes, yes, guess . . . ," Kent encouraged him."

"Oltraggio," he choked out. "I have heard them mention it several times. It concerns forty explosive charges," he added.

Kent eased pressure off the man's neck, repeating the word he'd seen in Cavalchini's original notes: *Oltraggio*. Then he thought about the mysterious deliveries to the base, the ones apparently disguised as bathroom fixtures.

"Fiadini, will you take me to this transmitter and help me disable it? In return, the Americans will help you and your family out of this mess."

Fiadini propped himself up on one elbow and took a look at the limp body of the other man. A pool of blood was forming alongside him. Then he looked back at Kent. "Yes. Yes, I will do it. For the love of God, we must leave quickly."

Kent grabbed the phone on the desk, dialed the number given him by the consulate, then asked to speak with Bartledge. He quickly summarized what he had just learned, then turned back to the task at hand.

Together, they dragged Fochner's body into a closet and locked the door. Fiadini pulled a small rug from in front of the desk and used it to cover the pool of blood, and the two men got into a gray company van parked in the alley behind the shop. The Italian driving, they headed toward the outskirts of town. Most of the traffic was heading inbound, and they were able to make good time. They turned eastward, went past the turnoff to the navy base, and turned toward the rim road that wound around the edges of the ancient, collapsed volcanoes.

Alessandro Bovio and Malcolm Bartledge decided they had fucked up royally by going to police headquarters concerning the slaying of their comrades. Not only were the police in the dark concerning how it had happened, but they insisted on detaining the two agents until they could be questioned formally later in the morning. Bovio and Bartledge finally got loose at the direct request of the chargé d'affaires of the American consulate. They drove directly to the main gate of the naval compound where they found the officer of the guard, Lieutenant J. G. Farwell. Farwell told them the admiral was current on the situation, but that he had not authorized an evacuation of the base, and that the two American civilians D'Amico and McCord had not yet been located.

"They've been located, all right," Bartledge said. "They, along with your Lieutenant Commander Harold Scheer, were dragged out of their car last night and shot."

The young officer was visibly shaken. "Who—"

"The police have no idea, but we do," Bovio said. "Why in the hell isn't somebody getting people out of these buildings? Don't you people understand what the fuck may be going down? We've got a goddamned Pearl Harbor about to happen!"

"Easy, Alex," said Bartledge. "The lieutenant here doesn't have the authority. Listen, son, do you think the admiral knows there's no search going on, that one of his officers and two of our guys were gunned down, that this whole base is a target for destruction, possibly in minutes, or at best a couple of hours? Do you think he knows all that stuff?"

"He's been told, sir. Not about the shootings, we didn't know about that. But the rest of it, yes, sir. He told me to awaken Captain Rosewell, which I did. But since then I haven't heard from him. The admiral will undoubtedly hold a meeting at oh-eight hundred, and then—"

"Shit. There may not even be a place to hold the fucker by then," growled Bovio in disgust. "Lieutenant, you know this base. Where are all the people right now? I mean what buildings, houses, barracks? Can't they be evacuated?"

The officer looked at his watch: about six-fifteen. "There are no houses, sir. And the only barracks is the VOQ. Everybody lives in town or up in the Gaeta compound. But we have people on duty every night, especially right now getting geared up for the fleet exercise."

"How many, and where are they?"

"Well, there'd be about a hundred fifty at the hospital, including patients, about thirty in the O&C building, maybe eighty-five in the supply facilities, fourteen on guard duty, and another twelve or fourteen in the main mess. What's that, about . . . three hundred?"

Bovio scowled. "Okay then, how many people you got coming on duty today?"

"By 0800 hours we'll have at least eighteen hundred on board."

A petty officer came in from the front office of the guard shack and told the lieutenant there was an urgent call. Farwell picked up the extension phone, listened, then said, "It's for you guys."

Bartledge grabbed the phone, said "Yeah, Mal here. Whatta you got?" Then he listened for a full minute, nodding, saying things like, "Okay, okay, got that, yeah, all right, yeah, I can remember that, all right. We'll do what we can from this end, but it'll be slow. Good luck on the hill, buddy. We'll send you any help we can. Be careful." The other two men looked at him with their mouths hanging open.

Bartledge looked at his own watch this time, then said, "Lieutenant, you've probably got about one hour to clear this place out, and I mean OUT. Kent, with our help, has a very slim chance of interrupting the detonation, but nothing to count on. He says even if we're successful, they probably have a backup—a default system, he calls it. Lieutenant, you now have the opportunity to get the width of your second stripe doubled, or lose the ones you already have, along with several hundred lives including your own."

The officer's face was white, his features grim. "The detonation . . . where will it be?" he stammered.

"Make that *detonations*," Bartledge said. "Forty of them, and simultaneous. All major facilities. You now have only fifty-nine minutes, Lieutenant."

CHAPTER SEVENTEEN

O n the way up the tortuous mountain road, Kent had Fiadini repeat several times what he knew about the transmitting equipment, and what they should expect on reaching the transmitter site. Fiadini explained that the transmitter was inside an abandoned goatherd's shack just off the crest of the mountain below the main electronic site that accommodated the transmitters of the U.S. Navy as well as those of several public agencies and private companies. He said the transmitter was quite heavy, and was powered by several large batteries that were built in. The radio equipment had been built into a steel container to be tamperproof, and had to be unlocked even to expose the unit's manual control panel.

"So they have to come up the mountain to the shack in order to activate the transmitter?" Kent asked.

"No. The unit can be operated remotely, from an automobile transmitter. It's a relay setup . . . receives the command on one frequency . . . from the car . . . then the main signal is sent out on another frequency."

"Why don't they just send out the main signal from the car?"

"Not powerful enough, first of all. Then, the transmitter in the shack is positioned perfectly to hit any location on the navy base."

"Well, if the outfit is tamperproof, how do we disable it?"

"Inside the locked panel there's a self-destruct switch, as well as ones to send out either a delayed or an immediate main signal manually. In either case, the unit can be set to self-destruct after fifteen minutes."

"And you know which switch is which?"

"They're not labeled," the Italian said. "But I found out from Fochner's notebook what they are. From left to right, they are the man-

ual main signal, the immediate self-destruct or boobytrap, the cancel
and reset switch, the delayed self-destruct and the delayed main signal
and self-destruct."

Kent repeated them back to the Italian, and he nodded. "You said
your partner was involved in this. Where is he now?"

"He left early this morning to tie in with the agent. He's the electronic specialist in our firm, and they wanted him along in case there
were any problems."

"Any problems? You mean they're planning to send out the signal
today?"

"In fact, this morning," Fiadini answered grimly. "We're getting
close, now," he said as they reached the main crest of the mountain.
Kent could see the antenna masts bristling from a dozen small buildings
positioned around the mountaintop.

"That's the goatherd's shack, right down there below that last group of
buildings," Fiadini said, pointing.

Kent could look back down and see the city stretching out to the west,
the Bay of Naples, ships standing in the harbor, and he could discern
the compound of the NSA not four miles away. The thought of dozens
of tons of high explosives detonating there sent shudders through his
spine.

Fiadini reached across in front of Kent and opened the glove compartment. "We need the key on a brass ring that's in there," he said.
Kent searched and could find none.

"Are you sure? It has to be in there," the Italian said.

"It's not."

"Shit!" Fiadini said. "That bastard Fochner! He must have taken it."

"Who?"

"Fochner. The guy you shot."

"God, you're right," Kent said. "He had a key on a brass ring in his
pocket when I searched him. Is that the key to the transmitter antenna?"

"Yes. We'll have to return for it. To get into that control panel without
triggering the explosive would be impossible without the key."

"Man, we don't have time!" Kent pleaded. "Can't we just drag the
thing out of the shack and send it rolling down the mountain?"

"That case weighs over a hundred fifty kilos, and it's welded to two
axles set into the ground with concrete. I know, because I supervised the

work myself. Anyway, it would explode if we tried to move it. We must go back for the key."

"Isn't there some way? I mean, what if those guys hit the relay from their car before we get back?"

Fiadini thought about it for a moment. "Well, we could slow them down a little," he said, his eyes lighting up.

They parked the van on the crest of the hill, and the Italian rummaged around in the back and came out with a two-foot-long piece of lead pipe. They walked down the hill to the shack and went inside. There was nothing there except a no-nonsense-looking steel case about four feet long, two feet wide, and two feet tall. An antenna about eighteen inches tall sprouted from one end of the case, and a steel cylinder about two inches in diameter and five feet tall extended upward from the other end. Fiadini carefully placed the lead pipe over the small antenna.

"Is this the main antenna?" Kent wanted to know, gesturing at the steel cylinder.

Fiadini nodded. "It extends clear through that hole in the roof before transmitting," he said.

They hiked back up the hill to the van, then headed back down the winding road. Kent studied the terrain below. No dust of ascending vehicles yet. But just then, Fiadini braked to a halt, staring intently across a half-mile-wide swale immediately in front of them. Kent followed his line of sight, and saw the car stopped at the high point across the swale. He knew immediately it was the one he had seen less than two hours earlier: the dark Mercedes sedan. Even from a half mile away he could see the long whip antenna jutting upward from the back of the car.

Fiadini looked at his watch. "They're trying to do it at this moment. They're in perfect position to transmit to the shack."

"Then they'll start up the hill, toward us, when they see they can't trigger the relay," Kent said.

"*Siamo fottuti!*" Fiadini said. "We're fucked. They undoubtedly have seen our dust already, and Giulio knows this van. But there is another road behind us, leading down the other side of the mountain. We can—"

"No!" Kent said. "We have to stop them, don't you understand?"

Fiadini searched Kent's face for a few long moments, then understood he would not be denied. He shook his head sadly. "Well then, American, how are going to do it?"

"You see that narrow spot in the road just down the hill?" Kent said, pointing. "Drive to that spot and let the van coast into the bank. When the Soviets arrive, tell them that . . . the steering gear is broken, or anything like that. I'll hide above the road in the brush. Leave the rest up to me."

Fiadini looked rather dubious, but saw that Kent was too fired up to be denied. He drove the van down the hill and ran it firmly into the cut bank, blocking the narrow road. Kent climbed the bank and found a suitable hiding place directly above where a vehicle approaching from below would likely stop.

"Giulio will be with them," the Italian called out. "Please don't shoot him. He's wearing blue coveralls."

"I won't. *In culo alla balena!* Up the whale's ass!" Kent said. It was an Italian wish for good luck.

Just three minutes later the Mercedes sedan came into view. From his position on top of the bank, Kent was able to see two men in the front seat. Neither had on the blue jumpsuit. He could see that there were two people in the backseat, but the upper parts of their bodies were obscured by the car's roof. However, he thought the one nearest his side of the road could be a woman.

The Mercedes stopped about thirty meters short of the van, its diesel engine clattering noisily. The brown dust slowly settled, but nobody got out. They obviously suspected an ambush, Kent thought. He waited. Still nothing. Then Fiadini crawled out from under the front end of the van, brushing the heavy dust off his clothing.

"Hey, you guys!" he called out. He came walking down the hill toward the Soviet car, waving his arms and speaking animated Italian. Still, nobody got out of the sedan. Fiadini walked up to the left side of the vehicle and, in a voice not loud enough for Kent to hear, seemed to be talking a steady stream, all the while pointing up at the mountaintop, then at his car. Then he would shrug his shoulders, his brow furrowed in six or seven lines, then point some more, talk some more. Then he shook his head violently, and seemed to be pleading. It was becoming clear to Kent that the men in the front seat were telling Fiadini to back his disabled van away from the bank and off the edge of the road. It was a steep hillside, and to do this would mean the end of the van.

Fiadini finally walked back to his van and got into the driver's seat. Kent had hoped the Soviets would get out and walk to the van also; then he would have room to operate. But they stayed put, and Kent had to simply wait for an opening. Fiadini got the van started, put it into reverse, and began rocking the vehicle to get it away from the bank. Kent watched, and thought the Italian was slipping the clutch, possibly trying to burn it out.

In a minute the right front door of the Mercedes swung open and a large, broad-shouldered man in slacks and a tan shirt got out and walked toward the van. He disappeared from Kent's view around the uphill side of the van, and Kent knew it was time to make his move. He could hear the clattering diesel, and could see the illuminated brake lights, which meant the sedan was in neutral and only held on the slope by the pressure of the driver's foot on the brake. Pushing the shrubs aside, he slid down the cut slope in full view of anybody who chanced to look behind where they sat in the big car.

Kent was now on his hands and knees moving up the road toward the rear of the sedan, his pistol in his right hand. Then he saw the van, its motor roaring, backing away from the cut bank. As it straightened out in the roadway, Kent could see the Soviet moving alongside the driver's door, gesturing how the steering wheel should be turned. It was now obvious they were trying to maneuver it for a downhill shot frontward off the edge of the road and down the hill. He expected to see Fiadini jump out as the van lurched forward, its front wheels cramped hard right. But then, at the last moment, the Soviet, running alongside, pulled out a handgun and shot the Italian in the head as the van headed for the cliff.

Kent seized the moment, aware that all eyes were on the van as it plunged over the side. He ran up the left side of the Mercedes and fired a single shot behind the ear of the driver, killing him instantly. Kent dived to his left off the downhill side of the road as the Mercedes began rolling backward. In the commotion, the Soviet who had shot Fiadini failed to see Kent, and only saw the car rolling backward. He started chasing foolishly after it, shouting in Russian. Kent caught a glimpse of the two backseat passengers leaning over the front seat fighting for control of the vehicle, but it was too late. Neither of them could reach the brake, and at the first crook in the road the Mercedes plunged over the side and began bounding end over end down the hill.

The big man in the tan shirt stopped running when he came to the spot where the car had gone over the edge, then simply stood there looking down the hill. Kent fully expected to see him head down after the car, but amazingly, he just started jogging down the hill in the direction of town. It was then Kent saw what the Soviet had undoubtedly seen, a column of bluish black smoke from the gully below.

He waited a few moments until the Russian had disappeared around a curve, then ran down the road to where the car had gone off. He plunged down the hill, following the swath of crushed brush, broken pine saplings, and scraped boulders. He had two things in mind: what any survivor of the crash could tell him about where Cris was, and whether they had another key to the control panel on the transmitter. If he could find the key, he could get back to the shack on foot before the escaped Soviet could get back in another vehicle.

In about two minutes he found the car, lying on its left side, the front end wedged between two huge boulders. The fire had broken out in the engine compartment, but it was not yet engulfing the rest of the car. Instead, it had spread to dry grass and was starting uphill away from the vehicle. Kent approached warily. He had to account for three people, and one of them, the driver, was already dead. The Italian, Fiadini's partner, seemed less a threat to him than the woman. But anyway, who could have survived such a chaotic plunge whole enough to be a threat of any kind? he asked himself.

Seeing nobody near the car, he took a look down inside. Nobody. All thrown out, yet the doors on the right side, the top side, seemed smashed shut. So he began searching the slope directly uphill from the wrecked car. First he came on the driver. The fire spreading through the grass had already caught his clothing on fire; Kent couldn't have cared less. He moved on up the slope quickly and found the man in the blue coveralls, Giulio Petrini. The flames were almost on him, but Kent decided not to try moving him. Instead, he kicked in a narrow fireline with his heels—enough to divert the short flames around them. Then he felt for a pulse and got one. The man was badly injured; it looked as if his entire chest was crushed and he was bleeding around the mouth.

"Can you hear me?" Kent said in Italian into the man's ear.

Petrini's head moved a little, then his eyes came partway open. He nodded perceptibly.

"I am American. I am going to help you."

Petrini nodded again, looking very helpless and bewildered.

"Is the Spanish woman still alive?"

The Italian nodded.

"Do you know where she is?"

He shut his eyes momentarily and made a very slight shaking movement of the head.

"Do you have a key to the transmitter?"

Answer: No.

"Does the driver have one?"

Answer: No.

"Does the woman, or the other man have one?"

Answer: No.

"Good, good. Listen, my friend. I am going to keep the fire from burning you. You must keep up your courage. Help will be here soon. Do you understand?"

This time the Italian seemed to be trying to open his mouth and form words. Kent put his ear close to the man's mouth. *"Guadalcanal,"* he uttered in a cracking voice.

"What?" Kent asked, pulling his head back to look into the man's eyes.

"Guadalcanal." Petrini stared at him, his mouth hanging open. In a moment Kent realized the man was dead. To be sure, he felt at the neck for a pulse, and got nothing. He was vaguely aware of the thumping sound of a helicopter rotor not too far away. Then a shadow suddenly fell across Petrini's face, and at the same moment Kent heard a noise behind him. As he turned, he looked upward in time to see Vera Vlasov lunging at him, her upraised arms clutching a large rock, swinging it down at his head in a huge arc. He didn't even have time to raise his arm in defense.

Shortly after 0800 hours, navy authorities called the U.S. consulate in Naples to let them know about detaining Bartledge and Bovio on orders from the chief of base security. Within an hour, the U.S. ambassador in Rome had Admiral Carl Hixon on the phone. The admiral agreed to have the civilians released, but he gave the ambassador an earful about the trouble they had caused trying to bring about an evacuation of his base. The ambassador, having been fully briefed by the consulate regarding the impending detonation of bombs on the compound, was quite perplexed by the admiral's comments.

"Then you've already located and disarmed the explosives, Admiral?"

"My God, man, are you into this too? What the hell is it that everybody knows about my base except me? You think I'm living in a goddamn vacuum down here? No offense, Mr. Ambassador. I'm sure you can understand what we put up with running a place like this. If we believed every rumor we heard about sabotage and—"

"Excuse me, Admiral. What do you make of the killings that took place last night off the base?"

"What are you talking about? People get killed every night in Naples."

"I mean two of our men. And by the way, Lieutenant Commander Harold Scheer was seriously injured."

"What? Scheer? How?"

"Dragged out of their car and shot on their way to dinner."

"Oh, Jesus. I didn't hear about that yet. God damn it, nobody tells me a fucking thing, and I'm going to have somebody's ass on this one. What happened, they get robbed?"

"It wasn't robbery, Admiral. They still had their wallets. Scheer and our guys were getting ready to run a shakedown on your compound. Are you getting the picture yet?"

"Well, I still don't see what—"

"Fine, Admiral Hixon. I'll let you go now, as I see you're quite busy. Also, I'm about to place a call to the secretary of state concerning your incompetence and apparent dereliction of duty."

"What? Mr. Ambassador, you have absolutely no right—"

"I have every right, sir, when it comes to the four hundred American civilians whose lives are in jeopardy there. Perhaps you'll be getting a call from your own secretary shortly. Meanwhile, my suggestion would be that you immediately remove people from your compound until security has been achieved."

There was a long sigh. Then the admiral said, "Anything else, Mr. McAllestair?"

"Just one other thing. I'd like to know the whereabouts and status of Mr. Arno Kent."

"Kent? Who's he?"

"He's the guy the Soviets have been chasing all over Spain and Italy. Don't you read the papers, or what?"

"Oh yeah, yeah. I recall. But how am I supposed to know where the hell he is? I'm his parole officer or something?"

"He's working for the CIA on this case. You remember, there's a plot to blow up your base? Well, this Kent is in the Naples area and our folks tell me he went up near your main transmitter site on the volcano to forestall the detonation of the charges placed around your compound."

There was a silence, and McAllestair imagined the admiral pouring himself a full tumbler of brandy to help get him through the rest of the conversation.

"Admiral, does any of this ring a bell, even a little one? Or am I talking into a tunnel with no outlet?"

"Kent, you said? Are you sure it was Kent?"

"He may be traveling under another name. Bennett, I believe. Yes, Bruce Bennett."

"Hold one, Mr. Ambassador."

McAllestair waited, hearing muffled voices on the other end, the admiral conferring with somebody. Then he came back on the line.

"No, we don't have anything on him at this time. There was apparently some sort of disturbance on the volcano road this morning . . . a car off the road and a fire or something, but evidently that situation is under control."

"Let me see if I understand you, Admiral. You're saying you're absolutely satisfied, following a rigorous search of your compound, that there's no explosives, no breach of security, no problem whatsoever, despite the definitive intelligence reports we've been giving you?"

"I'm saying nobody's told me a goddamn thing yet that convinces me there's been any kind of a breach on my base, and until they do, I've frankly got a lot more important things to do than chase rumors up and down my corridors. No offense by that, Mr. Ambassador, but I really think you ought to take a closer look at those spooks they've got turned loose on me here."

"I see. Well, it's been instructive talking with you, Admiral." Then McAllestair hung up.

* * *

At about two in the afternoon Kent began to regain consciousness. When he opened his eyes, he saw pale yellow walls, a large metallic light fixture staring down at him, an IV bottle hanging from a metal stanchion next to his bed, a tube leading down to his right arm, and a mixture of hospital smells dominating the ambience. Everything had a dreamlike quality, with nothing in sharp focus, and with all of the otherwise recognizable shapes distorted in all three dimensions. He was unable to integrate a recollection of recent events with the sights and smells that surrounded him and come to any idea as to what the hell was going on. On trying to move his arms and legs, he sensed a combination of numbness and pain that was overwhelming. Then, the image of Vera Vlasov hovering overhead came to him, and he lay there praying the image was only a bad dream. Then, he thought he saw a man in a very short haircut and a white smock lean over him and look into his eyes. Then he lost consciousness again.

Seaman First Class Billy Lundgren had taken it upon himself to replace the cracked toilet seat in the enlisted men's head in the main operations building. But he found the attachment bolts rusted, and had to apply enormous pressure with the wrench to remove the nuts. On his third try, the wrench slipped off the nut and struck the rim of the toilet bowl, producing a crack that ran from the rim to the floor. Water immediately began leaking out of the bowl. He cut off the supply valve, then mopped up the puddle of water and reported the problem to the petty officer in charge of building upkeep.

Petty Officer Second Class Phil Olson looked up from his paperwork and thought about it for a minute. "Shit," he said. "If we wait on the contractor to fix it, that thing will be out of commission for two or three weeks. Anyway, they're supposed to replace all that stuff in there."

"Yeah, I seen all those crates of fixtures in the storeroom. What about if we break out a new toilet and put it in ourselves?"

"You know how to do it?"

"I've helped my dad do it. It's no big deal."

"Okay, Billy. Get yourself some help and go to it. Try to get it done by 1700 hours; they may decide to pull an inspection in here in the morning."

Lundgren unlocked the supply room and flipped on the lights. In one corner were stacked eight wooden crates, the stenciled labels in some foreign language. Lundgren and his buddy, Tim Payson, gawked at the unfamiliar words, shrugged their shoulders as they grinned at each other, then started prying the lid off the crate.

"Easy with that pry bar," said Lundgren. "I already creamed one of these things today. That stuff is fragile like you can't believe."

Payson lifted off the boards he had pried loose, and the two young men peered inside to see a dark green heavy-duty fabric enclosing the contents of the crate. There was a large, red tag taped to the fabric that said in English: WARNING: TO BE OPENED ONLY BY CONTRACTOR.

"What do you think?" said Payson. "Check with Phil?"

"Know what kind of guy you are?" asked Lundgren. "You're the kind of guy that's afraid to tear the little tags off cushions because it says not to. Come on, wimp, open the fucker and let's get on with it."

Payson cut open the fabric cover and pulled it aside. Then they both looked at the contents in amazement.

"What the fuck is this?" said Lundgren. "It sure as hell doesn't look like a toilet. I wonder what's underneath this box on top. Help me lift it offa there."

"Won't come up. It's tied down somehow. Look here. There's wires running outa there to the ones below. This whole fucking thing is wired together. What is this, some kind of an electronic crapper, or what?"

"Let's take the top off this sucker," Lundgren said, applying the blade of a screwdriver to the cap of the small box. It came off easily. "Jesus H. Christ, will you look at this? Looks like the inside of a fucking TV or something. You know what? I think there's been some kind of a mixup. This here is electronic gear. Let's try another box. Could be the whole load is in the wrong place."

They pried open a second box. It had the same warning sticker as the first one, but inside they found six individually sealed packages bearing no labels.

"What the fuck is this stuff?" said Payson. "Ain't any one of them big enough for a toilet, or even a sink. Cut one open?"

"Might as well, we're in it this far."

They lifted out one of the packages, set it on the floor, and cut it open across the top. Inside was a clear plastic liner, which they also slit open, revealing a colorless cube of a dense but somewhat pliable solid. It had no odor. They opened another package to find the same thing. They opened a third crate and found it exactly like the second one.

"What do you think this stuff is? Ever see anything like it?" asked Lundgren.

"Beats me," said Payson. "Just a lot of blobs. Maybe glue, you know, for tile floors. Or maybe something to melt and use on roofs, or to mix with paint. How the fuck should I know?"

"But what about this electronic stuff?" asked Lundgren. "It just doesn't go together. There's something weird about this."

The two reported what they had found to Petty Officer Phil Olson, who told them he'd go down and have a look in a few minutes.

Lieutenant Gerald Farwell was lying on his bed in the BOQ brooding about having been restricted to quarters by that asshole Captain Rosewell, when he heard on the base radio station the following report:

Local fire and police authorities responded to an incident early today on volcano road about two miles below the main electronic site. Police reported that the bodies of two unidentified civilians, one of them badly burned, were found near a late-model Mercedes Benz sedan that apparently veered out of control off the mountain road. There was one survivor of the crash, an American civilian identified as Bruce Bennett, who was transported in a helicopter by firefighters to the base infirmary here. In other news . . .

Farwell leaped off the bed and hurriedly got himself dressed and ran to the Naval Hospital, two blocks outside the NSA main gate. He quickly located the wing where Kent was being treated. Shore police from the navy and carabinieri from Naples were milling about in the corridors smoking cigarettes and chatting with one another. Soon he was able to find the chief petty officer in charge of the ward.

"Chief, skipper sent me down here to check on the American from the wrecked car," he lied. "What's his status?"

"Serious, Lieutenant. Concussion, lacerations, about what you'd expect in a crash like that. Lucky he's alive. He's either unconscious or sleeping right now. Seems to be slipping in and out."

"You got ID on him?"

"Carrying a passport with the name Bennett. I just now called the consulate, and they told me someone would be here shortly."

"Has he said anything yet?"

"Just keeps mumbling. He wants to say something but it's just not making any sense."

The pair was interrupted when Bovio and Bartledge burst into the ward, demanding to see Kent. The CPO told them it was impossible, that not even the police could get in without the doctor's personal say-so. Bovio told him to produce the doctor, then, because this was a national security matter of the utmost urgency. The surgeon attending the case was brought to the scene, and he reluctantly agreed to determine if the patient was capable of being interviewed, even if only for a minute. The surgeon was back in moments, looking angry. "He's gone," he said.

CHAPTER EIGHTEEN

Kent only had to jump ten feet from the ledge near his hospital-room window to reach the recently spaded garden below. Then he crawled through the garden to a point from which he could observe the main hospital entrance. It would only be a matter of minutes, he concluded, before somebody would leave a vehicle unattended near the entrance.

As he lay in hiding, his head throbbed miserably despite the heavy medication he had been given, and his left shoulder was numb. He let his eyes slide closed, his head resting on his right arm, and tried to figure out what Korolenko would do. It had to be Korolenko who had shot Fiadini and got away. The guy exactly fit the description given Kent by Bovio following the hotel fracas in Rome. What would the Soviet operative do now? He seemed to have no choice except to do what Kent was planning: get another key to the transmitter, then go there and operate the unit manually. Evidently, Fiadini's lead pipe effectively shielded the receiving antenna on the unit. Would Korolenko have another key somewhere, or would he have to go to Fiadini's shop? Perhaps he already had a key, and had gone back for another car.

It was no use trying to explain any of this to the navy. They had already proved they weren't interested in this whole scheme. If anything was going to happen, he would have to do it himself. They may have killed Cris by now, he reasoned. If her life had meant anything, it had to do with saving all those other people's lives. He would not allow her to just slip away at the hands of these commie bastards without reaping that one benefit for which she had sacrificed herself.

Then his chance came. A navy sedan pulled up to the entrance, and a uniformed courier got out, leaving the engine running. Looked like a delivery of paperwork of some kind.. Kent hurried to the car, got in and drove away in the direction of Naples. He glanced back in the mirror and could see no sign of pursuit. He saw by the car clock that it was already past four in the afternoon. Korolenko would have had since about eight that morning to get back to town for new wheels, even if he'd had to walk most of the way.

Afternoon traffic was nightmarish, and Kent didn't know the city. It was only by dead reckoning and a minor miracle that he stumbled onto Via Francesco Crispi. He passed the Fiadini shop as he had done before, then turned right at the next street and slowed as he came to the alley that led to the back. A quick glance behind the shop: only a few parked cars and an old man hoeing weeds.

Kent parked the car and tried the back door. It was unlocked. He opened it slowly, stuck his head in and listened. Not a sound. He went through the now familiar supply room and into the little office. Everything looked just as it had been left earlier that day. The stuff from Fochner's pockets still littered the floor next to the little rug covering the blood. Kent snatched up the key on the brass ring, then headed out the back door and back into the navy sedan.

He got no further than the end of the alley when a wave of pain swept downward through his head and neck, and he thought he was about to lose consciousness again. He stopped the car and put his head down on the seat, but concentrated on staying awake. The vibrations and throbbing in his head were almost intolerable, but after a few minutes he knew he could fight it off. He straightened up and looked ahead at the cross street. Traffic was heavy and frantic-looking, and he dreaded entering the busy street. Then he glanced into the mirror and saw an ominous sight: a big Fiat sedan pulling up behind Fiadini's shop. One man got out and went to the back door. Kent could see the silhouettes of two others still in the car. They seemed to have their heads turned toward the shop. Kent eased the navy sedan out of the alley and into traffic. Now, if he could just remember the turns to get back to the volcano road.

Petty Officer Second Class Phil Olson was in no hurry to check out the situation in the supply room reported to him by Bill Lundgren; the

stack of requisitions he was working on were already overdue. So he sent
Lundgren and Payson nearby to the enlisted personnel mess building to
check for a spare toilet bowl. They returned in a half hour.

"Phil," Lundgren said, "it looks like the same situation over here, but
Marv wouldn't let us look in any of the crates."

"Why the hell not?" Olson said.

"The containers inside the boxes are all marked 'To Be Opened Only
by Contractor.'"

Olson scratched the side of his nose, still looking down at his requisitions. "What did you say those boxes in our storeroom have in them?"

"Well, most of them are just full of some kind of material, you know,
big packages of yucky-looking globs. Then, one of the boxes, the first
one we looked into, had a bunch of electronic stuff in it."

"You mean, like parts or something?" said Olson, getting a little bit
more interested.

"No, not parts, but like the inside of a radio or TV. Some kind of
specialized equipment, I'd guess."

"Okay," said Olson, pushing the papers into a neat pile. "I'll never get
this shit finished today anyway. Let's take a look."

Olson's phone buzzed just as he was getting up, and he grabbed the
receiver: "Olson," he said. "Yes, sir. Not yet, sir, should have them
ready to go in a half hour. Aye aye, sir." He hung up, a scowl on his
face. "Son of a bitch," he said. "That's all the bastard can think of, is his
fucking requisitions. Listen, Billy, forget the damned toilet. Just put an
Out of Order sign on it and we'll let the contractor take care of it."

"What about that stuff in the storeroom? Close the boxes back up?"

"Naw, leave 'em open. I'll try to get down there after I finish the
ensign's precious fucking requisitions."

Bovio, Bartledge, the CPO in charge of the ward, and Lieutenant
Farwell looked at the surgeon in disbelief, then simultaneously the
three went into the hospital room to verify his statement.

"His clothes are gone too," said the CPO staring into the closet.

Bovio was at the window gaping downward.

"I don't believe this," said CPO Slack. "The guy was all but comatose
not twenty minutes ago. He was mumbling something about a corral or
something."

"What exactly was he saying?" Bartledge asked.

"He was incoherent, barely conscious. He kept saying some Russian word, like Korochekov, or something. Then he said something like 'motel corral.'"

"Could it have been *Guadalcanal?*" asked the doctor.

"I'm not sure," said the CPO.

"*Guadalcanal?*" asked Bovio.

The doctor gestured toward the harbor with his thumb. "It's a helicopter carrier docked here."

"You know, he may have found out something from somebody in that wreck on the mountain," said Bartledge. "Maybe he's headed back up there right now."

"Well, he can't get far, not in the shape he's in," said Slack. "We'd better find him quick before he goes into worse shock than he was already in."

Malcolm Bartledge squinted at Alessandro Bovio. "How you figure it, Alex? Where's he going? What's to do?"

"He took a bad head wound. Must be delirious. Maybe going after the del Barrio woman. Anybody know where she is?"

"No idea. You know, he evidently intercepted the Soviets en route to the electronic site. If he's lucid, he has to be figuring they're trying to bring about a detonation."

Bovio turned to Lieutenant Farwell. "Lieutenant, this isn't over yet, not by a long shot. What has the navy done about checking out all these buildings for rigged charges?"

"Not a goddamned thing, as far as I know. I tried to get it started last night and this morning I wound up confined to quarters by the chief of base security. Neither the OD nor anybody else will even take my calls."

"What's the most important building on this compound?" Bartledge asked.

"Well, that would be C and O, Command and Operations."

"What would it take to run a quick shakedown on it?"

"You mean, check out the whole place for explosive charges? It would take a lot," Farwell said. "There must be thirty-thousand feet of floor space over there, spread out on four levels. Must be at least sixty separate rooms, not including storage, latrines, all that kind of stuff."

"Latrines," Bovio said, his brow furrowing. "Vince, you remember that delivery confirmation sheet del Barrio got a look at in Rome?"

"Yeah, I do. Listen, Farwell, could you rapidly locate the storage area or areas in that building where new toilet fixtures and supplies would be stored, waiting for installation?"

"No sweat. Let's do it. You guys got wheels?"

Eight minutes later the trio pulled up opposite the C&O building. It was change-of-shift time and the place was alive with sailors and civilians coming and going. They got out of the jeep and started across the street when a navy jeep came screeching to a halt right in front of them, and a four-striper jumped out to accost Lieutenant Farwell. It was Captain Bryan Rosewell, chief of base security.

"All right, mister," the captain was shouting, "you've broken your confinement, and I'm running you up, smart guy. You'll get a special on this one, and I'm personally escorting you to the brig. Get in the jeep, Lieutenant."

Lieutenant Farwell stepped up within a foot of the superior officer and said, "Captain, I have reason to believe explosive charges have been placed inside this and other buildings on this compound, and I'm here expressly to check that out and evaluate the buildings if necessary."

"What?" the captain roared, his face red with anger. "You're out of your mind, mister. Now—"

"Shut up and listen," Farwell said. The captain's mouth dropped open in astonishment. "I'm going to check out this building and I'm going to do it now. You can either help, or get the fuck out of my way." He turned toward the building but Rosewell grabbed his arm. Bartledge and Bovio were standing by Farwell taking it in.

"You've just blown your career, young man," the captain said hotly. "Do you realize just who the hell you're talking to?"

"I sure do, Captain," Farwell said, making the word *captain* sound sarcastic, as if the rank didn't fit, or wasn't even close. "I'm talking to as worthless a piece of shit as ever slithered into a navy uniform. Now get your slimy lunchhook offa my arm or I'll cold-cock your ass right here in front of a bunch of sailors who are under the mistaken impression you might *be* somebody."

Farwell strode away, leaving the captain in a fit of rage.

"Stop that officer! Stop that officer!" Rosewell was shouting, pointing at the lieutenant. People looked, but frankly didn't see why they should try to do the captain's bidding. Rosewell whirled around and ordered his jeep driver to stop the lieutenant, and the seaman hesitantly climbed out of the jeep, not exactly sure what he was going to do about it either.

At that moment two sailors in shore patrol arm bands and sidearms happened on the scene and quickly sized things up. They stopped the junior officer in midstride and held him for the captain.

"Detain this officer," thundered the captain. "I'm charging him with violation of a direct order, insubordination, conduct . . ."

"Maybe I can explain this," said Bartledge, taking his identification folder out of his pocket and approaching the SPs.

"And I also want these two intruders detained," said Captain Rose-well. "Take all three of them to the brig and lock 'em up until I find out what's going on around here."

As Kent worked his way through the crowded streets, he fought off the waves of tremors that seemed to be rattling his brain and optic nerves. His vision became blurry, then clear, then blurry again. He was amazed that he made all the turns correctly and found his way through the suburbs to the volcano road turnoff. Suddenly it occurred to him that he was desperately hungry, and that low blood sugar might explain his lightheadedness. He thought about stopping for something to eat, felt his hip pocket and said, "Shit. I don't even have any fucking money." Anyway, he thought, there was no time to waste eating. He had to get to the shack before the Soviets did.

Then another shocker hit him: he had no weapon, either. He thought back to the incident on the mountain that morning. After shooting the driver of the Mercedes, he had stuck his automatic in his waistband before starting down the hill. By the time he had reached the wrecked car, he recalled, he no longer had it with him. He remembered falling once; perhaps that was when he lost it. How far from the road had that happened?

As he drove up the winding road, he glanced in the mirror repeatedly, looking for the dust of any car behind him. So far, he saw nothing. When he reached the site of this morning's incident and still saw no dust behind him, it meant he had at least a fifteen-minute lead. He recognized the spot where Fiadini's van had gone off the road, and parked there. He got out and took another look down the mountain behind him, and still could see no dust near the road. Then he began retracing his steps, first back down the road to where the Mercedes had plunged off, then down the steep hillside. In a few minutes he found the place where he had fallen, and there, just down the hill a step or two, was his automatic. He snatched it up, blew the dust off the surface, and pulled out the magazine. He still had six rounds left.

By the time he had struggled back to the road, his head pounding terribly, the dust was there. He could discern a column of it about three miles down the mountain. He hurried back to his car and started up the hill again toward the electronics site. As he drove the last several miles he concentrated hard, trying to bring back into recall what Fiadini had told him about the unlabeled toggle switches on the control panel of the transmitter. Kent cursed himself for not paying closer attention and committing them to memory. Of course, at that time he hadn't foreseen Fiadini's death, but that's a piss-poor excuse at a time like this, he told himself. He still didn't have it solidly worked out by the time he got to the top of the hill.

CHAPTER NINETEEN

Kent parked the navy sedan at the end of the road above the old goatherd's shack at just about sundown. He took a last look at the road below, noting the advancing dust column still two or three miles away. He had no time to lose. He clambered down the hillside, a distance of about sixty meters from the road, and entered the shack. The lead pipe was still in place over the receiving antenna. Everything else was the same as he had seen it earlier that day. To unlock the control panel, he had to insert his hand into an opening the size of a short length of pipe, and found there was barely room to get the key inserted and twisted in the lock. Probably insurance against picking it, he thought. He opened the control panel and looked at the five toggle switches. One of them had the power to kill hundreds of people at the flick of his finger, another the same thing after a fifteen-minute delay.

There could be no mistake. He would take the necessary time to evaluate the consequences of flipping each of the three switches he was unsure of. He remembered clearly that number two was a booby trap, and that number three was just a cancel-and-reset switch. That left numbers one, four, and five.

One of those would immediately level most of the buildings on the base, and he would hear the explosion in a few seconds. Either of the other two switches would produce nothing for fifteen minutes. In one case, the transmitter alone would be blown up; in the other case, the detonation signal would be sent out, and then the transmitter would be destroyed.

Kent pondered the three switches, thinking back about Fiadini's explanation of them. But the more he concentrated on it, the harder his head was pounding, and the blurrier his vision was becoming. He staggered back out of the shack and looked toward the road coming up the mountain. The light was fading fast, but against the orange sunset still hovering above the horizon, the dust of an approaching vehicle was now plain to see. They must be within a mile, he told himself.

He went back into the shack to face the awesome-looking control panel, the brass plating seeming to leer at him as if to say, "Go ahead, idiot, flip one of my switches!" By chance alone, he had only a one-in-three chance of hitting the right one, the self-destruct, providing he was right about numbers two and three. That just wouldn't do, even for a gambler, and he wasn't a gambler. Then he had a thought: What about not doing anything? Defend the shack and hope to be lucky. Not very good odds there, either, he thought.

As he stood there leaning on the steel cylinder on the right side of the steel case, he began looking at it. What had Fiadini said? Wasn't it that the main antenna automatically elevated itself to protrude through the hole in the roof? Obviously that would be designed to happen before transmission!

Excited now, Kent rethought his tactics, then, steeling himself, flipped switch number one. He heard some electronic clicks, then some gears engaging. In a moment the main antenna mast began elevating. Quickly he flipped switch number three, and the antenna stopped suddenly, then retracted into its original position. So he was back where he had started, but now he knew that number one was one of the detonation switches, and that left only numbers four and five still uncertain.

He thought once again about Fiadini's rundown on the switches. What was the last one? Wasn't it the delayed self-destruct? He was almost sure of it. What he should have asked the Italian was, on the delayed detonation signal, would the antenna elevate immediately, or not until just before transmission?

There was simply no time to ponder it further. He had to act now. He flipped switch number five, and heard a similar electronic clicking sound. The antenna didn't budge. He was encouraged. He checked his watch carefully. It said seven twenty-one. The unit should self-destruct at eight thirty-six, and he would have to defend the control panel unit then. He slammed the control-panel door closed.

He had left the shack door open for light; he peered outside toward the road above. The dust was swirling around, and now he could see the roofline of the car that had just come to a stop. Obviously, they had spied the navy sedan parked at the end of the road only a short distance ahead of them, and would be aware somebody was already at the shack. He started looking around for a place in the rocks nearby from which he could defend access to the shack, but except for a few small boulders, it was fairly open terrain. He didn't relish the idea of staying in the shack until the last minute, but maybe it was his only good shot. He pulled the door closed, leaving only a narrow crack to see out of.

It was quiet on the hill above. Kent surmised they were checking out his sedan, talking about what they should do. He waited, then looked at his watch again: seven twenty-five. Eleven minutes to go. Then he rethought the situation. Eventually, he would have to make a run for it, or he'd be trapped in the shack when it blew. Better get out now, he decided, and take his chances in the rocks. He slipped out the door and, moving in a crouch, traversed the slope along a contour to a point about twenty meters away where he found a depression in the ground with a few modest-size boulders between himself and the shack. He stretched out in the depression and waited.

From his position in the rocks, Kent could not see the car; he could only listen and guess what was going on.

He looked at his watch: seven twenty-seven. Still no sounds from the road above. Then, footsteps. Somebody coming down the hillside toward the shack. Kent slowly raised his head enough to see outlines against the gray-pink sky to the west. Then, the silhouette of a man— the same man who had shot Fiadini. Korolenko! He was carrying a weapon, and it wasn't a pistol. More likely an automatic rifle or sub- machine gun, Kent thought. The man was moving along slowly, being careful not to stumble or kick any rocks, and to be silent. Obviously, because of the navy sedan, he expected to find somebody in the shack.

As the silhouette became larger against the sky, Kent was asking him- self who else was there, and where were they? Covering Korolenko from above? If so, with what kind of weapons? Would Korolenko have figured out that he'd best hit the number-three switch in order to cancel out what Kent had got started? If so, his next move would be to hit switch number one and get an immediate detonation on the base. Once Korolenko got inside the shack, therefore, Kent's game would be over. Obviously, the Russian would have a key to the control panel.

It was almost dark now, which favored Kent. He decided to try to get off the first shot before his position was detected. The silhouette was now only about twenty-five meters away, and at its closest point to Kent along the way to the shack. Kent needed to chamber a round in his pistol, and he slowly pulled the slide to the rear, intending to ease it forward slowly and quietly. But his hands were sweaty, and the unthinkable happened: the slide, controlled by a powerful spring, slipped through his fingers and clanged forward with a characteristic sound recognizable by anyone familiar with firearms.

About one second after Kent's mistake, Korolenko was flat on the ground and out of sight. It was quiet, deathly quiet for about ten seconds. Then Korolenko shouted something in Russian. A voice from the road above answered him—also in Russian, and it was the voice of a woman.

The Vlasov bitch, Kent muttered to himself. Who else would come all this way for the finale? Then Korolenko again, shouting what sounded like instructions. Kent looked at his watch: seven twenty-nine, seven minutes to go. He wished it were only two. Could he get a shot off at Korolenko's prone body? He raised his head for a split second, then jerked it back down, just as a burst of automatic gunfire shattered the rocks immediately below where his head had been.

He had chosen his spot badly, and now he was pinned down. While he wasn't exposed to anyone on the road above, there was no direction in which he could move laterally to get out of Korolenko's arc of gunfire. He looked directly behind, and noted that the hill dropped off somewhat in that direction. But if he retreated that way, he would no longer be in position to guard the door of the goatherd's shack.

As Kent squatted there, wondering if he could wait it out, he heard footsteps coming down the hill from the road. But this time they were not stealthy, careful steps. It sounded like several people, stumbling, almost struggling along. Then in a minute he could make out the silhouettes of three persons. But they were not in a column; rather, they were tightly bunched, almost clutching each other. They came closer and closer, still in a tight group, until it became evident that two of the people were dragging along a third one, pushing the person ahead of them. They stopped not far from where Korolenko lay training his weapon at Kent's rock barricade. There was a brief, almost matter-of-fact conversation in Russian. Then, quiet for a moment.

A woman's voice, directed toward Kent, and spoken in English: "Mr. Kent, we have your precious Spanish whore with us here."

It was like a knife piercing Kent's chest. He immediately felt blind rage, and it was all he could do to restrain himself from charging at them. A glance at the barely visible face of his watch: Seven thirty-two, four minutes to go. Could he stall them? He played for time, saying nothing.

"Mr. Kent, we know you are out there, and we know you are armed with a little pistol," Vera Vlasov said derisively.

Then, Korolenko's voice, somewhat muffled, but giving instructions again.

"We have no time, Mr. Kent," she continued. "Throw out your gun and stand up right now, or the woman dies in front of your eyes."

"Is it you, Cris?" Kent called out in English.

A moment of silence. That's Cris, Kent thought. She's not giving them a damned thing. Then he heard a dull thud, and Cris's muted grunt. Kent grimaced, having an idea what just happened.

"You can see for yourself, American," Vlasov said.

Kent stuck his head out to one side of the rocks and got a glimpse of del Barrio's face, illuminated with a flashlight. Somebody behind her was holding her head up by her hair. Blood was running down the corner of her mouth across her chin.

"Let her go," Kent called out. "Let her come over here. Then you can have my gun."

"Ten seconds and she's dead," Vlasov said.

"Don't do it!" del Barrio screamed out. "They'll—"

There was another dull thud, cutting her off in midsentence. Then Kent could hear movements. He chanced a look over the rocks and saw what he was almost sure was Korolenko and Vlasov dragging Cris along toward the shack. One more look at his watch: looked like eight thirty-four. Another look at the trio. They were only about ten or twelve meters from the door of the shack.

Kent picked up a rock and with his left hand, tossed it to a point about fifteen feet to the right of his position, at the same time coming up to a firing position. The man Korolenko had left to keep him at bay with the automatic weapon fell for it. Kent caught the man's reactive movement as he trained his weapon on the spot where he heard the rock hit, and, steadying his hand on the rock, got off two shots. The man grunted loudly when Kent's second round struck him, and slumped forward onto the ground.

Running now in a crouch toward the other three, Kent moved fast toward the shack. Del Barrio, her hands tied behind her, saw what was happening, and began struggling violently to keep Korolenko and Vlasov busy restraining her. But Vlasov, displaying amazing strength, pulled del Barrio in front of her as a shield with one arm, while pushing her pistol against del Barrio's neck with the other. Meanwhile, Korolenko jumped inside the shack.

Kent figured that Korolenko had about one minute to open the control panel, hit the reset switch, then go for the number-one switch. Vlasov was shouting in English that her hostage would die if Kent came any closer. Del Barrio was writhing, trying to give Kent a shot at Vlasov, but the Soviet woman was holding fast.

As Kent vacillated, waiting for an opening, he heard the grinding noise once again, and against the western sky he saw the ugly shaft of the antenna slowly rising through the roof of the little shack. Korolenko hadn't had time to open the panel and reset the switches. Kent perceived that he must himself have confused the last two switches. In only seconds, the charges would detonate and hundreds of innocent people would be killed or maimed. He lunged toward the shack in a last desperate move to reach the control panel, determined to let nothing stop him.

As he hurled his body forward, stumbling over rocks and uneven ground, Vera Vlasov stayed in front of the door, keeping del Barrio in front of her. She held her fire, awaiting the perfect moment, and when Kent got within three meters, two shots rang out. Vlasov's bullet missed the dodging Kent by inches, but she couldn't fire again because Kent's shot had pierced her chest. Both women fell to the ground.

There was no time to stop. Kent jumped over their slumping bodies into the shack, landing squarely on Korolenko's back as he crouched in front of the control panel. Disregarding the sprawling Russian, he felt for the toggle switches and flipped the reset switch just as the antenna reached the top of its traverse. Another second would have been too late. It was dark in the shack, but Kent saw Korolenko's shadow as the Russian lurched toward him. Their heads crashed together, each man's weapon clattering to the floor. Then they grappled furiously, their bodies alternately slamming against the transmitter casing, then the walls of the shack. At one point, the Soviet slammed Kent behind the neck with his fist, felling the American. As he groveled on the floor to get himself back to his feet, Kent found his hand on top of one of the pistols, that of his adversary. He grabbed it, pointed it at the Russian's silhouette, and squeezed the trigger. Nothing. Now, using both hands, he fumbled for the safety catch. Korolenko saw he had the gun, and dived out the door, rolling to one side as he hit the ground.

Kent had the gun figured out in seconds, but already, Korolenko was bounding up the hill toward the road. Kent got in two shots, missing with each. But at least, he had the Russian on the run, and unarmed.

He knelt down by del Barrio and felt her neck, hoping for the miracle of a pulse, but there was none. Before his one shot had stopped Vlasov, it had passed through Cristina del Barrio's heart.

He took Cris's face between his hands and gently kissed her bruised cheek. Then he checked Vera Vlasov. She was unconscious, but maintaining a steady heartbeat. Without giving the matter a second thought, Kent put the pistol to her temple and fired. Then he went back into the shack and set the control panel to self destruct in fifteen minutes, this time knowing for sure which switch to set. Finally, he locked the panel, and threw the key away into the night.

The sound of the car's engine starting gave Kent a new burst of energy. He staggered up the hill, falling twice among the rocks, getting to the top only in time to fire three futile shots at the silhouette of the departing Fiat. He hurried to the navy sedan, climbed in, and reached for the keys he'd left in the ignition. They were gone. He jumped out and began running wildly down the road, stumbling through the dark, and choking on the dust still hanging in the air behind the speeding automobile.

"You bastard!" he shouted into the night, punctuating his frustration with the last three shots from the Russian pistol. Finally he fell to the ground, exhausted, sickened, defeated. And then he felt the shock wave that rocked the mountaintop as the transmitter self-destructed in a tremendous explosion. Before giving way to complete collapse, Kent made a solemn promise: *Korolenko, you're next. I'm coming after you, and when I find you, you're going to pay.*

EPILOGUE

News reports the next afternoon quoted the CO of the Naval Support Activity as saying the navy had thwarted a terrorist attempt to blow up the entire base. The only damage actually occurring was when a helicopter attempting to deliver a crate of lobsters, purportedly a gift to the crew of the USS *Guadalcanal* from the mayor of Gaeta, was diverted from the ship to a nearby pier, where the crate later exploded. Fortunately, no one was injured.